PRAISE FOR GREGG ANDREW HURWITZ

AND

THE TOWER

"Compelling. . . . The narration is sharp, and the dialogue jumps off the page. . . . This is the kind of novel that will probably be snapped up by Hollywood, but, once word of mouth picks up, readers might not want to wait for the movie."

—*Booklist*

"*THE TOWER* is a terrific achievement, a big-scale psychological thriller that takes the reader on a roller-coaster ride at breakneck speed."

—Bill Eidson, author of *Adrenaline*
and *Frames Per Second*

"First-time novelist Hurwitz has created two very powerful characters in Atlasia and Marlow, showing their similarities as well as their obvious differences."

—*Library Journal*

"Gregg Andrew Hurwitz stages a gripping psychological battle between a serial killer and the tortured soul who pursues him."

—Kate Phillips, author of *White Rabbit*

"*THE TOWER* is a compelling tale of terror and suspense that illuminates the darkest shadows of the human psyche."

—Walt Becker, author of *Link*

GREGG ANDREW HURWITZ

THE
TOWER

A NOVEL

POCKET BOOKS

New York   London   Toronto   Sydney   Singapore

POCKET BOOKS, a division of Simon & Schuster, Inc.
1230 Avenue of the Americas, New York, NY 10020

Copyright © 2001 by Gregg Andrew Hurwitz

Originally published in hardcover in 1999 by
Simon & Schuster, Inc.

ISBN: 0-671-02321-7

First Pocket Books printing January 2001

10 9 8 7 6 5 4 3 2 1

POCKET BOOKS and colophon are registered trademarks of Simon & Schuster, Inc.

Front cover montage by Rod Hernandez

Printed in the U.S.A.

ACKNOWLEDGMENTS

My parents, for teaching me dedication by example.

My sister, Dr. Melissa Hurwitz, for being my first reader back when I supplemented text with crayon art.

Kelly Macmanus, for her general benevolence and precocious sagacity.

Jess Taylor, whom I will always consider my first writing teacher, for his professorial eye and (alas) rapier wit.

Stephen F. Breimer, my attorney, for his circumspection and occasional well-directed intensity.

Joel Gotler, Alan Nevins, and Irv Schwartz of The Renaissance Agency for all their hard work on my behalf.

My team at Endeavor —Adriana Alberghetti, Vani Kane, Brian Lipson, Dawn Saltzman, and Tom Strickler— for their persistence and endless support.

And my editors:
Chuck Adams, for doing the kind of editing that many claim no longer gets done, and for setting a standard of excellence I will strive to emulate.
Michael Korda, for his incisive notes, warmth of character, and inexhaustible talent when it comes to all things written.

FOR MARC H. GLICK,
A SUPERB ATTORNEY
AND FRIEND

What in the midst lay but the Tower itself?
The round squat turret, blind as the fool's heart,
Built of brown stone, without a counterpart
In the whole world.

—ROBERT BROWNING,
"CHILDE ROLAND TO THE DARK TOWER CAME"

HE didn't sleep well, but then he never did. He woke in the night and it seemed as if he had been awake all along. He tried to close his eyes and let sleep wash over him again, but it didn't.

Throwing back the covers, he swung his feet over the edge of the bed and rested his hands on his knees. The first light of morning showed through the blinds. Soft morning light, still dull around the edges. He shook his head, rubbed his eyes, and stood up.

The dim light cut him at the waist and shadowed the muscles in his stomach. He ran his hand hard across the back of his neck and stretched his shoulders. The greenness of his eyes was startling; they seemed to draw the dim light of the room into themselves. Green, flickering gems set in the dark silhouette of a face.

Picking up a thin chain from the nightstand, he examined it for a moment before putting it on. He had worn the chain for years, though he had long since removed the medical tags it once held.

He pulled the blinds up. It was 5:26 in the morning and the air was still a heavy gray. He went into the kitchen and took a healthy swig from a carton of milk. The house was impeccably neat, as if some divine hand had swept things into order. He placed the milk back in the refrigerator, pushing it gently into line with the other items.

The living room was adjacent to the kitchen, and he went and lay across the couch. The room seemed empty although it was filled with furniture. It was sparsely but well decorated.

He grabbed the remote from the glass table and flicked on the TV without looking at it. Blue light danced across his face and the hum of voices filled the room. He gazed at the ceiling, shut his eyes, and counted as he breathed. He was still for a long time. It was a forced restfulness.

Finally, he got up and went to the bedroom. Lying backward on the bed, he put his feet on the wall. He reached into a drawerful of papers in his nightstand. On top was a Phi Beta Kappa key. His dirty little secret. He turned it aside and dug deeper, pulling out a racquetball.

He squeezed it, then threw it at the wall, catching it in front of his face. The ball's rhythm relaxed him, the tick against the wall, the tock against his palm.

The television sounded from the other room. The sounds of six in the morning. "Tired of spending another night rearranging your sock drawer? Well, now's your chance! It's time to be social—but not in a way that'll make you uncomfortable, like in all those singles bars."

Tick. Tock. Tick. Tock. Each time he caught the ball, he gave it a firm squeeze, pressing his fingertips into its soft surface. *Tick. Tock.*

"I never thought it would be so easy. I just pick up the phone and I have a whole network of friends to talk to."

He looked over at his phone. It was like the President's line. It usually rang out.

Tick. Tock. Tick. Tock. He was into the four hundreds when he lost count. The ball became a blue blur, a line to the wall and back to his face. He threw and caught, threw and caught as the sun made its tedious ascent outside his window.

At about seven, he got up and went into the study. He pulled a pistol from the top-left drawer and felt its familiar balance in his hand. It was a Sig Sauer, government issue, a weapon he had learned to use and love in his Quantico days.

He went to the dining room and gazed out across his front yard. There was a difference in the air that he could taste, as if something was about to fall out of place.

He twirled the pistol around his finger, cocked it and uncocked it expertly with his thumb, and twirled it again. A mail truck made its way slowly up the street, stopping at each house. It passed his mailbox without slowing and went to the next.

Pulling a chair around the table to face the window, he sat down, leaning back so two of the chair's legs tilted off the ground. The early morning joggers were out: a tired middle-aged man, a mother with her daughter, a couple with a dog.

He played with his pistol almost unconsciously, turning it over in his hand, spinning it around his finger, catching it in his palm. Sometimes he held it at arm's length, sometimes he held it on his lap. But he always held it well.

The stream of light through the front window climbed his body slowly as the sun rose. Just before it reached his eyes, he got up and walked back into the study, pulling a maple gun case from the drawer. He slid the pistol back into the velvet lining. It fit snugly. His fingers perched lightly on the case's lid as his gaze lingered on the gun. He slammed the case shut.

There was a name emblazoned on its brass plate: JADE MARLOW.

ONE

FLIGHT

THE TOWER was magnificent, rooted beneath the swelling waves and standing proudly above the inconsistency of the water. It rose firmly and elegantly, layered with stone over metal, tall and sleek in the salty breeze.

Nicknamed "Alcatraz II" by law enforcers and government officials, and "The Boat Pokey" by inmates across the country, the Peter Briggs Federal Penitentiary was famous for one reason and one reason alone: the Tower. The Tower was conceived over a table covered with cigarette butts and half-drunk cups of coffee at 3:32 in the morning. It had been an election year. Peter Briggs had won the election.

The regular prison, Maingate, framed the end of a peninsula by San Francisco that jutted into the Pacific. It contained the expendable criminal element, those with life sentences doubled back over life sentences. Yet the worst of the worst had a special distinction even within Maingate.

The Tower was fifty yards offshore at low tide. Only about eighteen feet in diameter, it housed twelve levels of prison units, two cells on each floor. It sat within an inlet cut into the craggy walls of the peninsula. When the tide rose, it inched up the side of the structure until only the last two levels peeped out above the water.

A peripheral fence blocked the prison from the vast expanse of sea beyond, its enormous posts grounded with concrete plugs in the ocean floor. Access to the

Tower could be gained only by boat, and only from the heavily guarded grounds of Maingate. The guards shuttled back and forth on speedboats like little insects busy at work.

The Tower was constructed to be the most airtight security facility in the world. Like anything built with such exuberance, it had a few design flaws—a few places where overzealousness lapsed into an arrogant carelessness. However, for the most part, the Tower was what it was designed to be: a steel trap.

Level One was used for storage only, so the second level was the lowest floor that housed prisoners. Because it was the darkest, Level Two was referred to as "the Dungeon." The loudest prisoners were kept there so their noise wouldn't disturb the guards.

The first eight levels were always underwater, and the only natural light they received filtered through the steel bars from the floors above. The twelfth level remained empty, for security reasons. Despite the tremendous precautions, the warden felt Level Twelve was just too close to freedom and the guards above.

A large fan, protected by a steel gate, was situated underneath the first level. Piping ran beneath the ocean floor from the mainland, drawing air to feed the fan. But the sluggish movement of the blades was not enough to sweep the musk from the air. Only the top four levels had vents, though those on Level Nine were never opened, as they were almost always beneath the ocean's surface.

A single carbon gaslight was encased in bulletproof glass on every other level, slightly illuminating the metal walls. These bleak lights trailed through the dimness of the Tower, making it seem as thickly claustrophobic as a mine shaft. At night, they were usually turned off.

The interior of the Tower was constructed of thick

steel bars. There was barely a quarter of an inch between
the bars and the outer wall, which sat over the steel
intestines like a stone hide. Not only were the unit walls
made from such bars, but also the floors and ceilings.

Home to men who could kill with paper clips and
keys, the Tower was designed as the barest possible liv-
able environment. No plaster could be risked for walls,
no wood for floors. The steel bars that composed the
inside of the Tower had another advantage: They
allowed the guards to see through the levels to check on
the inmates. Initially, the architects had experimented
with an unbreakable glass, but they had found that it
fogged heavily with mist from the ocean and created a
ventilation nightmare.

The outside wall of each curved cell measured twenty
feet, and the cells were five feet in width. Each faced its
mirror image across "the Hole," an open cylinder of air
that ran straight down the center of the Tower. There
were spacings of eight and one-third feet between the
units on each side; this ensured that the prisoners never
established bodily contact, and that the guards could
always remain out of reach.

Due to the fact that the ceiling of each cell also served
as the floor for the one above it, the prisoners could most
easily communicate with the men directly above or
below them. Although this design element may have
seemed a lapse in the Tower's tight security, few of the
men were tall enough to reach their ceilings, even from
their beds. Those who were could hardly get their fingers
to the bars, let alone through them. The neck-strained
interaction between the floors served the Tower's design:
to break the spirits of nearly indomitable men by removing from them all the trappings of civilization.

The cells each had a minuscule toilet with a small tap

that swung into place above it, allowing it to double as a sink. The toilets caught the water before it spiraled down through the barred floors. Each unit had a single mattress on a steel frame, and a thick blanket for the chilly nights off the California coast.

The Hole formed the shaft for the platform elevator, four feet in diameter, which was operated by a handheld unit. Precisely framing the elevator was a two-foot platform between the Hole and the unit doors. When not in use, the elevator was raised out of the top of the Hole ten feet in the air, leaving only the dark emptiness below.

When the prisoners were unruly or when it rained (which rarely happened), the large Hatch was swung into place underneath the raised elevator, blocking out all natural light and moisture. However, when the sun was directly overhead and the Hatch was open, light shone through the metal mesh of the raised elevator, and the two men on Level Eleven could see clearly down into the units ten levels beneath them.

A prisoner was shackled around his biceps and wrists when transported, and his thighs were strapped together to allow only minimal leg movement. He was sent down the elevator with a guard on each side. He was always gagged, and often hooded. At all times, one of the two guards had a gun with the safety off trained on the prisoner. The necessity of such seemingly paranoid precautions had been learned at painful expense. Prisoners were only moved once, and they were only moved in.

Before a prisoner was taken to the Tower, a small sensor was surgically embedded in the tip of the ring finger on his left hand. If he escaped, this device allowed his movements to be tracked. The prisoners were put under general anesthesia while the sensors were installed, and were kept heavily drugged until a significant amount of healing had taken place, sometimes five or six days. The Maingate physicians feared if the prisoners fully awakened before then, they would dig the sensors out with their nails and teeth.

Food was delivered to the prisoners twice a day. It came in the form of a large loaf containing all the necessary nutrients to allow an animal to function. A cross between quiche and bread, the loaves were light brown when cooked correctly. They required no plates or silverware, part of the reason for their continued use. They were delivered by a guard at precisely 10:30 A.M. and 7:15 P.M.; he slid them through a small rectangular slot, barely the size of the loaf itself, at the bottom of each unit door.

A long metal arm with two outgrowths at the end was used to guide the loaves through the slot. The loaves were referred to by the inmates as "shithouse bricks." They had minimal taste.

When a prisoner behaved perfectly for a week, he was allowed a large sheet of paper and two crayons with which to entertain himself. A guard held a box through the bars with a metal arm to retrieve the crayons when the time was up. This was called "Sketch Duty."

Sketch Duty was perhaps the only activity that the prisoners unanimously held to be important. It was the sole end of the prisoners' lives to obtain this hour of distraction each week. They could keep the pictures in their cells for two days, then they were removed and taken to be analyzed at the criminal psychology department of the Ressler Institute on the mainland. The pictures were often used in lectures.

Aside from the occasional books they were allowed, Sketch Duty was all that the prisoners had to break the monotony. Inside the Tower, minutes could stretch to hours, hours to lifetimes.

Despair prevailed in the bowels of the prison; nobody would ever be released and nobody had ever escaped its dark confines. The inmates sat pressed against the metal bars of their cramped cells, reciting their tales in the broken tongues of idiots.

ALLANDER Atlasia sat on the bed wrapped in a frayed blanket, his knees tucked tightly to his chin. The small bed was more than ample for his wiry frame. Outside, the waves pounded ceaselessly against the side of the Tower, causing the structure to hum with a deep vibration. Allander braced himself against the onslaught, relaxing his muscles slightly before another wave caused the Tower to shudder anew.

His long, stringy hair curved in wisps to his cheeks, a dark brown cascade that accented his high cheekbones. His eyes squinted, just barely, making him look either sarcastic or like a child protecting his eyes from the sun. At first glance, many people dismissed Allander as a skinny adolescent recently grown to manhood, but he was in fact quite strong.

Allander's moodiness was the most terrifying aspect of his personality. When he'd been in the correctional ward as an adolescent, nurses had noted that he seemed to wake up as a different person every morning. He was a whimpering child when the rain hammered against the window, a sullen boy who poked frogs' eyes out with his finger, a sweet youth who cried against a nurse's bosom, an angry adolescent who painfully tweaked the incipient breasts of the girls in the ward.

He could be deathly frail or dreadfully powerful. After a year in prison, he came down with a case of pneumonia. A nurse who was new on rotation failed to see the security signs outside his room. She unlocked the door and entered alone to check on him. His face was tinged blue and his teeth chattered loudly, causing an echo in the sterile room. She sat at his bedside and rocked the boy (who was now close to twenty) against her breast until he warmed beneath his blankets.

When the security guard walked past the infirmary, he noticed the open door. Gun drawn, he charged into the room and pulled the nurse away despite her protestations. After she complained about the incident, the warden released several photographs of Allander's victims for her perusal. She sat down after the second one, requested a glass of water after the fifth, and turned in her resignation after the seventh. Through the bars on his window, Allander watched her leave the prison, shaking her head, her steps slow and unsure.

When he was moved to the Tower after the "lawyer incident" (as it was referred to in the vague prison memo), he rode the elevator down through the Hole, bound, with an armed guard on each side and a sack tied over his head. He didn't flinch as the other inmates taunted him and screamed, banging the bars. It wasn't often that a new visitor came for them to play with. Allander was thirty-three years old.

He was placed in Unit 10A, and asked to turn around and back up against the door. From the safety of the platform, the larger guard reached through the bars and unlocked his handcuffs and thigh strap, then pulled the sack off his head and untied the gag. Allander wore a mask of calm, apparently not intimidated by the shrieks that carried up and down the Hole.

The ruckus quieted as the prisoners tired of their new toy. They resigned themselves to bed, their heads settling to rest on the stained yellow pillows. After the shouts stopped echoing, after not an inmate stirred in the jet, black night, Allander drew the thin blanket to his face and shook uncontrollably.

On rare occasions, high tide was moderate enough that the top three levels stayed above the ocean's brink. The water would remain just under the vents of Level Ten, so the guards would open them to aid the air circulation. In the deathly heat of the summer, the prisoners would lie bare-chested on their cots, fanning themselves with their blankets and dousing their bodies with water from the toilets. But as dusk fell like a funeral veil across the sky, the cool San Francisco air crept through the vents and into the bones of the prisoners. The guards would laugh as the inmates shuddered and clamored in their metal rooms.

On these nights, Allander would retreat to the safety of his bed and stare through the thin gaps in the vents. As moonlight spread across the water, it engendered figures and shapes, creatures and monsters that crept in the swirls and eddies. He stifled his cries as he saw clowns dancing above the whitecaps, their long, white arms reaching toward him through the waves, their laughing red mouths rippling in the water's surface, mouthing threats and delights eternal.

Only once did he lose control, and he hurled himself against the metal bars, screaming in despair. "JUST COME IN! Come in now and take me. TAKE ME!"

He collapsed, cowering in the corner under the vent. His eyes bulged wide in dreadful anticipation as he slowly became aware of the laughter filling the air around him.

IN Unit 2A of the Dungeon was Tommy "Cuckoo T" Giacondia, perhaps the most famous living Mafia hitman. Tommy at one time had weighed over two hundred and fifty pounds, but since his imprisonment five years before, he had lost over a hundred. Now he looked thin and weak, his cheeks and eyes filled with shadow. His weight loss had no effect on his vocal capacity, however; he constantly bellowed complaints up the Hole, most of which dealt with the food. Evidently, Tommy was used to a more varied diet than a loaf for every meal.

"This shit," he would say. "I wouldn't feed this to my worst enemy. I wouldn't make his dog eat this shithouse brick if it pissed on my mother's grave."

This was perhaps because he dealt with his worst enemies (or those of the Berlucciano family) in far more colorful ways. His signature disposal method was an original one. He would tie up his victim in a closet of an abandoned warehouse, and then cut off the tips of his fingertips about midway down the nail. He would leave them to bleed to death or to die slowly of dehydration. They were usually found weeks after he left them, their fingers scraped down to the top knuckles from trying to escape.

Tommy ran into trouble on the Merloni hit. He had finished only the first two fingers of the right hand when the cops arrived at the scene. Tommy came out shooting and took two bullets to the gut, but was rushed to the hospital and lived to stand trial.

The victim testified with a large bandage wrapped around his hand. When photographs of Tommy's last hits were circulated to the jury, an accountant in the front row fainted. Needless to say, Tommy wound up with life, no parole. Perhaps even worse, he never found out who'd tipped off the police. This question consumed him, swimming through his mind on long afternoons until the bittersweet thought of revenge tightened his hands into fists.

But Tommy was a different man now. His time in the Tower had worn him down, like water over a rock. His edges dulled, he smoothed against opposition.

Although he was a horrible artist, he loved Sketch Duty passionately. One day, he refused to return his crayons when his time was up. And when he was supposed to relinquish his picture, he would not. Using his semen, he pasted his childish drawing of a single potted flower on his wall bars and admired it as if it were a Renoir. The guards could not have prisoners disobeying the rules, and although they wouldn't open the unit door to retrieve the picture, they could render it worthless from outside.

Tommy regarded them nervously as they rode down on the elevator trailing a thick hose usually used for washing down the inmates. "Whaddaya want? Whaddaya want with my flower?" They didn't answer him; they just turned on the water full blast, dousing the unit and drenching the picture.

He shrieked and tried to block the stream with his body, but it was too late. The colors faded into the darkening paper and the ruined picture fell in a wad through the floor bars. He started crying like a child, big, round tears running down his cheeks. "My flower," he said over and over. "My beautiful flower."

That was the last time Tommy got Sketch Duty. In the Tower, one chance was all you had.

Although he kept up his contentious front, Tommy Giacondia was gone on the inside, rendered totally harmless. That was a bad thing to be in the Tower, surrounded by men who smelled weakness more strongly than anything else. So, as a means of protection, Tommy kept loud.

Across from him was Safran Habbád, a bomb specialist who worked contracts for Third-World countries. During a South American coup in the early eighties, he had taken out an entire government cabinet.

He was captured in the United States a few years later, fulfilling a contract on a Massachusetts senator who was a strong advocate of gun control. Safran was cornered in the house after he'd set the bomb, and he'd refused to surrender. It exploded in the kitchen, and although he was on the second floor, he still lost half the flesh on his face to the blast, as well as a considerable amount on his back, arms, and legs. He'd attempted to burn down his hospital room to avoid his trial, hoping perhaps to rise from his ashes and spread his wings, but his escapade had failed and he was sentenced, ironically, to life.

The first day Safran moved to Level Two, Tommy greeted him in his usual manner.

"You stupid falafel-eating 7-Eleven prick. You shut the fuck up if you gonna live here by me. Bombing houses of families, you're a sicko. A *spaccone*."

Safran swore back at him in several languages before commenting on Italy's paltry effort in the Second World War, implying that it was due to the deficient genital dimensions of the soldiers. The two men were quickly embroiled in the first of many violent arguments in which neither understood much of what the other said.

Alone on Level Three was Mills Benedick. The guards decided to leave Unit 3A vacant rather than subject even a Tower prisoner to Mills on a daily basis. He stood hunched over, his rounded shoulders heaving as he loudly drew breath.

An unusual amount of body hair covered him, curling thickly around his shoulders and arms. There was no line where his head hair ended in the back and his body hair began. Mills ate by shoving his loaf against his mouth, grunting and sucking the food in.

Mills had escaped a high-security mental institution two years after he was committed. He'd become a serial rapist in his brief stint in the outside world, committing five rapes in the seven days he was free.

He would break into single women's homes during the day and hide until they came home from work and went to sleep. Sneaking to their beds, he would pounce on them, quickly pressing duct tape over their mouths and eyes. Once he had their heads adequately fixed to the beds, he would undress the women slowly and stare at their naked bodies. Then, from his heavy perch upon their chests, he'd begin to masturbate. Finally he'd unleash himself on their bodies, hurling himself into them and thrashing until he was relieved.

Four of the women had severe bite wounds on their breasts and faces; one victim had even died mid-act (the forensic pathologist concluded), when Mills had ripped out her larynx with his teeth.

The day he was captured, Mills had fled a rape scene after he'd heard sirens approaching. He'd run several miles over rough terrain with tree branches cutting his arms and cheeks. Sweat ran into his cuts and his eyes, and he'd begun to bellow with pain. A frightened farmer, believing there was a wild animal on the loose, had called the police.

The police tracked Mills to a church in the hills, and they positioned themselves outside, peering through binoculars to fix his location.

Inside, the sun bled harshly through the stained-glass windows, casting distorted images across the pews. Mills sat on the stairs leading to the altar, holding his head in his hands, dust floating about him in the multicolored air. When he raised his head, the light ran madly across his unshaven face.

The police burst in from their silent vigil, shattering windows and breaking down doors. Mills stood on the stairs and screamed, a terrified, primal roar, his face distorted as spittle flowed over the brink of his bottom lip, spilling onto his bristled chin. Before verbal contact could be established, a scared rookie sank two tranquilizer darts into Mills's upper chest. Mills woke up on Level Three.

Another personality in the Tower was Cyprus Fraker, a former Ku Klux Klan Grand Wizard from Alabama. His Klan chapter had grown to be influential at a local political level and, eventually, he was indicted on charges of embezzlement.

Cyprus was less immediately dangerous than the other inmates, but he wound up in the Tower because at Maingate he'd led the Aryan Fist organization, which had been responsible for several prison assassinations. The officials thought it better to separate him from his followers and his outside contacts, so they had placed him in the Tower. Racial violence at the prison had abated as a consequence.

Cyprus lived in Unit 9B, where, in his underwear, he would sit for hours, tilted back on his bed, singing country songs. He managed to catch a number of water rats that made their way into the Tower, and he snapped their necks and hung them by their tails from the ceiling bars. Whenever the Hatch was opened, they would twirl in the air like wind chimes.

When Cyprus had first moved to his unit, Spade, the powerful black prisoner in Unit 10B, urinated through the floor bars into his open mouth every time he fell asleep.

"You stupid fuckin' nigger. I ought to lynch your sorry ass. You're a fuckin' gorilla."

"Yes," Spade smiled back, "but who's the one with a mouthful of piss, 'Bama boy?"

Eventually, at the command of the guards, Spade had toned down his urinary assaults in exchange for more Sketch Duty.

CLAUDE Rivers lived right above Allander, in Unit 11A. After a killing spree in 1992, Claude had come home, decapitated his mother, and lived quietly in the apartment with her head impaled on a coat tree. He'd kept her corpse in the bedroom, using it to fulfill his sexual needs. He was captured after neighbors complained about the smell emanating from his apartment.

In the Tower, Claude spent his time sleeping. Balding, his gut protruding from beneath his shirt, his skin greasy and red, he looked more like a seedy hotel manager than an accomplished killer. Allander had heard stories about him back at Maingate, and was amazed that someone with such an egregious appearance could have committed that most challenging of crimes.

Spade lived in Unit 10B, across the hole from Allander. Like the pairs of prisoners on each level, they were both locked together and apart in their tight circle. Spade stood a solid six foot four, two-forty, and he was as bald as an eight ball. He was still known by his street tag, which he carried with him like a weapon. None of the prisoners knew his real name.

Through a rigorous routine of exercises during his eight years at Maingate and the Tower, Spade had maintained his muscle from his gangster days. In the late-night hours, Allander watched through the thick air as Spade contorted his frame, twisting backward and upside down.

Spade alone could reach through the bars that composed the ceilings of the cells. He did pull-ups on them until one day Jonsten Evers gleefully overturned his bed on top of Spade's hands, which peeked through his floor. Spade was stuck dangling five inches above the ground, swaying painfully back and forth. Jonsten had giggled hysterically during the thirty minutes the guards took to respond to Spade's roars. It was very hard to hear what went on in the Tower from certain areas of the roof (one of the flaws of its design), and this, in addition to the guards' general contempt for the prisoners, accounted for the slow response time when mishaps did occur.

After the tops of his fingers scabbed over, Spade stood on his bed for hours, his hand extended through Jonsten's floor bars. Jonsten, still under the sway of his heady delirium, played with Spade's hand at first. He taunted it with strokes, jerking back his hand as Spade's snapped shut like a Venus-flytrap. He would spit on the hand, pinch the back of it—even try to step on it and pin it wriggling to the floor. Spade's hand responded so quickly, however, that it avoided much of the punishment from above.

"On the street, you'd be my little bitch," Spade growled at Jonsten through the bars. "I'd own you. These metal bars protect you from the beast. Just a couple feet between us. If I could touch you, I'd rip you apart with my hands and teeth. Rip you apart. Come on, just reach down. Reach on down and touch my hand."

Jonsten tittered nervously, his high-pitched laugh echoing through the elevator shaft.

"But we're not. We're not on the street. You can't touch me. I'm up here and you're down. You're down on Level Ten." He giggled as he writhed about the floor, singing ecstatically. His halting song came in tortuously rhymed couplets: "On the street a wild killer he made. But in the Tower, Spade finds himself caged."

As Spade persisted in his efforts, Jonsten's hyper-delirious mood was replaced with concern, then fear, then despair. He began to obsess about the hand's minuscule intrusion into his world. He stopped playing with it, then touching it at all, and soon he withdrew to his bed and refused to leave.

"Spade, I didn't mean it. With the bed. The bed. The bed that tipped over. I'm sorry."

But Spade said nothing, and day after day, he stood on the bed with his hand extended patiently through the bars.

Jonsten began screaming and moaning in anguish, but he was generally ignored. This was nothing new in the Tower. "The hand. Make it go away. Away, hand! Away, Spade's hand. I'll bite it. I'll bite it off."

He never really slept anymore, existing instead in that bitter dream world that lies between sleep and waking. He squirmed in his bed, his disheveled hair flipping from side to side. "The hand! Don't! It's reaching for me. It's coming for me."

A chorus of shouts answered him. "Shut the hell up, Jonsten. Or I'll come for you. And I'm worse than some fucking hand."

Jonsten peered anxiously over the edge of his bed to see if the telltale hand had sunk away, but it had not. For days it did not depart; it stayed and watched him, a shark's fin emerging from a metal sea.

When Jonsten had to go to the bathroom, he leapt from the bed and made his way to the toilet, his back mashed against the wall bars so he could watch the hand. He balanced over the toilet, his bulging eyes still fixed on the hand as he defecated sloppily into the steel bowl.

Aside from such ventures, he remained sitting Indian-style on his bed.

All the while Spade waited calmly.

Jonsten got weaker and weaker. He was afraid to cross his cell to pick up his loaves; they accumulated just inside the slot in his door, collecting swirls of flies. After a few days, he became afraid even to make the brief journey to the toilet.

Eventually, his exhaustion caught up with him and he began to nod off. His head lolled forward and his weight started to shift him over the side of the narrow bed. He jerked awake in a panic, his wild eyes flashing, then orienting on the hand and setting themselves again with determination. He had glimpsed his final weakness, however, and now he knew, as Spade had all along, that it was just a matter of time.

Finally, one night he fell asleep completely and he slumped forward, his arm dangling above the floor. His eyes opened in terror as he realized where his lapse had landed him, and then the hand seized him around the wrist.

Spade leapt from his bed, maintaining his viselike grip on the wrist and bringing his two hundred and forty pounds to bear on it. Jonsten's body slammed flat against the floor, smashed by the force pulling his arm downward. His hand snapped back against his arm to accommodate the gap between the bars, and he squealed as his wrist broke in two.

Spade's size-fourteen feet were finally touching the floor. He gazed up at the limp piece of meat in his outstretched hand. His face and bald head were splattered with blood from the wound where Jonsten's bone had punctured the skin, and he laughed deeply as he licked the spray from around his lips.

Dropping his weight, Spade swung from Jonsten's arm, which was taking on the appearance of a grotesque chandelier. There was another pop (accompanied by more screams) when Jonsten's shoulder left the socket, and the flesh around his upper arm bunched up above the bars. It began to give way, and as it tore, bone, muscle, and ligament came into the dim light in front of Spade. He no longer had to stand on his toes.

He heard a series of whimpers coming through the ceiling, and he smiled before climbing on the bed and reaching through the gap again. He grabbed a handful of Jonsten's hair, and using his body weight again, ripped it out.

Jonsten passed out, giving the other inmates a break from his delirious screaming. Mercifully, he didn't have to be awake as Spade's meaty hands closed around his neck, and with a single quick jerk, snapped his spinal cord.

The only prisoners who actually witnessed the episode were those on the eighth and ninth levels and, of course, Allander. He lay on his bed, watching Spade's exertions with a mixture of amusement and contempt. The inmates on the lower levels realized something was wrong only as the blood made its way down, dripping from the ends of Jonsten's fingers through the floor bars. A few of them cackled and cheered, licking the blood gleefully from their fingers, remembering the flavor and the hot scent.

Spade settled down on his bed. Lying back, he opened a book and began to read as Jonsten's arm swung lazily overhead.

JONSTEN'S death came on Allander's tenth day in the Tower. Prior to that time, Allander had been largely ignored by Spade, who had been too preoccupied with the cell above to notice him. Shortly after the incident, the guards had arrived to view the scene. They reprimanded Spade, showering him with obscenities and turning a hose on him. Spade merely laughed and flexed in the water's spray. "Whatcha gonna do, put me in prison?" he taunted.

After the guards cleared Jonsten's mangled body from his cell (the warden decided to leave 11B vacant for the duration of Spade's sentence), Spade focused on the small, shivering prisoner across the Hole.

"So . . . you're the clown boy. We heard about you. Heard you all in the news and on the TV. I remember that. Young boy gettin' fucked in the ass, and not even in prison. We were waiting for you though."

Allander said nothing, remaining collected and distant.

"Let me ask you, child. You glad you don't live upstairs from me?" Spade tilted his head back, indicating the bars, which were still caked with blood and hair despite the hosing. "Guess I'm not too good a neighbor." He laughed his deep, booming laugh and climbed into bed.

• • •

Allander awoke to a tapping on his forehead. His hands moved over his face in a rush and he realized it was wet. He looked through the ceiling and saw Claude Rivers standing directly above him, his legs slightly spread so Allander was gazing up at his crotch.

Claude held his shirt, which he had doused in the toilet. He twisted it, forearms cording with muscles, bringing down another slow series of drops on Allander's head. Allander stood up, rubbing his forehead. It was sore, as if the water had worn a groove in it.

Claude watched him with interest, but said nothing. Allander crossed his unit to the vents. Overhead, Claude slowly shadowed his movement. He paused, wringing his shirt again, bringing a few plump drops down on Allander's head. Allander looked up at him, but no change of expression flickered over Claude's face. His eyes were light and wide, like holes through his head. When Allander went back to his bed, Claude did not follow.

Allander fell back into an uneasy sleep. When he jerked awake later, it was pitch black. He sat up in his cot quickly, glancing through the bars of the ceiling, but it seemed Claude was asleep.

The Hatch was open and the noises of the guards on duty drifted in. It was a moonless night and Allander peered around his cell, trying to adjust to the lack of light. He had the sense that something was in the cell with him, something was watching him. Finally, his night vision eased into effect, and he could see Spade's enormous meat-cleaver hands around the cell bars.

Allander sat up and stared across the Hole at Spade's cell. Spade's eyes slowly emerged from the darkness, then his white teeth flashed in a smile and Allander sensed a reflection from his skull. In that faint light, Spade looked as if he were made of only two hands and a floating head; the rest of his body faded into the black cell.

His voice came low and he articulated each word fully, playing with it in his mouth before releasing it to the air. "Welcome back, my child. Welcome to the cage. At first I didn't think you belonged here. But now I've seen you sleep and I know. I know you do. No one in here sleeps, and it's not the sound, it's not the"—he gestured grandly—"ambiance. And it sure as hell's not our consciences. You see, those of us in the Tower, we 'Boat Pokey boys,' we're different. We've *seen* too much to sleep. We *know* too much to sleep. What do you know, my child? What do you see?"

"Nothing," Allander said. "I don't see anything."

"BULLSHIT!" Spade boomed. The word echoed through the Tower. No one yelled for him to shut up, and the lapping water outside filled the silence. His voice dropped back to its deep whisper. "I see you turning and rolling and panting, and it's not from jackin' off. What do you see in your dreams, my child? What do you see in your heart of hearts?"

Allander remained quiet.

"Is it the clowns? The ones you're always drawing? There?" He pointed at Allander's drawing. Allander glanced over at it, amazed that Spade could make it out through the darkness.

In the drawing, an enormous clown loomed over the horizon of what appeared to be a medieval castle on a hill. The clown had dismantled one of the castle's towers and held it menacingly in its spidery fingers. Its long fingernails were wrapped around the tower, and a small maiden, hanging from a window, shrieked for help. The clown had a large, painted grin on its face. Its expression was that of a fat child about to indulge in an ice cream cone. The artwork was spectacular; the intricate details betrayed the labored minutes Allander had spent hovering over the paper.

"No," he replied.

Spade drew air in loudly through his teeth. "Clowns to the left of me, rapists to my right, here I am, stuck in the Tower with ya'll." He laughed. "Tell me, my child, why are you too good to talk to the rest of us murderers and molesters?"

Allander did not reply.

"I know your story. We all know your story. You're probably the most famous one in here. All the attention you got in court because of your—what'd the judge call it?—'environmental conditioning'?" He sounded out the syllables of "environmental," making it sound like en-vi-ron-mental.

"But you proved them wrong, didn't you, child? When you look inside, you know, you know like we all know. You know that even if you missed your childhood"—he paused, searching for the right word—"honeymoon, you know you'd still be a twisted, sick motherfucker. Now don't you?"

"How should I presume?" Allander chuckled softly, as if to himself, running his hands through his hair. He lifted his head, and for the first time, Spade caught a glimpse of what was behind his eyes. It made even him draw back, ever so slightly.

Allander continued quietly, but his voice warbled as if under great strain. "You think you can measure the range, the depth of my sickness?" He shook his head slightly. "I don't think you want to walk that landscape." His eyes darted back and forth, flashing over Spade's face, trying to gain entrance to his mind. He pried at it through Spade's eyes, his nose, his mouth.

"You wish what? You wish to explore the common bonds we share as outsiders in our society?" He waved an arm in the air for emphasis, his voice drenched in sarcasm. "Well, then, that much we have in common. Hooray for your insightfulness. But I'm afraid that's where our similarities end. You're a beast who beats the walls of its prison, but what would you do if you were free? What heights, pray tell, are you just waiting to scale?" Allander shook his head, making sounds of disappointment deep in his throat. "I must confess, darling, I find you a bit tiresome."

Spade's upper lip withdrew disdainfully from his teeth, and he scowled as his fury bubbled to the surface. "YOU MOTHERFUCKER! DO YOU KNOW WHO THE FUCK I AM? WHO THE FUCK YOU'RE TALKING TO?"

Allander remained completely still. "Evidently not."

Spade inhaled deeply, his chest rising and falling like a mountain in an earthquake. "I *owned* faggots like you on the outside. In the slammer, I bent men twice your size over the bathroom sink and *fucked* them. Because you're protected from me by this"—he motioned to the bars around him—"you think you can step up to me. You *know*, you *know* better."

Allander paused and gestured with his eyes, indicating the space above Spade's head. "I'm afraid I don't have Jonsten's delicate temperament." He thrilled at the "I," as if arriving at it after a long and tedious journey. "And, forgive me if I'm incorrect, but it seems that you can't touch me in here, not even through a ceiling, which makes those muscles of yours about as useless as your sluggish brain."

Allander let his last comment sink in before continuing. He spoke clearly and firmly, pausing dramatically between each word. "I can and will talk to you however I

want, whenever I want. Remember, we're . . . locked in."
He moaned the last words, raising his eyebrows and wig-
gling his fingers in mock horror.

He laughed once, sharply. "You pose no threat to me
standing safely under lock and key across the way." He
crossed to the front of his cell and slid his arm slowly
through the bars in Spade's direction. "At arm's length, if
you will."

Spade exploded in rage, his magnificent roars shaking
the Tower. Backing up, he threw his full weight against
the unit door, banging the bars with his shoulder. He continued to hurl himself against the steel bars, reaching
through and straining to reach Allander's extended hand.

Acknowledging at last the futility of his efforts, Spade
overturned his bed, hurling it against the wall with one
arm. He sank angrily to his haunches, glaring across the
Hole at Allander.

"Keep it the fuck down down there!" one of the guards
shouted into the Hole.

"Yeah, you shut the fuck up, nigger," Cyprus added
from below.

Spade threw water from the toilet over his head, then
sat on the cell floor as his breathing slowed to normal.
There was a long silence.

"Perhaps you would have had more luck had you used
your head as a battering ram." Allander smiled, then
walked to his bed and peeled the blanket back neatly.
"Now, if you could please restrain your impotent rage . . ."
He motioned majestically around his unit and climbed
into bed. Rolling over, he turned his back to Spade.

Spade's hands clenched and unclenched in the darkness. After several hours, to make himself feel better, he
loosened his pants and pissed on Cyprus again.

6

THE guards patrolled the top of the Tower, circling endlessly with their guns and cigarettes. Tom Hackett was Maingate's senior guard; he'd been selected because of his CIA training, and his experience in transporting and subduing prisoners. There are two types of enforcers—those who catch people, and those who keep and control them. Hackett was definitely one of the latter. When the Tower had first gone up, there were few who didn't suspect he would be called in to run security.

Toughness was written in every line on Hackett's face. The ruddy, tan skin of his cheeks drooped into jowls. Along with his pug nose, they gave him the appearance of a kind, but disgruntled bulldog.

The two guards talked as they circled, sometimes shouting above the roar of the waves, and bits and pieces of their conversation wafted down to the inmates.

Justin Greener pulled out a cigarette. "Got a light?" he asked.

"Of course," Hackett said, reaching for the toolbox. He removed a small cup of yogurt and placed it on the deck, then dug through a pile of tools to find the matches.

"You eat that shit?" Greener asked, pointing to the yogurt and trying not to smile.

Hackett stood up, straightening his green slicker indignantly. "Wait till you get a few more years on you and your doctor starts riding you like a bronco, we'll see what you're eating." He lit a match off his thumbnail and held it out unceremoniously.

Greener surveyed the darkening clouds as he cupped his hands around the small flame. "Looks like rain," he said, the cigarette jiggling slightly with his words.

"I told you. Better grab your jacket."

Greener crossed over to the small guard station and took a tightly rolled slicker from the wall. The jacket was packed into itself and tied with a cord; he flipped it once in the air casually and caught it.

"That new kid's a sick bastard," he said as he walked back to Hackett, the end of his cigarette glowing in the dusk.

"They all are," Hackett replied.

"No, I mean he's really psycho. He's calm as shit, all the time. I guess over at Maingate all he did was read all day and draw pictures."

"And kill five people in his two-year vacation over there. That's why we get him."

"What'd he kill, the shrink and some nurses?" Greener tapped the roll of the slicker against his thigh as he leaned back against the railing.

"No. Try his lawyer, two inmates, and two guards."

"This is the prick who killed both those guards?"

"Yeah. It's not officially released yet, so it's still a rumor as far as you know."

"What happened?"

"He had a meeting with his lawyer and took him hostage. Held the poor bastard's Mont Blanc pen to his carotid artery. I guess he broke the light in the room and hid with his hostage behind the door. When the first guard came in—"

"Gun first?"

"Of course."

Greener shook his head as Hackett continued, "He kicked the door closed on his arm and the stupid bastard dropped the gun. He shot him and his first backup before anyone else got there." Hackett looked down, studying his shoe.

When he looked up, Greener was surprised by the sudden intensity in his eyes. "You remember, Greener." Hackett stabbed his finger in the middle of Greener's chest. "A veteran never relinquishes his weapon." They stood silently for a moment.

"And the lawyer?" Greener asked.

"You know what always happens to the lawyer."

Both men laughed, their breath showing in the cool, misty air.

"The kid punctured his neck and was drawing pictures on the ground with his blood by the time anyone else showed up. When I got there, he was peaceful and as cooperative as a baby. Came with us, no problem."

"When did he off the prisoners?"

"Almost two years apart. He killed the first when he got there. In the shower. Gave him a forehead to the nose and put it through his brain. Put in seclusion for a week, and he was good when he came out. It really scared him, seclusion."

"The other?"

"About a month ago, he put a spoon through someone's eye in the cafeteria."

"Why a spoon?"

"Cuz what do you think, they give 'em knives to cut their prime rib with?"

"How 'bout a fork?"

"No forks either."

"How do you kill somebody with a fucking spoon?"

"You hold the spoon end like this"—Hackett prepared his imaginary spoon—"bending it so it sits flush against your palm, with the long end sticking out between your second and middle finger. Then you jab your fist at an angle. Hit the eye. Up and in."

Greener whistled. "I don't even know how they think of this shit."

"That's why you're out here, Greener, and they're in there."

Hackett turned and started another lap around the tight perimeter. As he passed Greener, he faked a jab at him. Greener, who had been flipping the slicker, flinched to the side. He shot out his hand to grab the jacket and knocked it over the side of the Tower. "Shit," he said as he watched it drift away, a green spot on the dark water.

Hackett laughed. "If you're that scared of an imaginary spoon . . ." He chuckled again as Greener started to smile.

"He must be a smart bitch to think that one up," Greener said.

Hackett pressed his lips together as he looked out over the rolling waves. "He's a fuckin' genius, that kid. Shouldn't have let him read so much shit at Maingate. They tested him at the ward. Twice. Thought they fucked up the first time. A genius." He wiped his mouth with the back of his hand. "Which makes him all the more goddamn dangerous."

They stood silently for a while, finishing their cigarettes as the sun dipped to the hazy horizon. A few seagulls flew overhead, then wrangled over some dead crabs that had washed ashore.

A burst of thunder swept across the gray sky.

"We'd better get dinner ready now in case we have to close the Hatch on account of rain," Hackett said.

"What's on the menu this morning, boss?"

"Yogurt," they both said together, and Hackett reluctantly joined in Greener's laughter.

Greener went into the small shed on the roof of the Tower and pulled out the tray with loaves on it, grabbing the pronged metal arm. The arm enabled the guards to deliver the loaves from the elevator, sliding them through the food hole at the base of the door. Maximum distance, maximum safety. It also had a plastic loop that the guard put around his wrist so a prisoner couldn't yank it away.

Greener checked the monitor that displayed the prisoners' location sensors. Eighteen blinking lights lined up in two rows. One red flashing light after another.

When he walked out of the shed, Hackett passed him the keys. "Why don't you grab another jacket out of storage," he said. "Last thing I need is you getting even more wet behind the ears." He grinned affectionately as Greener took the keys and hooked them through his belt. "And grab a couple of extras while you're down there."

"All right, hotshot," Greener said, leaning over to pick up the tray.

7

HEADING onto the elevator, Greener launched into what had become his customary routine: "Okay, kids, wake up! The menu today consists of, surprisingly, a fucking loaf. We were flying in a new recipe straight from Paris—that's in France, Cyprus—where they've been doing experimentation with escargot soufflés. Unfortunately, the plane crashed, so you get to eat this shit again."

"Fuck you, Greener—"

"Greener, you asshole—"

He smiled. "The choirboys speak."

He placed a loaf down on Level Eleven and, extending the arm, slid it under the door of Unit 11A. Claude Rivers did not stir.

"Here you go, Van Winkle. Try not to choke on it." He held the elevator control with its big red buttons in his left hand. It was a remote unit that could fit into a front pocket. "All right, here we go. More four-star dining. Looks like we'll be skipping Jonsten today." He shook his head at Spade as the elevator platform settled at Level Ten. "Spade, you sicko. Don't we feed you enough?"

"Yeah, fuck you."

"Well, it's good to see your vocabulary's expanding in here. I'll put in a good word to your parole officer—oh wait. That's right. You don't have a parole officer."

Spade sneered, his curled lip rising until its wrinkles

met those from his squinting eye. Greener looked over at
Allander, who was lying facedown on the floor with the
blue blanket draped over his waist. "Hey, Atlasia, you
want breakfast?"

No response.

"Hey, junior, you want some food? Come on, I'll even
let you eat with a sharpened spoon." No response.
Greener knew that the prisoners sometimes lay like that
to look at the man below—intimidating, hateful stares
that lasted all day. It wasn't like Allander, he thought, but
it wasn't that unusual either. "All right," he said. "Lie
there and I'll get you on the way up."

He pushed the big red button on the remote and the
elevator's gears clicked, lowering him another level. "Hey
there, Cyprus, ya big inbreed you. Sorry I couldn't bring
you a distant cousin to enjoy, but how about a nice deep-
fried fun loaf?"

"I could have you killed the minute you step foot off
this Tower, Greener."

"Well, Billy Ray—"

"I told you, don't you fuckin' call me that."

"All right, Sir Cyprus. I'm sure you could have me
killed, but unfortunately . . ." Greener surveyed the bleak
steel walls around him. "Unfortunately, I don't see a pay
phone around here anywhere. Or a quarter."

Cyprus scowled and ran his palm over his chin. "And
you're not due for a parole hearing . . . ," Greener said,
checking his watch carefully, "for about two hundred and
eighteen years."

"Two hundred seventeen, six months, and four days
or else when the good Lord Jesus comes to free the
Master Race. And he won't be taking you along."

"Now that hurts. I'm sorry to say it, Cyprus, but you're
off my Christmas-card list." Greener checked his sheet.

"Love to shoot the shit with you all day, farm boy, but I gots some grits to deliver." Smiling, he rode the elevator out of view.

He grimaced at the thick odor surrounding Level Three. Mills was down on his haunches in the corner, his hands resting on the ground. Greener said nothing as he slid the loaf through the opening. He didn't watch as Mills scurried over to it, but he could hear him start to eat.

When he finally reached Level Two, Tommy was ready with a complaint.

"Greener, you gotta listen to me. This food's fuckin' killing me. It's hurting me, it really is. Cruel and unusual, eh? It's bad for a man's soul to eat like this. To eat this. Bring me one good meal. One plate of fusilli, sausage and tomato sauce with oregano and basil. I'll make you a rich man. You know I can. One plate, Greener, one plate."

"I'm sorry, Tommy. Can't do it. But I did specially prepare this loaf for you. Unfortunately, I cut off the tips of my fingers making it, but you'll enjoy those, I'm sure. It'll remind you of old times."

"You *mameluke*." Tommy wrung his hands as he paced his cell. "It used to be you could bribe a guard. What happened, the Democrats back in office?"

"Sorry, not allowed to tell you. Remember, the 'no access to outside information' rule?" Greener glanced over at Safran, who was staring through the bars. Dried blood from a recent nosebleed had crusted around his lips and down his lower cheek. "Well hello, my little beacon of sunshine. A pleasure as always. Today's specials are—"

"Food. The food. Give me to it."

"Well, a little pronoun confusion going on, but I think you've earned your loaf anyway for your charming display of social skills. Come on, guys, let's give him a hand."

"Can you believe him, this guy here?" Tommy shook his head and gestured painfully at Safran as Greener clicked the button to lower the platform. "All the criminals in the world, I get stuck next to fucko over here."

The platform stopped on the first level and Greener unlocked Unit 1A, the main storage area. He grabbed a couple of slickers before swinging the door shut and relocking it.

"Jesus Christ!" Greener yelled as the elevator rose. "For a bunch of fuckin' criminals, you'd think one of you'd have a goddamn sense of humor." He snickered to himself. "Mr. Greener, you've just won the chance to be a prison guard. Where are you going to go? Well, Bob, I think I'll waste my life away in the Tower! That's right, ceaseless fun for the whole family."

As he came up on Level Ten, he noticed the last loaf by his foot. "Oh yeah, Atlasia. You want this? Last call. Come on, I'm gonna eat it myself."

Allander still lay facedown by his unit door, not moving. Greener called up the Hole, "Hey, Hackett! Hackett!"

There was no answer from above, just the rising wind sucking across the top of the Hole. He decided Hackett was probably leaning over the parapet, watching the waves crash against the stone.

He reached the metal arm through the food slot and prodded Allander before jerking it back out. No movement. He looked for an indication of breathing in the rise and fall of Allander's back, but there was nothing. He prodded him again. Finally, he relaxed, letting the arm come to a rest on Allander's back. He turned and shouted up the Hole, "Hey, Hackett, I think we got a dead one!"

The minute Greener's eyes left him, Allander seized the end of the metal arm. By the time Greener turned back, Allander was poised like an alligator. He faced Greener, glowering in the darkness.

"What the fu—"

Allander yanked the end of the metal arm with incredible force, pulling Greener by the strap around his wrist. Greener stumbled forward, losing his balance. As he fell, the elevator control slipped from his left hand and slid across the platform through the food slot under Allander's door. Allander gathered it with his hands like a hockey goalie embracing a puck.

Greener struck his chin on the steel bars of the platform floor. He shook his head, trying to clear his vision. The prisoners in the cages around him, sensing that something extraordinary was happening, began to scream with excitement, thrashing against their doors. The tightly wrapped rain slickers rolled around the platform, bouncing off the unit bars.

Allander clicked the big red button and the elevator started up. Greener hung doubled over the edge of the elevator as it left the Level Ten platform. He dug his hands at the elevator where it met his crotch, hoisting his body up briefly to orient himself. The last thing he saw was the rush of Level Eleven coming down behind his head. The powerful elevator rose quickly under his stomach as the eleventh level caught his lower back and severed him at the midsection. The air left him in a wet grunt.

The upper part of Greener's corpse fell to the Level Ten platform with a dull thud, landing in front of Unit 10A. Allander still lay on his stomach, a look of subtle amusement on his face. The twitching torso was splayed grotesquely behind its crooked neck, both of its arms outstretched worshipfully to Allander.

"I know, my little friend, I know," Allander purred as he managed to free the metal arm and pull it inside his cage.

Glancing up, he noticed Greener's keys dangling over the edge of the elevator, still attached to his pants. They swayed back and forth from what had formerly been Greener's crotch and legs, which remained somewhere around Level Eleven. Allander clicked the bottom red button and giggled obscenely.

Spade also noticed the keys, and he began moving madly around his cell as the elevator lowered, bringing them nearer and nearer.

"Atlasia. You forget that shit I said. You forget it. You let me out of here. You let me the fuck out when you get ahold of those keys. Don't you leave me caged up in here."

Allander ignored him and reached for the keys with the metal arm, which he had been holding reverently. The pronged end of the arm caught the ring easily. As he backed it away, the chain slid out of Greener's gory midsection.

Even the prisoners who could not see Greener's corpse had joined the clamor. Ironically, Claude Rivers, the only one with a good vantage point of what was happening, was dozing away in his cot.

"Hey, Greener, you all right down there? Move your ass, it's starting to rain and we gotta get the Hatch sealed." Hackett's voice echoed down the Hole.

Allander tensed up and the metal arm struck the top of his food slot. The keys lost their hold on the end of the arm and fell to the platform. They barely caught, dangling halfway over one of the flat steel bars.

"You promise. You give me your word you'll let me go when you get that bitch or I'll yell like a beast to high heaven."

"Interesting simile," Allander hissed.

"What the fuck's keepin' you?" Hackett bellowed from above. "You throwin' a party, or what?" Because it was dusk and a storm was coming in, it was too dark for him to see down the Hole.

"I'm not joking here," Spade growled. "I'll fuck you."

"Sounds ravishing," Allander said dryly.

The other inmates moved frantically about their units, trying to figure out what, exactly, had happened.

Leaning against the Hatch, Hackett heard only the crash of the waves against the side of the Tower and the noise of the stirring prisoners. He gazed up at the dark clouds gliding ominously through the sky.

"Must've dropped a fuckin' loaf down the Hole," he said, settling back against the railing and lighting up another cigarette.

Spade cringed as Allander reached for the keys with the arm. "Come on, Atlasia. You got this. You got this now."

Allander struck the keys with the metal arm, but he missed the ring, and they shifted dangerously on the edge.

"You motherfucker! You gotta be careful."

"Your perception of the obvious is admirable." Allander stabbed at the keys again, this time hooking the ring with the prong. Slowly, he brought the arm back, moving it hand over hand until the keys dangled just outside the bars.

They were right before him, just out of reach. He lowered the tilt of the arm and pulled it back sharply. The keys flew through the bars to his hand. Allander gazed at them affectionately for a moment, overwhelmed at all they represented. They glittered in the darkness.

Rising to his feet, Allander reached the keys through

his door to the lock. On the way through, they struck the side of one of the bars and slid from his sweaty palm. He crouched and shot his other hand through the food slot, grabbing the keys just before they disappeared through the bars of the platform floor.

Spade let out a gentle moan.

"It's hard not to be in control, isn't it, Spade? Frustrating not to be in the driver's seat?" His hand tight around the keys, Allander gestured as though he were holding a steering wheel. He pretended to lose his grip on the keys again, and Spade fell to his knees with a bang, arms uselessly outstretched. Allander caught the keys easily with a sweep of his other hand.

He laughed at Spade's expression as he inserted the key. The gears in the lock clicked loudly. He pushed the door and it swung open, creaking at the hinges. It was the first time a unit door had been opened from the inside. Only the dead had ever left the cells.

"Now open me. Free me." Spade reached for him, his fingers grasping at the black space in front of him.

Allander stepped onto the elevator platform and crossed the Hole, holding the keys inches from Spade's reach. Spade strained forward, turning his head and pressing his cheek to the bars.

"How much does all that exquisite muscle help you now, Spade? I'd bet that if your shoulders were a touch less beefy you could reach . . . the . . . extra . . . inch . . . to . . . the . . . keys." He swung them back and forth in front of Spade.

"You hand those. You hand them here, you motherfucker, or I'll yell. I'll yell my fucking lungs out."

"Calm yourself." Allander laid a long, bony finger over his lips. "I'm going to dispose of the final nuisance above and the last thing I need is to be struck on the head by one of your wayward muscles. I'll see to you after I've handled him." He motioned upward with a flick of his head.

"Bullshit!"

"Ssh."

"Fuck you, ssh! Why the hell should I believe you?"

"Because what choice have you got?"

"I could fuckin' scream—how's that for a choice?"

"Fine," Allander said loudly. Spade cringed, looking up the Hole. Allander crossed his arms, strumming his fingers. "Let's hear it."

Spade turned in a tight circle, then grabbed the bars, his chest rising as if he were going to yell. But he didn't. After a moment of silence, Allander placed the keys on the elevator platform by his feet. Then he stepped forward and extended his hand to Spade's unit. Spade saw that the keys were out of Allander's reach, and he cursed silently.

They gripped hands firmly around the thumbs, and Allander leaned forward, peering intently into his eyes. "I will free you," he said. "You have my word."

He clicked the top red button with his other hand, and the elevator whirred and began to rise. Spade held Allander's hand until it slipped up out of reach. Then he began to pace.

8

HACKETT heard the elevator engage. "About fuckin' time," he muttered, and peered over the edge. He saw a mound in the center of the elevator, covered with a blue jail-issue blanket.

"Oh shit, Mary Mother of God." His gun was immediately out, aiming at the mound as he fumbled for his walkie talkie.

"Come in, goddamnit. Come in *now*. Over." But the thunder brewing in the sky had given way to a rain shower, broken now and then by bolts of lightning. The reception on the handset was shot, and only static poured out.

"Fuck, fuck, *fuck!*" Hackett smashed the walkie-talkie on the railing. He looked longingly at the emergency phone on the wall of the shed, but then he glanced back down at the rapidly rising elevator and knew there was no time. He couldn't even check the location sensors to see which prisoner was on the loose.

His gun stayed fixed on the rising blue pile, which became clearer as the scant light from the sky spilled over it. Rather than rising to its usual perch ten feet in the air above the Hole, the platform clicked to a stop barely two feet above the top of the shaft.

Hackett fought to keep his hand from shaking. "Come out. Uncover yourself now! There are three of us up here and we have you surrounded."

Silence.

He advanced to the elevator, then stepped up onto it, his eyes locked on the blue blanket. His footsteps were measured and steady as he crept silently forward. The rain fell gently across his face, and he felt drops moving down his neck and mingling with the sweat on his back.

Behind him, an arm slid, spiderlike, out from the two-foot gap under the elevator, and Allander's head emerged after it. Allander strained to pull himself out from where he hung on the crossing support bars beneath the elevator. He managed to roll silently through the gap to the top of the Tower.

Hackett approached the blanket. His left hand inched forward, still shaking, as he held the gun steady in his right. He yanked the blanket back, revealing Greener's lower body. "Oh my God," he gasped.

Behind him, Allander pulled himself silently to his feet. Hackett started to whirl around but Allander ducked and swept his feet with a glancing kick, pulling the guard's legs out from under him. Hackett hit the ground flat on his back, banging his head.

Before he could raise his gun, Allander was in the air above him. He landed with the point of his knee squarely on Hackett's neck, collapsing his windpipe. Hackett twitched twice, then was still. His arms fell to his sides, the gun snug in his hand even as it clicked to rest against the metal.

Allander smiled. "I guess it's true. A veteran doesn't relinquish his weapon." He pried the gun from Hackett's grip and set it down beside him.

Then he paused and looked down tenderly at the fallen man. Reaching forward, he hugged him around the chest and neck, curling up on him momentarily as if to draw warmth from him. Hackett's head bobbed in the embrace, his blank eyes gazing ahead. After a moment,

Allander got up and raised the elevator to its resting position ten feet above the Hatch.

Spade spied Allander's dark figure silhouetted at the top of the Hole. "Come on now, Atlasia. Your word. I have your word," he cried, his voice pleading now.

"Indeed. I said I'd free you, and I will. You just have to be less . . . literal."

Allander smiled as he extended his arm over the Hole and opened his fist. The keys fell from it, rotating end over end as they plummeted into the darkness.

Spade roared below him, reaching desperately through the door at the keys, his fingers splayed, his shoulder and cheek mashed against the bars The keys brushed his fingertips as they passed and he screamed as he saw them disappear below.

Allander looked at his hand, feigning shock. "Whoops."

"YOU MOTHERFUCKER. YOU SENSELESS MOTHERFUCKER!"

"Well, at least my actions have prodded you to use a two-syllable word."

"I'LL FUCKIN' R—"

"YOU'LL WHAT?" Allander yelled, crouched intently over the Hole, the veins in his neck bulging with blood. Spade halted mid-sentence, shocked by the rage in Allander's voice. "You'll what? I apologize, I didn't quite catch that. Somehow, I'm failing to see the danger in your threats." He leaned forward and gazed into the Hole. "I couldn't even retrieve those keys now if I wanted to. And I certainly don't want to."

The prisoners below Spade recognized Allander's voice, and peered up the dark shaft. The Tower erupted with noise, like a madhouse on the evening of a full moon. Despite the clamor, Claude Rivers slept on in

Unit 11A. Spade strained to shout at Allander above the din, but realizing he could no longer be heard, gave up and settled heavily on his bed. His head collapsed into his open hands as he tried to shut out the insanity.

Allander roamed around the top of the Tower, laughing at the submachine guns hanging limply in the shed and digging through Hackett's tool kit. He pulled out a pair of wire cutters. The rain had momentarily stopped, as if gathering strength for a larger downpour.

Running over to the top of the Hole, Allander lowered the elevator and rolled Hackett's body off before raising the elevator again. Then he kicked the sprawled corpse over to the Hole, where it dangled over the edge. He laughed, and uttered a brief introduction. "Hackett, the Hole. Hole, this is Hackett."

Placing his foot firmly on Hackett's behind, he shoved once and the body fell over the side and dropped into the void. It landed with a loud thud at the bottom, where it lay like a discarded marionette.

The inmates went crazy, shrieking as the body plummeted past them. From Level Two, Tommy and Safran could make out the outline of the body below them, and they screamed with delight.

"Hackett, you fucking *mook!* How the fuck you like it down here? Always a tough guy. Well, look what happens to tough guys. Broken fuckin' neck in the sewer of a prison. By choice too. Could've just stayed on the outside, been a family man. Station wagon with wood paneling, picnics with pasta salad and marinated chicken." Tommy shook his head.

"Stupid. Fuck you quiet, Tommy." Safran glared across the Hole at Tommy through the tangle of black hair hanging over his eyes. "Stupid food all you say. All you say about. Food."

9

ALLANDER stood on top of the parapet of the Tower, balanced on one foot. A surge of energy flowed through his taut muscles and he rolled his head back, letting his hair catch in the wind.

Seeing the Tower from above for the first time, Allander felt its power entering his body through his feet and legs, rising through his groin and stomach into his rib cage. Now, standing on top of man's greatest effort at order and hierarchy, he felt a sense of domination.

The Tower was a prison, but to him it was also a house of worship, a place to celebrate man in divine trespass. It was a building of history, for all its inhabitants were caged by and for their pasts. They spoke only of memories, skewed interpretations whispered by their minds.

Above all else, Allander realized, the Tower was wildly and beautifully masculine. They had built it to restrain the human spirit, to punish those who danced to a different beat, to still the music that came to them in the dead of night. They never appreciated the fact that Allander had never shut his eyes to the secrets of the human soul. He had listened to the quiet babbling of creeks running deep through the crags of his mind. He knew that he was something grander, more majestic, than their prison built of rock and steel. He was a Tower of flesh and blood, rising above the emotional quagmire through which other men limped, thoughtless and impotent.

He inhaled deeply, pulling at once the dank air of the

Hole and the fresh ocean breeze into his lungs, feeling them merge, absorbing them into his body as if to incorporate some part of the Tower, to integrate some piece of this time and place.

The top of the sun was still visible above the line of the horizon, though it was a blurry glow. As Allander scanned the sea for approaching boats, a flash of movement in the hills behind Maingate caught his eye. A person, no larger than a dot, was plummeting from one of the cliffs, like a folded bird. Then, a small streak of black threaded out above the figure and exploded in a point of color that grew like a blot from a fountain pen. Allander realized that he was witnessing a parachute jump rather than a suicide. He found the sight captivating; it was like watching a painting unfold on the darkening canvas of the sky. He watched long after the jumper had disappeared into the trees below before turning his attention back to the Tower.

He crossed to the small guard station and foraged through its drawers until he found the first-aid box. He threw bottles over his shoulder and they shattered on the ground behind him. When he came to the procaine hydrochloride vial, he stopped.

The Maingate physician had insisted it be present in case emergency oral surgery were ever necessary for the guards; in addition to being a contained security unit, the Tower had to be a self-sufficient medical station.

Allander withdrew a needle from the small packet and fit it gently into a plastic syringe. He punched the needle through the rubber top of the vial and withdrew some of the liquid, then cleared the air from the syringe. A few drops squirted through, onto the floor.

Taking a deep breath, Allander inserted the needle into the tip of the ring finger on his left hand. He waited for the numbness to spread and settle. After a few minutes, he removed a scalpel from its sterile package and dipped it in the container of alcohol. Then he made a neat incision, cutting diagonally through his fingerprint.

Since the anesthetic had not fully taken effect, he felt a painful tingling in the pad of his finger, but feeling suddenly rushed for time, he continued. Using tweezers, he pried underneath the skin, grimacing as he saw his flesh rise along the straight line of the cut. The blood came and washed over the end of the tweezers until it obscured his view.

Once, he felt the tweezers close on something hard and he pulled gently, but when the tweezers emerged from the bloody gash, they held only fleshy material that looked like gristle. Allander hadn't anticipated that numbing the finger would have made it difficult for him to distinguish the location sensor from his own senseless tissue.

Beginning to lose patience, he pressed the tweezers in until they hit the bone. He applied too much pressure and they slid around the side of his finger next to his nail, pulling the flesh around and stretching the cut open. He heard a soft, metallic clink as the tweezers struck something distinctly alien, and he bit his lip in a mixture of pain and delight. Finally, working the tweezers around the metal, he withdrew the sensor, which was the size of a large pea. The flesh around the cut strained and whitened at the edges as he pulled the bloody orb through.

After pressing gauze to his wound, Allander wrapped it with medical tape, bandaging it thoroughly. Then he used the tape to affix the location sensor to the side of the Hole. It was close enough to its assigned location that the difference in position would not be detected from the mainland.

He began to move at a furious pace, sprinting back to the guard station. He opened the control box, ignoring the flashing lights and the warning stickers. Finding the knob labeled PUMPS, he turned it to DISENGAGE, then broke it off, flinging it out of the shed. It skidded across the top of the Tower and into the Hole. He found a pencil and jammed it in the hole where the knob had been, breaking it and lodging a small piece inside. That would be enough to hold them off until it was too late.

His finger was starting to hurt. Blood leaked through the gauze and tape, but he ignored it—he was almost done now. He turned back to the controls, finding the section labeled VENTS. As the pounding waves rose against the Tower's side, he pulled the levers, one by one. Twelve . . . Eleven . . . Ten . . . Nine. Level Nine was the lowest floor to have vents, but it was almost always underwater, so its vents had never been used. They jammed halfway open.

A torrent of water blasted down the Hole, dousing the inmates through their cages. It struck the bottom and roared upward, snarling and swirling about the prisoners. They screamed in terror, many of them running in circles, regarding their walls and ceilings with wild eyes.

Safran was knocked across his unit with the first blast of water. His head was smashed against the bed, caving in at the temple like a deflated basketball.

Tommy froze as the water rose under his feet, driving him up. His mouth opened in a silent scream as he rode the massive swell, his face striking the steel bars of his ceiling.

Allander rushed to the gaping mouth of the Hole and cried down: "WELCOME HOME, MY LITTLE ONES! WELCOME HOME!" What he said, however, was lost to the inmates, drowned out by the roar of the

water and their own screams. Allander scampered away
from the edge of the Hole.

On Level Three, Mills roared in terror as he watched
the river of water flow past his unit. He looked down at
his feet and saw the seething mass of liquid rising toward
him through the bars of the floor. It deluged Level Two
now, and it would be only another few seconds before it
reached him.

He seized the unit wall fiercely with both hands, his
hairy fingers squeezing the bars. The water flew up,
striking his bottom and groin, and he bellowed in pain.
He did not release his grip, even as the water yanked his
body from the ground. The void over his head filled, and
he slowly pulled himself back down to a standing
position beneath the ocean's roar. He finally opened his
mouth, forced to inhale, and a peace spread through his
body as his lungs drew the water inward.

Cyprus moaned and paced madly about his unit, feeling the walls and jumping to grab the ceiling bars and
hold his body up off the ground.

Above him, Spade laughed and stepped on his hands.
"He got us, Aryan boy. He got us good," he called down
tauntingly.

Cyprus squealed in pain and fear and collapsed to the
floor. The water appeared to be moving more slowly
now. It rose from Level Eight and when Cyprus's feet
got wet, he screamed as if they'd been touched by acid.
He jumped onto his bed.

"Any chance?" he cried, his breath catching in his
chest. "Any chance it'll stop, that it'll level off? Come on,
Spade, tell me. Tell me now. Oh, Jesus God."

The water reached his bed and continued to rise,
claiming his calves, then his thighs. Again he leapt up
and grabbed the ceiling bars. And again, Spade placed

one of his size-fourteen feet over both hands. Cyprus whimpered like a puppy.

"None at all, white boy. None at all. Maybe by the time it hits Level Ten, or maybe not. But you got no hope. No hope at all for Level Nine." He smiled. "And I'll be right here watching you go."

He lifted his foot from Cyprus's hand, but this time Cyprus did not fall away. The water buoyed him until he was pressed against the ceiling. Spade sat clumsily on the floor, his legs spread so he could see Cyprus's face between them, and he watched as the water slowly covered Cyprus's frantic eyes. His blond hair flowed gracefully in the water, making him look like a distorted mermaid. He struggled against the bars, and as Spade's pants began to soak up water, Cyprus's breath left him in a bubbled cough. Sucking in painfully, he jerked about before drifting away from the ceiling.

Spade stood up and pulled off his shirt, throwing it into the corner. He sloshed over to his bed and sat, resting his chin on his fist, his black body sculpted and organic against the sterile steel bars. The water had slowed, but each wave pushed another gasp through the tenth-level vents into the Tower.

He looked at his hands. Opening and closing them, he flexed them before his face, his massive fists like sledgehammers. He watched until liquid flowed over them and then he stood to face the water. It rose over his bulging pectorals, then over his deltoids and trapezoids. Little bubbles clung to him as he felt his feet leave the ground. He welcomed the cold water flowing over his body. It had been a long drought.

He rose, treading water though barely moving, until his head struck the ceiling and stopped his ascent. "Allander, my child," he whispered, his voice a deep rumble. "Allander, my child." Water rushed over the smile that had formed on his lips, and a small funnel of air pushed into the water as he breathed from his nose. His glassy eyes did not blink as they went under.

By then, Allander was already off in the transport speedboat that had been loosely moored to the side of the Tower. As the water rose to Level Eleven, he used a pair of wire cutters to make a hole in the fence large enough to guide the speedboat through.

Breaking from the reflection of the Tower that rippled in the day's last light, Allander steered into open water. He buzzed toward the bleak glow at the horizon, nibbling from a cup of yogurt. The high tide rose to its peak, and sat defiantly around and throughout the Tower.

ALLANDER stood in the rocking speedboat about a mile offshore and nosed it around until the bow faced open water. He wedged an iron rod into place between the floor and the wheel, turned the motor over, and started the boat again. It was getting low on gas. He tried to ease the throttle a bit higher, but the boat jerked forward and he fell over the side, banging his shoulder as it sped off.

The cold choked the air out of him and for a moment he thought he might sink. But then he felt his arms fight through the numbness, and he began to tread water. He floated for a minute holding his shoulder, moving with the waves. At least I disposed of the boat, he thought as he started the long swim to shore.

The throbbing in his shoulder intensified with every stroke and Allander realized he had underestimated his injury. He began to thrash, fighting with the rise of the waves to pull his body nearer to land.

The water splashed over his face, forcing itself into his eyes and nose and stinging horribly. His throat became raw from taking in water in little gulps. The cut on his finger throbbed as the saltwater entered the wound. The small lights of houses in the hilltops above the beach twinkled at him, as though jeering at him in his precarious situation.

Be calm. Just calm yourself, he thought. He rolled his tired neck from side to side and inhaled deeply, clearing his mind.

He kicked off his shoes when he'd first landed in the

water, and now he stripped off his socks, his shirt, and even his thin prison pants. He tied one leg of his pants in a knot and shoved his socks and shirt into it before throwing the whole ball of cloth aside.

Wearing only his underwear, Allander gave in to the rhythm of the ocean, letting his body flow with the swirling water, letting it seize his limbs and take him under its sway. He rose, barely moving his arms and legs, and twirled on the surface before dipping below again, his exhausted body washed about like a leaf riding a harsh autumn wind. But the ocean continued to press him upward. He drank the air greedily before the ocean moved him down, forcefully sweeping him to shore. He felt his limbs grow stiff with the cold and he hoped they'd keep moving.

Finally, he noticed that the waves were breaking and he had to fight for breath as they crashed, spouting a white mist into the humid air. His torso actually broke through the surface as he neared shore, pushed into the air by the force of a wave, and he saw the lights clearly before his body hit the water again. At last, he felt the sand beneath his feet, and the thick pebbles and grains surrounding his toes. He touched the ground with both knees and still the ocean pushed him forward, seething up his back and through his legs, propelling him to shore.

Suddenly, his legs and waist were seized by a large, dark mass. A slimy substance wrapped itself around him and squeezed him tightly, tying up his limbs and sucking him back out to sea. Allander dug his fingers into the sand and pulled himself forward, screaming and thrashing.

The mass slid from Allander's waist and briefly held his knees before he kicked free. He turned on his hip to watch as it slid from view. It was a patch of dark green seaweed, glittering moistly in the moonlight.

He pulled himself free of the water as it retreated to gather itself for another surge onto the beach. Scrambling on all fours and wearing only a ragged pair of underpants, Allander was delivered to shore at three minutes past midnight.

The water climbed gently to where his body lay and barely touched his side, as if sniffing him curiously. Allander stirred, coughing deeply, and winced at the dull ache in his throat and head. His finger throbbed even more now. He drew himself up to his knees and peered around the beach, admiring its fine, open expanse, its irregular shape and sloppy curves. Overhead, the moon broke through the clouds. Throwing his head back, he shrieked, something between a sob and a cackle.

He ran his hands through the water, petting it as it edged forward to meet him again. It rose through his spread fingers, climbing clingingly up his forearms, and he dug his hands shovel-like into the moist ground and clenched them loosely. The water drew the matter away to reveal two fists of small wriggling crabs, alive and free in every handful of sand.

THE first light of morning broke through the low clouds and cast a bluish glow over the beach. The storm had passed in the night, and the ground was damp with morning dew. A crab scuttled across the sand, back toward the water, its ragged claws leaving small trails in its wake.

Allander turned his head and coughed, then rolled over and threw up. His vomit smelled clean and fresh, his stomach acid diluted with saltwater. The swelling on his shoulder had gone down during the few hours that he had been passed out. He had slept deeply, but his eyes were puffy and sore.

At one point, from the depths of his stupor, Allander had thought he heard voices. Panic had washed over him momentarily as he'd imagined cops or security guards dragging him from the beach. But then he'd realized that the noise came from a group of passing teenagers, and they'd dismissed him as a harmless bum.

Rolling to his forearms, Allander rose to his haunches, squinting even in the dim morning light. "'Free at last, free at last. Thank God Almighty, I am free at last,'" he mumbled. He laughed, a choke thick with irony.

He pulled himself to his feet, but stood stooped, favoring his swollen shoulder. Facing the breeze with his bare chest, he wandered from the beach, looking much like a scarecrow that had freed itself from its post.

He gazed up at the houses in the hills as he climbed

the stairs that led from the beach to the residential neighborhood. Manicured bushes lined the sidewalks, but as the street wound higher up the hill, the neat shrubbery gave way to thicker underbrush. The houses sat farther back from the road behind larger gates. Their mailboxes were all that were open to the outside world, and even those were built into protective brick structures.

Blending with the shadows, Allander made his way up the street. It was early in the morning and no one seemed to be up yet. He could probably have proceeded up the middle of the road, but he kept to the shadows out of habit. He glanced at the gates as he passed them, amused at the false sense of security they created for their owners.

At the top of the hill, he stopped at a white stucco house that peeked out behind an elaborate fence. Reaching through the gate, Allander slipped the bar. He swung the gate slightly open and slid through, disappearing into the bushes at the side of the driveway.

He ran his thumb gently over the bloody tape covering his finger. It was damp and the edges were frayed. Ocean water was cleansing, he reminded himself thankfully.

Making his way slowly through the landscape, Allander flanked the house, occasionally peering between the bushes to scan the area. Although he knew nobody would be awake at this hour, he didn't want to risk a bold approach.

He made his way behind a garden shed twenty feet from the side of the house. Sliding open a window, he crept through, noticing the equipment stored within. He had always prided himself on being able to make do with anything he could lay his hands on. So many tools could be found around the average house—tools of death, destruction, torture.

After digging through a toolbox, Allander held up a lengthy awl, studying it in the light that filtered through the dust and cobwebs.

The doorbell rang.

"Who the hell? At this hour?" A shrill voice issued forth from beneath a white beauty mask and a set of rollers. Henry was startled until he remembered his wife's new habit of rising early to apply beauty products. "Go get the door, Henry," she urged.

Henry grunted and shifted heavily in the bed. "It's probably just the paper boy."

"Get the door, Henry."

Henry sighed and stumbled out of bed as his wife rolled back over on her side, her arms crossed on top of her red nightgown. It had been one pain-in-the-ass thing after another since they'd let the maid go last week for stealing a bracelet from his wife's bureau. Just can't trust people anymore, Henry thought groggily as he padded across the tiled floor of the foyer.

"Who *is* it?" he called, and then mumbled in the same singsong voice, "You annoying *ass*hole."

He looked through the peephole and saw nothing, then opened the door and stepped out onto the porch. Nothing. A bird called out twice from its perch in a tree and Henry relaxed and inhaled deeply, stretching his arms. He bent over and picked up the newspaper.

As he walked back down the hallway to the bedroom, the doorbell rang again.

"I thought I told you to get the door," his wife screeched from the bedroom. Henry winced at the sound of her voice, raising his shoulders above his neck as if to block out the noise.

"I got it. Just go back to sleep." He walked back to the

door muttering to himself. He leaned forward to check the peephole again; there was a tinkling sound as the glass from the peephole broke. Henry convulsed and slumped forward. His body seemed to hang on the door from his head.

Allander pulled the awl back out through the peephole. Poised in his other hand was the hammer he had used to force the awl through the small hole and into Henry's eye. The door shuddered softly as Henry collapsed to the floor. His body showed no visible sign of violence except for the small puncture in the iris, through which the awl had entered his brain.

Allander pushed the door open, shoving against the weight of Henry's body.

Vanity breeds contempt, Allander thought. If you hadn't wanted the white castle on top of the hill, you'd still be dreaming of breakfast.

He crept softly toward the master bedroom, holding the hammer tight in his fist.

A familiar sensation invaded him, filling him slowly, leaving him with a tingling in his stomach—the ecstasy of the kill. Somehow, he knew that it was what he was made to do. And he didn't feel angry. In fact, it was the only time he didn't feel angry.

The woman's form under the blankets was barely visible from the doorway, yet Allander could sense the inconsistency of her femininity. It scared him, the inconsistency. It always had.

He approached her slowly, his knees trembling. His left foot came down on a lipstick cylinder and it cracked like a walnut.

The woman rolled over in bed and saw Allander's sickly, pale skin covered with sand trails and dried seaweed. The white mask over her face opened to emit an enormous scream. Allander backed up, momentarily fearful, bumping against the cabinet.

Throwing the covers aside, the woman grabbed the phone from the nightstand and hurled it at Allander's head. She screamed her husband's name over and over: "HENRY! HENRY! GET THE CHILDREN! HENRY!"

The phone hit Allander in the face and split open his upper lip, spilling blood over his mouth. He cowered until he tasted its richness, then he felt himself energized.

The white mask was out of bed and running for the door. As she passed him, Allander stepped forward and swung the hammer's pointed end at the back of the woman's head. It struck her in the soft nape of her neck and stuck. He jerked it back and swung again, lodging it firmly in the wound.

The woman fell as if in slow motion, jolting momentarily on her knees before pitching face first to the carpet.

Her final scream reverberated within the room, then there was quiet. The silence was broken by the distant crying of children.

A young boy's voice sounded from around the corner, "Mommy? Are you all right? Daddy?" It was a beautifully pitched voice, a soprano full of prepubescent innocence. It trembled delicately, like a feather approaching the blades of a fan.

Allander was the man of the house now. He had established that.

He wiped the blood from his lips and headed for the door.

TWO

THE
TRACKER

"STAY BACK, YOU FUCK! DON'T EVEN THINK ABOUT IT," Jade Marlow yelled above the scream of bullets that ricocheted off the pavement and the open car door that shielded him.

"But I think I got it! I think I got an angle to the door," Dave Patrick said excitedly, his eyes fixed on the second-floor window of the Lilliputian Day Care building, behind which a team of gunmen held three children hostage.

Jade peered cautiously around the car door. The late-morning heat made the yellow window frame waver and distort, its peeling paint seeming to vibrate in the heavy air. A wooden sign was staked in the middle of the browning lawn. "For Growing Sirs and Madams," it announced in impressive lettering.

"You don't! You *don't* have it, and you're my cover. Don't fuck me on this! I'm the lead here, so stay put."

Dave glanced at Jade nervously, his blue eyes filled with more bravado than intelligence. "I got it. I got it, Jade!" With that he leaped to his feet and ran out from behind the car, sprinting for the building.

"No, you stupid fuck!" Jade hit the door angrily with his elbow, then quickly turned and fired several shots at the second-story window. The gunman upstairs stayed put.

As Dave neared the door, it swung open and he found himself facing a fat man with a goatee, a shotgun braced beneath his jiggling chins. Panic crossed Dave's face. He tried desperately to skid to a halt while raising his gun, instead losing his footing and landing on his ass. Before he could blink, Goatee had unloaded two quick shots into his chest, splattering his policeman-blue shirt with blood.

Jade pivoted around the car door and put one bullet neatly through Goatee's neck, dropping him before he could retreat. As Goatee toppled over backward, another man scurried around the body and slammed the door shut again.

Rising slightly from his crouch, Jade peered at Dave's body. His longish blond hair, brushed by the wind, was the only thing that moved. Poor dumb guy, Jade thought, an ex-high school running back who'd never learned to separate the playing field from the world that fenced it in. He was definitely dead. At least you got us one kidnapper, he thought.

The door opened slightly and the downstairs gunman showered bullets all over the front of the car door. Jade flattened himself against the ground; as he got ready to return fire, the door slammed shut again.

Peering through the shattered remains of his driver's-side window, Jade noticed a mail slot toward the bottom of the thick oak door. He raised his gun, holding it firmly while he aimed. He fired once. The mail slot pinged open and shut like a throwing game at an amusement park.

Hearing a scream, he rolled from the safety of his car and sprang to his feet. He ran toward the door, firing over his head to keep the gunman upstairs at bay.

As Jade got to the base of the steps leading to the door, he planted his foot on Dave's chest and leaped over the four steps in a single motion.

The gunman lay across Goatee's body, his shoulders propped up by the wall. He was crying silently and holding his knee, his gun on the floor a few feet from him. Dark streams of blood spurted from between his fingers. When Jade kicked open the door, the man scrambled for his gun, but Jade stepped on his hand and fired once into the top of his head. The bullet blew out part of his jaw as it exited.

The foyer was a large room with smooth beige carpeting. A curved staircase swept up to the second floor, which was set off by wood railings. An elaborate chandelier dangled from the high ceiling. Elegant, though slightly rundown, the Lilliputian Day Care building was a converted mansion. It provided day care for the more affluent families in Pacific Heights.

Jade assessed his position: lower location, limited sight—extremely vulnerable. Either turn back or bulldoze ahead. He stepped over the bodies and headed for the staircase.

He made his way up the stairs, holding his gun next to his cheek. His muscles were tensed beneath his clothes. "Shut up, you little shit," he heard as he reached the top step. A child whimpered softly. The noise came from the first room off the wide hallway.

Jade moved slowly toward the room, stepping quietly on the plush Chinese patterned rug. He paused beside the door frame and listened, carefully controlling the sound of his breathing.

"I know you're out there, asshole. Come in," he heard.

Jade dropped to his stomach and peered around the bottom of the door frame. He could see Michael Trapp. He was backed into a corner, one arm locked around a six-year-old girl's neck in a half nelson, a gun pressed to her temple. She dangled in his arms like a rag doll, her button eyes wide with fear. To Trapp's right, two boys knelt side by side, facing the wall.

Jade had studied Trapp's profile inside and out. He was a ransomer who'd never been in a face-off, although he'd killed kids before. Now his partners were dead and he was scared shitless. But Jade knew he wouldn't fire right off the bat. He'd want to negotiate. That's what ransomers did.

Jade stood up and whirled around the corner, his gun pointed. The girl screamed and struggled in Trapp's grip.

"Drop the gun or so help me God I'll—"

Jade fired once and put a bullet right through his mouth. Blood splattered the white wall and the floral painting behind him. Trapp's knees buckled and he collapsed to the floor, the girl still clutched in his arm. She flailed to get out from under him, screaming at the top of her lungs. Finally gaining her feet, she ran to Jade, embracing him around his waist.

He placed his hands awkwardly on her shoulders, pushing her away. He walked over to the body to make sure it was dead, laying two fingers on the neck to check for a pulse. There was none. "The real cops'll be here soon to take care of you," he said over his shoulder. He glanced at the two boys. They were shaking badly, still facing the wall. "You can get up now. He's dead."

They didn't move.

Jade released the cartridge so it tapped his palm, then clicked it back into place. He'd collect a twenty-thousand-dollar reward for four days of tracking. Not bad for an FBI dropout. He smiled and ran his hand over the rough stubble on his chin. To his right, the boys continued to quiver. Behind him, the little girl sobbed loudly.

Jade pulled Trapp's wallet out of his pocket and double-checked the driver's license, a formality since he was

already positive on the ID. Several hundred-dollar bills
stuck out, and Jade pushed them all the way into the bill-
fold and stuck the wallet back in Trapp's pocket. He rose
and walked downstairs as he heard the black-and-whites
racing up the street, their sirens screaming.

He stepped over the two bodies downstairs, giving
Goatee a kick that knocked his head against the wall.
Putting his gun in the back of his jeans, Jade stepped
through the doorway into daylight. Recognizing him,
the cops sighed in relief and lowered their guns.

"One of these days, I'm gonna beat you to it,"
Lieutenant Hawkins said, fumbling over his beer belly to
find his holster. Hawkins's eyes were as deeply brown as
Jade's were green. He had a thick black mustache. They
always have a mustache, Jade thought.

"I wouldn't count on it."

"Trapp dead?"

"Yeah. And the kid." Jade pointed with his gun at
Dave's body, still sprawled out, reaching for the door.
"The commissioner gave me him to work with. Almost
got me killed."

"He break cover?"

"Yeah." Jade shook his head. "They never listen."

Hawkins sighed, running a hand over the top of his
head. "Poor kid was just a rent-a-cop. Worked security at
night to support his family."

Jade's mouth tightened. "You guys took long enough
to get here. What, was there a cat stuck in a tree somewhere?"

"We didn't get the call till you'd already cornered
them, then we came as fast as we could. You should've
waited for us to back you."

"I didn't have the luxury."

Hawkins grimaced and glanced back at the house.

Goatee's arm was visible in the doorway, lying in a pool of blood. Cops stepped over the bodies and headed inside to examine the scene. The sound of the boys weeping upstairs became softly audible.

"Jesus Christ, Marlow, you left the kids in there?" Hawkins asked in disbelief.

"Oh yeah, shit, that's right."

"'Oh yeah'? You leave three kids alone in a room with a corpse and that's the best you can do? 'Oh yeah'?" Hawkins scratched himself angrily.

"Look, Hawkins, I don't see baby-sitter anywhere in my job title."

Hawkins gestured to a newly arrived paramedics team. "You three—upstairs. Let's go." He turned back to Jade, shaking his head. "You bounty hunters are sick fucks."

The paramedics rushed out carrying the kids. The children were sobbing freely now, all three of them. Jade looked down as they passed, studying the ground. "I'm not a bounty hunter," he said. "I'm a tracker. It's an art."

"A madness, Jade." Hawkins wiped his mouth on his sleeve. "A madness."

"TRACKER" was the term that Jade used to describe the new profession he had carved out for himself after resigning from the FBI. When he broke his second case, the media began referring to him as a "T&Der" or "tracker and destroyer," but the phrase was too strained for his style. His language, like his actions, was quick and efficient.

Being a tracker set Jade apart from the bumbling military Soldiers of Fortune and the trained dogs that the bail-and-loan companies sent out. He was the only one, and he worked alone.

Tracking didn't entail following a physical trail, it involved more subtle measures. Jade had learned that there was no straight line to a criminal's door. He began a case by going backward, studying a criminal's history—his motivations, his weaknesses. Once he got a profile, he could close in on him with the precision and determination of a shark circling its prey.

He said that he quit the feds because he couldn't stand the bullshit of hierarchy. But there was a truer, more difficult explanation: He didn't get along with people. And in general, they didn't get along with him either.

There were people in his life, of course, but they came and went as the weeks passed. He was always going somewhere else, always looking for something else. He was a hunter by trade, and hunters never stay in one place for very long.

Jade didn't like covering the same ground twice. And he didn't like the feeling that settled in once he stopped chasing. He pursued his prey with such fervor that it sometimes seemed he himself was fleeing from something. And it was true that he sometimes heard voices behind him, voices from his past. The singsong, manic voices of children spinning nursery rhymes in the hot summer air.

Eeni meenie minie moe, they sang, the notes of their song burning into his memory.

But eventually, after blisters, calluses form. They're much easier to live with.

When it came to himself, Jade didn't have time for complexity. Because he spent his days dredging society's murky waters, he had little energy for introspection. As a result, he viewed himself as fiercely independent, not isolated, as self-reliant, not difficult. It was easier that way.

Jade left the FBI after his rambunctious attitude landed him in trouble. He had upbraided the Head of Operations of the Hostage Negotiation Department for allowing a terrorist to escape. The incident came after the agents had been ordered to stand down because hostages were in the line of fire. So when Jade had seen his shot open up for a split second, he had forced himself to resist. The terrorist had escaped and had been taken down by another agent in Maryland the next week. There had been other casualties along the way.

"You always shoot," Jade had yelled at the balding Head of Operations. "You shoot and ask questions later. So he takes out a hostage, big deal. If you let him escape, who knows who he'll do next?"

The Head of Operations had replied without looking up. "You throw temper tantrums like a child," he said calmly. "You have no grasp whatsoever of public relations. You don't follow orders and when you do, you do so grudgingly. You were the top agent in your entire graduating class, Marlow," he said, finally raising his eyes to meet Jade's. "And for the life of me, I can't figure out what you're doing here."

Jade walked that day, and burned all his suits and ties that were part of the Bureau's uniform. He was on his own.

He was too good to be forgotten by law-enforcement officials, though, since during his five years as an agent he had had the top arrest record in the FBI. His combat skills and his abilities in criminal analysis and tracking were extremely well respected. He was best known, however, for his instinct. Jade had instinct like a tiger on the prowl; it seemed to come from the very blood running in his veins.

Local police units began hiring him to help take care of problems that eluded their own forces, everything from catching a burglar to tracking missing children. Eventually, even the FBI began to hire him for special cases, calling him in to coordinate and oversee operations. He felt a deep flush of satisfaction rise to his cheeks as he issued his conditions to them. He was the only outsider they'd ever hired for cases, and that knowledge was sweet revenge.

The FBI knew he was a risk. That was why they had asked him to resign. But in some cases, a risk was what was needed—an expert with a sharp tongue, a quick temper, and a quicker trigger finger. Sometimes, a threat arose that was so dangerous it was worth unleashing a tiger.

Jade Marlow was a tiger burning bright. He fed on the hunt, and his eyes sparkled green and yellow from the thrill of the pursuit. When he was angry, his face became downright cruel, and when he smirked, a thin scar across his left cheek rose slightly and highlighted the disdain on the rest of his face.

Jade left the San Francisco Fifth Precinct building, Hawkins and a group of officers behind him.

A brown Honda Civic squealed to a stop at the curb. The left-front side of the car's bumper was caved in, and one of the back brake lights was broken. A bumper sticker was stuck crookedly to the back, proudly declaring: MY SON BEAT UP THE STUDENT OF THE MONTH AT VISTA ELEMENTARY SCHOOL. A green, scented pine tree ornament dangled from the rearview mirror.

A woman in her mid-twenties fumbled at the door to get out. Her mouth was a red line, stretched thin with fearful anticipation.

"Oh my God." She saw Hawkins and ran to him, her arms outstretched. "Are you the lieutenant? Is it true? Oh my God. Where's Dave?"

Hawkins consoled her as the other policemen departed quietly.

"The rookie's wife?" Jade asked the nearest cop.

"Yeah. Eight-year-old kid too."

Jade swore under his breath. "He should've fucking listened to me."

"Well maybe he didn't—"

"He didn't fucking listen." Jade pressed the heel of his hand to his forehead. "I really need this right now."

The officer stopped and looked at Jade, not quite sure he had heard him correctly. "You know, Marlow, you're a real asshole."

Jade paused and ran his thumb across his bottom lip. "He gets himself killed breaking cover and I'm the asshole. Astonishing logic."

"He died."

"He was my backup. He should have listened to me. If he had, he wouldn't have died."

"You think you're fucking flawless?"

Jade leaned back against a police car, ignoring him.

The cop bit his cheek and looked away for a moment before facing Jade again. "I heard you were a prick, Marlow. But this is unbelievable." He pulled his shoulders back slightly, waiting through the tense silence for a response.

"You'd better move on, junior," Jade said, looking straight ahead. "You might hurt yourself."

The cop stepped forward. "You got something to say?" he asked, placing a hand on Jade's shoulder and leaning toward him.

The moment the cop touched him, Jade grabbed him by the shirt and slammed him into the police car. He moved his face right up to the cop's until he could see through the darkness of his sunglasses. The cop didn't move. His arms were out to his sides, hands opened passively. Jade held him for a moment, then let him go. He turned to walk away.

Dave's wife was walking toward him angrily, tears drying on her cheeks. She had overheard Jade talking about her husband.

"You bastard," she cried. "I knew it was trouble, him working with you." She stifled a sob. "And now. How dare you talk about him that way! He died helping you on this job."

"'Helping me,'" Jade said under his breath. He looked off in the distance, slowly shaking his head.

Her voice was wavering and her words blended together, but she forged ahead. "I knew it. I knew it would end in blood. But he was so excited to work with you. The great Jade Marlow."

"I think we should just—"

"How could you have let him die? He was there for you. He died covering you, and you didn't even try to help him." She raised a finger, pointing it at him. "You're a curse, a fucking death curse."

Jade finally looked down at her, his eyes narrowing. "I hate to burst your bubble, sweetheart, but he was breaking orders when he got shot."

She slapped him, her hand ringing loudly across his face, leaving a red outline. She pulled back to hit him again, but Jade caught her arm and threw it away roughly. She collapsed on the ground.

"You'll get over it," he snarled. "Start dating." He turned and walked slowly to his car, leaving her sobbing on the pavement.

THREE women clad in green-sequined bikinis gazed out from the yellowed poster. Its caption proudly announced: STRAUDERS FULL-BODIED BEER—IT GLITTERS AS YOU GUZZLE. The women held sparklers and curled their hands suggestively around the large brown bottles.

"You know, I never understood that shit," Jade said, indicating the poster with a flick of his head.

Tony Razzoni shifted heavily in his chair and turned to face him. "What shit, Jade?"

"Why they always put chicks all over when they advertise. Beer, cars, power tools. I don't get it. Are we supposed to be able to fuck these girls if we buy the shit?"

"No. No, I think if we buy the shit, then we're the kind of guys who can get laid by chicks like that." Tony stabbed a meaty forefinger at the poster to emphasize his last words.

Jade glanced at Tony's rugged face, then down at his belly, which was wedged subtly beneath the bar. "Oh yeah. Right."

Tony had gone through six months of FBI training with Jade before dropping out. He'd gone into the police force and now headed up a squad for the small town of Falstaff Creek. He had remained friends with Jade, and now was one of the few people relaxed enough to endure Jade's abrasive personality.

Tony was a large man, about six feet, two-fifty. Much

of his size came from muscle, though it wasn't readily apparent from his appearance. His face was round, his features soft. A thin sheen of sweat seemed always to cover his cheeks, and his snug-fitting shirt usually showed spots of dampness on the back. Jade couldn't remember ever having seen him when he wasn't sweaty.

Tony didn't lose his temper. Because of his size, he never had to. And he had a gentle touch, even when he wasn't being gentle. Tony's personality could be read right off his face. He was never mean, and fair all the way through. If he ever hurt someone, it was deserved.

"So . . ." Tony said. He paused to clear his throat. "I hear you were a real asshole at the day care shoot-out today."

"So I'm garnering the usual thanks already?"

"I hear you yelled at the dead kid's wife."

"She was being dramatic."

Tony realized that he was pushing too far and softened his tone. "I don't mean to be disrespectful, Jade, but—"

"Bullshit."

"What, bullshit?"

"Whenever someone starts a sentence with 'I don't mean to be disrespectful, but,' it really means 'I'm gonna be disrespectful, but let's pretend like I'm not.' So just cut the shit and say what you have to say."

Tony sighed and set his jaw. "Look, kid. How long I known you?"

"About eight years, Tony. About eight years."

Tony smiled affectionately. "How many people you known that long who still talk to you?"

Jade pretended to count them on his fingers. When he got to ten, he turned to Tony and smiled. "None."

"Now, Jade, that's gotta count for something."

"Sure, Tony. It does."

Tony smiled and ran his fingers through his hair. "Then shut the fuck up for a minute and listen to me. You can't go through life like a wrecking ball all the time. It'll fuck up your job, it'll fuck up your broads, and it ain't fuckin' professional."

Jade lifted his black and tan and stared with one eye into the dark brown liquid. "Well, maybe I can't do what I do and be nice."

"Believe me, I'd never expect that much from you. I'm just saying you don't have to be an outright prick."

"That's not my intent."

"I'm not saying it is."

Jade laced his hands together on the bar, his thumbs touching, and stared at them. His eyes, though, were somewhere else. "A fuckin' eight-year-old kid."

"What?"

"He had a fuckin' eight-year-old kid, Tony. The rookie."

Tony slowly tilted his glass back into the wet circle it had left on the bar. "I'm sorry."

"Yeah, well so am I." Jade knocked down the rest of his black and tan and rose, pushing back the bar stool. "So am I."

He rolled through the crowded bar and a path opened up for him as people leaned out of his way. It was a policeman's bar and Jade was known there, even if he was rarely spoken to. He was not the biggest man in the bar, but the look in his eyes was as hard as ice. It didn't invite greeting. As he walked, he brought his fingertips up to the scar on his left cheek and absentmindedly traced its length.

A cop with sharp features and sandy blond hair came over and sat down next to Tony. A cigarette dangled casually from his lips, so natural-looking that it seemed like a part of his face.

"Hey, Robert," Tony greeted him.

"Sharing a drink with the infamous Jade Marlow, huh?"

"Yup," Tony said. "Infamous. Ever met him?"

Robert shook his head. "No. And from what I've heard, I think that's just fine."

"He's a good man," Tony said. "Well, not a *good* man. He's a *decent* man, and a *great* fuckin' agent, so I always figured they averaged out."

Both men laughed.

"I hear you brought him in to crack a confession out of that robbery suspect. Falstaff Creek, right?"

"Yeah, I brought him in. Worth every penny." Tony ordered another beer and settled back to tell his story. "We had a guy robbed a string of Seven-Elevens. Shoots out the security cameras before they pick him up. Last one, he shoots the clerk too. We have no hard leads, but a pretty good suspect."

"Evidence?"

"Circumstantial." The two cops shook their heads.

"But I call Jade in. He doesn't charge us much because we came up together. I want to question the guy that Saturday, so I send Jade home with his file. Friday night I get a call. Jade says, 'Cancel the interrogation. We're doing it next Sunday.' I have the mayor breathing down my neck for an arrest and this guy's telling me to push it back a week?"

Robert leaned forward, drawn into Tony's story. "Why?"

"Jade found out it was the guy's mom's birthday the next Sunday."

"So the fuck what?"

"That's exactly what I said. But Jade says you get 'em close to a birthday, an anniversary, something like that, it gets them thinking about the time they'll have to serve. Gets them thinking it's their last one if they don't cooperate. Then you hit them with the 'We'll go easier on you with a confession' speech and bang. . . ." Tony slapped his hands together.

"So did you get him?"

Tony smiled. "That's not all."

"That's not all?"

Tony shook his head. "Jade says to get him in there first thing in the morning so the guy doesn't have a clear head, not thinking straight. I have someone pick him up at six in the morning."

"You let him stay out on the streets for another week?"

Tony waved him off. "We had an eye on him. We picked him up at 6:00 A.M. What time do you think Jade shows up at the station to get ready?"

Robert shrugged, his eyes riveted on Tony.

"Two o'clock in the fuckin' morning. I get in at 5:00 A.M. He's yanking folders off the shelves and stacking them on the desk. Papers are flying everywhere. I think he's gone fuckin' nuts. He's made copies of all the newspaper headlines about the robberies and he's taping 'em on these files and writing the guy's name under 'em with a big black marker. He even puts the original articles all over the walls."

"What's in the files?"

"I don't know. Traffic-ticket records. Blank memo paper. My dry-cleaning list. Whatever."

"Holy shit," Robert said. He ordered two more Strauders.

"So this poor miserable fuck comes in and he has no

idea what's in store for him. He's scared, he's tired, it's fucking early, it's his mom's birthday. He sees these files with the headlines all over them and about shits his pants. He thinks we have the whole National Guard on his ass. He starts fingering this cross around his neck like crazy. He's sweating and he keeps glancing at this one file labeled 'Seven-Eleven Shooting' in huge black letters, laying on the table all the way to his left."

"He's *turning* to look at the file?"

Tony demonstrated, swinging around his beer gut in exaggerated fashion and gawking behind him. He turned back to his beer and took a long swig.

When he continued, his voice was much softer. His index finger waved in the air as he spoke. "And Jade notices this guy's holding on to the cross around his neck like it's gonna come to life and carry him off to heaven. So he starts talking really biblical."

"Talking biblical?"

Tony nodded. "Yeah, like, 'Who could have committed such an egregious sin? Perhaps someone who feels cast out, who needs help and forgiveness.'" He waved his arms over his head as he imitated Jade.

"Giving the guy an out."

"Giving the guy an out," Tony repeated, nodding his head. "And when this guy's right on the edge, Jade circles the desk, walks over to him and 'accidentally' bumps a videotape off the desk where he hid it. It's got a Seven-Eleven security cover, it's got the date of the shooting on it, and the guy's name across the front in huge red letters."

"No."

"I shit you not. He practically knocks it into the guy's lap and then grabs it back real quick, all embarrassed-like, and acts like the guy wasn't supposed to see it."

"And he spills?"

"Like a glass of milk," Tony said grandly. "He starts crying about how he didn't mean to shoot him and it was an accident and it's his mother's birthday and he wants to see a priest and on and on."

"No shit?"

"None." The men drank their beers in silence for a few minutes.

Robert took a long final drag on his cigarette, then stubbed it out. "What was the videotape?" he asked.

"*Blondes Back on Top*. He got it outta my top desk drawer."

SETTLING into the seat of his '81 banged-up black 320i, Jade rolled the radio tuning knob through a cacophony of static. Giving up, he reached into his glove compartment, pulled out a CD, and slipped it in. Miles Davis, *Kind of Blue*.

The green lights floated overhead, one after another, as Jade swerved from lane to lane, darting between cars. He drove along the streets with his left arm extended out the broken window, his hand tapping the car roof furiously to the tune: *"Du nu nu nu nu nu nu na. So what. Du nu nu nu nu nu nu na. So what."*

The music was turned up so loud that even with the window down, Jade was sealed away in his own vessel of sound. It flowed over him, clearing his mind. Screeching down one-way streets and alleyways, he cut off cars, arriving first in line at red lights. Or he circumvented stoplights altogether by turning right, then zooming back to the street through corner gas stations and parking lots.

Du nu nu nu. His tires flew through puddles, spraying water into the air, reflecting the headlights of oncoming traffic and soaking the left sleeve of his shirt. *Nu nu nu na.* He rolled the wheel with one finger, bringing his steering hand down near his crotch to hold the turn as his car whipped around corners. And the movement he saw through his dirty windshield—the cars passing and the flare of the water and the pedestrians walking on the sidewalk—were all choreographed pieces of his dance, of his song, and he watched as they moved to the beat he pounded on the roof of his car. *So what.*

As he cruised, he focused on a green station wagon three cars back in the left lane. It had been with him for some time. Jade brought his arm back inside the car, and he hummed the music more softly as he tapped on the steering wheel. His eyes were glued now to the rearview mirror.

He made three consecutive lefts, which the station wagon followed, then he threw on a false signal. The station wagon imitated it, but also drove past the turn, just as he had.

"Rookies. Don't send me that," Jade muttered, smiling crookedly.

He jerked off the road suddenly, into the gravel parking lot of a small bar. The building was low-roofed, with flashing neon signs and an eternally pouring Strauders bottle in the window.

The two men in the station wagon had been baffled for some time.

"What the fuck is he doing?" Andrew asked, running his fingers through his greasy brown hair.

He wore a buttoned-up shirt with dark stains under his armpits; sweat dotted his forehead and cheeks as well. "You think he spotted us?"

"How the hell would I know any more than you? Maybe he's just drunk. He was in that last bar forever," his friend Kyle replied, scratching his neatly trimmed beard.

They both watched in horror as Jade's car skidded into the parking lot of the bar. They slowed, watching him as he got out of his car and headed inside.

"Keep going, keep going," Andrew hissed. "Speed up. Let's circle the block so he doesn't notice us."

Jade watched the car's reflection in the front window of the bar. He saw it slow to a halt, then accelerate rapidly, pulling out of view. Two men. Mid-thirties.

He pulled open the door, disappearing into the smoky haze. All right, you fucks, he thought, I'll wait for you.

He went up to the bar and signaled the bartender. A robust Greek man came toward him, grinning widely.

"Ahh. Mr. Jade. How are you, my friend? Would you like a black and tan? Your favorite, eh?"

"Actually, Nick, I'm okay right now. Just wanted to warn you I've got a tail. Might be a bit of trouble."

Nick's face darkened. Obviously, he had seen this drill before. "Fine. You keep it to the pool-table area." He started to go, then turned back, raising a finger. "And no guns. Mr. Jade. Not like last time."

"Don't worry," Jade smiled. "I'll behave."

Nick turned to go, but Jade touched him on the shoulder. "Hey, Nick, mind if I wait on your side of the bar?"

Nick hesitated for a moment, then shook his head.

The two men walked into the bar. Andrew whistled nonchalantly, then whispered to Kyle. They pretended to talk to each other as they peered around, surveying the room. Jade watched them through the ordering window of the kitchen, noticing the bulge in Andrew's jacket.

Walking over to the bar with a forced stride, Andrew casually leaned one elbow on the counter, right into an ashtray. He lifted his arm up and shook loose a cigarette that had stuck to his sleeve. The woman sitting one stool over looked at him, slightly perplexed, then bit her lip to keep from smiling.

"Oh," Andrew said, smiling back. "This must be yours." He held the crushed cigarette out to her.

"Thanks," she said, taking a sip of her drink. "I usually collect the butts when I've finished smoking them."

Kyle cleared his throat behind her, shoving his hands into his pockets. Andrew pivoted away from her and faced Nick at the bar.

"I'll have two beers."

"Well, sir, you see, we're a bar," Nick leaned forward to whisper. "And we have lots of kinds of beer here."

"Oh yes. Well, I knew that. I . . . I'll have two Coors drafts."

"We don't have Coors on tap, how's Strau—"

"Yes, yes, that's fine." Andrew played nervously with a coaster as he waited for the beers.

Kyle leaned forward, his beard brushing Andrew's shoulder. "Where the hell is he?"

"He probably went to the bathroom. Just shut up and we'll wait."

"Are these guys for real?" Nick whispered to Jade over the back counter. "Please, Mr. Jade, don't hurt 'em too bad."

"I'll try not to."

Nick returned to the bar with the beers. "Maybe you gentlemen would enjoy these frosty beverages over by the pool tables?" His smile was strained.

"Oh yes, that'll be fine." Andrew paid, then slid two quarters across the bar to Nick and winked at him.

Nick looked at the quarters, then put his fingers on them and slid them back. "You'd better hang on to these," he said. "It seems like you need them more than I do."

Andrew and Kyle made their way over to the pool-table area and pulled up stools. They sat on them awkwardly, sipping their beers. Gazing around, they tried to locate Jade inconspicuously.

A woman laughed heartily, throwing her head back and slapping her knee. She seemed faint from laughing, leaning into the large man next to her for support. Smoke, sweat, and the thick smell of beer hung heavily in the air, mixing with loud voices to form an oppressive atmosphere.

The kitchen doors banged suddenly as Jade kicked them open. Both Andrew and Kyle dropped their beers as they saw Jade's form moving swiftly toward them. Their glasses shattered on the floor.

Jade crossed the room in four strides, throwing the pan of greasy water on his second step and the pan itself on his third. They arrived on Kyle's face simultaneously, the water splashing over his eyes and cheeks, the pan smashing into his forehead. He screamed and rubbed his face, temporarily blinded.

Andrew remained frozen in his seat. Sweeping Kyle's stool over with his shin, Jade pivoted and threw a high side kick to Andrew's head. The outside of his foot caught Andrew just under the chin and smashed his head against the dartboard. Andrew's eyes bulged as he saw the dart stuck in the cork right next to his nose. Jade held the stretch, his leg extended to Andrew's jaw.

Jade cleared his throat once, then spoke. "If you move at all, I will break your neck into fragments. Understand?"

Andrew wiggled his head against Jade's foot. Jade decided it was a nod.

He turned his attention to Kyle, who had rolled to his hands and knees. Blood seeped through the back of his shirt, and Jade realized that he had knocked him onto his own shattered glass. Kyle staggered to his feet, wiping the grease from his eyes. He was too dazed to try anything, so Jade looked back at Andrew.

"Now, with a slow, even movement, reach inside your jacket and remove the gun."

With trembling fingers, Andrew reached inside his jacket. His hand emerged, holding a camera.

"Oh, for fuck's sake," Jade groaned. He slowly emerged from his zone, his vision widening, and he realized where he was. The bar had fallen quiet and everyone was staring at them, slack-jawed.

Jade lowered his foot from Andrew's jaw, remaining perfectly balanced on his other leg. Kyle tried to lean against the wall beside Andrew, yelping as the effort forced the glass deeper into his back.

Andrew tried a smile, but his quivering cheeks would not comply. "Andrew Straussman. *The San Francisco Daily.*" His wavering hand went to his front pocket and he held a shaking press badge before Jade's face.

Jade looked away with a laugh, but it turned into a snarl. The jukebox rolled over a new record in the background and the spectators shifted uneasily on their feet.

"I have people following me who are assassins, hit men. I've put away rapists, murderers, child molesters. Do you really think I'm not alert enough to notice two reporters? What if I'd fuckin' shot you? Do you know how much trouble you would've gotten me into?"

Blood matted Kyle's beard. "You're right. I . . . we . . . we're sorry."

"Apology accepted. Now what do you want?"

"We just wanted a statement about today's shootout," Kyle said, wiping his face. "Cover story. You know, 'The Day Care Affair.'" He spread his hands nervously.

"Why didn't you just ask?"

"Well, we wanted to see where you live."

"And looking in a phone book was too much of a mental leap?"

Andrew and Kyle looked at each other sheepishly. The people in the bar began to go back to their business, a few of them pointing over at Jade and whispering to their friends.

Jade turned to leave.

"Do you think you'll get the Atlasia case?" Andrew called after him above the din of the bar, his last hope of ensnaring Jade in conversation.

Jade whirled around. "Atlasia? Allander Atlasia? How'd he break? Where is he? What happened?"

A smile appeared on Andrew's face, broadening with each of Jade's questions. He finally had something Jade wanted. He thought for a moment and decided to press his advantage.

"Well . . . I can't quite release all our informa—"

His sneakers left the ground before he could finish his sentence. One shoelace had come untied and was soaked with blood and spilled beer.

Jade's grip on Andrew's shirt tightened. "Information," he snarled. "Now."

"Dusk. Last night. Not located."

The arms relaxed and the grip loosened. "Thank you."

Jade dropped Andrew, and he collapsed to the ground. By the time he got up, Jade was gone. The reporter turned and looked at his blood-stained companion.

"You look like I feel," Andrew said.

"Don't flatter yourself," Kyle replied, wiping his beard. "You look like shit too."

Jade heard footsteps crunching on the gravel behind him and turned to see a woman with enormous breasts wearing a red, low-cut dress. She twirled a lock of hair around a finger as she walked up to him, looking him up and down, noticing his six o'clock shadow, the hard line of his jaw, and his green, green eyes.

"I think you could have a really good night tonight," she said huskily.

Jade's eyes danced over her cheap outfit, taking in her costume jewelry and her ruby-red lipstick. "Yeah?" he said. "Thanks for the premonition."

He slid into his driver's seat.

A cloud of dust enveloped the woman as the car pulled away, and she felt the soft sting of gravel particles across her cheeks and in her hair.

HER blond ponytail swaying with each step, Agent Travers walked down the sleek black corridor with a briefcase handcuffed to her wrist. She ran her card down a slot in one of the large metal panels and a segment of the wall rolled back to reveal another long corridor. At the end of the second corridor, she placed her eye in front of a laser scanner. The check cleared with a series of beeps and a huge steel door clicked open. Travers entered the inner sanctum.

The room she stood in was the office of the man behind the men behind the scenes at the FBI. As far as anyone knew, the room was his home as well, for nobody ever saw him enter or leave the building. He seemed to be eternally present, a single beating heart within the labyrinthine network of subterranean corridors.

The room was empty except for a large black desk, with accompanying chair, that sat in the middle of a dark rug, and a single chrome-and-leather chair placed facing the desk. There was an enormous computer on the desk, and several video monitors were within easy view of the man sitting there, giving him access to an immense range of FBI intelligence that he could recall with the punch of a key. Though he was a solitary man in an air-tight room, he seemed to know everything.

There was a great deal of agency lore surrounding this man, but it was anybody's guess as to how much of it was true. After he'd lost an eye in a freak accident or an operation, depending on which version one heard, he had taken the code name Wotan, referring to the German god who had traded an eye for knowledge. His remaining eye had grown quite sensitive to light, so he kept the room dimly lit. There was, however, almost as much artifice to his surroundings as there was need, since Wotan enjoyed his status as the agency mystery. By remaining in the shadows, he appeared even more intimidating and powerful, which was precisely what he wanted.

"Sit down, Agent Travers," he said quietly, his voice that of an older man.

Travers sat in the small chair ten feet from the desk, dangling her arm to allow the briefcase to rest on the floor. She stared at the row of blank screens set into the wall. When Wotan took meetings, which was not often, he turned off the video monitors.

"Yes, Wotan?"

"Any leads on Atlasia?"

"Well, sir, we found the speedboat about ten miles offshore. It appears he had set it so it would be headed out to sea, so we can't exactly pinpoint where he got out. He may have drowned. We put out roadblocks and sent search parties through all the beachside towns in proximity to the Tower, but there's nothing so far."

"It appears we have a child in need of punishment," Wotan said softly. "And the Tower?"

"Everyone there died except Claude Rivers, an Eleventh Leveler. The sleeper."

Wotan nodded in recognition. "Peter Briggs himself has ordered Rivers back in there as quickly as possible. Plus, I don't want him mingling with other prisoners and guards. It puts them in danger."

"I'll inform Warden Banks."

"How'd Rivers survive?"

"It was an unusually high tide, so the water eventually covered up even his cell, but he ripped the U pipe out of his toilet and used it as a snorkel. The water's surface was only about four inches above the top of his ceiling bars. He spent the better part of an hour staring at the rippling air just out of reach before the emergency crew arrived.

"We notified all the prisoners' families, and no one should be a problem, with the exception of Cyprus's mother." She paused and pursed her lips. "She's a real bitch, sir."

Wotan leaned forward and light from the dim lamp fell on his face. Travers saw his bare eye socket, the skin stretched over the hole.

"I called Briggs first thing this morning. We're not going to fool around on this one." Wotan drummed his fingers on the desktop, then stopped. "I want Marlow on it," he commanded softly.

Travers shifted uneasily in her chair. "Sir, can't you give us more time on this? Marlow's a hell of a guy to unleash in this situation—it's like letting a fifteen-year-old loose in a whorehouse, if you'll pardon the metaphor."

"It's a simile. And I want him."

A moment of silence followed, broken when Wotan cracked his knuckles by pulling his fingers down at the joint with the thumb of the same hand, one at a time. He paused between each pop, letting the noise fill the air. When he finished his fingers, he made a fist with his thumb inside and tightened it. His thumb cracked sharply. Then, he cracked the fingers of his other hand in similar fashion.

Travers sat quietly in the chair and waited for this ritual to end. She cleared her throat nervously. "Very well, sir. We'll put out the retainer and update him. Marlow usually works alone when he tracks, but we'll give him the flexibility to take another agent-partner if he needs it. He usually doesn't like the distraction, though."

Travers rose from the chair. "Wotan, sir . . . we *will* keep intelligence on it, won't we?"

"Of course. Just don't interfere with Marlow. I want him well-oiled and on course as soon as possible." His fingers traced the edge of the weighty marble ashtray that sat always within his arm's reach on the desktop. "Marlow will bring him in. He always does."

Travers had to lean forward to hear Wotan's final words, his voice was so faint. She snapped her head in a quick nod and left the room as Wotan ran his fingers gently over the bare socket of his left eye.

ALLANDER laughed softly as he wiped the noses of the two children. Their arms and legs were bound with gray duct tape and they lay struggling on the couch. The tape was also wound around their heads several times, covering their eyes but leaving the rest of their faces exposed.

The bodies of their parents lay on the carpet next to the couch. The woman's body was sprawled over her dead husband, her limbs interlocked with his. Their heads, arms, and legs were positioned at unnatural angles. Although Allander had intended them to look like two people holding each other intimately, they looked more like broken action figures.

Before arranging this deadly embrace, Allander had carefully gouged out their eyes with a knife he had found in the kitchen. It had taken him some time to get up the courage to approach the woman. The first thing he had done was to wet a towel and smear the white beauty mask off her face.

Now, he sat on a love seat with his knees pulled up to his chest. He hugged himself and grinned as he addressed the children.

"I'm certain that your estimation of your mother and father was rather hyperbolic anyway. Parents are deified by their children, but as you can see, the idols in the temple have come tumbling down." He extended a foot and touched the woman's corpse.

The little girl choked on a sob. "What did you do to my mommy?"

Allander chewed his cheek and squinted. "Let's just say I did nothing you didn't want to do yourself. I only put your desires into action. You see, that's the worst part about being a child—you're too small to have an impact on anything. Just a confused mind and a weak body with tiny little fingers insufficient to grasp and swing a blunt object."

He took the girl's hand and caressed her trembling fingers tenderly until she jerked them away. They brushed the ragged tape that covered his ring finger and a jolt of pain shot through his hand.

The boy was clearly too petrified to speak. His legs poked out of the large leg holes in his shorts, looking foolishly small and unimportant.

"I'm afraid I'm going to have to dispose of you both for the time being," Allander said.

The girl's chest began to shake uncontrollably and she jerked around on the sofa and pulled at the tape on her wrists.

"Oh no. Oh no no no." Allander threw his head back and laughed a deep, rolling laugh. "I'm not going to kill you. Just move you to the bedroom, away from the watchful eyes of your parents." Standing up, he faced the children and his voice dropped. "They see not what they do."

The girl's bedroom was pink and yellow and splendid. The wallpaper had grand stripes of dancing color, and the bed was adorned with a flowing canopy. Above the girl's desk were several cut-out letters that had been colored with crayons.

The letters were aligned with an ordered sloppiness that only a child's hand could have accomplished. "L-E-A-H." They were proud, bright and confident. Allander stared in fascination at the girl's name, standing with one child tucked under each arm. "Astounding." He shook the girl gently. "Such self-affirmation. To be admired in a budding woman."

He laid the children side by side on the mattress underneath the canopy and unwrapped their wrists, allowing their groping hands to meet and clasp together. Then, he secured their fearful handhold and taped their other arms down to their sides.

After kissing both children on their foreheads, he stood back and admired his work. His fingertips moved lovingly over the boy's face, lingering for a moment on his lips. Running his other hand smoothly down his own stomach, Allander fondled himself. He moved his hand from the boy's lips, across his rosy cheeks to the back of his head and held it there for a moment before turning away.

It would be easy, but not quite what he wanted. The woman in the mask had scared him, but he had dominated her. The boy was nothing next to that.

He cleared his throat and found his voice again. "Brother King, Sister Queen. So much contradiction harmonized in a single pair. Play, children, and see each other not."

Allander stood naked in front of the full-length bathroom mirror and stared at his pale, bruised body. His dirt-covered feet had left marks on the white carpet. Gazing at the mirror through his tangled locks, he looked at the crusted blood on his bottom lip, the swirls of dried salt that clung to his chest, the small leaf of seaweed pasted by his left nipple, and the thin, wiry stubble that sprouted unevenly around his jaw and throat.

Peeling off the tape, he looked at the red slit in his

finger. It was a brand, he decided. They had marked him like an animal, right across his own fingerprint.

He reached out his hand and touched the mirror. "What have they done to you?" he said aloud, his query bouncing off the white walls of the bathroom.

Allander sat on the love seat in the living room wearing a royal-blue silk shirt and a loose pair of pants with a drawstring. He had showered, shaved carefully, and re-dressed his finger. He had decided on the exotic outfit after trying on several; he felt it looked somehow princely on him.

He swirled some milk around in his highball glass and leaned back against the sofa, closing his eyes. After a few minutes, his head lolled back, and in his mind he caught a glimpse of an overweight man pulling a clown mask over his unruly hair. Images of heads with the eyes gouged out and a hand wiping a white mask from a woman's face flashed rapidly through his mind. He awoke with a start, the glass of milk sliding from his grasp. He watched the milk spread across the carpet, sinking into the soft fibers. It reminded him of semen.

He was instantly alert, his eyes darting around until he realized where he was. "Ah, there's the rub," he said, and walked to the kitchen to make himself a cup of coffee.

The boy and girl lay next to each other, the sound of their breathing all that interrupted the perfect silence of the room.

"Leah?" the boy said.

"Sssshhhh, Robbie. Don't talk. We don't know what the man will do."

"Is he gonna—" Robbie's breath caught in his throat and he started gasping, sucking air in and out through his wavering lips. Leah pressed his hand tightly.

Robbie finally regained control of his breathing and continued. "Is the man gonna hurt us?"

Leah didn't respond right away, but squeezed Robbie's hand again. Their palms were both sweating profusely and the moisture mingled to make a slick seal.

"I think he already has," she replied.

JADE awoke as sunlight filtered through the curtains and fell across his eyes. He threw back the thick black comforter and rolled out of bed. Stretching his arms over his head, he cracked his back from its base to just below the line of his shoulders. Then he rolled his arms back over his head to pop his shoulder sockets. He let his head go limp and swung it back and forth, groaning with pleasure as he felt the little snaps running up the sides of his neck.

He enjoyed waking up alone now. He had had any number of girlfriends in the past, but stayed with them only until they got in the way. Eventually, of course, they all got in the way.

His last relationship had reached the point where she stayed over several times a week. But then she began to get annoyed when he got called out at night. He could hear her sighing and rolling under the covers as he spoke on the phone.

She had been there the night he got the call on the Black Ribbon Strangler. Three o'clock in the morning, he was out of bed and dressed in seconds. She looked over at him, eyes and jaw set firmly. "It's just not normal, Jade. You're not even with me when you're with me. You're consumed with your job. *Consumed* with it. I can't stand it anymore. Not like this."

His back was to her as he pulled on his shoes.

"Guess that doesn't leave me with much of a choice,

does it?" he answered, and she started to smile. "Door locks behind you on your way out." He got up and left without even turning around to look at her.

"Without even turning around," she had sobbed to her friends later.

That was the last time he had spoken to her. And the next night seemed like the best night of sleep of his life.

He especially appreciated his solitude in the morning, like now, as he walked over and opened the blinds, letting in full sunlight. His bedroom, like the rest of the house, was sparsely furnished. Bookcases, filled with psychology and forensic pathology texts, faced his bed from the left side. A few pictures were arrayed on top of the shelves: Jade and Tony at a baseball game, Jade running the hundred for the UCLA track-and-field team, Jade at the batting cages. Next to them was a picture of a young boy with drooping features. It was an old snapshot with creased corners, and the small metal frame around it was greatly worn.

Jade walked over to his bookshelf and picked up the framed picture of the boy. He held it tenderly for a moment, then ran his thumb across his lip and set it back down. The normal scowl returned to his face.

After jumping into his Nike cross-trainers and a pair of running shorts, Jade mixed himself a fruit drink and swallowed it in a few gulps. The screen door banged twice behind him as he took off down the street, enjoying the fresh morning air.

His knees rose with his hands at the apex of his stride. His arms swung, relaxed, his elbows bent to perfect right angles, betraying his background in track and field. The sound of his breathing echoed in his head as he made his way through a network of streets, and he timed his step by it. He barely saw the trees and mailboxes as they whistled by; he kept his eyes focused on the ground, about ten feet in front of him.

Beginning to speed up his pace, Jade legged his way up a steep incline, driving himself against the slope. He reached a near sprint and the veins stood out against his thighs and calves. A silver chain danced against his neck as he ran.

He swept the back of his arm across his forehead and the diver's dial on his watch cut into his flesh. He didn't even notice the blood seeping out as his feet jarred on the pavement.

Turning the corner, Jade eased into a slower jog as he entered La Vista de los Árboles, a community park. Although it was in a bad part of San Jose, Jade stopped to stretch. He was accustomed to far worse places. The park was located on the edge of a gang zone, but Jade wasn't easily intimidated. Even gang members wouldn't want to tangle with someone like him.

He leaned forward against the fence to stretch his calves. He liked to stretch once he was well into a run. The park was a little under the halfway point of his workout, so it was a good place to break and loosen up.

A kid leaned back against the fence about twenty feet down from Jade, talking to a friend. He wore low-slung jeans and a sideways baseball cap, and he had a beeper latched to his front pocket. A cigarette was stuck awkwardly in the corner of his mouth underneath a bad teenage mustache. The smoke carried all the way up to Jade. He hated smoke.

The park was usually quiet this early in the morning, but as Jade glanced around, he noticed a group of boys gathered in the jungle-gym area, past the kid with the cigarette and his friend. The boys wore buttoned-up shirts, sweaters tied around their waists, and blue corduroys. They weren't quite in their teens, yet their faces had the early trappings of apathy. They looked very out of place.

Jade started to walk over to them. As he passed the smoker, Jade reached out nonchalantly and plucked the cigarette from his mouth. He broke it in half with a flick of his thumb and dropped it, never turning his head.

"Hey, fuck you, Homes!" he heard from behind him. "Yeah, that's right. You'd better keep walking." He heard the kid's hands slap to his thighs after he finished each sentence.

Jade approached the group of boys slowly. There were five of them, four sitting with their shoulders angled toward the fifth, who stood with one foot in the bucket of a swing. If you check the body posture, you can always find the ringleader, he thought.

The boy's thickly freckled face squinted up at Jade. He had reddish-brown hair flipped defiantly to one side. "Yeah? Whaddya want?" he sneered.

Jade sighed and shifted his jaw forward. "You kids from around here?"

"No," the boy replied. "Are you?" His friends guffawed, sinking their mouths into their hands to cover their giggles. Definitely private-school material, Jade thought.

"Look, you self-righteous little cocksucker," Jade said. The smirk on the boy's face vanished. "I don't really care where you're from. This is a dangerous park and you're gonna get hurt if you hang around here. What are you doing here?"

The boys all looked at each other. Finally, a pudgy kid who was sitting cross-legged spoke. "We have a debate today at St. Bellarmine's," he said, digging at his sneaker with a stick. "It doesn't start till eight, though. Our parents dropped us off early."

St. Bellarmine's was the all-boys private school across the street. A junior high school in downtown San Jose, it was in a league with some of the top schools in the Bay Area. These kids were probably from San Francisco or across town, Jade decided. They didn't know what a dangerous neighborhood was yet. They'd probably never seen one before.

Jade checked his watch: 7:50. "You'd better wait over at the school," he said.

The ringleader let his breath out through his teeth. "Yeah. Whatever. I don't think we have to listen to you." The other kids looked scared, but they wouldn't move against their leader's will. "Just keep running," the boy said. "You're not in charge of us."

Jade scowled. "You're right. You're not my responsibility. Get yourself knifed. I don't give a shit."

He walked off, a nervous silence lingering behind him, and started jogging when he passed the front gate of the park. He ran for a few blocks, then stopped, cursing. He turned around and ran back to the park, stopping on a side street.

He watched the kids through a chain-link fence, keeping an eye out for gang members. No signs of trouble. After a few minutes, the kids got up and went across the street to St. Bellarmine's. Jade watched them until they'd safely entered the school, then turned to finish his run, cursing himself for stopping mid workout.

He felt the sun warming his shoulders as he made his way home. Jade always ran without a shirt, and as he passed, women watched his chest and stomach muscles flex with each step. They would stop walking and stare until their dogs pulled their leashes; they'd gaze through their kitchen windows and turn around in their cars.

But Jade didn't notice. He didn't think about anything

except where his next seven steps were landing, and he didn't hear anything except the rush of his breath as he inhaled and exhaled.

As he came up on his house, Jade saw a shadow behind the front curtain. He kept jogging with his head forward, straining his eyes to the side to watch the figure in his house. He noticed a black Oldsmobile parked well up the street.

After passing his house, Jade circled back around to his driveway, carefully lifting the latch on the gate. His backyard was spacious, a lawn stretching from one fence to the other, broken only by a small cement path. A rectangular patio stood out from the back of the house, edging the lawn. Running along part of the back wall of the house, underneath the kitchen window, was a thin, tiled counter.

He tiptoed across the back patio and peeked through the glass sliding door. He could see over the kitchen's countertops and into the dining room at the front of the house.

A figure stood in his dining room, facing the window.

Jade reached under the tiled counter and removed a Glock, which he had kept from his training days in the FBI. Access to a pistol, he thought. First and foremost.

After checking through the other windows in the house, Jade carefully approached the glass sliding door, holding his breath as he eased it open. He slipped inside and moved cautiously to the doorway directly behind the stranger, who stood gazing out the window through the blinds. Because the room was unlit, Jade couldn't clearly make out much more than a figure, but he did see the blond hair spilling over the back of the man's collar.

Keeping his eyes trained on the stranger, Jade let his right hand wander over to the desk by the doorway. He brushed a glass paperweight that sat next to the phone, and his muscles tensed as it started to slip. His fingers closed over it swiftly as it balanced on the edge, just about to fall.

He allowed himself a deep exhale, pacing the rush of air through his mouth as his shoulders dropped. The calmness returned to him after he waited for a few seconds, and he felt his vision narrow to the target. Then, he threw the paperweight to the left side of the stranger and stepped silently up behind his right shoulder.

It hit the floor and the stranger jerked to the left, his hand expertly diving inside his jacket. He was good, Jade thought. Gun motion—like reflex.

Jade wrapped an arm around the stranger's neck and picked him up off the ground, twirling him 180 degrees to slam his head against the dining room table. He pressed the metal tip of his pistol firmly to the stranger's temple.

"Relax. Let's see your hands."

The stranger put his hands next to his face, which was pressed flat against the table. From the muffled voice, Jade realized that the stranger was a woman. She wore slacks and a loose-fitting jacket over a white shirt.

"Jesus Christ, Marlow. Calm down. I'm FBI." She turned her head and Jade saw the delicate line of her cheek.

Although Jade believed her (who the fuck else but an FBI agent dressed up to break into your house?), his hand went to her pocket and fished out a badge. He flipped it open and held it up to read, "Agent Jennifer Travers. Top Clearance." He snickered. "Evidently. Boy, I really had my hands full with you."

He realized he still held Travers's face pressed against the dining room table and he let go of her, flaring his hand apologetically. Travers stood up and straightened her slacks, running her palms over her hips to smooth the wrinkles.

He tossed the badge on the table and walked back into the kitchen. "You people need to learn how to use a doorbell," he called over his shoulder. "Now what, exactly, can I help you with?"

"We want you on—"

"Atlasia. I know. I've been waiting."

Jade took a few gulps of orange juice from the carton. "I hope you brought the file and retainer. You can leave them on the dining room table. Same rules as always. I work alone and have unrestricted access to all privileged information, labs, forensics, all that shit. And I'll need a badge—one that doesn't say 'temporary' across the front of it. If I need a partner, I want an experienced agent, not a rookie." He poked his head back around the corner. "It's been a bad week for rookies," he said.

It was the first time he'd really looked at her face, and he was startled by her beauty. Her features were simple, yet stunning. Her high, proud cheeks were still red from the struggle. He turned away before she could read anything in his eyes.

"Marlow, you understand that this is a larger case than you've handled in the past."

"So pay me more."

"We've taken care of that. But we need you to stay in line with the press. Handle them gracefully and we'll keep all pertinent resources open."

Jade smiled sweetly. "I already have been handling the press."

Travers reached into her jacket and pulled out a brown envelope. "Here's fifteen thousand. You'll get another twenty for locating him, and twenty-five for bringing him in or taking him out."

"So if I get him, I cash in forty-five thousand more?"

"You should've been a mathematician."

"You should've been an FBI agent."

He was impressed by how well she ignored him. "The bottom line is, we want you inside Atlasia's head. We want to know what he likes, what he eats, what he dreams about. As some of our more uncouth agents are prone to say, we want to know how many times he wipes his ass when he shits.

"You run the background checks and figure out what he's about and where he's going. That's what we're paying you for. And we'd like to see you at headquarters for a briefing at two o'clock this afternoon."

Jade checked his watch. It was just after nine, which gave him a little more than four hours before he'd have to start driving.

"Fine," he said, turning back to the refrigerator. "I assume you know how to let yourself out."

After Travers left, Jade jumped rope for a while in his garage, then boxed on the speed bag that hung suspended next to his car. He felt his shoulders working and held the burn for a while, stepping lightly with the punches. He toweled off, then went inside to shower.

The living room held a set of glass tables with black, metal frames, and a matching desk sat in the study. The bookcases in his bedroom, which he had built himself, were made of wood and painted black. The shelves got shorter as they rose, giving the impression that they were receding into the wall. In the kitchen, the countertops curved in and out, adding a sense of organic disorder.

Jade could think more clearly in a neat environment. Every last item in his house was in place, from the books lined up in decreasing size to the silverware divided in a black mesh container in the kitchen drawer.

His study was particularly well ordered. On his desk, a Macintosh computer sat on a swivel, elevated slightly above the keyboard. A blank legal pad was laid in the middle of a desk mat, and a small box held pens and pencils. They were returned to the box after each use.

When the pencils wore down or the pens got low on ink, Jade threw them out and bought new ones. He found them much easier to work with. You can't write down a new idea with an old pen, he figured, just like you can't start a thought on a half-used pad of paper.

Stepping from the steam of the shower and wrapping himself in a dark gray towel, Jade wiped off the mirror and shaved in short, neat strokes. He ran a comb down the top of his head to find the part and then flicked his hair over to one side. He brushed his teeth, cleaned his ears, blew his nose, and cut his nails. Then he washed his hands again, got dressed, and filled a glass with crushed ice.

He went into the living room and sat in a black leather chair facing the file on the table before him. He crunched the ice deliberately. Exhaling deeply, he flipped the file open and felt the eyes of Allander Atlasia meet his.

THREE

THE
SHADOW

JADE found the preliminary psychology reports from Allander's first institution to be revealing. When reading them, he could almost hear Allander's voice rise from the pages of the transcript. The stenographer had noted that Allander laughed a lot during the interviews.

The doctor had used the Rogers technique of questioning, pursuing a kinder, gentler approach. However, questions such as "Allander, how did that make you *feel?*," "What were your *emotions* at this time?" were too basic to allow insight into a mind like Allander's.

It seemed also that Allander understood the logic behind the doctor's methods. He'd allow the doctor to think he was making headway, then he'd say something to confuse him. He was using Skinnerian conditioning on a goddamn psychologist, Jade realized. Allander wasn't giving a great deal away, wasn't giving much up for interpretation. Instead, he guarded his thoughts like jewels, hiding them in a wash of worthless words.

Jade moved on to the tapes. Often, prison psychologists hide their tape players when interviewing subjects. Jade hoped that Allander would be less reserved if he didn't know he was being recorded.

The tapes proved to be a little better. Once in a while, Allander's answers seemed more honest. But the sincerity was not cooperative, Jade thought, just fueled by annoyance. His expressions of disgust were very real indeed.

On the third tape, Jade finally found a lapse, just one moment when Allander's language changed. His sentences got short and choppy, and Jade could tell he was truly enraged.

The doctor had asked him about the source of his anger, and Allander had exploded in a fit of verbosity.

"So, *Doctor*," Allander had replied, "if that is what we can call you—you're certainly not a healer, but that's a different tale, isn't it? You'd like to know the source of my anger? I can speak your tongue. See if you can keep up.

"Repression, projection, catharsis. Dr. Schlomo taught us to probe and dig. He was right on. He just never should have backed off. Well, I've shone the flashlight deeper than you can see through your round little spectacles. What there is in every little boy, I've seen it. So I can act it. Put me onstage and I'll toe the line of the unconscious. Take a peek at the future of my delusion.

"Sublimation. We forgot sublimation. The divine deflection of earthly longings. Build a tower, buy a motorcycle, sculpt a voluptuous pear. No thank you. My art doesn't mirror reality—it *is* reality. What I carve, I'll carve in flesh. What I paint, I'll paint in blood.

"Don't look at me with those eyes, Doctor. Take notes. Write this down. It's the key to your trade. Indulge in it, you hollow man. That's all you are. No insight except that which you want to see. Looking in rooms with the lights already on."

There was a long pause on the tape. Jade would have thought it was over except for the fact that he could still hear Allander's harsh breathing. The doctor said nothing.

Finally, Allander continued in a much calmer voice. "When children are born, they're too pure to distinguish themselves, their true selves. They try to conform their image to a societal mold. But they step forth as hollow as a chocolate Easter bunny and they need time to fill themselves with appropriate proportions of love and anger, hate and rage, kindness and despair.

"But no one speaks to the child. No one guides him through this time. He must be spoken to if he's not going to be protected. Or given a set of bearings upon which to impale his limbs. Those are the choices."

One phrase in particular caught Jade's attention: *He must be spoken to if he's not going to be protected.*

As a child, Allander had not been protected—he had undergone a terrible experience. On the tapes, he had said that children were pure. He seemed to pride himself on his ability to act out what others couldn't even see, as if his childhood trauma enabled him to see what only lay dormant for others.

What is it that's there in every little boy? Jade wondered. Allander made it sound worse than cancer.

At this point, there were only questions. Like who the hell was Dr. Schlomo? Jade couldn't find his name anywhere in the files, so he wasn't one of Allander's doctors. He had also run a check of the psychologists in the area, but he'd come up with nothing.

It was almost time to head to the San Francisco federal building for his meeting. He removed the tape and set it in line with the others. Three down, fourteen more to go. So far, only one bright spot in the midst of a lot of verbal manipulation, he thought, and it wasn't even that bright.

20

JADE sat with fifteen agents around a large table in a room on the thirty-fourth floor of the federal building. The room was stark: No pictures hung on the walls and the table was bare. The air conditioner was blasting on high, and Jade was relieved that he had jeans on instead of the thin dress pants that the agents wore.

Waiting for Jade on his seat was a folded sheet of paper. He opened it to find the home phone numbers and addresses of the agents heading up the task force. There were seven names on the list, and Jade memorized all the information as he waited for the meeting to begin.

The list was a gesture of good faith, he realized. For this case, they were letting him all the way back into the fold, and while he had mixed feelings about it, it made him acutely aware of just how much Allander scared them.

A tall agent sat down across the table from him. By watching him, Jade could tell he didn't work with any of the other agents. No eye contact. Uncomfortable gestures. He scratched his forehead a lot and laced his fingers together. He ignored Jade. Probably called over from admin to oversee things, Jade figured. He heard one of the other agents address him as Fredericks.

A secretary entered to bring everyone bottles of water. When she left, Agent McGuire locked the door behind her and opened a refrigerator-size steel door in the wall, revealing a large cabinet of files. He selected several and returned to the table.

"Here's what we got," he said. "Agent Travers, would you like to brief everyone?"

"Sure," she said, her tone serious.

Although she wore a plain suit and no makeup, Jade thought she looked as if she'd just escaped from the pages of *Elle* magazine, career women's issue. Jade caught himself admiring her neck and turned his eyes back to the table.

"We found the boat early this morning. It was seven and three-quarter miles offshore, about twenty-three miles up the coast from Maingate. The wheel had been jammed to ensure that the boat would continue to travel out to sea after its occupant departed. We don't know how far it drifted after it ran out of gas, but we're estimating Atlasia got off somewhere along a twelve-mile stretch."

"How can you make that estimate?" Fredericks asked.

"Well, it started with a full tank—we got that from the Maingate maintenance crew—so that gives us some idea of the outer limits of the distance he could have traveled. We looked up and down the coast from the Tower to find the more reasonable areas where he could have gone to shore. We believe he took the boat in close to shore, then set it to travel out. In the engine, we found traces of seaweed from inland and grains of sand that were picked up after the boat departed from the Tower."

"It just seems like it's too large a range to be very helpful," Fredericks said.

"It's a lot more helpful than you're being right now. Any objections to my finishing the briefing?"

Fredericks turned scarlet and looked down into his bottled water. Jade laughed.

"Is something funny, Mr. Marlow?" Travers asked.

"Yes, something is funny, but you can go ahead, Ms. Travers."

"*Agent* Travers."

"I was not aware of the fact that agents can't also be ladies, but I apologize. *Agent* Travers."

She was seething, but she shifted her jaw and continued. "Atlasia's prints were all over the boat and the metal bar used to set the wheel."

"Where did you get his prints for comparison?" an agent in the back asked. Everyone in the room turned and looked at him. "I'm just kidding. A joke."

Travers continued, ignoring him. "I think we're all clear on what happened at the Tower. He killed both guards and opened the vents on the prisoners. He also disabled the pumps. Hackett was a very experienced guard, so this guy's dangerous as hell. He collapsed Hackett's windpipe, probably by stepping on it after knocking him down.

"We'll have the complete forensics back from pathology tomorrow. He cut the location sensor out of his finger using surgical equipment from the guard station. He also stole some supplies from the Tower, but we accounted for everything on the speedboat."

The agent beside Jade leaned forward, resting his elbows on the table. "Great," he said. "So where are you set up?"

"We have roadblocks on every road leaving the coast, and we're keeping local law-enforcement officials on lookout in every town within thirty miles of the Tower. If that net's not large enough to catch him, then he's already slipped through anything we can throw up."

"Are we definitely ruling out the possibility that he had outside help?" Fredericks asked, finally recovered from being reprimanded.

"Well—" Travers began, but Jade interrupted her.

"Yes," he said shortly. The clock was ticking. He wanted to cut through the shit.

Travers looked over at him angrily before continuing in a calm voice. "There's no outside contact from within the Tower, so it would've been nearly impossible to coordinate, and if Atlasia had any outside help they would've probably met him where he cut the gate."

McGuire rose from his chair at the head of the table. "As all of you probably already know, Mr. Marlow here has been brought in to profile and track Atlasia. Obviously, I expect you to cooperate fully with him."

He looked over at Jade. "I assume you have a few things you'd like to say."

"Just a few." Jade leaned back in his chair. "What you're doing is chasing, which is fine. What I've gotta do is turn the tables. He's too smart. Forget the roadblocks. If he's had this much time, it's too late. It's been over forty hours since the break. To snare him, we have to make him come to us."

A few of the agents looked at each other.

"Well, then I'll just cancel the whole operation, Marlow," Travers said. "Maybe we could send him a polite telegram asking him to turn himself in."

Jade laughed. "He broke through seven levels of security with no tools except his own mind," he said. His voice lowered to a snarl. "Seven. Count them." As he listed them, he ticked them off on his fingers. "One, his cell door. Two, Greener. Three, getting up the Hole. Four, Hackett. Five, getting off the Tower. Six, the fence. Seven, the ocean.

"He killed Hackett, who was good at what he did: containment. Hackett was larger, stronger, and armed. Atlasia knew he would've ripped him apart. So he took him up here." Jade tapped his temple. "Must've got behind him.

"Basically, he escaped from a goddamn security safe and killed a master guard to do it. Forgive me if I'm not optimistic about Joe Cop scratching his crotch and sitting out on the road waiting for him to drive by."

Travers's face was white. "It's a little more complicated than that, Mr. Marlow," she said, punching her words angrily.

"What are you going to do, look around to see if he dropped a matchbook? We don't have time for this, Travers. Why don't you sit down and listen? This is what I do."

Travers started to speak but McGuire shot her a sideways look and she closed her mouth.

"We gotta go proactive," Jade continued. "Starting tomorrow, I want you to organize discussion groups for the nearby communities. To talk about their fears and concerns."

"That's all well and good," the agent in the back said, "but we don't exactly have time to console the community right now."

"I couldn't care less about the community," Jade said. "Atlasia's a megalomaniac. Nothing would be more attractive to him than a big group of people talking about him. Admittedly, it's a long shot—he's on the run and he doesn't have a base yet—but it's worth a try to see if we can lure him in.

"Second, I want my face all over the press. As fast and as much as possible."

"What was that about megalomania, Marlow?" Travers asked.

Jade ignored her and continued. "I need to be painted as a supercop. The best of the best. It shouldn't be too hard. Throw my record around, my credentials. I want to challenge him to contact me. We have to feed him all the information. I want my house on the news, my address, my phone number. No, scratch that. No phone number— I don't want any weeping mothers calling me. I'll leave it listed. But I want my location advertised."

"You have a death wish, Marlow?" the agent next to Jade asked.

"'Want,'" Jade replied. "I prefer 'death want.'"

"How the hell are we gonna get press to comply?" McGuire asked.

"I don't know. That's your job. Why don't you run a check and see if any TV field reporters have fathers or relatives on the force? Press tend to be independent, so if we want someone to cooperate, we gotta cross their loyalties or trade an exclusive."

McGuire scribbled notes furiously. He finally stopped and looked up. "That it?" he asked.

"Badge. Where's my badge?" Jade asked.

Travers set her briefcase on the table and snapped the locks open. She pulled out a badge and looked at it. Sighing deeply, she slid it down the long table to Jade, who caught it as it flew off the end.

Jade checked it. His full name, "temporary" nowhere in sight. He slid it into his back pocket, where it bulged uncomfortably.

McGuire stood to leave.

"His parents live in San Jose. Have you set up twenty-four-hour surveillance on them?" Jade asked.

"The minute we heard about the break," Travers said. McGuire sat back down. "But we'd like you to go down and talk to them."

"Obviously. I'll go later. I'm heading to the Tower after this meeting."

"Well, we'll certainly miss your company at lunch. Mr. Marlow, you have—"

"Excuse me. It's *ex-Agent* Marlow."

"Oh for fuck's sake!" McGuire yelled, pivoting around in his chair. "You two stop it. We don't have time for this shit. See them tomorrow. I thought Trav—"

"Thanks, I'll go alone," Jade interrupted.

After a moment of icy silence, Travers continued. "Mr. Marlow, you have the manuscripts and tapes from the prison's psychiatric department to study. Unfortunately, we can't get access to reports from any private psychologists Atlasia may have seen before he was imprisoned."

"We'll see about that," Jade said.

"Did he have any relationships with other prisoners who may currently be free?" Fredericks asked.

"None of any significance," Travers and Jade replied at the same time. They glanced at each other.

Travers continued, "There are very few prisoners who have received parole from the kinds of jails Atlasia has been in for the last six years. The few who have been paroled didn't overlap with him very much at all."

Jade paused and ran his thumb across his bottom lip. "This kid's a reject. He had no visitors at Maingate or at the two jails before that. No friends, no family, nothing. He spent half his time in solitary. Clearly, he doesn't like people much."

"Funny, *ex-Agent* Marlow," Travers said, "that's just what some people would say about you."

21

THE first briefing had gone well, Jade thought. The agents seemed willing to give him access to the materials he needed. In the past, whenever they'd hired him, the FBI had tried to exert control, but evidently he had earned their trust.

For much of the ride to Maingate, Jade thought about Agent Travers. He found her severity amusing, and once he got out on the highway, he actually laughed out loud. His laugh came in three descendent atonal notes. He didn't laugh much, but when he did, it was always the same. Travers had a quick mouth and a caustic wit that rivaled his own. And clearly, she could get extremely pissed off in a hurry. A few times, Jade had seen her clamp down her teeth to hold her temper inside.

Maingate was in disarray when he arrived. Men with equipment ran back and forth through the front gates, barking instructions. Trucks drove down to the shore where there were several large cranes. Two guards armed with Win Mag .300s paced the top of a small guard tower. Extra prison-security officers oversaw the operations, their bright-blue jackets standing out against the colorless prison.

Jade glanced at the Tower and saw men scurrying over it like ants. A black security guard ran by him, yelling into his walkie-talkie. Jade reached out and touched him softly on the arm.

"What?" he asked.

"I'm looking for Walker Banks."

"That's good to know."

"I'm Jade Marlow."

"Oh shit. Damn. Sorry. Warden's tied up right now on the Tower. We'll have to run you out on a boat."

Four more security guards walked by briskly, their sleeves whistling against their sides. "What's all the panic?" Jade asked.

"Looks like we're evacuating the prisoners. Too much activity. Trucks and equipment all coming and going."

Two white buses with thick bars across the windows pulled in. "Looks like a big operation," Jade said. "You moving 'em in small groups?"

The guard smiled. "Just ten at a time. We got over two hundred men to clear out of here. Not exactly juvenile delinquents, either. It's a big job." He looked over at Jade. "Even for you, I'd imagine."

"I'd imagine," Jade said dryly.

A sudden blast sent Jade into an instinctive crouch, his pistol drawn and at the ready.

"Hey, relax, man," the guard said. "They're just blasting out some of the rock to get the cranes through."

The ride out to the Tower was bumpier than Jade had thought it would be. The speedboat flicked over the water's surface like a skipped rock, and by the time they reached the ladder leading up the Tower, his clothes were soaked.

The guard pulled in close, and Jade had to make the transition from the boat straight to the steel ladder. There was no true dock, only a thick rubber strip for the boat to bump against. Jade clung to the ladder as the boat sped away. He felt very alone hanging above the ocean on two steel rails. For the first time, he realized how desolate the Tower really was. He surveyed the water stretching around him, then began the long climb to the top.

The frenzy at Maingate was nothing compared to the activity on top of the Tower. Divers were geared up in wet suits and tanks, dangling their flippers in the water that filled the Hole. An FBI team had been there since shortly after Allander's break was discovered.

Won't do much good, Jade thought. Already know who, what, and when. There was nothing new they'd discover about the scene of the crime—they'd created it. Won't tell them anything about what Allander's doing now.

A short, burly man charged around barking orders. A cigar was wedged in the side of his mouth almost parallel with the line of his molars. Sweat and moisture from the sea air dotted his bald head.

Jade walked over to him, noticing that his soggy cigar had long since gone out. Still, between barking out commands, the man chewed it with vigor.

"Walker Banks," Jade said.

"Marlow. Jesus fuck, what took you?"

"I just got the job seven hours ago."

"What took them?"

"The FBI, Warden. Moving at the speed of bureaucracy."

"No shit. I got a stack of papers on my desk could sink the *Titanic*."

"The *Titanic* is sunk."

"My point, Marlow. My point."

One of the divers surfaced, his arms looped underneath those of a corpse.

Walker pulled the cigar out of his mouth and stabbed it at the body. "Mills Benedick. Smells like a Tijuana whore."

Jade grimaced.

"On a good day, I mean," Walker said.

Another diver pulled Mills from the Hole by his hairy arms and flopped him on his stomach. Mills's hair stood out against his pale blue flesh. His naked back was humped like a buffalo's.

"Must be fun getting the cells unlocked underwater," Jade said. "Then pulling the bodies up."

"You shoulda seen the first ones, Marlow." Walker circled his head and shoulders with his damp cigar. "Head trauma from the force of the water." He shook his head.

"Look, Warden, I know you're tired—"

"Marlow, the past forty-three hours have been a bigger pain in the ass than hemorrhoids. I got two guards dead. I got sixteen prisoners drowned, one in lockdown, and one on the loose. Not to mention the fact that I'm gonna lose my standing at the Warden Hall of Fame. So yes, I'm fuckin' tired."

He looked over at the divers, who were resting at the side of the Hole. "Move your asses. We got eight more bodies that need to be up before we roll the pumps. I'd like to get home while my wife still recognizes me."

He walked away, speaking to Jade over his shoulder. "We had to bring in outside pumps—the internal ones can't get out from under that much water."

Jade stepped in front of him. "All right, Banks. Give me a quick tour and I'll be out of your hair."

"My hair?" Walker rammed the cigar back in his mouth and placed a thick hand on Jade's shoulder. "Come on, hotshot. Let's peek at the sunken treasures."

He took Jade around the top of the Tower, his voice gruff as he explained guard procedures, equipment use, and prisoner containment mechanisms. In about twenty minutes he had given Jade a full summary of the Tower's operating procedures.

The other workers and guards glanced over at Jade

from time to time. Even though he was quietly listening to Walker, Jade had a very loud presence. His eyes were penetrating; they seemed to pick apart the disaster site, noting and filing clues invisible to everyone else.

Walker finally wound up his procedural review and his account of what had happened during Allander's break.

"The survivor. What's his story?"

"Claude Rivers. Typical Boy Scout—mass murderer, postmortem fornication with his mother's headless corpse. We pulled him out safely. He's in lockdown at Maingate, but we're gonna get him back in here as soon as possible."

"Even during evacuation?"

"Peter Briggs's direct orders," Walker said. "Called up in typical fashion, ranting and raving, saying *his* prison wasn't gonna be shut down by some psychopath, even if it meant keeping the Tower up and running for one prisoner. Don't matter anyways. I'd prefer to have Rivers here. Tower prisoners are a different breed. You might think this place was built for them, but it wasn't. They were built for it." He gazed at Claude's submerged cell. "Won't eat up much manpower, having Rivers back here. One guard could handle it."

"He talk? Rivers?"

"No. Literally. Not a peep since we stuck him in here in '96." Walker groaned, putting his hands on his sides and arching to stretch his back. "There's one thing that's just not sitting right with this, Marlow. How the hell did Allander get Hackett? I came up with Hackett. He could eat scrap metal and shit bullets."

"Must've got him from behind. Swept his legs or took out a knee."

"No, no," Walker replied. "Knee was fine." Using his tongue, he brought his cigar to his front teeth, straining his mouth to breathe around it. "How the hell'd he fool

Hackett to get behind him?" he asked himself, looking down at the moist stone.

"Maybe we'll find out from the TV movie," Jade said.

Walker shook his head, then went to the shed to call for a speedboat. Jade followed, waiting as a man rolled another drum of diesel fuel over to the enormous water pump.

A diver came over and met them at the door. He pointed at the levers that controlled the vents. "Warden, I just wanted to let you know that these levers move automatically when the vents open. They could have . . . I mean, something could have pushed the vents open from the outside. Like they could've just given way or something. Are you sure Atlasia did it?"

Walker turned around, rolling his cigar from one side of his mouth to the other. He looked at the diver, then at Jade, then back at the diver. "Did Rose Kennedy have a black dress? The odds of a spontaneous implosion with such impeccable timing are fairly low, I would have to say. Yes, we're sure. Would you not agree, Marlow?"

Jade bit his lip to keep from smiling. "Yes, I would."

The diver blushed, retreating to the Hole.

Walker chomped on his cigar. "You see the shit I've been wading through here? I'm getting screwed six ways from Sunday, Marlow." He sighed deeply. "Problems. We've got problems."

Jade glanced at the flashing red lights above the vent switches. "Well, consider this," he said. "Allander had been locked up for fifteen years. Fifteen. And he took the extra time to come back to the shed just to kill everyone else. He could've been caught, but he risked it. He risked it all. Killed people he didn't even know, just to send a message. You think we've got problems now, Warden? This is just the beginning."

Walker met his stare. A look of recognition passed between the two men.

"How'd he get Greener, Marlow? We got the body parts, we got why he was down there, even how he got cut in half. But how'd the kid get his hands on him?"

Jade ran his thumb across his bottom lip and squinted as he thought. "I bet you'll find one of those metal arms for the food down there," he said. "I'll say Greener's concentration wandered and he hung it too close to Alland—Atlasia's unit."

Walker nodded sharply. "Good man. He's a good man here," he said over his cigar to no one in particular.

A guard called over from across the Hole. "Hey! Docker on the line!"

"Your ride, Marlow. It's here. I'll walk you over."

"I appreciate your time, Warden."

"I appreciate yours. Call me if you need anything else."

Jade swung his leg over the parapet and rested it on the ladder's top rung. "Hey, Banks!" he yelled.

The warden stopped and turned around.

"I'd check for prints underneath the platform. You might be surprised what'll turn up."

Walker snapped his fingers. He stood shifting his cigar around his mouth long after Jade was out of view.

22

THE children finally dozed off, their palms stuck together by their sweat and the duct tape. Since comfort was nowhere to be found, they retreated to the anesthetic of dream. The boy shivered occasionally as his eyelids flickered. His cheeks were a shade of red that normally would have been described as cheerful.

Allander watched the two children sleeping side by side on the bed, tape still covering their eyes. They had found a way to escape their physical bondage, and Allander was proud of them.

Leaning forward in his chair, Allander shook their knees gently and the children jerked from his touch as if they'd been burned. Robbie immediately began sobbing, and Allander moved next to him and placed the boy's head on his chest.

"Don't worry. I'm not here to hurt you. Only to serve as an informant into the little world of your mind, the world that lies beneath your thoughts. The world of your wishes."

His voice was soothing, and the heaving of Robbie's chest lessened. Allander sat the children up on the edge of the bed and returned to his chair opposite them.

"Why can't you take this off our eyes? Why can't you let us see?" Leah asked. Now that Robbie had calmed down, she was stronger, more defiant.

"I will let you see. That's precisely the purpose I serve. I came to your house in need of only the barest essentials." He started to say something else, then stopped as a new thought grabbed him. "Your parents would have stood in the way. Parents create, but can't see the barriers they erect. They pretend to serve and protect but, in reality, they do neither. They can't see, and it's better." Allander's voice trailed off. "If they could, they wouldn't be able to endure the vision."

"What'd you do to them?" Leah asked timidly, not really wanting an answer.

"I spared them the pain of visual catharsis."

"I don't know what that means," Leah said.

"That's all right," Allander said. "Neither do they."

He leaned over and picked a tray up off the floor, sliding it onto his lap.

"Now, I cut up some fruit for you, to replenish you in this"—his hand circled as if trying to pluck the right phrase from the air— "time of exhaustion."

At first, the children resisted being fed, but Allander waved the ripe fruit beneath their noses, and the smell became too enticing. Their small mouths opened and he patiently lowered the tidbits in, one at a time, occasionally feeling the brush of their soft pink tongues against the sides of his fingers.

This was his time, he thought. His perverted communion.

"Now revitalize again, little ones," he said, then giggled uproariously as he pushed them gently on their backs. "You must sleep. You have a learning experience before you."

Noise from the bustling workers outside carried into the building and echoed up and down the hallways. The administration building was adjacent to the cell blocks within the Maingate grounds. It attempted to be more inviting than the prison that surrounded it, but there was something unpleasant about it, an odor that couldn't be scrubbed away, even from the shiny floors. The smell of discomfort.

Jade hooked a quarter into the pay phone and punched in a number, followed by a seven-digit code. "McGuire."

"Goddamnit, Marlow, we told you to check in every—"

"Why don't we just drop that misconception right now. I'll check in for information when I need it. I don't have time to fuck around calling in like a sixteen-year-old girl on a first date."

"You will stay in correspondence with us."

"I will check in for updates when I need them, McGuire. If you have a problem with that, take it up with your superiors and get back to me. Until then, I'm calling the shots."

Such an aggressive attitude was a slight gamble, but Jade figured that someone pretty high up was pushing for his involvement. For the first time, it occurred to Jade how fortunate it was that he had not met his high-ranking FBI proponent. Given his track record with bureaucrats, Jade probably wouldn't like him very much. And he was fairly certain that the feeling would be mutual.

"All right, Marlow."

"Now what'd you get me for a reporter?"

"Alissa Anvers. Channel 5. Had a relative on the force."

"Father?"

"Mother, actually. She can get you on the news tonight. Piece together some old clips and run a special story—whatever they call that shit. She was actually glad to get an edge on the report. Press blackout so far. They're only being allowed within helicopter range."

"Well, information is our only weapon right now. Let's be careful with how and when we give it out."

"We'll consult you. Where are you right now?"

"At Maingate. Took a look at the Tower already. I'm waiting for a printout. They're getting Atlasia's library list together for me."

"They keep track of all the books he read there?"

"Of course."

"All right, Marlow, I want to . . . I'd like to hear from you within the hour if that's at all possible."

Jade dropped the phone back onto the hook.

An attractive secretary walked over to him with a messy sheaf of papers.

"Sorry that took so long to print out. He was quite a reader, I guess," she said.

Jade took the pile and started leafing through it. The woman continued to stand beside him, waiting for him to look up. She tapped a pencil against her full bottom lip as she waited.

"There's a psych institute near here. A college, I think. Where they analyze the prisoners' drawings," Jade said, his eyes still glued to the papers.

"Yes, the Ressler Institute."

"How do I get there?" he asked flatly.

She glanced at her watch. "Well, they'd be closed by now. You'll probably have to try tomorrow."

Jade continued to page through the book list. "What's the name of it?"

"The Ressler Institute," she repeated.

He nodded without looking up.

She watched him tentatively. "Got it?" she asked.

"Yeah," Jade said slowly, his finger tracing down a page. He walked up the long corridor mumbling something to himself.

"Uum. Sir. Sir. SIR!"

Jade snapped his head around, visibly annoyed. "What?!"

The woman's forehead wrinkled as she frowned. "The door's that way," she said, pointing to the other end of the hallway.

23

SESAME *Street. Hill Street Blues.* A commercial with a balding man resisting the enticements of a healthy cereal. Allander watched the latter until the balding man was won over by the cereal's "crunchy naturalness"; then he continued his journey through the seemingly endless channels.

A shot of the Tower flashed on the screen, filmed from a circling helicopter. A team of men in orange suits could be seen frantically working an enormous pump to empty the Tower of water, while a woman's throaty voice provided commentary.

"—everyone died in the flooding except for two prisoners."

"Two?" Allander bolted upright in the chair. He cursed when they flashed the front and profile mug shots of Claude Rivers. "That corpulent wretch. Level Eleven. I should have known."

"—finally announced in the face of media pressure that Allander Atlasia has escaped from the Tower. Atlasia is a convicted murderer and sex offender who authorities say may have made it to shore. The FBI and local police have launched a massive manhunt. They've put out an all-points bulletin and placed roadblocks on every street leading out of the coastal area."

She paused, clearly readying herself for a dramatic conclusion. "After remaining an iron-clad detainment center for years, Maingate's much-touted security has been breached. Reportedly, the prison is now being emptied while new safeguards are installed. This is Jessica Allende, for *Channel 5 Eyewitness News.*"

The TV cut back to the anchorman, a gentleman with graying hair and sincere eyes. "We'll keep you updated on this fast-breaking story." He straightened the papers on his desk, then looked up. "Law-enforcement officials report that they are doing everything they can at this point to apprehend the escaped prisoner, who is considered extremely dangerous. For a look at the man who may bring Atlasia to justice, here's Alissa Anvers."

A brunette with big, dark eyes stood in front of a quiet, single-story house. She wore a yellow jacket, and the wind was blowing her long hair across her face.

"Thank you, Andy." She raised a hand to indicate the house behind her. "This may look like just another sleepy San Jose home here on Blake Street, but the man who lives behind this door is anything but typical. Who is he? Jade Marlow, former FBI agent and America's self-proclaimed top 'tracker and destroyer.'"

Allander leaned forward in his chair, his eyes focused intently on the TV.

"Marlow has been called in by the FBI to locate Allander Atlasia," Alissa continued. "He came to fame tracking the Black Ribbon Strangler, and has since been involved in over half a dozen high-profile cases."

A tape of Jade at an awards banquet appeared. He was seen attempting to smile as an older agent pinned a medal to his chest. Action footage of Jade leaving the federal building and pushing his way through a sea of reporters followed.

"No comment. No comment. NO COMMENT!" he shouted to them. The reporters cleared as he got into his bullet-riddled black car.

Alissa's face appeared onscreen again, and she smiled into the camera. "FBI Chief of Homicide Brad McGuire had this to say."

Standing behind a podium, McGuire straightened his tie. As he spoke, his face was illuminated by dozens of flashes. "Jade Marlow is the nation's best criminal tracker, bar none. We are extremely confident that he'll locate Atlasia and bring him in."

The TV cut back to Alissa. "California's senior senator, Peter Briggs, also expressed optimism about Marlow's involvement."

She paused momentarily and brushed her hair out of her face. "It looks like we can all sleep easier with Jade Marlow on the case. For *Channel 5 Eyewitness News*, this is Alissa Anvers."

Allander was flushed with anger. He tapped his fingers on the arm of the love seat as he spoke to the television. "How precious," he sneered. "I've become a pawn in *their* game."

He couldn't believe the audacity of Agent McGuire and the press. The impudence. They'd all but promised he'd be caught. Didn't they understand what they were up against? He was a mastermind. He'd broken out of a facility that nobody had ever left alive. He'd virtually destroyed it. And they thought that a bumbling agent could track him down like a foolish animal. Some imbecile named Jade, Jade Marlow.

As quickly as his rage had flared, it subsided. He sighed. "I do love games," he said softly to the empty room. "Let's see if Mr. Marlow can keep up."

Rising suddenly from the love seat, he began to pace about the room, chuckling softly and shaking his head. He stopped mid-step and whirled to face the television, which was rolling old publicity footage of Jade. His smile fled.

• • •

On the edge of sleep, in the fringes of the dappled orange-and-yellow light that flickered across the insides of Allander's eyelids, something waited, something terrible, like a dead body in a closet. Years had passed during which he had hardly slept at all, but as he had grown older and stronger, he had learned how to relax himself in the right ways. With all that had happened in the past two days, however, he found that relaxing was not easy.

Allander lay on the bed in the master bedroom and watched the fan make lazy circles above his head. Every time he began to drift off, he'd awaken with saliva flooding the sides of his tongue and a shallowness in his chest that restricted his breathing to short gasps. He knew that this time he couldn't push it down. After struggling himself awake a few more times, he surrendered to the terror. He knew that when it came this strong, it was going to have its way with him. He dozed off, and it seized him.

Allander had been taken when he was seven. The man was thick through the hips and buttocks and had a potbelly that hung over his belt. But worst of all was the gray stubble that peppered his puffy face.

They had tracked him for three days before they'd caught him. A checkout girl at the grocery store had recognized him from his sketch. They'd followed him to a filth-ridden motel behind a large freeway. When they'd broken in, he'd reached under his pillow for a gun and they had opened fire, making him dance, his body jiggling foolishly as the bullets entered it.

What they had found inside the motel room was unlike anything the veteran police staff had seen in their careers, and unlike anything they would see again.

Allander had been tied tightly to a chair, thick rope binding his wrists and ankles. He'd been naked, and a small shock of pubic hair had been painted, with a black permanent marker, above his prepubescent penis. He sat in his own defecation; it was later surmised that he had not been allowed movement except when molested or forced to perform acts.

The room had seemed the harrowing entrance to a world beyond reality, perhaps even the doorway to hell itself. It had been scattered with feces and blood, and illuminated only by a blinking television screen. Pornographic videos and magazines littered the floor, showing men with chains, women with animals, children with men. Sex tools of extreme perversion lay beside the more traditional handcuffs, whips, and blindfolds. Sets of masks were also discovered—leather masks with zippers crisscrossing the front, masks that merely covered around the eyes, masks of women's faces.

Most disturbing of all, however, had been the clown masks found beneath the stained sheets. Months later, some of the policemen still would awaken in a deep sweat, seeing the smiling faces and blank eyes of the clowns laughing at them through the darkness. And through the memory came the stench, and the realization of a horror that went beyond human comprehension.

Young Allander had been freed from his torture, and was returned home and to counseling. The thick red marks the ropes had left around his limbs soon cleared up. The whip scars on his back took a little bit longer, but eventually they, too, faded. He had seemed perfectly serene for his first three weeks home, his young mind brilliant in its repression.

Then the clowns had come to visit him.

He'd awakened screaming himself hoarse and his

mother had rushed in and pressed his face to her bosom and made the clowns go away. His father had flicked on the light switch and stood in the doorway, his fists clenched in impotent anger and unfulfilled rage. Tears had traced a path down his face.

The clowns had come again and again in the night, and soon his momma couldn't make them go away anymore. Allander would cry hysterically at any prompting. He wouldn't watch TV because the cartoons sometimes had clowns, and he couldn't go near McDonald's because of the laughing white-faced clown that lived there, and even when his momma wore lipstick he would cry and try to smear it off with his child's fingers, sometimes digging his nails into her skin and leaving red welts.

The therapy had at first yielded no results, no reactions from the catatonic child. But once the clowns had begun to come in the night, the therapists' questions had probed like a flashlight shone into widened eyes.

An older man with long gray curls and a beard had tried to get him to play with dolls and make the dolls act things out. Then he'd tried to get him to draw, but Allander had taken the pencil and put it through the man's eye when the man's attention lapsed. He still remembered how the man's shattered spectacles had dangled from the end of the pencil as he'd screamed and clutched at his face.

Soon, the dolls had begun to look like clowns with accusing eyes, and so had his stuffed animals. One night, before the clowns could come, he had ripped the heads off all his stuffed animals and hidden them, with their placid, questioning eyes, in the bottom of his closet.

But still the clowns had come that night.

When his parents found him in the morning with his toys defaced, they had looked at him, eyes filled with concern and accusation, and had bestowed guilt upon him. He had screamed at them, "I HAVE SEEN THINGS, MOMMA. I HAVE DONE THINGS." Things incomprehensible, things unimaginable. But of course they could not understand, and they couldn't make the hurt go away.

Allander had increasingly felt his difference, for he'd been avoided by his former playmates, and twice a week was sent to a special school where he would talk to adults about ink blots and about "The Period." There were so many faces that finally he could not tell them apart, or remember what they wanted. When he was nine, he had sodomized a younger boy in the school bathroom during recess. He had been taken away from regular school for good, and had had to spend more time at the special school.

One of the men who had come and talked to him was different. It was only to him that Allander could show the depth of his darkness. The new man was mostly interested in the monster, though, and not much in the child. He hadn't stayed long, but Allander remembered him and his gently slanted eyes.

When he was older, Allander had attacked his mother. He had come up behind her when she was putting on makeup, pursing her lips and winking first one eye, then the other. He had beaten her about the face and had shoved her down, but before he could reach resolution, he had heard the hard, punishing steps of his father on the porch.

He had fled out the back door into the darkness, traveling through what seemed one endless night of alcohol, prostitutes, sex, and drugs before he'd gotten caught with the five-year-old girl and his pockets stuffed full of her hair. He had been eighteen.

And still the clowns came.

• • •

Allander slept deeply, more deeply than he would have imagined possible. As he awakened, he had the distinct sensation of swimming upward, rising through levels of water as distinct and varied as the stripes of a rainbow. When he surfaced, he had a tremendous sense of focus.

He loaded the gray Mercedes he found in the garage with the supplies he needed. He slipped the roll of duct tape into his pocket, where it bulged conspicuously. It would come in handy, he knew.

He returned to the house and cut up food in little pieces to leave for the children. Gazing out the living room window, he could see teams of policemen with dogs prowling the beach in the distance, and he hoped that his clothes had sunk as he had planned. It was time to move to a less vulnerable position before they discovered a clue and started calling door to door.

Allander noticed the stench as he reached Leah's room, the food he had prepared neatly arrayed on a black tray. The children had desperately needed to go to the bathroom, but with no sign of Allander for several hours and no imminent hope of being freed, they were forced to pee themselves. Robbie had also defecated, and the odor rose from the damp bed and filled the room. Both children were crying freely as Allander tiptoed in and slid the tray across their laps.

"Here's your food. Stop your tiresome weeping. And about this mess, you could've called me and I would have untaped you like before. I'm not barbaric."

He looked at them disdainfully. "Well, you've made your proverbial bed, so lie in it. I'm leaving you here, but when I'm safely away, I'll call and have you delivered to the authorities."

Allander paused for a minute and rubbed his eyes

with his fingers. He began to pace around the room, running his fingers through his hair and letting it fall back over his face.

"I'm sorry, my dears, that time doesn't allow me to continue your education. Just remember that your parents—or 'mentors,' whoever they'll be—will try to 'bring you up right,' but they'll have no concept of what that is. They'll raise you to be functional and to imitate them and indulge in petty little successes. Resist them with all your might.

"They won't ready you for the time when reality rears its head. They've worn blinders for so long they've become a part of their heads. Maybe that's what they desired all along—to have their vision restricted, expurgated."

Allander's words rose in excitement. He felt his voice come to him, clear and strong. The children began to cower from his voice, but the direction kept shifting as Allander moved around the room, sometimes even circling behind them. He didn't really address them; he seemed to be thinking aloud.

"God and country will step in to fill the void, offering you laws and equations, rules and punishments to carry you through those lonely, restless nights you spend tossing and turning in bed as the moon slides whispering in your window.

"They're worse than an opiate for the masses. They'll turn you into deaf sheep standing in line as the truth bleats fearfully at the altar. They'll have you standing in line for slaughter." His eyes narrowed. "They'll deafen you to the roar of your inner voice. That's what they do. Soon, you won't even be able to hear yourself."

Robbie choked on a sob and Leah clamped down on his hand. Not now, not here, she was telling him. They had to go unnoticed. She squeezed Robbie's hand, closed her eyes, and pretended she was shrinking away to nothing.

Allander continued, his words taking on the color of a rant. "Your educators will embark with you on a supposed journey for the truth, but they'll deceive you. They'll say things that mean nothing—they always do—and you'll be forced to nod and agree as if they're profound."

Leah held Robbie gently and quieted him as Allander paced and raved. "Sssshhhh," she whispered. "Just don't say anything and the man will go away."

"They'll tell you that when people are moved by the spirit of art or the Good, they are speaking in tongues," Allander continued. "What is it to speak in tongues? It's to babble incessantly, to fill the air with phrases and words that mean nothing, nothing at all. Your educators will think that they've been moved by an intellectual spirit, and they'll speak all the time, but in truth, they'll say nothing."

He paused and his shoulders rose and fell with his deep breaths. His nostrils flared and his eyebrows furrowed with rage.

"BLIND, DEAF, and DUMB!" he shouted, pounding his first into his palm. The children jerked violently.

"They don't want to see or admit that which is difficult. And what happens to you when you're touched by an evil, one of *their* evils? They get you out of the way, sweep you under the carpet, into the closet, into *prison!*" His voice broke and he paused before continuing softly. "They repress you."

Allander felt the tears rising, but he fought them back. The children suffered through a long, painful silence as he gazed at the carpet.

Robbie whimpered again, and Allander's eyes snapped up to focus on him. He was suddenly back in their world again. Back where he could hurt them. His jaw shifted forward and his bottom lip stuck out as he clenched his teeth. He started toward the children.

Sensing his movement, Leah shook her head vehemently, warding off the uneasy darkness. Allander saw the line of duct tape around her eyes move back and forth, and halted. It would be too easy.

He cleared his throat and started again. As he heard his words, he relaxed.

"What I hope I have done is to *show* you, to show you what lies beneath all this corruption. Others want you to see, or hear, or speak *their* truths. I offer you no values, no workbooks, no catechisms.

"Peel back the unblemished flesh that covers the face of reality, and *then* you'll see the real truth pulsing beneath. More than that, you'll feel it, and that's my lesson for you—always reach for what you desire, what you *truly* desire. Your wishes lie like fish beneath the water's surface. Call to them and they'll come to you, and you'll understand and be alive.

"That's what I've done. I've looked beneath the surface and I've seen what's really there. I'm one of civilization's discontents, but I'm not forging any false paths. What we've called fantasy is reality. It always has been. We've just forgotten that." His eyes were distant, impassioned. "Well, it's time to remember. I've seen who's wrong and what needs to be done to them. And now I have the power to make them see, to understand."

The back of Allander's shirt was darkened with a circle of sweat; the fabric clung to him. He had been running his hand through his hair, pulling it in the back as he spoke. It was wildly disheveled now. A small trickle of blood ran from a scab on his upper lip that he had chewed open.

Allander focused again on the children. They squirmed at the sudden silence, for they couldn't see the expression on his face. The air was choked with tension.

Allander leaned over them and patted their cheeks, and both children drew back from his touch. "You'll be seeing me again, I'm quite sure of it," he said. "Not in body, of course, but surely in spirit."

The children felt a rush of air across their flushed cheeks as the door swung shut.

JADE pressed on the accelerator and gunned his car to eighty-five. He swerved between lanes, cutting in and out to pass cars going the speed limit.

Joe Henderson blared from the speakers, and Jade tapped the wheel enthusiastically as he sped along, occasionally adjusting the treble and bass dials. His fingers stole to the line on his left cheek and ran gently over it.

After driving south on 280, Jade cut over to Highway 17 and exited at the Alameda. As he drove through back streets, he checked the directions that were lodged in his ashtray. He was looking for 624 Pepper Lane.

Through his windshield, Jade saw a small one-story house that looked comfortable, if slightly decrepit. A white knee-high fence ran along the front of the yard, blocking off the spotted brown grass from the street. A little gate stood open at the head of the walkway. It hung at an angle, clumsily but warmly inviting visitors.

Suspended from a large maple in the front yard was a rope swing. Jade could imagine Allander as a child swinging from the tree, kicking his legs up toward the summer sun, the smell of lemonade and mown grass in the air.

Jade adjusted his rearview mirror and noticed the dark Cadillac parked behind some bushes at the corner of the street. He opened his door, swinging his legs from the car. Admiring the sunflowers growing from the brown planter boxes, he walked along the sidewalk up to the gate. Decent place, he thought. A little midwestern, but decent.

Above the doorbell a small placard proclaimed, "Our House." A welcome mat showed a gaggle of geese in a pond.

He stepped up to the door.

The coolness of the white beauty mask calmed Allander. He saw the flashing red lights ahead and slowed the Mercedes to a halt before maneuvering it into the lineup of cars.

A young policeman with a mustache was peering intently into each car before clearing it with a thumbs-up. They always have a mustache, Allander thought.

He heard the officer shouting above the noise of traffic up ahead. "Yes, ma'am. No problem, ma'am. We're just on the lookout for somebody. No, you shouldn't be concerned."

Allander's eyes peered out from behind the beauty mask and he counted the cars in the line in front of him. There were four. He drummed his fingers on the steering wheel.

Allander wore a white terry-cloth bathrobe over a long nightgown that ran up to his chin. He had stacked two sets of shoulder pads and taped them to his chest to make an outline of breasts beneath the folds of cloth. He wore thin leather gloves to conceal the wound on his finger, and the white beauty mask over his face had hardened slightly. His hair was tightly curled in rollers.

He rolled down his window as he approached the young officer, and switched the radio to a soft oldies station. Smokey Robinson's voice wailed through the speakers singing "The Tears of a Clown." Allander hummed along.

The officer peered in and pressed his lips together to avoid smiling at the ridiculous outfit the woman was wearing. Allander smiled amiably at him.

"Go ahead, lady," the officer said, his voice hinting at both disgust and amusement. He waved the Mercedes through with his baton, shaking his head as Allander sped away on the open highway.

The young officer's walkie-talkie squawked, and he picked it up. "Yeah. All clear so far. I will, I will."

THE wooden door swung open as Jade rang the bell, and he felt a sudden rush of humidity on his face. The air was thick with the scent and feel of food, like a heavy stew.

A pleasant-looking man with graying hair stood, barely visible in the darkness of the house. Jade knew from his research that he was in his early sixties, but he appeared much younger.

"Like to keep the lights off when it gets hot out. Keeps the house cooler," he said, smiling. His lips were full, and Jade noticed the distinctive curve of his Cupid's bow. It matched Allander's exactly.

The man had on a well-worn apron that proclaimed, "Freeman & Jobbers Real Estate. We put the OWN in HOMEOWNER." The "OWN" in "HOMEOWNER" was colored red, in case the puzzle proved too much for some people.

The man looked down at Jade's white buttoned-up shirt. "I hope you're not selling any of those study books because our little one's already gone and moved out."

Jade covered his smile by scratching his nose. "No, sir. No, I'm not. But I did actually want to talk to you about your 'little one.'"

The man's face darkened. "Goddamnit, I told you hounds to keep away. I'm afraid I'm going to have to ask you to leave."

The door started to swing shut, but Jade caught the

handle and pushed. The man stumbled back, his eyebrows raised in surprise.

"Well, I'm afraid I'm going to have to stay for a while." Jade pulled his badge from his back pocket. "Jade Marlow, FBI."

The concern on the man's face lessened. "Oh. Thought you were one of those fellows from *A Current Affair* or *Hard Copy*. They've been calling all morning."

"I can imagine," Jade said. "I just need a few minutes of your time."

"Well, I suppose I should invite you in. I'm Thomas Atlasia. You like soup?"

"You keep the lights off to cool the house and then you cook soup?"

The man laughed. "If you eat hot, your body cools."

Jade nodded politely at his logic, or lack thereof. "I see. But I think I'd better pass."

Thomas showed Jade to the living room. Brown furniture and thick brown carpeting made the room darker than it should have been; it seemed to devour all the light let in by the windows.

The fireplace was composed of large white-and-beige rocks that stuck out at strange angles to form an uneven surface. A Haydn symphony played in the background, the roll of a drum momentarily filling the air.

Jade sat in a large brown chair, sinking in until he felt as if his knees were touching his chin. Mr. Atlasia sat down on the hearth. Apparently, he wasn't bothered by the jagged edges of the rocks.

"Now," he said, then paused as if summoning his courage before turning his mind to the subject. "My son. I would like to reiterate that my son has not tried to contact me. I haven't visited him or spoken to him in over eleven years, nor has my wife."

"Deborah?" Jade asked, just to break up the rehearsed speech.

"Yes. Darby. She just went to the store. She'll be back soon. What exactly can I do for you?"

"Mr. Atlasia—"

"Please. Call me Thomas."

"Okay. Thomas. What was he like before his childhood incident?"

Mr. Atlasia paused and cast the line of his memory back, disturbing still waters. Jade watched his face to see if he told everything that was dredged up.

"I'd like to say that he was a normal boy. Well-adjusted."

"You'd like to or you are?"

"I'd like to. You see, he was always extremely sensitive. We used to joke that he was trouble from the first because he was a C-section delivery. Made him more . . . fragile, I guess. One foot still in the womb, so to speak."

He raised his head and smiled. "I remember when he was in kindergarten, one of the beefy kids called him 'The Salamander.' He used to come home crying even though he didn't know what it meant."

Allander the Salamander. Kids' true brilliance shows in how effectively they hurt each other, Jade thought.

Thomas laughed a sad, hollow laugh. "I still don't know what the hell it means. But anyway, Mr. Marlow, he would react to everything. He was very fragile and very alive."

Jade was impressed that Thomas had remembered his name from the informal and rude introduction he had forced at the door.

Thomas continued. "You see, we're simple people, Mr. Marlow. We believe firmly in education and hard work. We had that boy reading from the day he could stand up.

By kindergarten he was at the reading level of a sixth-grader. And what a voracious reader he was. He used to go to the library every other day and stack the books right up to his chin."

His eyes sparkled fondly at the memory. "The librarians used to tease him that he would have read everything in there by the time he finished high school."

He paused for a moment reflectively, then chuckled. "Well, he never finished normal high school, but I'll be damned if he didn't read every book in that library by the time he was sixteen. That was before . . . before he left, you see."

"We got hold of some of Allander's IQ tests from before he was committed," Jade said.

He noticed Thomas tense up as Allander's name was said aloud. It was as if Jade had released it into the stagnant air of the house for the first time in years. So far, Thomas had used only euphemisms for his son's name.

Jade continued with his question. "Was he always so bright?"

Mr. Atlasia smiled, the side of his mouth twitching slightly. "He takes after his mother's father. That's whom he was named for. Allan Darby, God rest his soul. He was a kind man, a brilliant man. He taught English literature at the state college here for a number of years. His students loved him passionately. He died the week before Allander was born. Heart attack."

He shook his head slowly. "So young. Such a wonderful man. He was the youngest professor ever to get tenure there. I recall one of his colleagues said at his funeral that he was the only man he knew who could recite *Paradise Lost* beginning to end."

Jade shuddered. "A dubious distinction." He was testing Thomas, but even this jab didn't draw an angry response—only a disapproving stare. Very level man, very controlled, he thought.

Mr. Atlasia squinted over at him, his voice becoming serious. "That's the kind of man he was. He was fascinated by everything. He beheld life through the eyes of a child. Reminded me of that picture of Einstein on a bike."

Jade cleared his throat. "I'd like to see Allander's room if that's all right with you."

"Please, Mr. Marlow. This isn't *Great Expectations*. We weren't exactly going to keep a boy's room untouched in our house to remind us. Memories can be painful. We cleaned out his things years ago."

Jade leaned forward, placing his thumbs under his chin. He stared intently at Thomas and the small yellow ring in his green eyes seemed to glow with anticipation.

Thomas, obviously intimidated by Jade's glare, braced himself for the next question.

"How do you feel about your son, Mr. Atlasia?"

The door from the garage banged open. "Hello, honey, I'm back. You should've seen the look the kid at the counter gave me when I went through the whole line just to buy a single carrot." A pocketbook banged down on the kitchen table and then some keys. "Thought I was some kind of pervert or somethi—"

Mrs. Atlasia came around the corner into the living room, and upon seeing Jade, stopped mid-sentence. She blushed, covering her mouth with her hand.

Although she was in her sixties, Deborah Atlasia was an extremely attractive woman. Her smile radiated charm and grace, and she had a becoming self-assurance. She could fill an empty room with her smile. Her warmth carried over to her eyes. Jade recognized her eyes—they were Allander's down to the crow's-feet that wrinkled from the sides.

It was eerie looking at those eyes, Jade thought, wondering how Thomas Atlasia could look into them every night and not see his son's reflection. Maybe he did.

Jade struggled to rise from the plush seat.

"I am dreadfully sorry. And rather embarrassed, too, now that I think about it. I'm Deborah, but you can call me Darby." She extended a hand and several elegant silver bracelets jingled around her wrist.

"Jade. Jade Marlow. You go by your maiden name, Mrs. Atlasia?"

Again, Jade was unsuccessful in his attempts to stand. She walked over and gently pushed him back into the chair, placing her hand on his shoulder and applying pressure.

"Please. Not Mrs. Atlasia. It makes me want to look for Tom's mom." She laughed an elegant, womanly laugh. "And believe me, I'd rather not."

Thomas tilted his head and gave her a look of mock warning.

"Just kidding, hon." She smiled at her husband.

Pushing her light brown hair behind her ear with a cupped hand, she looked at Jade as if for the first time. "So what do you do, Mr. Marlow? I mean, why are you here?" She stopped. "Oh no. That sounds atrocious, I don't mean that." She smiled again. "I mean, what allows us to be graced with your presence?"

"Nice recovery," Jade said, smiling and still trying to stand up.

"Thanks. I thought you wouldn't notice."

"FBI. Sorry—I notice everything."

She widened her eyes and pulled her head back a little. "Well, I must say that caught me a bit by surprise." The room was silent for a moment. "Your mother know what you do?"

"No. She thinks I'm a pimp."

Darby laughed uproariously and slapped her husband on the shoulder. Mr. Atlasia was in a more solemn mood than his wife, but he smiled nonetheless.

"Well, I suppose she'll be elated to learn of your shift in vocational emphasis." Her smile finally faded. "I must admit your name did sound familiar," she continued. "As much as we try to block it out, the media still manages to creep its way in here—the radio, the television, on our doorstep. So we've heard of you. You're the one they call 'The Tracker.'"

Jade cleared his throat and thumbed his silver chain absentmindedly as he considered how to make the transition back to Allander.

"A necklace, Mr. Marlow? I wouldn't expect a man like you to wear jewelry."

"It's a chain. My mother gave it to me." And I'll never forget what she said when she handed it to me, he thought to himself. He could see it draped over her outstretched hand, his brother's medical tags swaying beneath her fist. "Something like a parting gift," he added.

"Oh. You're not close?"

"No. We don't . . . no." Jade cleared his throat a second time and was immediately angry at himself for doing it. Relax, he told himself. You sound nervous. "Well, I'm—"

"I know. You're here to 'ask some questions,'" she said, mimicking a businesslike voice and moving her head up and down as she imagined men did when filled with a false sense of importance.

"Just a few. I'll try to make them as painless as possible."

"That could be difficult, Mr. Marlow. You are hunting my child." She said it softly, yet sharply, and it stung a little. She wasn't angry, merely stating a fact. Clearly, she was used to hard facts, although after all that Allander had done over the years, Jade hadn't expected to find her quite so defensive.

Thomas began to trace the rocks on the fireplace mindlessly. He hadn't spoken a word since his wife had arrived, but Jade could sense they had a warm relationship.

"Well, obviously it's about your son."

"Obviously," she said, her smile returning. "Of course no one would want to ask questions about *us*."

She disappeared into the kitchen for a moment to retrieve makeup from her pocketbook. As Jade asked questions, she put on lipstick and blush, facing away from the men into a round mirror on the wall.

Darby's mood, like her husband's, was oddly giddy, Jade thought. They were all over the map emotionally, still trying to process the feelings moving through them.

"Have you been worried since he broke out?" Jade asked.

"Well, I suppose *worried* isn't quite the word for it. Concerned. Concerned is a better word."

"For yourself and your husband?"

"And for him," Thomas said, finally breaking his silence. He repeated himself as if explaining something to a child. "She's concerned for him as well."

"So you still feel close to him?"

"No," Darby answered. "But it is our blood running in his veins. We raised him, and he was a sweet, sensitive boy. He was always a little vulnerable, but he was so uncorrupted." She put her makeup back into her purse and turned around. "So pure."

Still she did not sit, but crossed the room and played with little trinkets on the mantel. She seemed to be trying to avoid eye contact, especially with her husband. "It's hard to let go of that. You understand, Mr. Marlow?"

"No. But I hear you."

"Fair enough."

Jade shifted in his chair to face Thomas again. "How about you, Thomas? How do you feel about your son?"

Thomas didn't look up from his fingers, which still roamed over the curves of the fireplace rocks. He hunched over and grabbed his ankles, looking up at Jade.

"Son . . . I just don't know. Years of therapy haven't helped me figure that out, and I sure as hell can't give you a three-sentence answer now. But I do know that when . . . that when your child does a thing, a thing like he did—"

"I think that's enough, dear," Darby said, cutting him off, her voice maintaining its sweet tone.

Jade sensed something in the brief exchange. The couple wasn't in agreement about Allander. Darby had looked away when she spoke of him, as if she were ashamed for still having motherly feelings toward him. Showing this kind of guilt before her husband seemed strange, especially in light of the closeness Jade sensed between the two of them.

And now she had interrupted her husband—not rudely, but as if she were worried about what he might say. What was "the thing" that Thomas said Allander did?

"We don't need to get into all that right now," Darby continued. "I'm sure Mr. Marlow can read between the lines. Anything else, Mr. Marlow?"

Jade noticed that her tone had changed. Though she was still polite, her warmth had departed.

He had a lot more digging to do; he hadn't even

touched the tip of the iceberg. The Atlasias seemed pretty disturbed just by the mention of Allander's name, however, so Jade decided to wait and give them some time to adjust to talking about their son again. He would come back, though, and he would get them to talk, however painful it might be. That was his job.

Jade leaned forward and, with great effort, pulled himself free of the chair. He took a card from his wallet and wrote his home phone number on it.

As he handed it to Darby, he took her gently by the wrist. "Your husband said he doesn't think Allander will try to contact you. Do you agree?"

The name unnerved her, as it had her husband, and her hand shook ever so slightly.

"We haven't spoken to him in years. I can't imagine what he would want from us now."

She paused, looking at Jade for a moment. "You know, Mr. Marlow, we've done a lot to move on, to integrate ourselves back into the community. A lot of charity work, social service—that was our road back to sanity. People don't forget things easily. So you'll have to forgive us if we're less than enthusiastic at the prospect of opening some of these doors again."

"Yeah." Jade nodded once. He ran his hand over the back of his neck. "If you need anything, please call me. Anything. Any hour." He glanced over at Thomas, who was studying the carpet. "Thank you both for your time."

Thomas looked up at Jade and his eyes were strikingly empty. "Good-bye." He snapped his head down again. "Good-bye, Mr. Marlow."

AFTER Leah slid her hand into the noose of the tape so that it gathered around her wrist, she worked it back and forth for what seemed like hours. Robbie whimpered as the tape chafed his skin.

Finally, it had stretched enough to allow Leah to slide her sweat-lubricated hand through, freeing it. She ripped the tape from around her eyes and left it dangling from her hair. After yanking on the remaining tape around her waist, she pulled out her other arm. Once she had both arms free, she kicked off her shoes and slid out of her pants rather than trying to extricate them from the coils of tape. She stood, feeling pins and needles through her legs, and pulled the tape from around Robbie's head.

His blue eyes watered as he squinted in the light.

"Before I untie you all the way, I'm gonna go get help, okay?"

Robbie was too weary to scream that he wanted to go with her, so he bit his lip and nodded as the tears began to spill down his cheeks.

Clad only in her shirt and underwear, Leah tiptoed down the carpeted hallway. As she rounded the corner to the living room, she screamed and sank to the floor, landing on her rear. Immediately, her legs began churning, backing her to the wall, away from the horror that lay in front of her.

The corpses of her parents lay grotesquely intertwined. The empty holes of their eye sockets gazed blankly at her like those of the skeletons she had seen on the pirate ride at Disneyland. Her mother's stomach had been cut open, and there was blood splattered everywhere—all over the walls, on the white blinds, on the fireplace and mantel, seeping into the carpet.

Smeared across the window overlooking the beach were the letters "S N E." The blood had crusted already, and was beginning to flake.

Leah ran back down the hallway to her room screaming, "DON'T LOOK, ROBBIE! DON'T LOOK AT IT! DON'T LOOK!"

The dam of Robbie's emotions broke when he heard the panic in his sister's voice, and fear overwhelmed him. He sobbed with complete abandon, twisting on the bed, his face swollen and red.

Leah ran screaming into the room and pulled the tape from her hair, not even noticing the sting as it yanked a clump from its roots. She fell on top of Robbie and stuck the tape over his eyes. The scream kept coming, "DON'T BE SCARED, ROBBIE! JUST DON'T LOOK! DON'T LOOK!"

Then she ran back down the hallway, closing her eyes when she again passed the room in which her parents lay. Feeling the rest of the way with her hands, she reached the kitchen and called 911.

It was quiet and the dimmed green lamps glowed across the dark wooden bookcases. The occasional clicking of footsteps was all that interrupted the perfect silence of the Josephine Public Library.

Allander's book list was set evenly in a black folder. Jade pulled it out, placed it on the big oak desk, and reviewed it again. He was amazed by its contents. Though the Tower restricted reading, Allander had checked out an incredible range of books during his time at Maingate proper. Library resources were unlimited at the main prison; officials even borrowed books from local libraries if the prisoners requested them.

It seemed Allander had read everything: Victorian literature, biographies of composers, art theory, legal journals, historical analyses. He had also read a number of computer journals, Jade noted. Even from within prison, Allander was trying to keep up with modern technology, probably so he could be self-sufficient if he ever escaped.

He scanned the rest of the list, his finger running down the page. One author's name appeared over and over: Sigmund Freud.

At first he didn't think it was so unusual; the study of psychology was encouraged because of Maingate's association with the Ressler Institute. But as Jade glanced down the page, he realized that Allander must have read Freud's entire canon. The materials by and about Freud far outnumbered those of any other author.

Lacking a familiarity with some of the works listed, Jade asked the librarian for help. "I need a brushup on Freud. I've read him before, but I was hoping I could get something like a summary."

"I should recommend a reader," the librarian said. "Peter Gay edited one. He's fantastic on biography and—"

"Peter Gay. Good." Jade turned and left.

He found the suggested reader after spending a few minutes poking around the dusty shelves. He also grabbed *Introductory Lectures on Psycho-Analysis*. He settled into an armchair by a window and didn't move for an hour and a half as he leafed through the books.

Much of Allander's recorded interview came into focus as Jade read. One piece of the puzzle fell into place almost immediately. The first footnote he came across stated that

Freud's given names were Sigismund Schlomo. Freud was the "Doctor Schlomo" Allander had spoken of on the tape. He had been taunting his psychologist, daring him to discover the hidden clues.

Jade had already recognized some of Allander's language as Freudian, but now he uncovered more of its meaning. For example, Allander had expressed disdain for sublimation. "What I carve, I'll carve in flesh. What I write, I'll write in blood," he had said. He felt that his art was reality; by his art, he meant his violence. Instead of sublimating his violent tendencies into something productive or healthy, he prided himself on acting them out. While others distracted themselves with fantasies, he alone indulged his true self. His way was more real, he thought, more courageous.

So what was it he admitted? What did he need or want to act out?

On the tapes, Allander had talked about something that's "there in every little boy." The Oedipal complex? The complex, like the myth, was certainly filled with sexual violence.

Jade jotted notes down on a pad. He'd have to run a lot of this by a psychologist when he got a chance. Setting down his notes, Jade stood up and cracked his back all the way up from the base. He stretched his arms over his head as he walked back to the front desk.

"Where's a phone?" he asked the librarian.

"There isn't a public phone in the building," the man replied, folding his thin arms across his chest.

Jade looked down over the counter at the white phone in front of him. He pointed at it.

"I'm sorry. No public use."

Jade flipped his badge open as he reached across the counter and grabbed the phone. "Yeah, well I'm not the public."

• • •

"Goddamnit! Where is he? Why hasn't he checked in?" Travers circled the conference room, eyeing the telephone that sat silently on the middle of the table.

McGuire looked over at her. "He said something about going to the library."

"Well, that's helpful. We're knee deep in shit and he's off reading books."

McGuire raised a finger. "I told you, we need to cooperate," he said sternly. He grabbed his briefcase and checked his watch. "You keep an eye out. I gotta run home. The boys have a baseball game."

He walked out of the room, then stuck his head back through the doorway. "As soon as you hear from him, I want him to go over to the crime scene to see those kids."

"I know, I know," Travers yelled down the hall after McGuire. "He needs to—"

The telephone rang, the shrill sound echoing off the walls.

Travers grabbed it before the first ring ended. "Marlow, where've you been?!"

"I missed you, too, *Agent* Travers. Where's McGuire?"

"Actually, he's at his kids' baseball game. Think you can lower yourself to talk to me?"

"I'll try."

"Well, while you were out, Atlasia committed two more murders and held two children captive."

"Fuck! You got him?" Jade grimaced at the thought of missing out on the capture.

"Glad to see your priorities are in place," Travers said sarcastically. "No, we didn't get him. He tied up a little girl. She freed herself to call nine-one-one after he left."

"He tied her?" Jade sounded surprised.

"Well, he taped her," Travers replied.

Jade pushed his hair out of his eyes as he adjusted the phone on his shoulder. "Yeah, that figures. He was tied himself. He wouldn't re-create that experience. Not with the same constraint. He'd adapt it and make it his own."

"What the hell are you talking about?"

"Nothing. Where's the hospital? I'm there first, then I'll check the scene."

"St. Mary's. And Jade these kids are traumat—"

Travers heard the dial tone and let her breath out in a hot rush. She had to get over to St. Mary's to protect the children from Jade.

JADE drove his car onto the curb directly in front of the hospital's lobby entrance. As he stormed through the sliding glass doors, he flashed his badge and shouted at the lady in the reception booth, "If you tow that car, I'll arrest you." A silence fell over the lobby and lingered even after the elevator doors had closed behind him.

The trauma unit was on the second floor. Jade had been there many times before to interview witnesses and suspects, so he knew the drill. The first person who tried to stop him was the woman at the front desk, but she was new on the job, and not quite clear on patients' legal rights.

Jade faced her, slamming his badge down on the counter. He leaned forward on both hands, his eyes focused on hers. "I need to see a kid who got brought in here this morning from the hostage situation. Immediately."

The woman cleared her throat nervously, her hand hovering in front of her nose. Jade knew he had her.

"I'm sorry, visiting hours are—"

"I'm not a visitor, I'm an FBI agent. And I need to talk to this child immediately. We need her in order to apprehend a murderer and child molester. Unless you want to be personally responsible for wasting my time while this suspect flees, Ms."—his emerald eyes lowered to her name tag—"Doren, then I suggest you don't jerk me off any longer and tell me the room number."

She gasped. "Well . . . I . . . There's two . . . children. A little boy—but he's in deep posttraumatic shock and not speaking. The girl is eleven." She paused and her eyes flicked around nervously to locate her superiors. Finding nobody to bail her out, she surrendered. "She's in room two-twelve."

Jade was gone, running down the corridor. Ms. Doren stood up abruptly, knocking over a pencil holder. The pencils rolled across her desk and fell to the floor, chattering like rainfall.

"She's very fragile right now," she called after him. "You can't just—"

Realizing that Jade was not listening, she sank back into her chair and paged a physician.

When the door to her room flew open, Leah sat up in bed, drawing the blanket protectively around her chest and up under her chin. Her eyes regarded Jade with fear and suspicion. She was shaking violently.

"It's all right. It's fine. I'm on your side." Jade flipped out his badge and flashed it at her. Crossing to her bed, he stood over her for a moment, then gripped her shoulders firmly. She continued to shiver.

"Don't be afraid. I need to know what happened."

Her bottom lip quivered, and tears began to roll down her cheeks.

Jade let go of her shoulders and sat on the edge of the bed, swearing softly.

A team of doctors burst into the room, knocking the charts from the back of the door. The largest doctor stepped forward. He wore wire-frame glasses and had a decent physique. The other doctors crowded behind him.

"Who are you, the intimidation factor?"

"I'm Dr. Levinson. I'm going to have to ask you to leave the room immediately or I'll call security."

"Now maybe they lied to me in training, but I always thought the FBI took precedence over the security team at St. Mary's. And I'd suggest you stand back a little. I don't like your posture."

The doctor stepped back. "Sir, you cannot be in here right now. This patient has just undergone a horrible experience. The last thing she needs is offensive external stimuli."

"I haven't even begun to get offensive," Jade said. "But try me."

The doctor shook his head nervously. "Not that kind of . . . that's not what I meant." He paused, assessing the situation, trying to figure out the best tactic to follow.

Jade ran his thumb across his lip. "Look, Dr. Levin-whatever. I'm pursuing the most dangerous—"

"Sir, look at the girl."

Jade looked over at her. The tears were flowing, and her face was swollen. He noticed the red marks around her wrist, the only part of her body exposed from under the blanket. His breath started to come harder as he felt the anger flooding his veins.

"Please," Dr. Levinson said.

The door opened behind them and Travers pushed her way through the team of white coats cowering behind Dr. Levinson. Leah began to sob.

Travers's badge hung from the pocket of her white blouse, and her blonde hair was down across her shoulders. She was dressed more femininely than Jade had seen her before. She saw Leah and her jaw tightened. "Marlow. Outside. *Now.*"

Jade looked at the doctors and then at Travers. He could tell she was somewhere between livid and incensed. Impressive. He opened his mouth to say something, then changed his mind. Quietly, he got up and followed her out of the room.

The minute they turned the corner, Travers spun to face Jade, pressing her finger into his chest.

"Did you see that girl, Marlow? You scared the shit out of her. Your tactics are fine for harassing adult suspects, but they don't work on small children who are victims. VICTIMS! This girl found both her parents dead."

Jade's jaw shifted over and he bit his cheek. "First of all, take your finger off me. Second, you didn't tell me her parents got iced. I would have been more—"

"More what?! Like you can be more anything. The doctors are furious, the girl is probably too scared to talk now. Great piece of work, Marlow."

She was right. He should have proceeded more gently if he wanted to get the kid to talk, and he knew it. She unbuttoned the top of her shirt and pulled it in the back so it shifted on her shoulders. "Well, I'm handling this now. I'll deal with the girl. What do you need me to ask her?"

She unbuttoned her cuffs and rolled her sleeves up, then took her badge from her shirt pocket and slid it in her back pants pocket.

Jade paused for a minute, then answered very seriously. "I need to know how they responded. The kids. What they said. And ask her if... ask her if he explained what he was doing as he did it. If he gave them any insight into his rationale. He'd want to, I think. He'd want them to know, to understand."

The rage behind Travers's eyes subsided. She nodded and turned to go, but Jade caught her arm.

"You look good," he said.

"Well, thank you, Jade," she said sarcastically. "That's what I'm here for."

"Don't flatter yourself. I mean you look good. Maternal and caring. Perfect for the kid. Smart move."

"Oh. Thanks. I try to go for that Nancy Reagan look." She turned and walked away.

ONCE he was safely past the roadblock, Allander removed the bathrobe and nightgown and peeled off the beauty mask. Underneath, he still wore the comfortable blue silk shirt and loose pants. After taking out the curlers and applying a generous amount of gel, he parted his hair to one side and slicked it back neatly over his ears. Big sunglasses covered his eyes, and he had pushed cotton balls into his cheeks and under his lips to change the shape of his face.

Having already taken care of an important stop that he had planned, he relaxed and hummed along with the classical music pouring from the car's topnotch speakers. Closing his eyes, he breathed deeply, allowing himself to enjoy the simple perfection of a Mozart symphony.

A green sign appeared over the highway just ahead of him, announcing the next exits. It was followed by a smaller blue sign with crude symbols for food and transportation. Having still not fully adjusted to driving again, he gripped the steering wheel tightly as he put on his blinker and cautiously pulled over, exiting the freeway. He passed a Greyhound station and found a deserted factory several blocks from the main road.

He slid open the rusty gate, leaving the car humming. The gate's lock had been smashed open already and it hung from the fence. Allander inched the Mercedes through the gate, pulling up in an alley between a warehouse and an old building. He climbed in the backseat and curled up on the fine leather, content to pass the night planning and dozing.

The house was crawling with agents by the time Jade got there. He wandered through it, thinking that only hours earlier Allander himself had walked through these very rooms, had seen the same table, the same flower arrangement, had probably gone to the bathroom here and eaten from the refrigerator.

So close in time, so far away. Allander's presence still hung about the house the way a man's shape fills a shirt after it's been worn. Jade could sense him, sense that he had been here, and he walked around the house as if in a trance, feeling the walls and floor.

When Travers arrived a half hour later, Jade ignored her. He didn't have time for distraction until he'd made his first complete pass through. The other officers weren't sure what to make of him, but Jade hardly noticed their presence. He was alone in the house with the scent of Allander.

The door to Leah's room was slightly ajar, and Jade rested his forearm on the frame as he gazed in. The letters of her name on the wall made him smile. Allander would have appreciated them.

The bed was still wet with urine, and Jade crossed the room heavily and looked at the stain, a dark mass spread across the soft pink comforter. He touched it absentmindedly, gazing around the room.

Jade closed his eyes and imagined Allander's approach to the house in the early light of morning. The ground was cold under his bare feet. He rang the doorbell and waited. He heard approaching footsteps. His stomach was nervous but excited. The footsteps stopped and he leaned forward, driving an instrument through the peephole. He pushed the door open and it stopped when it hit the man's body. The body slid as he opened the door the rest of the way. He stepped over the corpse and he was inside. What was he thinking? Was he imagining the feel of children's skin against his fingertips? Was he nervous at the likelihood that there was a woman in the house?

An agent with a clipboard bumped Jade as he passed and Jade spun around, startled. The agent saw Jade's wild eyes and backed around the corner, mumbling an apology. Jade turned back to study the letters on the wall.

These killings were his worst fears confirmed. Allander had spent his years in jail developing an elaborate fantasy, and these deaths were the result. This was not an immature murder. Younger, inexperienced killers start with older women, prostitutes, or kids. Easy to target, easy to isolate, easy to dominate. That's where Allander had been when he'd first gone to jail at the age of eighteen. But he had matured since then, Jade thought. Matured into a master killer.

His feet sank in the thick carpet as he made his way back to the living room. He noticed two brown lines on the love seat, edges of foot marks. The bloody letters remained on the window. The woman's body lay crookedly beside the man's, her stomach open in a bloody gash. Jade heard Thomas's words rolling around in his head: *One foot still in the womb, so to speak.*

He mumbled to himself and wandered back into the foyer. The other agents looked at him expectantly.

"You. What's your name?" Jade asked, pointing at one of the younger agents.

"Daniel Harris," he said nervously. After a short pause, he added, "Dan."

"I figured. Check for the toolbox. See if there's a hammer missing."

"Where would it be?" he asked.

"You're an FBI agent. Figure it out. Start with the garage."

Dan looked angrily at his colleagues before leaving the room.

Travers walked in from the back bedroom. "Still working on those people skills, Marlow?"

Jade turned to her. "The girl. Leah. She didn't talk to him much, did she? The kids were scared and quiet."

Travers looked at him, surprised. "Yes. That's what she said. Why?"

"Because they lived. As for the woman, magnet on the refrigerator says 'Ask Mom, She's the Boss.' Next-door neighbor described her as the ice queen of the decade. Exact words.

"Check the bedroom. Phone ripped out of the socket, traces of blood. Both wounds on the woman are from the hammer. She woke up in bed, saw Allander, and threw the phone at him. She was tough. She would've reacted tough. She scared him, so he killed her.

"Look at the marks on the love seat. Marks from his dirty feet. He killed the parents, dragged them out here, then stood on the sofa and looked down on them. Got the upper hand, so to speak.

"The kids both lived. He must have felt complete control over them. He wouldn't kill them if they were completely nonthreatening. Nothing for the anger to grab hold of. Plus, it wouldn't be a challenge. He's after a challenge here."

Travers nodded.

"Bullshit," an agent in the foyer said. "He's a fucking coward. Held little kids hostage."

"A coward," Jade repeated, shaking his head. "He's cold, hasn't eaten, just broke out of a prison and swum to shore in freezing water. He walks up to a house and takes it on. Full frontal assault. No idea who's in here. Do you know the balls that takes?"

The room was silent for a moment before Jade continued. "If he was a coward, he would've just beaten an old lady to death and I wouldn't be bothering with this case. You clowns could handle it yourself. We're dealing with a powerful mind here, Agent."

Dan stumbled through the front door. "Found the toolbox out in the shed to the side of the house. He definitely went through it. Hammer's missing."

Travers sighed. "And probably a screwdriver. That explains the broken peephole." She glanced into the living room at the bodies. "Pretty gruesome sight. The posing and the letters. It's horrible."

"It's fantastic," Jade replied. "The more he does, the more he leaves me to analyze."

Travers started to respond, but her beeper went off. She checked it and went to the kitchen to answer the page.

The other agents stood around awkwardly. Dan coughed nervously, bringing his fist to his mouth.

"Notified family?" Jade asked.

"No, not yet," Dan replied. "Not looking forward to explaining this one."

"Well, I want full grave-site surveillance. Get those bodies in the ground so you can watch them."

Dan shook his head. "Well, I don't think—"

"That's good, Harris. *Don't* think. It's a long shot, but killers sometimes go to the grave sites. Could be a hook."

Travers came back in from the kitchen. "That was McGuire," she said. "We have another body. Doesn't look like our boy's work, but it's in the area, so McGuire wants us to check it out."

"I'd be surprised if it was Atlasia," Jade said. He expected Allander to have some kind of cooling-off period, as most serials killers do. At least twenty-four hours. If he was cycling this quickly, they were really in trouble.

"It's a different MO and a robbery, so I don't think so. Local police on it already."

"Let's go," he said. "I'll give you a ride."

"Why don't you come in my car," Travers said. Before he could respond, she continued. "Radio contact."

She turned and walked out the front door. Jade followed.

A cluster of agents stood in the shadows, to the side of the garage. They turned away when Jade passed.

IT was getting dark when they reached the house. Typical of the neighborhood, it sat back from a full lawn that stretched all the way around to the backyard. A sprinkler chopped back and forth over a yellow Wiffle-ball bat that lay in the middle of the grass.

Kids, Jade thought. More kids.

The upstairs windows were lit, two golden rectangles shining into the evening. Travers parked behind three police cars. They got out and headed to the house, passing a green station wagon in the driveway.

There were three cops downstairs. "Up in the bedroom," one said, pointing to the stairs. "Body first room to the right. Kid's out on a sleep-over, doesn't know yet. We're with the husband in the master bedroom. He's pretty broken up."

Travers nodded and headed upstairs.

"We also got a glove by the back door," another cop said.

Jade walked back and glanced at the glove. It was black, medium-size. Definitely a man's.

He headed back for the stairs. "Anything been moved?"

The cop shook his head. "Nothing. Husband's name is Royce Tedlow. Says he hasn't touched a thing either. Just the phone when he called us."

The body was upstairs, lying on a bed in a boy's bedroom. A thin woman with dark bruises around her neck.

Her shirt was neatly tucked into her pants. She looked peaceful, as if she were sleeping.

Jade and Travers looked at the dead woman for a moment, then headed for the master bedroom.

The husband sat on the bed, face buried in his stretched undershirt. An unbuttoned blue shirt was curled back from his body, and his hairy chest was distinguishable beneath the thin white undershirt. He had a medium build, a nice frame layered with muscles gone slightly soft with middle-age. Jade put him in his late forties.

The bedroom was nicely furnished. A large mirror stretched almost the length of one wall above a marble cabinet, and a huge television faced the bed from beside a window on the other side. An elegant lady's watch curled around the base of a large brass lamp on the nightstand.

Travers spoke softly with two of the cops. They'd been at the scene for at least a half hour, and had yet to get anything from the husband. Every time he started to speak, he collapsed back into tears. They surrounded him, their faces supportive and sympathetic.

"I just . . . just can't believe that some . . . some MANIAC!" He yelled at the top of his lungs, his voice hoarse from crying.

"Calm. Calm down," Jade said. "What happened?"

Royce Tedlow looked at Jade and took a deep breath.

"Come on," Travers said. "Let's walk through this together, okay?"

The husband nodded and started speaking, halting occasionally to fight back tears. "I work down . . . downstairs in the basement, in my office. I came up to get Susan—"

"For what?" Jade asked. Travers and a burly officer shot him hard stares.

"I don't . . . I don't remember." The husband collapsed back into sobs.

"Nice touch, Marlow," Travers said under her breath. She turned back to Royce, laying a hand on his shoulder. "I know this is hard, and I'm sorry to have to push you like this, but the sooner we find out what happened, the better chance we have of finding the killer while the trail is still hot. So see if you can go ahead."

When Royce continued, his voice was steadier. "She wasn't answering, so I went upstairs. When I came in here, I saw my wallet and I knew something was wrong." He pointed to the floor, where a leather wallet was spread open. Business cards, an ATM slip, and credit cards were scattered on the floor.

A cop walked over and picked up the ATM slip. "Twelve hundred bucks," he said. "You always carry this much cash?"

Royce shook his head. "No. I just went to the ATM this morning."

The cop looked at Jade, then back at the husband. "Anything else missing?"

Royce looked up. "A clock."

The cop looked surprised.

"It's Waterford crystal."

Jade bit his cheek to keep from laughing aloud.

"Then you went to your kid's room?"

Violent nodding from Royce. His cheeks were flushed and the tears kept coming. Jade was amazed they hadn't run out.

"There she was . . . strangled." More sobs.

"Don't you think strangulation's a pretty personal way to kill someone?" Jade asked.

The husband gave him a horrified look, then collapsed back on the bed, burying his face in the comforter. "I'm not talking to him," he sobbed.

"Look, buddy," the burly cop said to Jade in a loud

whisper, "I don't know what kind of training they give you in the FBI, but—"

"Yeah, okay. We got a car in the driveway, two lights on upstairs, and you want me to buy that someone broke in for petty theft. Someone who'd leave a watch on the nightstand but take a clock. Thieves generally don't know their crystal, Tedlow. They have a hard time telling Waterford from Baccarat."

He circled the bed, trying to get a look at the husband's eyes.

"That body was laid on the bed with care. With guilt. Robbers don't treat bodies like that. He would've just knocked her, robbed the place, and split. Not taken time to lay the body out." He paused. "We all know this wasn't a random offender."

Travers watched Jade as he spoke. Her anger faded as she realized where he was going.

"You want to know who killed her?" Jade continued. "It was someone who knew her, someone who wanted to look at her face-to-face when she died. Someone who knew the boy was out, someone who has to sob nonstop so he can stall for time when he's being questioned."

He turned to leave.

The burly cop shouted after him, "What are you implying?"

"Oh please. Don't pretend this is news to you. You know you're gonna head right back to the station, meet with your captain, and discuss exactly the same shit," Jade said. He had very little patience for a bad murder.

The burly cop was quiet, still glaring at Jade, but with doubt starting to show on his angry face. He ran his hand across his bull neck.

"Look, we don't have time for this shit," Jade said. "Brand-new glove downstairs." He looked over at Royce.

"At least you could have come up with something a touch more original. Give me a break."

"The robber had time to separate this from the stack of bills just to leave it for us?" Travers asked, assuming Jade's aggressive tone. She picked up the deposit slip, careful to hold it only by its corner. "No way. The only people who have to try this hard to point at someone else are the most obvious suspects." She waved the deposit slip in front of the husband. "Like the glove. Bull*shit*."

Jade looked at her and grinned. He was beginning to like her.

Another cop cleared his throat, then spoke softly to the burly cop. "Look, Ed, we might have enough to move on this now. Some pretty glaring discrepancies. I mean, if the robber knew people were home, he would've gone after the man first. Why go after the little woman?"

Jade nodded. "Exactly. Always neutralize the biggest threat right away. Then take your time with the valuables and the woman."

Everyone stared, first at Jade, then at the husband, his face still buried in the comforter.

"What about the money?" the burly cop asked.

"Probably buried somewhere with the other glove," Jade replied. "Check for a shovel with fresh dirt on it. Might even find dirt in the trunk of his car. See if they match."

Travers nodded. She was beginning to understand how Jade operated, how he cast himself as the killer in order to understand how the murder was carried out. She realized that even as they had walked up the driveway, he had been thinking about how he was going to break into the house, how he was going to get upstairs, how he was going to kill the woman if he had to. She glanced at the husband; he was a murderer, but he wasn't a predator. Not the way Jade was. Travers felt a cold shiver run across her back, and she realized that she was sweating.

The burly cop turned to his partner. "All right. We'll run a few more questions on him while the crime scene's fresh."

"Whatever," Jade said. He turned to Travers. "Let's go."

The husband was suddenly on his feet, facing Jade. The tears were gone. His eyes were alive now. "You don't know. You don't know anything about this."

"Look, pal," Jade said. "I'm sure you're right. But I also really don't care. I'm just in a rush here." He tapped Travers on the shoulder and she followed him out of the room.

They heard one of the cops reading Royce his rights as they stepped into the hallway.

"Nice, Marlow," Travers said out of the side of her mouth as they descended the stairs.

"Glad you finally spoke up there, Travers."

"Anything turn up?" one of the cops downstairs asked as they headed for the door.

"Nothing important," Jade answered as he swept by.

WELL rested after a comfortable night's sleep in the Mercedes, Allander whistled the first motif of the *Jupiter* symphony as he emerged from the alley and walked past the broken-down machinery that littered the grounds. The blue of his shirt was resplendent against the dreary colors of the deserted lot.

A DANGER DO NOT ENTER sign lay in a patch of weeds by the side of the gate, and Allander picked it up, admiring it in the waning sunlight. He wedged its corners between the links of the fence, then smacked his hands together to rid them of dust.

Having whistled his way well into the recapitulation, he turned and headed toward the bus station.

Jade began the next morning by carefully studying the photographs from the first crime scene. He sat on his couch in the middle of his living room, chewing ice from a cup that he rested against his crotch.

The room was becoming cluttered as Jade collected more background information. He had stacked books on the glass table in front of him, and the files he had gotten from the FBI were piled up everywhere. It seemed as if the first one had reproduced, spawning an extended family. Now files littered the floor and the couch, many of them opened to important pages.

Jade was trying to hold all the material in his head, but it was difficult. There was just too much to absorb—

audiotapes of Allander's psychological interviews, video-tapes of his trial and old crime scenes, photographs of Allander, jail records, psychology reports, and victim profiles and photographs.

Once Jade had reviewed a photograph carefully, he taped it to the wall. The first photograph in the upper-left-hand corner was Allander's mug shot at age eighteen. The rest of the photos progressed in a more or less chronological order: Allander through the years, his victims through the years. His killing pace had slowed when he went to prison, but still his victim count rose steadily—here another prisoner, there a guard.

Jade looked at the files, books, and photos spread out around him and closed his eyes. What was Allander proving? What was the pattern of his pleasure? And most important, what was his weakness?

The phone rang and Jade snatched it off the hook.

"What."

"I got a good one. In light of your case and all," Tony said. "Okay. This guy comes home, finds his girlfriend packing. He's shocked. He says, 'What's going on? What are you doing?' Girlfriend says, 'I'm leaving you.' He says, 'You're leaving me? Why?' She says, 'Because you're a pedophile.' 'Yeah, yeah,' he says. 'Big word for a nine-year-old.'"

Jade laughed, tilting his head back. "You're a sick fuck, Razzoni."

"Thank you, thank you," Tony said. "And how's the case heard 'round the world?"

"Gonna have my hands full. I think we have a serial."

Tony whistled. "Well, I knew he was a killer of serial killers—he got three in the Tower, didn't he?"

"Five."

"I just thought little kids were more his speed."

"Well, he's progressed. Those years in prison helped

him evolve. We had a scene last night that looks like it could be the first in a string. Time will tell, though. Press blackout, so keep a lid on it."

"Consider me lidded. Just wanted to check in, make sure you're not howling at the moon or anything."

"Not yet, but I'll let you know." Jade hung up the phone, then stood and circled the living room, staring at the pictures on the walls.

Heading back to the couch, he stretched out so that his legs were sticking up in the air over the back of the sofa, and his head was slanted off the seat. He picked up *Introductory Lectures on Psycho-Analysis* and began to read intently.

It had been years since he'd read Freud. Most of the psychology he kept up with was much more practical, but if the prison records showed that Allander had read it, he had to at least review it. He needed to get inside Allander's head so he could use his own thoughts against him.

The ring of the doorbell startled him. Shifting his weight, he twisted awkwardly, landing with a crash on the floor. Rising sheepishly, he went to answer the door.

"Hope you didn't hurt yourself," Agent Travers said as she brushed past Jade into the room. "I know how difficult answering the door can be."

"Only when you're behind it."

Reaching the center of the living room, she stopped and looked about her, admiring Jade's intensity—intensity so great it led him to transform an entire room into a virtual shrine to the man he was hunting.

"Love what you've done with the place." She glanced at the stack of books on the table. "Learning to read?"

"What the fuck do you want?"

"Your patience runs out quickly."

"I'm gonna run you out quickly."

She stuck her bottom lip out in a mock pout. "Now

we wouldn't want that to happen," she said, sinking into a chair. "Then you'd be denied the afternoon with me."

"Look, *Agent* Travers—"

"Cut the shit, Jade. You can call me Jennifer."

"Fine. I'm in the middle of something here, Travers, and I don't have time to—"

"Oh please. You think I stopped by on a social visit? There are files to go over, and—"

"I've already been over all of them. I don't need your help, and I don't have to help you. It's not in the deal."

"'It's not in the deal,'" she repeated, mimicking him. "For Christ's sake, you sound like a ten-year-old."

Jade bit his lip as he looked at her, then he laughed and fell back on the sofa. "Fine. You got a half hour. Then I have some business to take care of."

They were silent for a few moments, staring at each other.

"I got him pegged as a classic *DSM-IV* antisocial personality disorder, but it's really hard to define him neatly," she finally said, moving to sit on the floor.

"What's that give us?" Jade asked.

"Lacking empathy, social responsibility, conventional morality. Displaying impulsiveness, abusiveness, sensation-seeking, and sometimes showing charm and seductiveness."

Charm and seductiveness, Jade thought. Allander had sounded very captivating on some of the tapes. He had argued several of the psychologists to a standstill without ever raising his voice or using rude language. He'd just overpowered them with intelligence.

"Sounds like a pretty good fit, but I'd imagine he's also got some form of anxiety driving him, maybe a simple phobia. The combination means it won't be long until his next strike."

"Unless he flees."

"He's not going to flee," Jade said. "I can feel it. The timing of his prison break, the method of his killings—everything indicates he's playing out a fantasy."

"What's with the timing?" Travers asked.

"He's thirty-three. Guess how old his molester was?"

"Oh God."

"Thirty-three. All this has been brewing inside him for a while. He's not roaming too far."

"But why here? Why can't he play out his fantasy anywhere?"

"Because serial killers usually confine themselves to one geographic area."

"We don't know that he's definitely a serial killer," she said in a neutral tone.

Jade raised his eyebrows and gave her a disbelieving stare.

"Sorry," she said. "I've been dealing with McGuire all day."

"The Federal Bureau of Procrastination. Don't act on a hunch unless it's proven beforehand," Jade said disdainfully.

"Why did you join, then?"

"Welding school was full that week." He glanced at the files. "Look, are we gonna get down to business here? We both know he'll kill again, and probably soon. It's a game for him; it's up to us to figure out the pattern. He's choosing his victims to fulfill some symbolic equation he's worked out in his head. We gotta get into that game. Into his head."

"What's the deal with 'S N E'?" Travers asked. "We ran it through the computer as initials of friends, relatives, prisonmates, everything. Came up empty."

Jade shook his head. "I don't know. Could be a red herring. Also could just be something that only has relevance to him. Fuck it for now. Let's start with the kid. What'd she say?"

Jennifer leaned back against the sofa, her white oxford-cloth shirt loosely untucked. Jade caught himself staring down at the line of tan flesh that led to the curve of her breasts. He blinked hard and focused on what she was saying.

"Leah blocked out a lot of what he said to her. It was so close to the trauma I didn't want to push her. Evidently, he lectured them. She said it was like her teacher at school. I guess he raved about the law, parents, and teachers."

Jade heard Allander's voice inside his head: *He must be spoken to if he's not going to be protected.* He had spoken to the kids, just as Jade had thought. "All forms of authority, huh?" he said.

"And hierarchy," Travers added. "I think he's still trying to get in touch with what he's all about. The children were just passive observers. Leah said it was as if he didn't really notice they were there at all."

"His game right now is power. He's testing us, testing himself. He didn't find the kids threatening. They weren't a challenge. Too young. I say he kills anyone who's gone through puberty."

They sat for a moment in silence.

"Well, how does that help us?" Travers asked.

"The more we understand him, the closer it brings us to him."

"At the scene, it sounded like you thought he was next to invincible."

"Not invincible. Just intelligent. I hate to see criminals simplified. It's dismissive."

"So where do we start?"

"With his weaknesses."

"It sounded like you didn't think he had any."

"No. That's not true. You can see his fear in his anger. He went after the parents. Why? You can argue that these were murders of opportunity. He didn't plan how he was going to kill them; he picked up the weapons right at the site. This was especially true of the woman. Totally spontaneous. I bet she scared him. But!" He held up a finger. "Look what he does with the bodies afterward. He studies them. He defaces them. He poses them."

"He's sadistic."

"Sure, but he puts out the eyes *after* death. It's more about possession. He's working through an advanced sexual fantasy here, one that's taken him years to develop. He *does* have a weakness—he's scared of the woman."

"How do you know?"

"The man he kills to get in. But then he's alone in the bedroom with a woman. What does he do? He kills her right away. As quickly as he can. With the hammer. His concern is to render her motionless as quickly as possible. He could have kept her alive and played with her."

Travers looked at him, her unease showing. It must be harder as a woman, Jade thought. It was her choice, though. He couldn't work with her on this if he had to temper his language.

"I bet they don't find any semen in her," he said. He picked up his cup, tilted it back, and shook it. A piece of ice slid into his mouth and he crunched it loudly.

Travers looked impressed. "I just got off the phone with forensics," she said. "They didn't."

"No rape. He can't do it. Wishes he could, though. He has a lot of sexual insecurity. Just wants her unconscious."

"But he did show remorse," Travers said. "The posing of the bodies."

"I don't think so. Remorseful killers usually cover the faces."

"But not always."

"But not always," Jade agreed. "I just don't think it fits. I think the positioning of the bodies mocks what he perceives to be the parents' hypocrisy. He left them as he sees them: blind to the truth, but going through the motions as if everything's all right."

"Let's talk about Allander's parents."

"No serial killer's profile is complete without them."

"Abusive, neglecting, violent?"

"Kind, normal, healthy," Jade said.

"That's a first."

"Literally."

"What gives? Does it all have to do with his molester?"

"Honestly?"

"Honestly."

Jade crunched another piece of ice and spat it back out into the cup. "I think he's just fucked."

"That's your professional opinion?"

Jade nodded. "I think he was fucked before that even happened. I think the problem was already there; the molester just brought it to life."

He glanced at his watch. "I'm heading up to Ressler to interview the prison shrink."

Travers was quiet.

"I guess you can come," he said. "Just try not to talk too much."

"Won't be hard with you around."

THE Ressler Institute's main building was mostly experimentation labs and classrooms. The doctors themselves enjoyed a small cluster of offices a few blocks away. It looked almost like a park; thin walkways threaded around open quads filled with lush vegetation. Beside the complex, a small brook made its way over a bed of gray rocks pushed into the soil.

A thick wooden directory stuck out of the pavement beside the parking lot. Jade ran his finger down it until he saw the listing he wanted: "Dr. Kim Tai Yung. Ph.D. A-18."

"Looks like we're here," Travers said as Jade strode up the narrow walkway and barged into the waiting room. He was a practiced barger, Travers thought as she followed him in, realizing she actually admired him for it.

He walked past several children reading *Highlights for Kids* and Dr. Seuss, and banged on the glass partition separating the receptionist from the waiting room.

The woman slid the glass over and peered out angrily.

"I need to see Dr. Yung. Now," Jade said, flashing his badge.

"Do you have any idea what his schedule is like this week?"

"Do you have any idea how little I care?"

Her head reared back. "Well, he's in with a patient. You can't just—"

"I can *just* whatever I want. And I suggest—"

"I'm sorry, ma'am," Travers said, sidestepping Jade as she pulled him back by his elbow. "We're FBI, you see, and we're in the middle of an intense manhunt. I realize that the doctor must have a tight schedule, but we really need to see him as soon as possible."

"Immediately," Jade added.

The receptionist glared at Jade, then turned a smile to Travers. "I'll let him know you're here."

"Thank you," Travers said.

The kids in the waiting room stared uneasily at them. After a minute, a young East Asian man led a small boy who had been crying out into the waiting room, where a concerned mother folded him in her arms. Jade rolled his eyes.

"Hey, pal," Jade said to him. "We need to get in now to see the doctor."

The Asian man wore a pair of corduroys and a pin-striped shirt with no tie, unbuttoned at the top. A pair of silver-framed glasses perched neatly on his nose. His hair was slightly disheveled, but it didn't look messy. Jade calculated the man to be in his early twenties.

The man chuckled softly. "And everyone's schedules should bow to your needs?" he asked. "The doctor spends weeks working with children to get them to the point of catharsis. The point which you so gracelessly interrupted."

"Well, why don't you tell the doctor we'll make it up to him later. I'm sure he'll forgive us," Jade said.

"I'm afraid that's not possible."

"And why not?"

"Because I'm the doctor. And I have an unforgiving nature."

Travers closed her eyes. Jade looked over at her, then back at the doctor. "You'll have to excuse my colleague,"

Travers said. "If it's any consolation, I have to work with him."

Dr. Yung smiled and nodded at her gently. "I can imagine it's quite taxing."

He ushered them down a hallway and into an office.

"Well, how was I supposed to know?" Jade whispered roughly to Travers. "He looks like he's not old enough to shave."

Although the room they entered was dark, it didn't have a heaviness to it. An open window allowed a breeze to move through the room, carrying with it the smell of the foliage outside. Jade and Travers sat down on a brown leather couch, and the doctor took his place on a large, comfortable chair.

A poster of the yin and yang symbol hung on the wall behind Jade and Travers. In the darkness of the yin curled an immense dragon with red and orange limbs unfurled. Its glaring eye doubled as the white circle of the symbol.

Dr. Yung cleared his throat and spoke, hiding whatever anger he might feel under the calmness of his voice. "Needless to say, I hope that the matter before us is an important one."

"We're here about Allander Atlasia. I'm Jade Marlow. I'm in charge of the investigation."

"Yes." The doctor leaned back in his seat, arms crossed. "My office manager mentioned something about your waving a badge."

"Actually, there are several matters we'd like to speak with you about," Travers said.

The doctor was silent.

"First of all, if you're one of the prison psychologists, why are you here treating kids?" Jade asked.

"Because you cannot study criminals without starting

with children," Dr. Yung replied. He chuckled. "I have a private practice, Mr. Marlow. Since I spend most of my time with the prisoners, I like to treat children on the side. More optimistic." He twirled the point of a letter opener against his thumb. "Now if the details of my practice are sufficiently clarified, perhaps we could get down to business?"

"Uh . . . gentlemen? Maybe I could offer a different approach," Travers said. She caught Dr. Yung's eye and nodded. "Jennifer Travers."

Crossing her legs delicately, she leaned back on the couch. "Why don't we forgo the pissing contest and remember we're dealing with a serious matter here. We need your help, Doctor, before more people are killed."

Jade and Dr. Yung looked at each other sheepishly.

"Now, how familiar are you with Atlasia?" Travers asked.

"Very. I'd say he was my reason for going into psychology."

"Excuse me, Doctor?"

He laughed. "I'm sure you weren't expecting that response at all. My father treated him when he was a child. Dr. Pan Yung."

Jade nodded in recognition. "Of course. The only psychologist who got anything from him as a kid. That was your father?"

"Yes. They had excellent rapport. I was in high school when my father was treating him. Of course, I shouldn't have known that, but the case was highly publicized. I found out watching the eight o'clock news. I saw reporters forcing their way into his office."

"Can we interview your father?" Travers asked.

"He passed away," Dr. Yung and Jade said at the same time. Jade shook his head regretfully.

"I'm sorry," Travers said. The doctor nodded gracefully.

"So why was Allander the reason you went into psychology?" Jade asked.

"Well, I must confess I exaggerated slightly for dramatic purposes. But it was worth it to see the looks on your faces." He chuckled kindly. "It was during this period that I became interested in my father's work. He studied the effects of trauma on children, but I was interested in studying those who perpetrated the acts themselves. As you can see, my practice ended up being a mix of these two goals."

"Were you surprised to see Allander when he got transferred to Maingate?"

"Well, he was already there when I arrived, but I wasn't surprised." He stopped for a moment and thought. "It was a strange coincidence, but I wasn't surprised. Many of the abused become abusers. I just try to break the cycle."

"So you think that Allander's experience as a child led him to be a criminal?" Travers asked.

The doctor laughed. "I only wish it were that simple. A lot of children have endured much worse and put their lives back together." He paused, then caught himself. "Well, not worse, perhaps, but for a longer period of time. Some children are molested for months, years."

"You think Atlasia's experience is one of the worst you've ever seen?" Travers asked.

Dr. Yung rubbed his hand across his forehead. "I don't know how, exactly, I should rank them, Agent Travers. Is forced oral sex worse than a prolonged whipping?"

Travers's eyebrows raised and her mouth tightened.

"I'm sorry," Dr. Yung said. "That wasn't fair."

Travers nodded and indicated he should continue.

"My father's files were confidential; they were destroyed

after he passed away. However, I do know that Allander was a very precocious youngster at the time of the incident. He remembered everything. It was a horrific molestation—the extent of what he was put through we can only imagine. We do know there was forced oral and anal penetration. Some of the . . . objects found in the room where he was kept . . . ." The doctor's voice trailed off for a moment as he recalled the crime-scene photos. "Well, let's just say that what purpose they served is well beyond the reach of my imagination. When I first saw Atlasia about six years ago, he dismissed those events as insignificant."

"Insignificant?" Jade asked.

"What a psychologist does, Mr. Marlow," Dr. Yung said, tilting back in his chair and pressing his hands together, "is listen to the spaces between the words. Allander is bright enough to hold together on the surface, but he's in turmoil. I fear he never put those problems to rest."

"Evi-fuckin'-dently," Jade said.

Dr. Yung continued, ignoring Jade's interruption. "You see, people develop by grappling with their unconscious, their darker half. The shadow. It consists of all their deepest desires and fears. We're all made of good and evil, of both parts. The yin and yang." He gestured to the poster on the wall behind Jade and Travers. "Most people are a blend of both sides. But some, some people allow one side to take over."

"What do you mean 'take over'?" Travers asked.

"They are devoured," the doctor said darkly, "by their shadow."

"So Allander has a problem differentiating reality from his fantasies?" Travers asked.

"Not exactly. He can differentiate between the two, he just has nothing holding him back from acting on his wishes. His shadow is no longer held in check by his persona, or superego. So it roams free."

"A runaway libido with no brakes," Jade mused.

The doctor looked surprised. "Yes, Mr. Marlow. Something like that. I'm afraid I can't be more helpful, but Allander was quite guarded, particularly when he spoke to me. I'm sure you've found that in the tapes."

Jade leaned forward and put his hands on his knees. "Let's get into specifics, Doctor. Atlasia has made a number of Freudian references that I'd like some input about. He seems really proud of the fact that he's in touch with his unconscious, that he can see all the parts he's made of. And he's not afraid to act on his desires— the real way, not through sublimation. He's very aware of the difference, which I think is bad news. And he also said he's seen 'what there is in every little boy,' but if he's talking about the Oedipal complex, I'm not really sure why."

Travers helped Jade fill in the blanks as he presented the entire case, beginning to end. They showed the doctor photos of the crime scene at the house, and Jade played him the segment from the tape of Allander's interview that he thought was significant.

For a long time, the doctor didn't say anything. He picked up the photographs and examined them closely. "You said that the girl claimed that Allander spoke of parents, educators, and the law, correct?"

Travers nodded.

"Well, none of them stepped in and protected him when he was a child, when he was in need. So this is his payback. On the tape, he references Freud, discusses probing his unconscious and coming up with the truth— the truth that everyone *should* see, but doesn't. Allander has made his own diagnosis of society. Like Freud in

Civilization and Its Discontents. And he's made a diagnosis of himself."

"What is that diagnosis?" Travers asked.

"That he can see man's true nature and act upon it. He feels that others cannot. They can't see their true needs, just as they could not see that he was in need as a child. He's gouged out their eyes to illustrate that. He's written it on the bodies.

"And the pattern starts with the family. This may be a stretch, but maybe he arranged the bodies to mimic his parents. They have a healthy relationship, you've said. Maybe he's mocking that by posing the bodies in an embrace. He's portraying them as being happy in their ignorance."

"Ignorance is bliss," Travers said.

"Yes. Very appropriate cliché."

Jade was quiet. Something was not fitting all the way. Something was missing.

"So it all comes down to Mom," Travers said. "Seems like it always does. Remember Kemper in Santa Cruz?"

Jade nodded. "Fed his mother's larynx down the garbage disposal. Also Rivers, the Tower survivor. He got his mother."

"With Atlasia, it's not just his mother," the doctor said. "Atlasia's anger was directed toward both parents. He included the father in the posing."

"And the gouging," Jade said. "Well, we have full surveillance on the Atlasias."

"I don't know if that's a concern." The doctor shook his head. "I agree with you that he references the Oedipal complex—'what there is in every little boy'—but serial killers almost always displace. They rarely kill the people they're really furious at. They pick others and vent their anger on them. It's easier."

"Warden Banks told me that you hold on to drawings the prisoners make when they have Sketch Duty. I'd like to see some of Allander's."

"Sure, sure," the doctor said. "Though I don't know how useful they'll be to you."

He excused himself and returned a few minutes later with three drawings under his arm. He unfurled them on his desk. "We have only three of Atlasia's," he said.

The first drawing showed an enormous clown holding an uprooted tower under its face. A woman flopped carelessly out of a small window beneath the clown's curling fingernails.

The next picture was a sketch portraying hands. The first set of hands faced one another horizontally, fingers together, fingertips a few inches apart. The hands were expertly drawn, right down to the lines in the palms. Beside them were two hands that seemed to be pointing at each other. The last image on the sheet was a solitary hand, its fingers together and thumb apart, pointed upward at a forty-five-degree angle.

The final drawing was an intricately detailed picture of a mountain range shaped subtly like the curves of a woman. Although it was at first difficult to notice the corporeal suggestion, there was something immediately erotic about the work. The drawings were made with crayons, but their clarity was exceptional. They were clearly the work of a skilled hand.

"The clown, of course, recalls the clown masks of his childhood captor," Dr. Yung said.

Travers nodded. "How about the others?"

"Well, this really isn't my forte," the doctor said. "But I find the mountain range interesting in how it incorporates female sexuality into the earth."

"Like it's the basis for everything," Travers said.

"Yes. That from which all else springs. An Earth Mother of sorts."

"How about that one?" Jade asked, pointing to the sketch of the hands.

"For that one, Mr. Marlow, your guess is as good as mine."

After studying them for a few more minutes, Jade rolled them up. "Mind if I hold on to these?"

"Not at all, Mr. Marlow, that's why I brought them."

Jade stood up. "Well, I'll definitely be in touch." He extended his hand. "About that little mix-up in communication . . . ."

"A mix-up, was it?" Dr. Yung smiled and took his hand. "I'm sorry I couldn't be more helpful. I'll take some time with it, think it over. I'm usually more insightful once I've sat with something for a while. Why don't you call me later this week?"

"**HAS** Marlow checked on the house yet?" Wotan asked. Smoke rose from the cigar in the ashtray on the side of his desk, curling like a white ribbon in the dim air.

"Yes, Wotan," Travers said. "He has some ideas about Atlasia, but he hasn't shared them with me. You want me to put pressure on him to reveal more?"

"I don't think that's a realistic option for you."

Travers blushed.

"He is not our enemy. He is in charge of this investigation and you will assist him, not interfere with his efforts." Wotan leaned forward slightly into the light, but the hollowness of his cheeks remained filled with shadow. The hole of his left eye was lost in darkness.

"We hired Jade Marlow for this case because he's an obsessive tracker. He has no hesitation about descending into the mind of the killer. Right now, his waking hours are spent thinking about Atlasia, and I am certain that when he sleeps, if he sleeps at all, he dreams of him. If you recall the Black Ribbon case, we almost lost him. That's a risk we run when we send someone into dangerous territory. But Marlow can go into the house of the enemy and not eat from his table."

Wotan plucked a bullet slug from the ashtray and raised it to his face. He blew the cigar ash from it, then dropped it back in the ashtray, where it landed with a loud clink. A small puff of ash clouded the air, then dissipated.

"You shall not impede him, Agent Travers, even if it is at considerable cost to your ego."

Travers nodded, biting her lip. "I was not implying anything like that, sir."

"Give him his space if he needs it."

Allander stepped off the Greyhound bus and regarded the dimly lit station. Two chubby little boys ran after a shrieking girl in a yellow dress while their parents stood by and smiled.

Woodside had seemed like the most arbitrary place within the Bay Area that the buses stopped. Allander needed to put a safe amount of distance between himself and San Francisco, at least until the manhunt slowed down, but he also didn't want to stray too far away. Not while there was more work to be done.

He checked the crudely drawn map on the wall, which displayed the public buildings in the area. Two churches, a library, a small residential school, town hall. Quite a cultural hub, he thought, sneering inwardly.

The bus ride had gone well. It was a direct route, so although there were stops, he hadn't had to transfer. He had passed the journey in a back seat, his body pressed against the cushion so that his face remained in shadow.

FOOD, DRINK, TICKETS: Allander read the words on the large sign outside the station. All the necessities of a bare, forked animal. I am a man more sinned against than sinning, he thought. More sinned against than sinning.

He headed up a winding road that ran into the hills behind the bus stop. Turning off the road, he walked about a mile into a wooded area before curling up underneath a large tree. He lay on his side, breathing the crisp air. Finally, he dozed off. For the first time in years, he slept soundly.

• • •

Darby Atlasia sat quietly in the study, nursing a glass of red wine. The detective had stirred old memories, and now they swirled about, refusing to be laid to rest.

She thought about the days when her seven-year-old son was missing. They had feared the very worst, but even their grossest speculations couldn't match the reality. Death would have been preferable. She slid the glass back into the indentation it had made on her Pottery Barn catalog.

There are so many things you wish for as a parent, so many dreams and aspirations, she thought. You want your child to grow up to be a doctor, or a senator, or a judge. You hope, you plan. And then a sick man steps in and tinkers with your son's mind. Damages it irreparably.

True, Allander's behavior had indicated some problems even before the incident. He had not been right, had not been normal. And then his natural predisposition had been encouraged and further corrupted by "environmental factors." That was what his first psychologist had called it. "Environmental factors." Like being raped by a thirty-three-year-old man at the age of seven, Doctor? she'd wanted to yell. Is that an "environmental factor?"

The guilt at that memory still gnawed at her from time to time. What could I have done differently? she would ask herself defensively. Did I do all I could to protect my boy, to treat him normally afterward? Did my feelings of disgust filter through the mask I wore at home? Did Allander feel my anger, my irrational fury that he had brought all of this to our lives?

After the boy had . . . after the incident between her and Allander, Darby had known that Thomas considered his son dead to him. In fact, he had felt that Allander was no longer his son. After that, Thomas had told her, he felt that Allander drew his inspiration from some source beyond Thomas's comprehension.

"Hon, are you all right?" Thomas's soft voice at the door startled her, and she knocked over her glass of wine. She watched as the liquid darkened the papers on the desk—the bank statements, the mortgage papers, the letters and magazines. She made no effort to stop the flow, but watched it as the keen smell of alcohol rose to her nostrils and permeated the room.

Thomas walked over and leaned on the desk beside her. He cradled her head to his chest as the tears came, and they cried together softly. Finally, Darby leaned back and looked at him, then wiped the tears from his cheeks with her thumb. She spread her hands and used her fingers to erase the tears beneath her own eyes.

"Well, hon," she said. "I guess we're just one big dysfunctional family, aren't we?" They laughed together for a while. Gradually, their laughter fell back into tears.

JADE lay draped across his leather couch in a daze, surrounded by the clutter of books and papers. A taped recording of a psychiatric interview played, and Allander's voice resonated through the room. Three of the walls now held black-and-white photographs of Allander and his victims, and the television blinked images of his trial, the bluish glow mapping erratic patterns of light onto the room.

Jade's eyes closed briefly and his hand, still grasping the document he had begun to examine, fell to his chest. His eyelids fluttered as he tried to fight off sleep, but his exhaustion was too great.

He was reclining in the middle of a massive rose garden, a peaceful oasis that seemed to exist out of time and place. Row after row of roses stretched before him, roses of different sizes and colors. A stone wall surrounded the fertile soil of the garden.

Lying propped on his elbows, Jade surveyed the calm surroundings and inhaled the fresh air. Suddenly a roll of thunder broke from behind the clear sky, and Jade searched overhead for any trace of darkness. There was none. The sound of tiny footsteps became slowly distinguishable, a cavalry of small feet pounding a ground unseen, accompanied by the whistle of thin legs pumping vigorously.

Then they were there. Hands grasped the top of the stone wall, hoisting to elbows, then elbows to knees.

Bodies poured over the wall, spilling down the ten-foot fall and bouncing effortlessly to their feet.

Boys. Scores of boys flooding the garden from all sides.

A look of panic flashed across Jade's face, an unfamiliar expression that sat awkwardly on his features. He rose quickly and twisted to glance around.

He watched as the boys continued to tumble over the wall. Righting themselves, they attacked the rosebushes, breaking off stems and gripping them tightly, the thorns puncturing the flesh of their hands. Using the stems like sickles, they lopped off the heads of the flowers. The blossoms fell and the petals came apart, littering the ground. The boys laughed as they raced through the rows of bushes toward Jade, who was frozen in place.

The boys bleated in pleasure as they raised their voices to the heavens, breaking into a chant of nursery rhymes. "Eenie meenie minie moe," they sang, repeating the lyrics in a near scream.

Rosebush after rosebush fell before their marching feet, plowed down by the vanguard. Droplets of blood from the boys' hands fell to the ground and dotted the trampled petals. The rose stems snapped through the air like whips. Jade recoiled before the onslaught, lifting his hands to his face, peering out through the prism of his fingers.

He awoke from his dream with the noise of Allander's voice filling his ears and with Allander's eyes gazing at him from the pictures spread about the house. He didn't lurch awake as many people do after a nightmare. Instead, his eyes opened and he waited silently for the world to flood back to him.

Jade rose from the couch and walked to his study, crunching papers underfoot as he moved. As he crossed the living room, his pace accelerated until he was running.

Inside the study, which, unlike the living room, was still neat and clean, Jade picked up from the desk a small box that held pencils and pens. He dashed its contents to the desktop, then struggled to keep them from falling to the floor, fencing them in with his forearms.

Slowly, he relaxed. Pulling the black desk chair to him, he sat down. He leaned forward on the desk and began lining up the pens and pencils, separating them by color and type. They were all different shades of black and gray, and there were five of each kind.

As he organized them, his breathing slowed to normal and his fingers stopped shaking. By the time he reached the black pens, he was ordering them with machinelike dexterity.

When he had all the pens and pencils lined up perfectly, he removed a ruler from his top-left drawer and pushed it against the erasers of all the pencils. He let his breath out through clenched teeth as the ruler pushed them into a perfect line, the tips lined up like little soldiers. Picking up the pencils, he slotted them neatly into their division of the box. He did the same with each type of pen until all sat in order—once again the way they had been. He leaned back in his chair and ran his thumb across his bottom lip, pressing tenderly.

The rollers on his chair grated noisily in their plastic sockets as he pushed back from the desk. He got up and centered the swivel chair in the space beneath the desk. Closing the door to his study very gently, he walked into his bedroom. Like the study, this room, too, was neat, orderly, organized. All was as it should be—except for one thing, which Jade noticed immediately. Some of the pictures were missing from his bookshelf.

He felt his heartbeat pounding in his ears. The sound of the chase.

He moved purposefully through the living room and into the kitchen. Pulling the glass sliding door open, he stepped out onto the back patio. A small note sat on the counter that ran underneath the kitchen window, held in place by two of Jade's framed pictures.

"Of course," he said aloud as he slid his hand under the counter to the space where his Glock should have been. He lifted the note—a plain white piece of stationery, folded in half—to his eyes.

The front of the note said simply, "Welcome." Jade flipped it open and saw Allander's familiar scrawl lining the page:

Full fathom five thy father lies;
    Of his bones are coral made;
Those are pearls that were his eyes:
    Nothing of him that doth fade,
But doth suffer a sea-change
Into something rich and strange.
Sea nymphs hourly ring his knell:
    Ding-dong.
Hark! now I hear them—Ding-dong, bell.

He looked at the two pictures on the counter that had been removed from his bedroom. In the photograph of Jade sprinting the hundred for UCLA, two circles to the sides of his head had been cut out. Next to this photo was the small picture of the boy with drooping features. It had not been altered.

A chill ran down Jade's spine and he felt the cold

moistness of his sweat under his arms and on his back and shoulders.

He ran through his schedule of the past few days. He had not been outside on the patio since early yesterday, before he'd left for the meeting. He'd gotten in so late last night that he hadn't even turned on the light in his bedroom. He had simply undressed and gone straight to sleep, so he hadn't noticed the missing pictures. That meant he had slept in a room last night that Allander had stood in, had walked around. The note could have been there waiting even while he met with Travers this afternoon.

He cursed himself for not checking the house thoroughly. He just hadn't expected Allander to come so quickly. By arranging the TV news story, he had practically dared him to come to his house. It had paid off. The hoped-for opportunity had come, and he had missed it.

Jade's rage rose suddenly and uncontrollably, and he yelled. He brought the edge of his hand down to strike the counter, breaking it from the wall. The top of the crumpled note protruded from Jade's clenched fist as he walked in tight circles around the patio.

JADE checked his watch as he stepped briskly across the campus of the University of the Gate at San Francisco, heading toward the building that housed the English department. Eight-thirty A.M. Bright and early, and he had already completed his run.

He hadn't been able to sleep last night, and he had lifted weights in the garage between one and three-thirty in the morning. When he was tracking, he was usually fine on three to four hours of sleep, but two was a little light, even for him.

After the workout, he'd touched up the paint on the bookshelves in the study. Painting always soothed him, like ironing wrinkles out of a shirt.

He had examined Allander's note under a loupe just to double-check the handwriting. He hardly needed to cast his mind back to the few scattered handwriting lectures he'd sat in on at Quantico to conclude that it wasn't a fake. The handwriting was very neat, spread in clean lines across the sheet. Allander was obviously very organized now that he'd had a little time to settle down.

A stone building loomed at the head of the campus quad, the large lettering carved above the door announcing the department of English and American literature. A few college students readjusted their backpacks over their shoulders as they left the building, and Jade's eyes followed two brunettes making their way across the lawn.

Distracted for the moment, he almost walked into a tree, but was given a heads-up by a branch that knocked his sunglasses crooked. After putting them back in place, he glanced around to see if anyone had noticed.

Jade couldn't stand coffee, but knowing he needed caffeine this morning, he had drunk three Dr. Peppers in the car on the way over. Already, he could feel them widening his eyes and quickening his step.

He had been excited last night, too excited to sleep. This note was important. Often, killers make a subconscious cry for help. Or they send out a dare. Allander's note seemed to qualify as both. At the very least, it was an attempt to broadcast intent. "Welcome," the note had said. Welcome to my mind. Here's what I'm thinking, catch me if you can.

I can, Jade thought. I will.

By the time he reached the building, he felt energy running through him like a current. He ran his fingers compulsively through his hair. A female student exited through the door as he entered, and turned to admire him as he passed.

The signs on the corridor doors indicated the professors and their fields of study: "Sacks—Romantic"; "Vendleman—Restoration"; "Caston—Medieval"; "Lithemeir—Elizabethan." The lines from Allander's poem sounded older, but they were still modern English, so Jade headed for Lithemeir's office.

The secretary almost dropped her cup of coffee as Jade entered, flinging the door open.

"FBI. I need to see him. Now," he said, flashing his badge quickly.

The secretary was not an attractive woman, nor did she do much with what she had. She also looked nervous; her eyes darted about the room as though she were looking for a means of escape. Jade almost smiled as she struggled to respond to this unusual situation.

"Dr. Lithemeir is an exceptionally busy man. You'll know from his latest book that he—"

"Lady," Jade cut in, "I didn't read his book and I don't care about his book. I just need a few minutes of Dr. Lithenhaur's time."

Her hand darted up to push a strand of hair off her forehead. "It's . . . Lithe*meir*," she said cautiously.

"Right. And as I said, I'm with the FBI and I need to talk to him about a murder case—right now. So please don't give me a hard time about it. Now, I'm sure he's a pretty impressive guy or he wouldn't have a secretary, but—"

Her eyes widened, outraged. "I'm an academic assistant," she said. She appeared extraordinarily offended.

"Look, honey. I don't care what you are to him, but I gotta get in to see him right now or else I'll—"

"Please. Come in. There is no need to berate my assistant. And in fact, Ms. Jennings *is* an academic assistant." Dr. Lithemeir had emerged quietly from his office, and stood leaning against the door frame. A good, solid lean. He looked amused at Ms. Jennings's inability to handle the situation. Jade got the sense that most things amused him.

He was a large man, more rotund than fat and more ruddy than flushed. He carried a large cane with a duck's head on the end. It was apparently more useful for affectation than support, as he waved it about to punctuate his words. A thick gray beard and mustache sprouted from his face, giving him a pleasant appearance.

Jade would have bet that he had moonlighted as Santa Claus to work his way through his Ph.D. program.

Dr. Lithemeir smiled and beckoned Jade into his office with a grand bow and a long, sweeping gesture of his arm. Jade ignored him as he entered his office and pulled up a chair.

Dr. Lithemeir seemed pleased to have a guest different from the students and professors he usually saw. He closed the door and hobbled excitedly over to his desk.

"Now, before we begin and you devour some of my most valuable time . . ." He chuckled lightly to let Jade know his assumption of importance was feigned. "You must allow me the pleasure of knowing your name."

"Jade. Jade Marlow."

"Wonderful, wonderful. Does your namesake hail from the wonderful legacy of Joseph Conrad . . ." He stopped and clicked his tongue several times. "Or is your 'Marlowe' more Faustian in orientation?" He smiled broadly, evidently pleased with his question.

"Actually, it just happened to be my father's last name."

Lithemeir chortled. "Well, of course. I was merely inquiring from whom you drew your intellectual heritage. But let us move on. I believe I heard you bellow that you are an FBI agent?" He seemed to take great pleasure in everything Jade said and did, no matter how banal, trivial, or offensive.

Jade considered cutting straight to his own questions, but then he decided to give Dr. Lithemeir some play. That way, he might be more helpful when it came time for Jade to get some answers. Besides, Jade enjoyed sparring with him, especially since he was still wired from the caffeine.

"I'm a cross between an agent and I guess what you would call a private eye," Jade said slowly, wondering how to explain his occupation to a sixty-year-old professor.

"Splendid, splendid," Lithemeir said, rising and twirling his cane overhead until it caught the fan on the ceiling with a mighty clang. "A private eye." He ran his hand excitedly up his chin and scratched his gray beard. "Do you spend restless hours fingering a set of dimly lit venetian blinds, gazing over the city like the ever doleful eyes of Dr. T. J. Eckleberg?" He spun to his window and dug his fingers through the blinds, bending them irreparably. "Or do you lean back in your chair with a glass of whiskey—which long ago replaced the opium pipe—delicately perched beside your crotch as a delightful blonde legs her way into your office with a piece in her purse?"

Jade stared at the professor for a while. "Actually, no. I track suspects, Professor."

Lithemeir waved his hand blindly as he moved a stack of papers over to one side of his desk, allowing a clearer path through which to see Jade. "Please call me 'Doctor' if you must." He suddenly froze and then sat forward excitedly. "By the club foot of Lord Byron," he said emphatically. "You're Jade Marlow!"

"Yes, *Professor*." Jade was losing patience. Patience was never one of his virtues, but on two hours of sleep and an empty stomach, he didn't even know what the word meant anymore. "I did introduce myself. Recall?"

"Yes, yes. Marlow. 'The Tracker.' I recognize you from the papers of late. I'd imagine you're all over the television but I haven't turned one on in years."

"It's not really that hard. All you have to do is push the power button on the remote."

"Yes, yes," he answered eagerly, ignoring Jade's sarcasm. "I would be honored to help you, my dear Tracker. I confess 'I am a gentleman and a gamester, for both are the varnish of a complete man.'"

Jade decided just to proceed blindly and ask questions. He cleared his throat and began. "I'm tracking a man by the name of Allander Atlasia." He felt a rush when he said the full name, as though he were mouthing a taboo and a desire simultaneously. "He's a cruel man. Extraordinarily cruel. And he's intense, intense as all hell." Jade leaned forward and grabbed a loose pencil from Dr. Lithemeir's desk, then began to play with it. In his eyes was the look of a man speaking of his absent lover. "He refuses to stop short of anything. He'll act on all his fantasies, giving them full range at any cost. He pushes, he pushes to the edge and doesn't worry about the fall."

Jade was pressing the pencil with his thumb, and it gave way with a resounding snap. Half of it clattered to the floor and rolled under his chair.

Dr. Lithemeir looked down at Jade's thumb, which was bleeding from where it had struck the jagged end of the broken pencil, and was startled to his feet. "'Which is the merchant, here,'" he said, "'and which the Jew?'"

Jade jammed his thumb into his mouth and applied pressure on the wound to stop the bleeding. Pulling it from his mouth, he regarded it for a moment and then spoke calmly again. "Just let me ask a few questions, then I'm out of your hair."

"Proceed."

"He left a quote I need—"

"A quotation, Mr. Marlow. 'Quote' is a verb. 'Quotation' is a noun."

"Thanks for the grammar lesson. Now I know my day's not a total loss." Jade reached into his pocket and pulled out the crumpled piece of paper which he smoothed on his knee but did not look at as he started to recite. "'Full fathom five—'"

"'Thy father lies,'" Dr. Lithemeir picked up the verse. "'Of his bones are coral made; Those are pearls that were his eyes: Nothing of him that doth fade, but doth suffer a seachange into something rich and strange. Sea nymphs hourly ring his knell: Ding-dong. Hark! Now I hear them—Ding-dong, bell.'"

When he finished his recitation, he closed his eyes, still enjoying the afterglow of the piece. The fan overhead limped in circles. Jade noticed several dings on its blades from the professor's cane.

"*The Tempest*," Dr. Lithemeir said.

"Shakespeare?"

He nodded briskly, "The last romance, the last play. Shakespeare's farewell to the stage."

The last hurrah, Jade thought. It seemed appropriate to Allander's situation.

"Can you clue me in on its significance?" he asked. As Lithemeir started to speak, Jade cut in again. "In plain English, please. Pretend you're speaking to your daughter."

"My daughter is preparing her dissertation in the Romantic visual arts, Mr. Marlow. I don't find myself speaking down to her very often." He punctuated his response by thumping his cane lightly on the floor. Another thought grabbed him and he no longer looked offended. "In fact, my son is the intellectual unfortunate in the family," he confessed heavily. "He's a banker."

He settled into his chair. "Now in *The Tempest* we find a young man by the name of Ferdinand. This Ferdinand is washed up on the shore of an island, having survived a shipwreck. However, his father is nowhere to be found." A wistful look crossed the professor's eyes as he contemplated the pain of getting washed ashore without one's father. "This so-called 'poem' which you present is sung to Ferdinand by Ariel, who is a fairy."

Jade started slightly in his chair.

"No, no. A fairy as in a flying elf. A Tinkerbellesque fairy if you must."

"So it's a song about his dead father?"

The professor shook his head vehemently, as if allowing Jade's response to hang in the air uncontested, even for a moment, might validate it. "No no. His father is quite well. He washes ashore elsewhere."

"So if this . . . fairy is a fairy, then wouldn't it know that?"

"Precisely."

"Then why's it telling Ferdinand his father died?"

Dr. Lithemeir grinned, pleased by Jade's curiosity. "Perhaps because he represents Ferdinand's fantasy world. Ferdinand must allow himself a clean break from his paternal tie in order to properly mature and come to manhood." He smiled self-consciously. "That's the Cliff's Notes version, of course. Please don't quote me."

Interesting, Jade thought. Another image of a dead father. The father having to die in order for the son's development to progress. *What there is in every little boy.* The Oedipal complex again. Why was Allander so fixated on it? he wondered.

Jade wasn't so sure that Dr. Yung was right in his assessment; he had a feeling that Allander might direct his rage toward his real parents. It seemed more and more that he was pointing back in that direction. Getting ready to go home.

"That's why he's able to win the fair maiden in the end," the professor concluded.

"Either that or he used a really good line," Jade said.

"Several of them, in fact," Dr. Lithemeir replied. "He couldn't help but score with the Bard of Avon writing his verse for him."

Jade rose to leave.

"A rather suitable quotation from a man who submerged a large tower to effect his escape, don't you think, Mr. Marlow?" He looked at Jade with his head bent slightly and one eyebrow raised. You're not getting this at all, his look said.

"You know, Professor," Jade said. "I'm not as dumb as I look."

Lithemeir laughed. "Well, I suppose we should all be grateful for little miracles." He rose from his chair and crossed to a shelf of books. He ran his thumb over the top of them, finally pulling a dusty paperback from the row and tossing it to Jade. Glancing at the cover, Jade saw that it was a copy of *The Tempest*.

"The play's the nook, wherein we'll catch the conscience of the crook," Dr. Lithemeir said with a smile.

"I don't know if he has one, Professor," Jade said. He tossed the book back. "Don't really have time. I think I got the gist."

The professor's smile faded as he remembered that the situation was more than a game.

"Thank you for your time."

"It was a pleasure," Jade heard the professor say as he swept past Ms. Jennings's desk. Again, she nearly dropped her cup of coffee.

"We'll have to do cocktails sometime," he muttered over his shoulder.

ALLANDER awoke with the first light of morning, feeling the coolness of the breeze across his face. He sat up. His first instinct was to spring to his feet, but he restrained himself. A feeling of unmitigated freedom washed through him like an orgasm, leaving his head humming and his fingers tingling. He had no reason to be anywhere except right where he was. Propping his head on his arm, he lay back again, listening to the breeze in the leaves and smelling the thickness of nature all around him.

Jade watched the rest of the tapes from Allander's trial, but they were not very helpful. Allander barely spoke at all, choosing to rely on the skills of the lawyer his parents had hired for him. He was too unstable to speak to the jury, Jade thought. Although it wasn't like Allander to play a peripheral role in his own show, it was a smart legal decision. He was capable of toning down his act when he knew it was good for him. Not that his silence had helped—he was convicted of the rape and kidnapping of a young girl. The kidnapping was what had landed him in federal prison; he was only eighteen years of age at the time.

Needing to hear Allander's voice, Jade switched back to the psychology audiotapes. In the next hour, his pen never stopped tapping against his knee, even to take notes. Finally, in the sixteenth tape, his suspicions were confirmed, when in another momentary lapse, Allander's true voice shone through. There'd been a different interviewing psychologist on that tape, one who was much more aggressive.

For the first ten minutes, Allander didn't respond to any questions. The psychologist started going through material from old interviews to try to goad Allander into speaking.

Jade, who had almost fallen asleep during the last three tapes, leaned forward, suddenly excited. He knew Allander was one to take a challenge. He'd already proved that.

The psychologist spoke loudly, an edge of sarcasm in his voice. "So let me get this straight, Atlasia. You're the holder of human truth. You know the foibles of the human heart, its yearnings, its errors, its desires. And since you know them so intimately, you're not afraid to act on them." He paused dramatically. With interviews, timing was everything, Jade thought. "What makes you so special?" the psychologist continued. "Why should you know any more than I?"

"Any more than you?" Allander sneered, rising to the bait. "You're a personified superego, a walking shadow that's run out of gas. Compare you to me. Hyperion to a satyr. I've lived through more than you can dream. I've lived the fantasies. I'm the only one to do it without a Greek wrap and I don't need any forks for my eyes. Try checking that at the door, Doctor. Let that roll around on your back for a while."

Then he was silent. Just like last time—one outburst and back to silence or dispassionate interaction.

But that one lapse was all Jade needed. The Greek wrap indicated Oedipus. Allander must have raped his mother. He *had* raped Darby. That's why Thomas was so unforgiving when Darby spoke compassionately about her son. Allander had literally fulfilled part of the Oedipal complex.

Jade thought back to the books he'd read on Freud. Freud used the Oedipal myth as the basis for his theory of development. Every boy desires his mother and wants to kill his father. Once the father is dead, the boy can fully possess his mother. Boys must learn to sublimate into other avenues, to break the fantasy in order to live in reality.

But Allander wasn't about sublimation. "What I carve, I'll carve in flesh," he'd said. "What I paint, I'll paint in blood." His reality *was* fantasy—he'd alluded to this many times. Others sublimate because they are scared of their fantasies. Oedipus put out his eyes when he realized that he'd killed his father and slept with his mother. But Allander wasn't scared to face his fantasy, to recognize it as a part of himself. *I don't need any forks for my eyes.* He'd already acted on part of it, but he was a perfectionist. He needed to finish the job.

Jade thought about the fact that Allander hadn't molested the children in the house he'd broken into. The children weren't enough of a challenge anymore. He was after a challenge ages old, a challenge that he thought fundamental to all humans. All humans had the yearning, none the courage to act on it. Except him. Except Allander Atlasia.

And though he had stripped her, Allander hadn't raped the mother at the first house, a fact that pointed to his sexual insecurity. Maybe something had gone wrong when Allander tried to rape his mother. Maybe he couldn't go through with it, maybe he was impotent. Whatever it was, something had happened that he was trying to fix after all these years. He was building up his courage for the second round.

And Jade knew right where he was headed.

He picked up the phone and called Dr. Yung. The secretary put him on hold. Jade's knee bounced up and down as he waited.

"Mr. Marlow, I'm so glad you called," Dr. Yung said when he finally picked up. "I was about to call you. I went through some of the materials again and I think I came up with something."

"Go ahead," Jade said.

"On the tape you left with me, he said that Dr. Schlomo—whom you identified as Freud—'just never should have backed off.' I didn't give this much thought at first, but then I went back to it. Freud initially thought the sexual content of his patients' dreams was based in reality, that many of them really had sexual interactions with their opposite-sex parents. But then he switched his position and posited that these thoughts were just fantasies, just wishes.

"I think that's what Allander meant by 'he just never should have backed off.' He thinks Freud was right the first time. That these sexual thoughts are the reality, not the fantasy. Which means he doesn't think you outgrow them."

"But you can act them out."

"Exactly. Now if he's ready to take on the Oedipal complex, we could have a dead father and a raped mother on our hands soon. Or on your hands, I should say."

"*His* father and mother," Jade said. Dr. Yung was quiet, so Jade continued. "I think there's already a history there that we haven't begun to penetrate. In one of his interviews, he said that he's lived all the fantasies. He said something like, 'I'm the only one to do it without a Greek wrap'—pointing at what Oedipus did. I think he's talking about intercourse. I think he actually raped his mother."

Dr. Yung was quiet for a long time. "It could be. But we shouldn't take anything he says literally. You never know how much the lines between fantasy and reality have blurred, Mr. Marlow."

"That's exactly what I'm concerned about."

Jade hung up the phone. He had been studying Allander's files ever since he'd gotten back from Dr. Lithemeir's office. The sleep he'd missed last night was starting to affect him. His eyes ached and his head was throbbing. He felt as if he'd just finished a boxing match.

But he was fitting pieces into the puzzle, getting a full picture of Allander's mind. Now that he felt he was really getting to know how Allander thought, he needed a plan. The first killings had happened before he'd been called in on the case. But now the game was live.

His breathing tightened and he felt a sudden heaviness across his shoulders. He was disgusted with its familiarity. A flash of cold tickled across his lower back and he shivered, shaking it off. He was hired to track Atlasia. There would be more bodies before he got to him, but that's just how it worked. They could pile up for all he cared, as long as he let blood in the end.

Allander peered back at Jade from his mug shots, his voice rattling around in Jade's head. Jade looked around the living room and saw only Allander. And corpses.

The pain in his head intensified and he grunted out loud, pressing his fists to his forehead to slow the dull throbbing. He stumbled toward the study, accidentally stepping on the remote control and turning on the TV. Allander's trial tape continued.

The mother of the molested girl sobbed on the witness stand, her cries following Jade down the hall. He banged through the study door and fell into his chair. He took deep breaths, counting them backward. He started with twenty and worked his way down. As he counted, he pulled himself slowly to the desk.

Above his pounding heart, his mind carried him back to a place from his youth, a place that smelled like wood sweepings and burning leaves. It carried him across a field where foxtails waved in the wind, catching the sun in all its yellow splendor and reflecting it back so brightly one needed to raise an arm against the glare.

Four boys cut a path through the high weeds, leaving a small trail behind them as foxtails fell beneath their feet. Looks of preadolescent cruelty sat across their freckled faces. Raised on country breakfasts and yellow school buses, boys like these were too naive to have empathy. All four had the same haircut, a side part with hair flared across in the front so that it spiked up or dangled over their foreheads.

They were voiceless to Jade as they screamed, though he noticed the strain in their necks and the rise and fall of their Adam's apples. With a sweeping aerial view, he saw up ahead to where the children were running.

The field led to an enormous mound with a large scarecrow planted in the middle. The scarecrow's arms cast a fierce shadow from its ten-foot perch. The enormous clothes hanging limply from the wooden frame were the product of hours of Mrs. Joe Allen's work on the sewing machine.

The scarecrow was stitched for the town fair back in '61, and the Allens left it out among the weeds as a sort of eerie landmark about which the locals could weave stories to entertain travelers. Mr. Hollow, they called him. He was surrounded by a circle of rocks, making the mound look like some mystical shrine to an ancient deity. Large crows would settle over the vast span of Mr. Hollow's arms, setting him alive with fluttering motion.

Mr. Hollow didn't come down until '79 when Slick James and a crew of his friends ran him over during a drunken ride in their Ford pickup. He was so big he left a dent in Slick's front bumper and Slick bragged for weeks about the size of the deer he hit on Highway 74.

In the vast expanse of weedland between the four running boys and the scarecrow there was a smaller figure, an animated dot in Jade's view. It was another boy, about eleven years old, whose run was clumsy with fear. A silver chain with medical tags bounced around his neck as he moved.

Jade could see his face more clearly now, the droop of his cheeks, the full upper eyelids, and the lolling lower lip. It was a miracle that his awkward legs found footing at all, but he lurched along with a spastic rhythm. A thin line of drool spun from the retarded boy's lip, draping across his shirt, and he grunted like an animal fleeing a predator.

In the distance, another boy ran down a countryside path into a quaint two-story home. He carried a baseball bat across his shoulder, his glove hooked on the end of the bat through the wrist hole. The boy looked tough; he was definitely a scrapper, and he wore a baseball hat cocked defiantly backward on his head.

The screen door slammed behind him as he casually loped into the house. His eyes were green, as green as emeralds. Jade looked into his eyes and his pulse raced.

A pair of hands grabbed him, nails digging into his arms. The face of a woman, distorted with rage and fear. *Goddamnit, where's your brother? I told you to watch your brother!* Over her shoulder as she bent to swat his face, the boy could see a bedroom door open, a frayed cord dangling from the doorknob. Behind the swinging door, yellow-and-pink striped wallpaper—the wallpaper of a circus tent—was visible, suited to a child much younger than eleven. On the floor a small music box lay on its side, thrown down in the child's rage at being trapped alone in his room. A brightly colored porcelain circus tent was glued on top of the lid. The woman's hand drew back to land another blow on the boy's reddened cheek.

The images scattered dreamlike across Jade's mind, every detail unfolding with excruciatingly slow clarity as the scene started to come apart.

The slap of his hand on the desk brought him back to reality. Jade shook his head as he raised it from the desk. He had been counting. Forward or backward, he didn't know, but he was on 153.

The box of pens and pencils faced him and he ran his fingertips across it. He had to move, had to keep moving. There was still a lot of digging to be done at the Atlasias', with Darby in particular. He pushed himself back from the desk and stood up, walked out of the study, and closed the door behind him.

After a minute, he came back in, picked up the phone, and dialed.

"Yeah. Travers. I'm heading back to the Atlasias'. You coming? Yeah, whatever. I just want a driver."

DARBY had greeted Jade and Travers coolly, but with forgiveness in her smile. We're all doing our jobs here, her smile said. Let's not forget that. She had just come in from a visit with neighbors and she was breathless. She seemed always to be slightly breathless, Jade thought.

Now he and Travers sat side by side on a brown couch, facing Allander's parents as classical music played softly in the background. It was a shame to interrupt the peaceful sound with words. Especially these words.

As soon as Jade said Allander's name, the makeup came out again. Darby turned away, looking into a small mirror. Arching her eyebrows, blushing her cheeks, painting her lips.

"Mr. Marlow, you have a propensity for ruining my afternoons," she said with a wicked grin.

Jade didn't respond.

"Oh, come now. I'm just teasing you. Since you're down here to make me miserable, you should at least allow me the occasional tension breaker."

"All right. Fair enough." Jade was being gentle. He found that he liked Darby and Thomas more each time he saw them. He wondered why. It might have been the sad but honest life they had managed to put back together for themselves. Like resurrecting a house after a tornado blows through, he thought.

"I need to ask you a few questions about Allander's childhood."

"Why?" Darby asked. "Is it really necessary to get into all this?"

"Well—" Travers started.

"Yes, I'm afraid so," Jade said, shooting Travers a warning look. "I'm trying to get a profile of how he thinks. I need your help."

"And why . . ." Darby's voice trailed off.

"Should you help me?" Jade finished. "Because you don't want him to kill more people. Because you feel responsible every time he does. Because he should be caught. Because you know you agree with me."

He was going out on a limb, but he thought he was right. He and Darby stared at each other for a long time, momentarily forgetting that Thomas and Travers were in the room.

"You're going to kill him," Darby said simply. "And you want me to help."

"I don't know if you've been watching the news, but—"

"Please, Mr. Marlow," Darby said, cutting him off sharply. "Let's not play these games. I am well aware of what is going on and you are well aware that I am. So why don't you reconsider how you're going to ask for our help."

Jade sighed and rubbed his forehead. He noticed a hint of a smile on Travers's lips.

"Look, Darby. My job's not exactly a picnic—"

"Oh. That's right. You have to make the difficult decision to sacrifice people you hardly know."

"Look, goddamnit." Jade pointed at her, and Thomas leaned back. "That is *not* fair and you know it. You want to stop playing games? Let's cut the one-upmanship."

Darby nodded, her mouth shifted to one side. "You're right. That was unwarranted. I apologize."

For a moment, Jade wasn't sure how to respond. Then he nodded his acceptance. "I know that you and Thomas want to help end this," he said. "However painful it may be, I'm going to need you to open up." Of course, he knew that what he really needed from them involved more than just "opening up," and he had a suspicion that Darby knew, too, but there was a sort of unspoken agreement between them to take things one step at a time.

They locked eyes for a long time as Darby thought. "I will help you," she finally said, "if you promise not to kill him. If you promise to bring him in alive."

Standing suddenly, Jade threw his arms up and walked away from Darby. "Jesus *Christ!*"

"Look, Jade, I think—" Travers said, but Jade waved her off violently.

He turned and approached Darby, his hands and voice shaking with intensity. "Do you know what that means for an investigation like this?" he asked. "It's like sending me into a war zone with my hands tied." He realized that he was coming dangerously close to pleading.

"Do *I* know what it means?" Darby asked coldly, her eyes indignant.

Jade's sigh sounded like a growl. He turned and walked toward the fireplace, having a heated dialogue with himself under his breath. He ran his hand through his hair, stopping to grip the top of his head with his fingers.

"Mr. Marlow," Darby said calmly to the back of his head. "I think we both know you don't have much choice. You need our cooperation. We might as well begin."

Jade turned around. "Fine," he said shortly. "Fine. I'll try to bring him in alive."

"You will not *try* to bring him in alive, Mr. Marlow. You *will* bring him in alive. Don't equivocate on that point."

"I'll bring him in alive," Jade repeated, feeling like a punished schoolboy.

Darby stood and approached him, her head cocked, looking deeply into his eyes, asking if she could trust him. "Do you promise?"

"What the hell? You have my word. You want me to swear on a Bible?"

She shook her head. "No," she said. She reached out and tapped the outline of the silver chain under Jade's shirt. "On this."

At first Jade thought she was joking, but her eyes were dead serious. He matched her expression and nodded solemnly. "All right." He glanced at Travers, who had a puzzled expression on her face. "I promise."

"His childhood," Darby said, picking up the conversation as if there had been no interruption, "was turbulent, often frightening."

"Let's start with physical disorders. Anything major?"

"No. He got sick a lot, but nothing serious. Just the flu and colds and things. He wet the bed until he was twelve. Does that count?"

Jade wasn't surprised. He knew from his training in psychology that many disturbed criminals had had bed-wetting problems when they'd been younger. Jade figured he'd probe further to see if anything else turned up.

He nodded. "Predictable. Any pyromania?"

Darby looked surprised. "Yes."

"And?"

"He liked to set things on fire," Thomas said. "Toys, shoes, branches. He'd sometimes get mesmerized by the flames and burn his hand. We thought it was all fairly normal 'boys-will-be-boys' behavior until—"

Darby shot him a glare and he stopped mid-sentence. He sat down on the fireplace with a small grunt and began tracing the pattern of the rocks.

"Until what?" Jade asked.

The Atlasias looked at each other. Thomas's eyes implored her to speak. "Honey," he said. "We talked about this."

"All right. Fine." Darby looked at Jade and forced a laugh. "We already agreed that if I could exact my promise from you, we'd try to help. More. More than we have in the past."

"I . . . well . . . good," Jade said dumbly. Travers looked at him affectionately. He could have killed her for it.

"So what happened?"

"I came upon him one time in the backyard," Darby said. "I remember I was all dressed up—a silk outfit. We were heading to the symphony benefit dinner. It's something we did every year as a family. It was really important to us, still is."

"And?" Jade asked impatiently.

"Just because we're trying to share these things with you does not mean they're easy, son," Thomas said. "Give her some time. She's—we're trying."

"We're sorry, Mrs. Atlasia," Travers said.

"Please, hon. It's okay," Thomas said to his wife.

"And what was he doing?" Jade asked.

"Well, he had cornered a squirrel on the porch, right against the house. I think it had a broken leg or something, and he—" She took a deep breath. "Allander," she said. "Allander had trapped it against the house." Her voice was getting shaky. She looked angrily at Thomas. "Oh, Jesus, do I really have to do this? Is it really so important to bring this up now?"

"It could be," Jade said. Virtually any childhood story might help him understand Allander better. But more important, it established trust with the Atlasias and got them talking. He was just paving the way.

"Sweetheart, please," Thomas said.

"Fine." Darby's hand shot up and nervously patted her hair in the back. "He got a can of Lysol or something from under the kitchen sink and a match. He held the match under the spray and set the poor little thing on fire." Her voice cracked. "I came out when I heard it scampering around the deck. He was . . . he was . . ."

"Masturbating?" Jade said.

She looked quietly at Jade. Her cheek was quivering and he could see the pulse beating in her temple. "Yes," she said.

The phone rang in the kitchen and she was gone instantly.

"Well, hello there! Yes, yes, we're fine. Fine. Great. Uh-huh. Oh really?"

Jade, Travers, and Thomas sat quietly in the living room as Darby's conversation continued. Jade caught Thomas's eye, but he lowered his head and began his mindless tracing again. Darby's laughter filled the room. After a few minutes, she hung up and returned.

Her smile faded as she entered the room. She locked eyes with Thomas.

"Sorry," she said softly without taking her eyes off her husband.

"What'd you say when you found him?" Jade asked her, picking up right where she'd left off.

"I told him he'd burn in hell forever," she said. Then she laughed, a mature giggle. "No, no. We're quite liberal people, Mr. Marlow. I told him that the masturbation part was normal, even healthy. I believe it is," she said, as if someone had disagreed with her. "I didn't want him to feel guilty about it. But I was very upset about the poor animal, and I scolded him for that. A lecture about cruelty to animals. If only I'd known. That should've been the least of my concerns."

A long, awkward silence ensued. Thomas cleared his throat twice but said nothing.

Jade finally broke the silence. "That was before Allander's kidnapping, wasn't it, Darby?"

She looked down for a while, then turned and walked to the mirror. "Yes," she admitted. "It was."

"That's interesting," Travers said.

"Actually, I think it's quite disturbing," Darby said, cutting her off curtly with a smile.

"No, I mean about how you responded to him masturbating. One of Allander's elementary school teachers caught him masturbating and gave him a big lecture," Travers said. "And a spanking, if memory serves."

"It does," Thomas said. "He was quite upset about that. You've certainly done your digging, Ms. Travers."

Travers bit her lip. They were trying to build trust, and she had just made it seem as if the FBI was digging through all the family laundry. Which, of course, it was.

Although Jade was irritated with Travers for her interruption, he realized that it was an important point. At an early age, Allander had received conflicting messages regarding his sexuality from two female authority figures. And his mother was more sexually open, less restrictive than the other. He was bound to be confused.

"It's okay," Thomas said. "We know you have to pursue all avenues." He chuckled though nothing was funny. "Actually, Allander always said he wanted to be a policeman when he grew up."

"Many killers go through periods where they're infatuated with the police," Jade said. "They're attracted by the fact that cops have authority and power, and that they deal with death for a living. It's quite a common interest."

"Not in our family," Darby said. "Umm. No offense."

Jade smiled. "None taken."

"So there you have your incident," Darby said in a rushed voice. "'Beating-Off Boy Burns Furry Animal.' But that was the last of that. Then we had the summer, those three days that stretched to a lifetime. And I'm sure you know the rest."

And they did. Allander had been kidnapped from a shopping mall, lured by one Vincent P. Grubbs into a blue van and taken to a filth-ridden motel where he'd been held for three days. The Columbus Motel. If those three days had seemed like a lifetime to the Atlasias, Jade could only guess what they had felt like to Allander.

"What store were you in when you first realized you'd lost him?" Jade asked. It might have been a cruel question, but he wanted to gauge how they spoke about it—especially if he was going to ask the big question later.

"Shoes. A shoe store," Thomas said. "I was looking at a pair of brown tasseled shoes the fourth row up from the bottom and I fail to see the significance of this, Mr. Marlow." His voice rose, ever so slightly.

That was good. It gave Jade a chance to isolate Darby. If Allander had, in fact, raped or attempted to rape her, he wasn't sure she would've told her husband. She was strong enough to have carried it around by herself to save Thomas the agony. Judging from their closeness, Jade would've bet she had told him, but it just wasn't worth taking the chance.

He would ask Darby, and he would ask her in private. Dr. Yung thought it was a gamble to pursue this point, but Jade felt it in his gut, and his gut had yet to be wrong.

"Thomas, I can see this is hard for you. Perhaps I'd better speak to Darby alone," Jade said.

"Is that okay?" Travers asked.

Thomas looked as if he'd just been betrayed. His face turned red as he fought for words. "I want to be by my wife's side when she discusses our son. As you can see, it's quite trying."

"I know it must be," Jade said. "But I really think it's better that I speak with her alone. Just for a minute."

Darby winked at Thomas. "I'll be okay, love. Just for a minute."

The living room had a sliding glass door that opened onto the backyard. Thomas rose to his feet and went outside. The door slid behind him with an airtight thunk. Jade looked at Travers. "Alone, please."

She stared at him with calm fury, her mouth clamped shut so tightly that it distorted her entire face. She stood and exited. The door closed with a louder thunk.

Jade rose and walked over to Darby. He rested his hand on her shoulder and she received it gracefully, as if it were an invitation to dance.

"How do you know, Mr. Marlow?" she asked.

Jade looked at her quietly before speaking. "I just pieced it together."

"If you're that good, then God help my boy because that's the best-hidden skeleton in California." She was totally calm.

"Do you really want God to help him?"

"When I believe in God?" She nodded. "Sometimes. I think that's the only thing Thomas will never forgive me for. My son was made who he is by the prisons, the psychologists. He can be salvaged."

She grasped Jade's arm around his elbow, leaning for support.

"When did he do it, Darby?"

She tightened her grip on Jade, but her voice was unflinching. "He was seventeen. It was . . . before he fled from here."

"He couldn't do it, could he?" Jade asked. "Allander."

For a moment, he thought she was going to faint. He could only imagine what memories were flashing through her mind. And how much they hurt.

She shook her head. "I'm sorry. Your reasoning has failed you."

"He couldn't finish then, could he?"

"No, Mr. Marlow. He could not. He did not ejaculate. In me. Thomas came home and Allander fled." Her jaw was squared, her eyes firm and courageous. "Thomas knows," she said. "But I do appreciate your sensitivity."

They sort of laughed together ironically.

Jade's mind was racing. Allander had not ejaculated. And he had not killed his father. His Oedipal complex had yet to be fulfilled. He hadn't had the courage to finish with either his mother or his father, and it had haunted him ever since. Now these killings were practice runs to get his courage up, to get him past his sexual insecurity. To get him ready to come home again.

"Thank you, Darby," Jade said. He couldn't remember the last time he'd thanked someone. "You're doing the right thing, helping me this way."

She blinked rapidly several times to keep the tears back. "There comes a time, I suppose, when you must let them go."

That's right, Jade thought, Allander's in my hands now.

He remembered his agreement with Darby and felt a sudden claustrophobia. He'd have to deal with that when the time came.

"Don't worry," he said. "I called for two more cars to watch the house. You're very safe."

She smiled and waved him off. Then she went to the door and called Travers and Thomas back inside. As they were getting ready to leave, Jade turned to Thomas. "Do you mind if I use your bathroom?"

• • •

Jade's face looked back out of the small mirror above the toilet as he urinated. The bathroom was decorated with floral wallpaper, and carved seashell soaps adorned the marble sink's counter. A wicker shelf protruded from above the towel rack by the sink, and it was cluttered with small, graceless figures that would have been out of place anywhere else—a twirling porcelain ballerina; the three monkeys of lore; a Rockwellesque doctor examining the ear of a freckle-faced youngster.

As he leaned forward to flush the toilet, he was struck with a moment of insight. It was right there in front of him. He turned around and plucked the figure from the shelf, holding it to the light before sliding it into his pocket.

He walked back into the living room, untucking his shirt slightly so that it would hang down over the bulge in his pocket. The Atlasias sat silently side by side, and they did not look up when Jade entered the room. He signaled Travers with a jerk of his head.

Darby showed them to the front door. When she swung it open, she let out a startled cry. A photographer had jumped from his car onto the front walkway. No more than twenty yards from Darby, he raised the camera to his eye.

Jade quickly stepped forward, blocking Travers from view. He slid his arm across Darby's shoulders just as the photographer started shooting. Although Darby was too shocked by the photographer to notice, it made him feel sleazy. It was a cheap move, but given the opportunity and the potential payoff, it was one he had to take.

The photographer ran back to his car and hopped in, tossing the camera into the passenger seat. The car had been left running.

Travers pushed past Jade just in time to see the car pull away. "Press?" she asked.

Jade nodded. "Wouldn't have gotten past the men if they hadn't checked him out," he said. He pointed to the black Oldsmobile across the street and the driver waved, then gave a frustrated shrug. "Not much they can do to stop them if they're clean."

Travers shook her head. "Only two kinds of people need getaway cars," she said. "Bank robbers and paparazzi."

Darby placed a hand on her chest to slow her breathing. "It's okay," she said. "Madonna and I, we're used to it."

Travers laughed. "Well, thanks for your time."

Darby looked up and caught Jade's eye. He was alone with her for an instant, alone in her private world. He could almost sense the depth of her pain in the slight wrinkles around her eyes.

She mustered her strength and smiled.

He smiled back.

IN the afternoon, Allander's hunger pangs finally distracted him from his quiet reflections. Rising and stretching, he headed back to the main road. He whistled as he walked, enjoying the lightness of the sound and the freedom of the notes as they drifted on the wind.

As he rounded a bend in the road, a large field spread before him to his left. He hopped the mossy wooden slats of the fence and made his way slowly through the field, skimming an open hand on top of the waving yellow foxtails. His feet sank slightly in the rich ground with each step. The far end of the field sloped up to the top of a little hill, and a farm-style house sat at its peak.

Allander resumed whistling and headed for the house. He rapped the door with his knuckles. It was a large wooden door, with lines and ridges, worn with time and use. The sign posted along the country road had advertised a "learning school."

Allander imagined that the teacher lived and taught in the same house, for it had been described as a "residential school" on the map he had seen at the bus station. The door was opened by a homely, middle-aged woman who wore her hair pulled back neatly in a bun.

"Hello. My car broke down and I was wondering if you would do me the great favor of allowing me to use your telephone."

She glanced down at him. She was a rather sturdy woman, and she stood with her arms crossed, pushed out from her chest by enormous breasts outlined like boulders beneath her apron.

"Well, sure. I'm just getting dinner ready, but why don't you come in and use the phone right down that hallway there."

Allander made a half bow, placing one hand on his stomach and extending his other hand open from his side. He nodded his head slightly. The gesture was meant to convey "thank you" and "you can trust me" and "I'm charming" all at the same time.

The woman smiled in amusement and stepped back, opening the door the rest of the way to allow him to enter.

Once in the car, after leaving Thomas and Darby, Jade told Travers of his private discussion with Darby, and of her secret. Though she tried not to show it, Travers was shaken by the story of the rape. When they arrived back at Jade's house, they both began to read through the psychology books that Jade had taken out of the library.

Travers shot Jade a look of annoyance when he began to chew on an ice cube. He, of course, didn't notice.

"What was the deal with that promise?" she asked. "Why did Darby tap your chest?"

Jade shook his head dismissively.

Sensing she wouldn't get any more out of him, she turned back to *Totem and Taboo*, and they read in silence.

"The style and location of the house suited him, I can tell you that," Jade said after a while.

"The whole castle on a hill thing going on? Family as royalty?"

"That's what I'm thinking. I'm betting he chooses another elevated house. Set apart from the others. And there's all this"—Jade leaned closer, holding the book up to his nose—"errant prince-child complex shit."

"The prodigal son avenging himself upon the king and queen—"

"—or mother and father," they said together.

Jade's face clouded. "He's like a fuckin' plague descending on the house. Punishes the parents, then toys with the children like playthings."

"Do you think he'll always kill the parents?"

"If you'd like, you're welcome to join me for dinner. Earl and the kids are at a baseball game, so they won't be back until later. Earl always says there's nothing like baseball at dusk, but I think . . ." Her voice droned on incessantly in the background, carrying through the house to Allander.

He walked right past the antique phone on the little wooden table and began opening doors to the rooms off the hallway. He found the laundry room and leaned over the dryer to open a cabinet. A large iron sat back safely from the edge. Allander smiled as he removed it and began to wrap the cord around his wrist.

"I thank you so much for your hospitality," he called down the hallway as he walked toward the voice still emanating from the kitchen, the iron swinging freely at his side.

Jade paused for a second, biting his cheek pensively. He grimaced as he ran his thumb across his bottom lip. He had come to trust Travers with more and more information.

He rose to his feet. "I have something to show you."

The iron, matted with blood and tangles of hair, swung back and forth, still wrapped around Allander's wrist. It dangled just above the floor as he peeled a piece of crisp skin off the turkey and dropped it into his mouth, savoring its rich flavor.

He turned on the radio, and a Beethoven piano concerto, *The Emperor*, played loudly from unseen speakers.

The woman's arm protruded from around the corner of a large cooking block situated in the middle of the kitchen. Thin, dark hair stood out against the forearm, and the wrist wore a gold watch. It ticked, and Allander took comfort in its consistency.

He stepped around the corner of the block to admire the rest of the body. The face was severely battered. Allander thought he could discern the distinct shape of the iron from the indentations in the forehead and right cheek. One of his swipes had missed the head and punctured one of the generous breasts, but it bled far less than the other wounds.

A pool of blood drained from her head and ran along the seam where the floor met the cooking block. Allander waved his hand to the music as he bent over, delicately dipping his index finger into the blood like a paintbrush.

Jade returned to the room with the small wood carving he had stolen from the Atlasias' bathroom. The detail on it was extraordinary, the solid chunk of wood transformed to a lifelike rendering. From the etched initials and date on the bottom, Jade knew that Allander had carved it, and had done so when he was only fourteen. Already, it showed the hand of an imaginative thinker.

Jade set it down on top of Allander's sketch of the sets of hands. The carving showed three monkeys sitting side by side, blended together at the midsection. The first one covered his eyes, the second his ears, and the third his mouth. Their hands matched those in the drawing perfectly—one set facing each other, one set pointing at each other, and a solitary hand angled up at forty-five degrees. The three monkeys looked as if they knew a great secret. As if they spied someone stalking you, lurking in shadows behind your back.

An ideal symbol for repression. Allander's own parody of the Freudian process.

"Oh my god!" Travers exclaimed. "See no evil, hear no evil—"

Allander stood before the large pane of glass that provided most of the light for the modestly decorated family room. His finger was covered in blood, and it ran down his forearm, dripping off his elbow.

He stood back and admired his lettering. "S N E." Same initials, different meaning. *Speak no evil.* Not much risk of that happening.

In the kitchen, the woman's mouth drooled profusely, spilling blood onto the wooden floor. It leaked from the hole where her tongue had once been.

Allander felt no sexual desire for her. The killing was easy, so the thrill it brought was lessened. Her screams brought ecstasy, of course, as did the sound of her body being battered. But without the sexual challenge, it just wasn't the same. He'd be moving on soon, moving on to the real object of his desires.

But she was an educator; she had the hypocrisy written thickly across her face. He detested educators who spewed forth nonsense. He had warned little Leah about them too. They talked just to hear themselves speak, but they feared the truth like all others. Well, he had stopped her tongue at last.

He finished his lettering and wiped his hand on his shirt. Then he went into the kitchen, stepped over the woman's body, and fixed himself a drink. After taking care of the body and the floor, he found himself a clean shirt in a drawer and put it on. Heading back to the front of the house, he pulled a large wooden chair around to face the front door, and began his wait for Earl and the kids to return home.

JADE continued to chew ice. It helped to keep him focused. He cooled himself by running the cup across his forehead occasionally, enjoying the drops of water that rolled down his face.

"You want something to drink?" he asked Travers. He got up, peeling his bare back from the couch.

"Sure. Iced tea?"

"Water."

"Water's fine."

She heard the shoveling of ice cubes and sighed. She didn't know how much more ice crunching she could endure.

"We're at a standstill," she said when he returned.

"What are you talking about? We just figured out his pattern, what he's doing."

"Yeah, but how does that help us in catching him? In stopping him?"

Jade looked at her disdainfully. The doorbell rang, and he left to answer it without responding to her question.

Tony smiled broadly as he pushed past Jade and walked into the entranceway. "There's these two sperm swimming. And they're exhausted. They've been at it forever, seems like hours. Finally, one turns to the other and says, 'Hey! How much longer we got?' Other sperm looks back at him and says. 'Who you kidding? We just got past the esophagus!'" His laughter started as soon as he finished the joke.

Jade laughed, three notes descending the scale.

"Aren't you going to ask me in?" Tony said.

"You are in."

"Farther in?"

"Would you like to come farther in?" Jade asked flatly, turning his back on Tony and heading to the living room.

"Why certainly. I'd be delighted." Jade watched Tony's face when he saw Travers sitting on the floor. He could tell Tony was impressed by her.

"You didn't tell me your partner was here," he said.

"One of your friends, I'm surprised he doesn't think I'm the maid," Travers shot back without looking up.

Tony turned to face Jade, his eyebrows raised. "And all the charm of a rottweiler."

"Rabid," Jade said. "A rabid rottweiler."

Travers kept flipping pages.

Tony took a step back and pointedly looked Jade up and down. A pair of ripped shorts, no shirt, no shoes and socks. "You didn't have to get all dressed up just because I was coming over."

Jade grabbed the leg of his shorts. "What, this old thing?" he said.

Travers smiled, but still refused to look up.

"I gotta hop in the shower," Jade said. "Play nice with the rottweiler." He disappeared down the hall.

Tony sat down heavily on the couch. "So. I see you've met the ever unpredictable Jade Marlow."

Travers looked up at Tony and studied him carefully. There was a softness to his face, and she wasn't surprised to see the wedding band on his finger. She decided she liked him. "You could say I've had the pleasure."

"Frustrating, huh?"

"And more. Sometimes he's impossible. I take that back. He's always impossible."

Tony laughed and extended his hand. "Tony Razzoni."

"I know. You're one of the only people he talks about civilly. Anyone else I figure he would've shot at the door."

"I've dodged a few of his bullets," Tony said. He chuckled. "He's very intense."

Travers slammed down the file she'd been studying. "Intense? About what? About himself? He doesn't give a shit about anything else. The victims, the families—nothing."

She immediately regretted her outburst, embarrassed to be showing emotion about someone she presumably didn't like.

Tony ran his hand over the stubble on his chin, and looked at her knowingly. She hated that he knew Jade was under her skin.

"I met a guy a few years back, ran track with Jade at UCLA," he said. "Said Jade trained like nobody else—put in five-hour practices six days a week. In his junior year, he was a strong candidate for team captain. That's rare, you know, for a junior. The night of the election, he didn't show up. Most guys woulda killed to be captain, but he didn't even show up. Guy I talked to said he just didn't want it. But I think he was afraid of the responsibility, didn't want to run the risk of letting anyone down." Tony paused for so long that Travers thought he was done with the story.

"He won every single regular season meet in his junior and senior years. And he knew he would, the guy said. Even back when he missed that election on purpose."

Tony looked away from her, leaning back and spreading his arms across the top of the couch. "Guess he just didn't care, huh?"

They sat in silence, Travers flipping through a criminal psychology textbook and Tony picking at his nails.

ALLANDER heard a truck pull into the driveway and then a man's deep voice followed by children's laughter. He had found a shotgun mounted on the wall of the study, upstairs, and a box of shells in the cabinet beneath. Now he sat in quiet anticipation, shotgun across his knees.

The front door opened and Earl entered the house. In his late fifties, he had a head of curly gray hair, and his skin was wind-blasted from years of working outside. Like his wife, Earl was a teacher. Allander had determined this fact earlier by looking through the photo album in the living room. That's why he waited for him.

Earl stopped when he saw the outline of Allander's figure in the darkness of the living room ahead. The boys hadn't noticed Allander's presence, and Earl's eyes closed regretfully as he heard the door click shut behind them. With one muscular arm, he swept his two boys, aged ten and sixteen, behind his back.

"You know," Allander said, uncrossing his legs and leaning forward until a sliver of light fell over his face. "You shouldn't allow guns in the house. There's an overwhelming likelihood that they'll be used against members of your own family." He smiled sweetly and waited to see a change of expression sweep across Earl's face. He was not disappointed.

"You'd better pray you didn't touch her," Earl said, his voice lowering to a snarl.

"I don't pray," Allander replied. "And I did touch her."

Earl lunged forward, his fingers spread in fury. The hatred in his eyes was extraordinary. Allander knew the man would have no qualms about tearing the flesh from his body with his bare hands.

The first shot hit Earl in the stomach and stopped his momentum, knocking him backward. He landed in a sitting position about two yards in front of Allander's feet.

His fingers pushed in and felt the rush of blood where his stomach wall had been. He raised his head to look at Allander just as the second shot blew much of it from his shoulders. Chunks of flesh landed in the entranceway, skidding past the children's feet before sticking to the wall behind them. Blood sprayed the large mirror on the left side of the room.

"Well, that was certainly a helpful exercise," Allander said cheerily as he loaded two more shells into the shotgun and recocked it. "I hope no one else loses his head over this little matter."

The sixteen-year-old started to cry, his shoulders heaving. The younger brother remained silent, staring at Allander with wide eyes. He stepped back against the door, and Allander smiled as he saw his little pink fingers grasp the older boy's hand.

The boys sat back to back in two of the kitchen chairs, bound to their seats by thick duct tape coiled around their bodies just under their chests.

The thrill of power rushed through Allander's body, touching him to the bone. He almost had to shake it off like a chill. He had come to settle another score, to revisit the teachers with a bit of retribution. The children had just been an extra. He liked having them just as they were; he could perform any action he desired on them and they could do nothing about it. Very few people had ever experienced such complete control.

Allander had been considerate enough to remove the mother's body from the kitchen before he took the boys in there. He had even mopped up the blood. Fathers received their retribution publicly, but he could never show children their dead mother. She was safely out of sight, one room over in the family room.

The older boy had stopped crying, but his breath still came with sobbing urgency. He shrank back from reality, shock glazing his now vacant eyes. The little one had not made a sound.

"Well, my young friends, what are your names?" Allander asked politely. He was perched on a high stool facing the boys and he dug a kitchen knife into his seat absentmindedly, cleaving little peels of wood from the surface.

"We're not your friends, and we're not telling you our names. We're not telling you nothin'." The ten-year-old jerked his head toward his older sibling. "Don't tell him nothin', Ted."

Allander smiled. "Well, if he doesn't tell me *nothing* then he would, in fact, be telling me *something*. A double negative makes a positive. Your advice isn't concordant with your desires."

The ten-year-old looked at Allander and squinted his left eye to form what he thought of as an intimidating glare. "Well, we're not tellin' you *anything* then."

"So young, and so untender?" Allander laughed. "Very well. But I don't think this one has much choice given his present condition." Allander gestured to the older boy with a flick of his head. "They don't talk much, you see, when they're in shock." His eyes narrowed and he dug the knife deeper into the stool. "It's a very trying time."

He raised his eyes to the younger boy. "I will ask you

one more time and then I will kill you and I will find out what your name *was* anyway by hunting around in your room and it will all have been an exercise in futility. So you'd best respond."

He leaned forward and stared at the boy eye to eye, their noses almost touching. "What is your name?" he purred.

"My mom said not to give out my name to people."

"Oh yes. You might find yourself in a dangerous situation," Allander said, laughing. "Besides, I don't think your mother's in a position to punish you anymore. Come now. Out with it."

The ten-year-old bit his lower lip for a minute and didn't respond. Allander flipped the knife over once and caught it by the handle. He began to step off the stool.

"Alex," the boy said quickly. He never once removed his eyes from the knife's blade.

"Well, Alexander, you and I are going to have some fun. But first, I must take the precaution of removing your brother."

Alex still kept his eyes trained on the knife. A look of horror was creeping into his eyes; Allander could see it blossoming beneath the clear green irises.

"Don't you hurt him. Don't you hurt Ted."

"Now whatever makes you think I would hurt Theodore?" Allander asked as he unwound the tape from the older boy's torso.

Ted stared blankly ahead. He stood and walked upstairs when Allander led him by the hand. As soon as Allander was out of view, Alex thrashed madly against his restraints, but could barely get the tape to stretch. He finally sank low in the chair and waited for Allander's return.

After what seemed like an eternity, Allander walked back into the kitchen. "Please pardon my absence," he said quietly.

He went over to the cupboard to get a glass, and as he lifted his arm, Alex saw the telltale splash of fresh blood. The young boy began to scream—long, drawn-out, blood-curdling shrieks of terror.

Allander glanced down at his shirt and noticed the blood. "Well. I'm sorry you had to see that. Horribly inconsiderate of me, but you see, it's important that it's just the two of us. We wouldn't want Theodore butting in and ruining all our fun, now would we?"

He drank his water, setting the empty glass on the counter when he was done. Turning swiftly, Allander yanked a knife from the cutting block. He crossed the room in a flash, pressing the point of the blade to Alex's throat. "WOULD WE?" he roared.

Alex tried to stop his sobs. He was drooling now, and he tasted the salty mucus running down the back of his throat. He tried to speak, but he couldn't get the words out because of his rapid breathing, so he just shook his head back and forth. No, no, we wouldn't, his actions said.

"Well, finally our tough little soldier has begun to crack under the pressure. But don't feel badly. You've put up an impressive showing for a boy who has just lost a parent before his eyes. You'll bless me for it one day. It's what you really want."

Allander bent down and began to unwrap the duct tape from around Alex, talking as he worked. "We're going to have a little wedding, you see. You'll need to find some white clothes to put on and a veil—yes, yes, we do need a veil—and we'll undergo a brief ceremony in which boy is wed to man." He looked up and smiled at Alex lovingly. "We'll be married in virgin splendor suitable to the Renaissance."

Allander worked at a particularly stubborn piece of tape that was stuck to Alex's side. It ripped free, and he continued. "We'll fuse before ourselves, before our own naked eyes, and we'll find *truth*. We'll find truth, not happiness, for the two rarely, if ever, coexist."

When his upper body was freed from the chair, Alex stood, the tape falling from his lap to the ground. Allander was still bent over, pulling the last pieces from the boy's legs. When he finished, he rose slowly, bringing his mouth to Alex's left ear.

"I want you to know you're going to die. For pulling that tough-soldier routine, for trying to intimidate me. Me." Allander pointed at himself sharply, stabbing his chest with a finger. "I'm going to kill you no matter what you do. If you act cute, if you act tough, if you act nice—you're going to die all the same. But if you cooperate, then I'll kill you swiftly. Painlessly."

Alex stood dumbly in Allander's grasp, and it took a moment for the words to sink in. Then, he suddenly seized Allander's shoulders and brought his knee up, squarely catching his captor's testicles. Allander grimaced, waiting for the wave of pain to hit him.

As he fell to the floor, the boy slipped from his hands and disappeared. The searing pain took hold in his groin and spread like wildfire through his lower stomach, and Allander screamed in agony, clutching himself.

"YOU STUPID CHILD. I'LL CATCH YOU. I'LL CATCH YOU AND I'LL KEEP YOU FOR HOURS AND HOURS." As he screamed, he sprayed droplets of saliva on the wooden floor.

Alex raced to a rounded room off the hallway and leaped inside, swinging the thick wooden door shut behind him. He let the large two-by-four fall into place in its iron holdings, and his muscles relaxed once he knew he was safely locked in. The circular room was the earthquake emergency zone in the house.

The room was small and well-supported, so it had the stability of a door frame. Alex had practiced locking himself in during the earthquake drills that his mother ran from the small schoolroom downstairs.

He reached up and felt for the wire chain that dangled from the single naked lightbulb. He pulled it, and the small room was cast in a dim yellow light. Shelves of food surrounded him, dozens of boxes containing snacks and meals.

He sat back on a canvas bag of sugar and turned off the light. He noticed the knotted rope that extended through the small hole in the ceiling and he smiled. The school bell.

Still on the kitchen floor, Allander rolled over on his back, clutching his injured testicles. He heard a soft ringing float through the air as the clapper struck its first tentative blows, and then the full glory of the school bell burst forth. Allander pulled himself to his knees, swearing loudly.

He limped down the hallway, pausing at the door that he had heard swing shut. He pressed his ear to the door and whispered in. "Alex. I know you're in there. I'm leaving now, but I'll be back. You won't escape me. I'll find you. And we'll have even more fun then."

Alex felt the coolness of his sweat layer his body, the rope sliding through his hands. Allander waited until the break between strikes of the bell, and then leaned forward until his lips touched the thick door.

He whispered, his voice just audible to the boy inside. "I'm going to hurt you, Alex. Hurt you in ways you can't even imagine." He waited until after the next toll, then continued. "I don't think you understand. I'm *really* going to hurt you."

As Allander's words reached him through the dank

air of the small room, Alex realized that he would never have another night of restful sleep. Dead or alive, Allander would haunt him in his dreams and visions, in the waking and sleeping moments of the rest of his life.

Alex sank down to a crouch and hugged his knees tightly. The trembling set in as he heard the front door open and close. He rang the bell again, then sat and waited for help.

THE first light of morning broke from over the mountains as Jade veered across four lanes to exit Highway 280 at Woodside. Travers kept a relaxed expression on her face, but Jade saw her hand gripping the side of the passenger seat. They'd gotten the call from headquarters less than five minutes before. Already there were dogs out combing the woods and hills.

He raced to the rural community, flying over dirt roads and potholes.

"Woodside? Why Woodside?" Travers asked.

Jade shook his head. "Don't know. Could be he wanted to get somewhere random to throw us. Widen the range of our search, make it less effective."

"We have forty minutes between here and the first crime scene," Travers said. "That's a lot of room. It'll be a pain in the ass to cover an area that large."

"McGuire said they were teachers," Jade said, thinking aloud.

He always does that, Travers thought. Ignores whatever he considers a digression. Just moves right on to whatever he's thinking about. But it works, she reminded herself. That's how he does it.

"At a home school, whatever the fuck that is," Jade continued. "Educators. The second group Leah told you he talked about."

"I hope to God there weren't more children."

Jade swerved around a large pothole without slowing. "Yeah, well," he said.

When they arrived at the scene, the house was already swarming with FBI and press, among the latter the two men Jade had terrorized at the bar. The pack of reporters fought their way over to Jade, tripping through the tangle of cords and cameras.

Although they were still at least fifteen yards away, they started with the questions.

"The city's in a panic and—"

"Investigation dragging into the sixth day—"

"Are you sure it's Atlasia—"

Jade cleared his throat calmly. "NO COMMENT!"

The group of reporters halted and looked at one another, trying to decide whether or not to proceed. They decided on not.

Travers spoke out of the side of her mouth as they walked past the frozen flock of reporters to meet McGuire at the front door. "Excellent poise, Marlow. Just what we meant by handling the press tactfully."

"Thank you, Travers. That's how it's done."

"I was being sarcastic."

"I wasn't."

"Hello, McGuire, what do you have for us inside?" Travers's tone changed from grumble to greeting without missing a beat.

"Similar scene. Parents, one boy dead. Another boy survived—ten years old. Atlasia was going to kill him, but he managed to lock himself in a closet. Alex, I think his name is."

"Let me guess," Jade said. "Ears cut off, 'H N E' written on the wall in blood."

McGuire looked at Jade for a moment. "Pretty close, Marlow. Tongues, and 'S N E' again."

Jade raised a finger to brush the scar on his left cheek. That made sense, he thought, in light of the fact that the ears had been cut out of the picture of him that Allander had left on his back counter.

"Huh," he said. "So the teachers are the speakers. That leaves us with the lawmakers who can't listen."

McGuire looked at Travers as Jade wandered trance-like into the house. "What the hell does that mean?"

"It means," Travers replied, "that he's not as dumb as he looks."

Jade headed through the entranceway, staring into the mirror splattered with blood. He wasn't looking at the blood though. He was watching the reflection of Allander as he moved through the house.

The scent of Allander lingered about the bodies. I just missed him, Jade thought. He walked around this house less than an hour ago.

He squatted over the mother's body, on the floor. Linda Johnson. The name, like the woman, meant nothing to him. Looking at her lifeless form, Jade could not even imagine her as having once been alive. The battering she had received from the iron had left her somewhere outside of reality. She was grotesque now, something out of a fantasy.

Jade turned his gaze to the bloody letters, and his hand absently went to the woman's face, brushing her cheeks. He felt his fingers dip into the pool that filled her vacant mouth, and a sticky warmth spread over them.

Some of the agents turned and looked at each other with raised eyebrows, but Jade didn't notice them. He inhaled the heat rising off the body as he felt the moisture of Allander's making. Even the air seemed to hold its breath during the long pause before he rose from his haunches.

The fingers of Jade's left hand dripped blood as they lifted from the mouth. He held them up before his face as the blood made its way under his cuff. The last three fingers on his hand had been submerged in the woman's mouth, and the line of the gory sheath ended neatly before his thumb and index finger.

With this ring, I thee wed.

He wiped his hand on his jeans. More agents scurried in.

Jade paced around the family room, walking laps around the woman's body and the forensics team working on her. He would have killed for a cup of ice right now.

The mother and older boy both had had their tongues cut out. The boy was past puberty, so Allander would have found him intimidating. He would have felt that any sexually potent male posed a threat. But Alex was young, like the children from the first house. Why had Allander told him he was going to kill him? Why would he want to kill a prepubescent child now, but not earlier?

"The boy," he asked one of the other agents in the house. "What was he like?"

"See for yourself," she replied. "He's out back."

"He's still here?" Jade said in disbelief. "Why the hell didn't you tell me?"

The agent shrugged, her eyebrows drawing together in a frown.

Jade stormed through the sliding glass doors that opened to the backyard. Rather than ending at a fence, the backyard sloped off into a grove of trees and the hills beyond. Jade felt as if he had just stepped into a forest; the lawn and a toolshed were the only indications that a home was nearby. He spotted a small huddle of adults on the far corner of the lawn by the toolshed. He assumed Alex was in the middle.

A woman turned and saw him coming, and she straightened up, blocking Alex with her body. She had bags under her eyes that Jade noticed even before he crossed the lawn. Brown curly hair, streaked with an occasional glimmer of white, fell randomly over her face. She did not look as though she were familiar with a brush.

"Oh no, Mr. Marlow," she said. "I was warned about you. You absolutely cannot talk to him now."

Jade was almost impressed with himself. He was practically famous.

"Look, Ms."—he pulled the tag clipped to the front of her cheap suit so he could read it—"Perkins of the Emergency Children's Advocate State Agency." He stopped and whistled. "That's a lot of capitals."

"They told me you were charming," she said flatly. "You can't talk to him. I'm sorry." She waved some piece of paper at him. "He has his rights."

"Then why's he still here?" Jade asked, standing on his tiptoes to peek at the kid. Alex was sitting Indian style on the edge of the lawn with his arms crossed, refusing to be moved.

"Well . . . he doesn't want to go. We're talking things through."

"I need to speak with him."

"That's certainly possible, Mr. Marlow, just not now. We're trying to move him somewhere more neutral. After he settles down, if he's ready, you can speak to him then."

Jade groaned. "You'll dilute him. That does me no good."

"I'm sorry. Those are his rights."

What was it about this kid that made Allander want to kill him? Jade stared at the woman's determined face and considered busting past her. If he could just get the kid alone for a few seconds, he might see what Allander had seen.

"Then how come you're letting the agents interview the little girl in the house?" he asked.

"A little girl?" she asked dryly. "Inside?" She looked fairly hesitant, but she was worried despite herself.

Jade nodded.

"This better not be a game, Mr. Marlow." She walked vigorously across the lawn toward the house.

As soon as she was out of earshot, Jade walked through the group of adults gathered around Alex, hooked a hand under his arm, and hauled him toward the toolshed. It was only about five steps away, and the social workers and EMTs were so shocked they didn't even respond until he tossed Alex into the small room and swung the door shut behind them. Alex fell to his bottom and skidded toward the far wall.

Jade grabbed a hoe and slid it through the metal door handles. He turned back to Alex. Several hands thudded the door outside, rattling the hoe fiercely. It wouldn't hold very long.

"Open up immediately!"

"You open this fucking door, now!"

Jade stepped toward him and Alex bounced to his feet, backing against the far wall. His back struck a protruding shelf, and his arms went to it, groping for something to grab hold of. His right hand found an ax handle that had been leaned against the wall. Jade smiled as he saw his little fingers tighten around the wood. That's my boy, he thought. That's my boy.

"Okay," Jade said, holding his hands out to his sides passively. "That's it. It's okay." Alex slowly lowered the ax handle, and Jade stepped forward and rested his hands on the boy's head. "It's okay."

The hoe broke, sending splinters of wood scattering across the floor, and a group of people rushed past Jade, almost knocking him over. They surrounded Alex protectively, as they had on the lawn. Ms. Perkins was back, leading the charge. Jade resisted a smile as he thought about the reception she must have received from the agency men inside. Trying to run into a crime scene after an imaginary girl.

Her nostrils flared angrily and her hands were clenched. For a moment, Jade thought she might strike him. "This is entirely unacceptable," she said. "You *will* hear from our legal department, Mr. Marlow."

"You keep me away from that asshole," Alex yelled over her shoulder.

"You are not to see him again," she continued.

"That's fine," Jade said. "I don't need to." As Jade headed back to the house, the group remained huddled together in the shed as though they'd been caught in a storm.

Alex was a tough little bastard, Jade thought. After witnessing his own father's murder, he wasn't in shock. And that was the least of it. He was a fighter. Of course, he was extremely upset, but he wasn't the kind of kid to fold right away. He reminded Jade of himself at that age.

Jade bet it would have been difficult for Allander to keep full control over Alex. The whimpering brats at the first house weren't worth Allander's time. But he would have viewed Alex as a challenge. And Allander loved rising to challenges.

Jade stepped back through the sliding doors into the family room. The bloody letters on the window partially blocked the light shining through, causing it to fall unevenly across the room. He stared at the iron tangled around the woman's feet. It was covered with blood and wisps of hair.

Allander had had time to plan, but he hadn't brought

any weapons to the crime scene. Again, they had been taken from the house. An iron, a shotgun, two knives. He was striking the family from within, killing them with their own tools. It was another way to show a family's repression and hypocrisy. All the tools for self-destruction lay behind their very own doors.

One of the forensics agents worked on the mother's body. He withdrew a swab from the corpse's vagina. "Looks like he didn't rape her," he said loudly to no one in particular.

Jade looked down at her and grimaced. "Would *you?*" he asked.

"That's completely inappropriate and unprofessional," Travers yelled from across the room. "Even for you, Marlow."

"Oh yeah, I forgot. He's a totally different animal. We shouldn't think like him," he said, his voice laced with sarcasm. "Let's hold him at arm's length while we try to run him down. Good thinking."

The forensics agents stopped mid-procedure and looked at one another uncomfortably. Jade sensed their unease and realized that his and Travers's tempers ran a lot hotter than he thought. It took a lot to make these guys uncomfortable.

"I just don't think of contemplated rape as casual conversation," Travers shot back.

Jade gestured to the surroundings. "Good. Then look around, sweetheart, 'cause this isn't a place for casual conversation. If we're gonna get to him, we're gonna have to think in ways that aren't pretty."

"I'm well aware of that, Marlow. You're not the only agent in town with field experience. I'd appreciate it if you'd stop talking to me like I'm two steps out of Quantico."

"Fair enough," Jade said. "And I'd appreciate it if you'd stop talking."

The same controlled anger that he had noticed at the meeting at FBI headquarters flashed behind her eyes. They faced each other across the woman's corpse, which looked up at them blankly.

"The weapons," she said. "Taken from the house. They're not a choice for power, not like Berkowitz's forty-four."

Jade nodded. "So where does he derive his power?"

"From the actions themselves. From a prolonged sense of control."

"But he doesn't enjoy the usual intimacy with the victims. Doesn't track them, lure them, keep them alive and savor them. Why not?"

"Because he's self-aware. He's committing patricides and matricides, but they're very conscious. He's not displacing. He knows he's implicating his parents. He knows his killings are symbolic—even illustrations of Freudian thought. That's why he thinks he's so much smarter than other killers. His killings don't divulge who he is. They affirm who he is. They're part of his self-definition."

"Bravo," Jade said. His tone was so genuine that Travers didn't even find him condescending. "And that's probably why he leaves the bodies in the house. The killings are about the family and home. But even though he's highly conscious of what he's doing and how he's going about it, it still doesn't put him that much ahead of us. He can't help himself. He acts as if he's leading us along, but that's only because he doesn't want to admit just how much he loves this. How much he needs it."

"How do you know?"

Jade pointed at the corpse between them. "The

answer is always in the body. Multiple wounds this time. A full battering with an iron. At the first house, the killings were very neat. One awl through the eye, two swift swings of a hammer. His rage this time is less controlled. There's more anger here. The fewer the wounds, the more controlled the rage."

Travers looked at him. "Aren't you known for only shooting once, Jade?" she asked.

He matched her smile, then his eyes narrowed and a serious expression spread across his face. Travers would have been scared if she hadn't recognized that expression. She left him alone with the body.

Jade finally left the house as night filtered in through the windows. On his way out, he went to the earthquake room and yanked on the rope. The deafening clang of the bell startled the agents still on the scene, and they glared at Jade as he walked to his car.

He didn't notice though. He just wanted to have the sounds of the bell in his ears as he left the scene.

ALLANDER placed his toe in the hole of the faucet as he settled back among the bubbles in the steaming bath. He whistled a lighthearted tune, filling it with baroque trills, his notes resonating off the bathroom walls.

It was astounding how easy it had been. He had hot-wired an old truck he'd found in a neighboring barn and had sped off before anyone had even noticed the chiming bells, let alone phoned the police so they could set up roadblocks. It was doubtful that anyone would notice that the old truck was gone before tomorrow, and even more doubtful that it would be noticed *and* reported before then. The owners would probably consider it a blessing that the decrepit thing had been removed from their property.

As he had driven slowly through the streets of Palo Alto, Allander had noticed a Land Rover with suitcases and surfboards on the roof, and inside a smiling family. He watched as the car pulled out of the driveway of a somewhat secluded, colonial-style home.

After circling the block, Allander returned. He was about to break a window to get into the garage when he noticed a thermometer on the wall. Even though night was drawing near, it still showed eighty-seven degrees. He tapped it, holding a hand underneath; a plastic hatch opened on the bottom and a spare key fell out.

It fit the garage door, so Allander opened it and moved the truck inside, parking it next to a beautiful red

Jeep. Getting into the main house was not a problem given that he had access to a full set of tools in the garage, and he smashed the alarm unit out of the wall and clipped the appropriate wires before it fully activated. The things you learn growing up in and out of prison, Allander thought. A practical education.

The large calendar on the refrigerator indicated that the family was gone for the week. He would steal nothing and leave everything precisely as he had found it, ditching the old truck when he got a chance. The only thing he couldn't fix was the alarm unit downstairs, but he doubted that would attract much police attention if everything else was in order. It pleased him immensely to realize he was brilliant and uncatchable, daringly irresponsible and wildly imaginative. And he was relaxing in a warm bath.

He pulled himself out of the tub and walked around the upstairs without toweling off. Glancing at the cut in his fingertip, he noticed that it was healing well. He stopped in the hallway underneath a ceiling fan. The coolness of the air on his moist skin felt wonderful. He walked into the study, admiring the dark wood bookcases and the shelves of hardbacked books.

On an antique wooden chest in the corner sat two matching cell phones. How cute, Allander thought. His and hers. He walked over and checked the numbers, written neatly in the slots on the back. They were different. He picked up one phone in each hand, bouncing them lightly to feel their weight. They might come in handy.

Crossing the room to lean over the imposing oak desk, Allander turned on the computer. An Internet icon came up on the desktop, and he double-clicked it. He bit his lip and concentrated, casting his mind back to the computer magazines he'd read in prison. It made him sad to realize how much of the world he had missed during his years locked in a cell. There was so much he'd never seen.

The Internet screen came up, complete with a search box. Allander carefully moved the cursor to the box, then typed in a name. Jade Marlow.

After searching through a few dead ends, Allander came upon several entries from the *San Francisco Daily*. He was not surprised to see his own picture in the most recent newspaper article featuring Jade. The headline, "Marlow in Hot Pursuit of Serial Killer," stretched above an extremely unflattering photograph of Allander taken at one of his many court appearances. Allander read the caption aloud in a deep, booming voice, then chuckled. "Serial killer," he repeated disdainfully. "Don't these people have a sense of humor?"

He clicked through the rest of the newspaper headlines. "Black Ribbon Strangler Identified." "Michael Trapp Dead in Shoot-out." "Missing Girl Found."

Quite an American hero, this Jade Marlow, Allander thought. He did everything but rescue cats from trees. He was about to shut down the computer when he saw one entry dated several years prior to the rest. January 2, 1973. A painfully familiar year.

He opened it. It was a small story, buried on the sixteenth page. "Retarded Boy Bullied to Death," the headline read. The picture showed a mother embracing a boy around the chest as a father rested a hand lovingly on her shoulder. The boy had light brown hair, and the drooping features of a developmentally delayed child. It was the same boy he had seen in the picture he had moved from Jade's bedroom.

Also in the picture, but in the background, stood another boy by himself, a baseball cap backward on his head. He faced sideways, unaware of the camera. Although the picture was blurry, Allander recognized him right away.

Jade slammed the door behind him and headed straight to the boxing bag in the garage. He attacked it relentlessly, driving lefts and rights, not at the bag, but straight through it. His form was perfect, his rhythm exact. Fuck. Fuck. Fuck.

Travers had seen Alex at the hospital, her interview mediated, of course, by Ms. Perkins. After leaving Alex's house, Jade had waited for Travers by her car in the hospital parking lot. She'd filled him in briefly and they had decided to break for the night.

At the first house, Allander had been able to perform his act from beginning to end. In Allander's view, it was a finished work. But at Alex's house, Allander had been interrupted. It was a shame almost, Jade thought. It didn't leave him as much to go on. How would Allander have fulfilled this crime?

The wedding business Alex had described reminded Jade of what Dr. Yung had said about a marriage of the different sides of the personality. Allander seemed to be trying to combine his brutal experience with the child's innocence, a sort of return to a lost past. Maybe that was why he'd told Alex he was going to kill him. Since Allander wanted to absorb him metaphorically, the boy couldn't exist afterward as his own physical entity. If you find someone threatening, make him your own. It was like psychological cannibalism.

Jade had to admit that the second "S N E" had thrown him a little bit, since "hear no evil" was supposed to be next in line after "see no evil." At first, he'd thought that Allander might be saving "H N E" for his parents, but then he realized that Allander was committing his crimes in the order in which he felt he had been betrayed—first by his parents, then by his educators, then by the courts and the police. The self-consciousness inherent in such meticulous planning showed that Allander wasn't truly a serial killer; it was more as if he were poking fun at the very notion of serial killers.

Jade pictured Allander's face on the speed bag as he snapped it back repeatedly to the suspended platform. His shoulders were burning and his wrists were getting sore.

Allander was unbelievably slippery. Though he hated to admit it, Jade was having a hard time pinning him down, locking him in. One moment he'd feel he was right there inside Allander's head, but then he'd turn a corner and be lost again. Jade had always believed that killers' actions were illustrations of their thoughts. But when it came to Allander, it wasn't that simple.

Just as Jade was struggling to figure out Allander, Allander was working on him. He knew what Jade looked for and what he wanted, and that made it difficult to interpret the crime scenes he created. Usually, Allander was deadly serious. But sometimes, Jade had learned, he was only playing.

He had called Allander by his first name again twice today at the crime scene. Publicly. Both times it had drawn funny looks, which he didn't care about, but it showed he was getting too close.

Leah had said that Allander raved about parents, teachers, and the law. So far, he had killed four parents, two of whom were teachers. Who would he find next? Who to him represented the law? Lawyers? Too easy a target. Given his overblown ego, Allander would probably go for the biggest challenge and kill a cop or maybe a famous judge. To match the pattern, it would have to be somebody with a family. Unfortunately, that ruled Jade out.

Jade had already ordered protection for all parties involved with Allander's criminal trial. The judge had passed away, which was too bad, because he was known widely as a "family man." He would have been a perfect lure.

The prosecutor and defense attorney had both wanted protection for their families. Jade had put two cars at the defense attorney's house, since criminals usually go after their own lawyers rather than their prosecutors. They figure a prosecutor is just doing his job; if their case goes poorly, they often hold their own lawyers responsible.

Jade also wanted coverage for all policemen and guards involved with Allander over the years, going back as far as the bust on Vincent Grubbs, Allander's molester. In fielding his request, McGuire had been his usual cantankerous self, pointing out that the FBI had already overextended itself on the case. Initially he had said he couldn't come up with the manpower, but Jade had pushed him on it. He didn't want anything left open, no matter how unlikely a target it was.

Despite the pain in his arms and shoulders, Jade continued to hammer at the bag. Something in the regularity of its sound and motion soothed him. Jab jab *jab*. Jab jab *jab*.

He couldn't get the images out of his head. Walking past the red skid on the entranceway floor. The woman's body sprawled out, maroon covering her chin and throat. The sixteen-year-old taped to a chair, his tongue also cut out. Allander had struck the boy on the head first to stun him so he'd be unable to bite.

The forensic pathologist concluded that his tongue had been removed before he received the terminal slit across the windpipe. Jade wondered what that had felt like. To feel someone's fingers prying into your mouth, removing some part of yourself and holding the bloody pulp before your eyes.

Allander's rage was flowering, bringing with it a new flush of sadism. He had started dismembering the sixteen-year-old before death. Up until now, he had mutilated his victims only after he'd killed them.

Jade switched to the power cross and hammered as hard as he could. Jab jab *cross*. The platform shook and he felt sweat streaming down the sides of his face.

Jade didn't care about the victims, exactly. He cared about them inexactly. They were grains of sand in an hourglass, scars to be tallied like points against him. Sometimes, he even hated them. They were glaring symbols of his imperfection. And right now, he couldn't shake them out of his head. He turned them over in his mind obsessively.

The ache in his shoulders brought Jade back to the speed bag. It was a blur of motion, but he seized it quickly between his hands. He lowered it slowly to a resting position.

Jade had a plan, but he didn't want to set it in motion until he was sure the time was right. Once he started that ball rolling, there would be no stopping it. However, with the way things were going, he wasn't sure how much longer he could wait. Most of all, he couldn't stand the waiting. And now that he'd made the promise to Darby, he felt restricted, almost muzzled.

He had taken preemptive measures to try to protect Allander's next potential victims. As far as the lawmakers were concerned, he had covered all the bases. What he had to do now was come up with a situation so compelling that Allander would not be able to resist it, even if it meant he had to alter his plans. Jade's options were fairly limited. There was only one thing that could tempt Allander like that. When it came down to it, there had always been only one thing.

After showering for a half hour, Jade moved into his living room and gazed at the pictures and files that lay scattered on the floor. The TV droned on in the background.

Not a fucking trace. Not one. Allander had just disappeared into the countryside. There were enough woods and mountains to hide an intelligent convict for weeks, and this time they were dealing with a genius. He also had a whole network of roads and old farms to work with.

The cops and the feds had gotten there too late; no one had even responded to the ringing school bells for thirty-five minutes, and then it had taken them another twenty to get the experts in. Fifty-five minutes. No way. Maybe if they'd gotten there within twenty minutes, but even that would have been tough given the rough landscape. There were also enough streams and rivers to greatly reduce the effectiveness of the dogs.

Jade was pacing when a news story on TV caught his interest. He grabbed the remote and turned up the volume.

A photograph of Royce Tedlow flashed on the screen as the news anchor's soothing voice reported, "Forty-seven-year-old Royce Tedlow confessed to the murder of his wife, Frieda, early this afternoon. He cited her wearing of short skirts out in public as his reason for killing her. According to inside sources, he confessed in the face of overwhelming evidence."

Jade chuckled and shook his head. "Must've found the other glove," he mumbled. He turned back to the crime-scene photos of Allander's latest killings, only half-listening as the report continued. When he recognized Alissa Anvers's voice, he looked up again.

She stood before the front arch of a cemetery, the words "Midland Hills" curved in gold letters on top of the gate.

"—Henry and Janice Weiter, the first victims of Allander Atlasia's latest killing spree, were laid to rest today as their children looked on."

The camera cut to a shot of Leah and Robbie standing side by side, holding hands. Robbie was wearing an ill-fitting black suit and Leah a dark dress. Jade saw the wetness of the girl's cheeks beneath the broad-brimmed hat she wore. Some nondescript adults stood behind them, hands on their shoulders.

Jade's breathing quickened. The victims kept piling up like a weight pressing on his chest. The first ones hadn't been his fault, he told himself. He hadn't even been on the case yet. But now the father, the mother, the boy. He shook off the thought. That's not what he was here for. It wasn't in the job description.

Just points to be tallied, he reminded himself. Points to be tallied.

"SIR, I'm afraid we may lose him." Travers drummed her fingers on the top of her briefcase as she addressed Wotan. "Have you looked at the photographs?"

A hand appeared in the thin light and lifted one photograph from the desk. It was a picture of Jade stooping over Linda Johnson's battered body, his eyes gazing at nothing in particular, yet seeming completely focused. It was an impossibly intense gaze, like that of a prophet descended from a mountain summit. The last three fingers of Jade's left hand were steeped in the bloody pool of Linda Johnson's mouth. The photograph also captured the horrified expression of an FBI agent in the background.

"Yes," Wotan replied.

"Well, sir, can't you . . . is there nothing odd to you about the picture?"

"He works on instinct, Agent Travers."

"Does instinct include touching evidence without gloves? And looking like Charlie Manson on crack?"

"Sometimes. Perhaps. I don't think one really knows."

Travers's voice didn't rise, but her tone betrayed her anger. "He's driving the field agents up the wall. He's a public relations nightmare—all the subtlety of Mussolini. We've had complaints from forensics, the press, even St. Mary's Hospital." Travers bit her lip and blinked rapidly several times, gathering her courage. "I'm not recommending dropping him from the case, I just think we need to rein him in a little. He's a loose cannon, sir."

"That's precisely why we hired him."

"Why are you so committed to him?"

"BECAUSE HE SUCCEEDS," Wotan boomed, causing Travers to jump back in her chair.

Wotan lifted the slug out of the marble ashtray and held it to the light. "Do you see this, Agent Travers?"

Travers was still stunned. She had never heard Wotan raise his voice, let alone yell. She didn't move a muscle.

"Do you see this?"

She nodded.

Wotan flipped it like a coin and banged it on the desk. "This is the roulette wheel to which we're all attached, Agent Travers. The divine deck of cards. Heads or tails?" He waited for a moment before asking again. "Heads or tails?"

"Heads, sir."

Wotan shook his head. "You just don't get it, Agent Travers. It's not that easy."

"Not that easy, sir?"

Wotan sat for a while with his hand covering the slug on the desk. "Do you think he's effective?" he finally asked.

Travers threw up her hands, frustrated. "Yes," she confessed. "I do."

"Do you think he's getting close?"

"Yes."

"Then with whom exactly are you arguing, Agent Travers?"

Travers opened her mouth, then thought better of it and closed it again. She looked at Wotan, but the room seemed to fade into darkness around the massive desk.

She rose to leave.

• • •

Through the living room window, Darby saw the mail truck pause at the end of the walkway before continuing up the street. She pressed her hands firmly to her eyes as she headed to the front door. It felt good, like scratching an itch. When she removed her hands, her vision dotted for a moment, then cleared.

The amount of pressure she'd felt over the past few days was so great that she sensed it physically, pushing in on her from all angles. She stepped outside, nodding to the agents parked up the street as she headed to the mailbox.

She flipped through the mail, pausing to examine one envelope in particular. Though there was no return address, she knew immediately who it was from.

Jade leaned over the kitchen sink and peeled an apple with a hunting knife he kept in the kitchen drawer. The weight in his hand felt better than that of a kitchen knife, more substantial.

As he raised curls along the knife's edge, he felt the firmness of the blade through the thin red skin of the apple. His hands moved quickly, like a chef's. When he'd worked his way around the apple several times, he flipped it over and deftly cored it with a single deep thrust and twist.

The doorbell rang and he went to answer it, still holding the knife in his hand. Travers stood on the porch looking out at the street, a newspaper in her hand. She wore a pair of jeans and a white shirt, loosely tucked in. He recognized the shirt from the last time she'd come over. Not a woman much interested in clothes, he decided.

Her hair was still pulled back in a ponytail, but several

strands had escaped and curved down the side of one cheek. She turned to face him, and the morning sun shone across her blond hair, catching its golden highlights. She smiled, lips parting back from perfect white teeth.

Jade bit the apple because he couldn't think of anything to say. She entered the house, brushing his shoulder with hers. As she passed him, she impaled the newspaper on the hunting knife.

"Smart move, Marlow."

Jade was surprised that there was no sarcasm in her voice.

He pulled the newspaper off the knife and opened it. The brightly colored headlines betrayed that it was a tabloid—*The Globe*. Half of the front page was taken up with a color photograph of Jade and Darby standing in the doorway of the Atlasias' home, Jade's arm across Darby's shoulders. "Jade Marlow's 'Private Investigation' of Allander Atlasia's Mother." "*True Details of the Daring Affair Inside!*" the subhead screamed.

When he entered the living room, Travers was sitting on the couch, flipping through a legal notebook. On it, Jade had profiled all the victims' personalities from information he had pieced together from the houses, and from friends and neighbors. He needed to know how they had reacted to Allander; that might help him to understand his actions.

"Excellent move, Marlow," she said. "The photo. Creates an urgency and an attraction for him."

"Urgency is what I'm hoping for," Jade said. "Right now, he has us just waiting for him to strike again. I want to light a fire under him and get him moving."

"Moving where?"

Jade shrugged, averting his eyes.

"I guess that's the challenge, huh?" Travers said, continuing to flip through the notebook. "How'd you come up with that? Putting your arm around Darby?"

"I thought about the emotion that most overwhelms him."

"Rage?"

Jade shook his head. "His rage he can control."

"What then?"

"Jealousy."

"Of whom?"

"Not of whom. Of what. Of his mother's attentions. Of her time. Of her person. That's his Achilles' heel. His jealousy."

Travers smiled, and for a moment Jade thought he detected a softness in her eyes. "At times, Marlow, I almost like you. But don't quote me on that."

"I won't." Jade grinned and lowered his eyes. When he looked up, he started to say something else, then stopped himself.

"What?"

"Nothing." He shook his head. "Where were you this morning? I tried reaching you."

Travers shrugged, glancing at the notebook. "Chores."

"Yeah, you strike me as the real housekeeper type."

She pretended to be absorbed in his notes. After a few moments, she didn't have to pretend. Underneath the personality charts in the notebook, Jade had written the information from forensics. Nothing much to match right now—no traces of dirt or carpet fibers. Since Allander wasn't settled into a base yet, it wouldn't help that much anyway. Given the time frame, he had moved almost directly from the first house to the second, with a quick stop at Jade's. Jade bet he'd move to a safe zone for a while now. To wait. To plan.

Travers looked at Jade's extensive notes, flipping over

page after page of his comments and thoughts. One of the last pages was filled with scribbles and doodles that he had made while he did phone work.

Travers stifled a smile. It was just like Jade to confine his doodling to one page.

Jade crossed his arms, facing Travers's back as she looked through the notes.

Hidden in the doodles were the names of the victims: "Henry Weiter." "Janice Weiter." "Linda Johnson." "Theodore Johnson." "Earl Johnson." They were written in a scrawling hand, much different from Jade's usual neat writing.

"It was tough there yesterday," she said over her shoulder. "The bodies . . ."

Jade shook his head, inhaling deeply. "I missed. Just missed."

She turned to him and a look of understanding passed between them. Her eyes lit with a sudden realization. "It's not your fault, you know," she said softly. "There was nothing you could do."

"I could've gotten there earlier. I could've figured out where he was heading. I could've been here waiting when he stopped by my house. I could've—" His voice broke off. He opened his hands and turned them to the ceiling before slapping them against his hips.

Travers rose and walked slowly over to him. She placed her hand gently on his side. Jade admired how her hair curled around her neck. The edge of her palm was on his stomach, her fingers resting tenderly across his ribs. He lowered his eyes and cleared his throat awkwardly. "I had a . . . brother who died when I was younger."

Travers's forehead wrinkled with sympathetic lines. "I'm sorry."

"Yeah, well, aren't we all." Jade scratched his forehead

at the hairline, blocking his eyes with his wrist. "It was my fault. He was retarded. I was supposed to be watching him." He took a step back. "Allander's story broke the next week. His kidnapping. I remember that the outpouring of public support made me fucking ill. It was a lot . . . more. My brother, that wasn't such a big deal because he was just a retarded kid."

Travers took a small step forward, raising her hand to Jade's face. Just before it touched his cheek, the phone rang on the coffee table, startling her. Jade stood motionless for a moment, his eyes on hers. He walked to the phone slowly, picking it up on the fourth ring.

"Yeah?"

"Hello, Mr. Marlow. This is . . . this is Darby. I got something in the mail today."

Jade leaned forward, speaking intensely into the phone. "Is it a body part?"

A nervous laugh. "Oh, no. Nothing like that. Just a broken pencil. Looks like an eyeliner. It's probably nothing, but it came in a plain white envelope and I just thought—"

"Did you show the agents there?"

Darby laughed. "No. I don't find them very personable."

"All right. I'll be right there," Jade said, hanging up the phone. He turned to Travers. "Let's go."

On his way out, he grabbed the entertainment section of the newspaper from the kitchen table and jammed it in his back pocket.

It was time.

Pushing the gas pedal to the floor, Jade raced onto the highway heading toward the Atlasias.

"Fuck! I should've known."

"Known what? What's going on?"

"Trophies. He's mailing her trophies from his victims. It's common, really common. Gives him a thrill, mixing his world with theirs. Allander's linking them to the model of the monkeys. An eyeliner—has to do with the eyes. 'See no evil.' Family number one. I bet she gets lipstick from the second killing."

Travers shook her head. "Who cares? So he's sending her trophies. We already knew she was marked. It doesn't help. Why are we racing over there?"

"It's time to light the fire."

"What? What fire?"

"Under Allander. The one that'll get him moving."

"I already asked you—" Travers cut short her question and her jaw dropped. "No. You wouldn't. Even you."

Jade looked straight ahead at the road. "Come to Mama," he said.

"No way. We just increased protection on them," she said. "Everywhere they go. He's not stupid. There're too many men."

He looked over at her and groaned. "Jesus Christ, Travers. We'll pull them off."

"Excuse me?"

"Believe me, I'd like to."

"You're going to risk their lives to lure him in?"

"You're a quick study."

She laughed a single note, completely unamused. "Are they people, Jade, or instruments?"

"Let's be honest, Travers," he scowled. "What's the difference?"

"Don't you care about them? Any of them?" She shook her head and another disgusted laugh escaped her.

"I only care about one thing right now. And that's catching him."

"And you don't care who you have to kill to do it?"

"Risk, Travers. Don't you mean 'who I have to risk'?"

"And why, exactly, is that *your* decision?"

"Because no one else wants to make it."

They sped between two large trucks on the freeway, the noise rising as they passed them, then fading away.

"Christ, Marlow. I thought you liked them."

"I do like them. What the fuck does that have to do with anything?"

"Pull over."

"What?"

"Pull over. Let me out. I'm not doing it. I'm having no part of this."

"Oh, for fuck's sake."

"PULL OVER! *Now.*"

"With pleasure," Jade snarled. He yanked the car over onto the shoulder of the highway and skidded to a halt. He was off again before she could slam the door behind her.

THIS time they sat in the kitchen. Thomas prepared dinner, washing salad and whistling along with Beethoven's *Pastoral* symphony. Darby sat at the kitchen table across from Jade, her elbows resting on the white tablecloth. She closed her eyes and let her head sway from side to side in time to the music.

"I love this," she said. "'The Shepherd's Song.'"

Jade sipped his glass of water. "It is nice."

"Where's your friend?" Thomas asked.

"My partner. Ex-partner, I suppose."

Darby smiled. "Could have read that one from a mile away."

"That we didn't get along?"

She shook her head. "Not quite."

Jade let it go.

"Have you seen *The Globe?*" Thomas asked.

"Of course he has, dear," Darby said over her shoulder. "Haven't you, Mr. Marlow?"

"Yeah. Yes, I have."

Darby looked at him, shaking her head.

"Well, we can't help what they print."

"No," Darby said, watching him knowingly. "We can't, can we?"

Raising her hand, she gestured casually to the envelope on the table. Darby's name and address were printed in block letters on the front. It was postmarked San Francisco, but Jade was reluctant to attach too much importance to that, given that Allander had already proved that he was mobile.

"So you think he sent it? The eyeliner. Another image of repression? Makeup. Reminds me of Glenn Close smearing the makeup off her face in that movie. What was that movie?"

"*Dangerous Liaisons*," Thomas called from the sink.

"*Dangerous Liaisons*," she repeated.

"Why do you think it has to do with repression?" Jade asked.

"Why did you steal the carving from our bathroom?"

The question caught him off guard. "I didn't quite steal it," he said slowly. "I just took it to examine."

"Yes, yes. Police business. I understand. My child is a killer so we no longer have the rights that ordinary citizens can expect. Freedom. Privacy. The right to our own property." Her voice rose. "We have guards around all the time—walking through the yard, peering in the windows."

Thomas dropped the salad in the sink and watched her, concern spreading across his face.

"It's fine, Mr. Marlow. I'm used to it. About twenty years of people looking at me with . . . with those eyes. 'From forth the kennel of thy womb hath crept a hellhound that doth hunt us all to death,'" she said in a purposefully deepened and dramatic voice. She was speaking loudly, louder than Jade had heard her speak before.

She laughed, then slid her hands down around her lower stomach, giving them an emphatic shake. "'The bed of death,'" she said quietly.

Thomas walked over to her and placed his hands gently on her shoulders.

"Shakespeare?" Jade asked.

Darby nodded. "I used to read the plays to Allander

when he was younger. I don't usually remember quotations, Mr. Marlow, but I've learned that one really well." Her eyes lowered to the tablecloth and she played with one of her nails.

Thomas rubbed her shoulders, leaning over her.

"So you took the carving." She gestured to the room around her. "It's okay. Everything's public property. How I punished my child, how I talked to him, when I stopped breast-feeding. Do you know what the mothers of most murderers are like? Do you know what it's like to have everything assessed, Mr. Marlow? Do you?"

The sharpness of her words carried around the kitchen for a while. A tear escaped from Thomas's eye and he wiped it away.

Jade cleared his throat and looked at her. "I'm sorry," he said. "I'm sorry."

She reached out her hand and placed it on his arm. "It's okay," she said. "*I'm* sorry. That was unfair. What can we do? Just tell us what we have to do."

Jade couldn't make himself meet her stare. It was a very uncomfortable feeling for him. He wasn't used to it at all. "Well, I'll be honest. I think he's coming for you and I'd like to make that possibility even more likely. In fact, I want to lure him. I'd like to pull some of your protection off and see if we can get him to move in."

She pursed her lips and nodded, as if she had been expecting this all along. "Will you remember your promise?"

Jade bit his lip in irritation. "Yes, but I hoped you might reconsider. I lost . . . he killed another family yesterday. A sixteen-year-old boy. It's only going to get worse."

Darby and Thomas took this news together. Though their expressions barely changed, he could read the pain on their faces. At this point, he could only imagine what they were feeling.

Darby tried a smile and failed miserably. "I won't lure my son to his death, Mr. Marlow. I cannot." She looked to Thomas for support, but he looked down at the table. "Besides, when you get close enough to capture him, it won't save any lives to kill him." Her eyes dropped to Jade's chest. "You're much bigger than he is. It'll be just as easy for you to bring him in alive."

That may or may not be true, Jade thought, but he didn't say anything. He and Darby had made a deal, and he would uphold his end of it.

"So then will you help me get close enough to him?" Jade asked. For a moment, he hated himself for bringing this much pressure to bear on them. They looked so weary and they had already endured so much.

The symphony ended and the room fell silent. The clock ticking across the kitchen suddenly sounded incredibly loud. Jade looked at the tablecloth and waited for their answer. He wasn't sure what response he actually wanted.

"Will you be there, Mr. Marlow?" Darby reached her hand across the table toward him.

Jade grasped it awkwardly. "Yes. Of course."

Darby looked up at Thomas. "Then I'll do it," she said to her husband.

Thomas nodded once, just down. "We'll try, Mr. Marlow," he said.

"Jade. Call me Jade."

Darby was drumming her fingernails on the table, but she stopped and looked up at him. "Jade," she repeated thoughtfully. "Unusual name. Because of the color of your eyes?"

Jade nodded. "My father didn't like the name, but my mother can be quite stubborn."

"Now why isn't that surprising?" Darby said with a smile.

"Back to business," Jade said. "How often do you go to the movies?" He wanted to get the Atlasias out of the house. The more variables he could introduce into their environment, the more appealing they'd be to Allander as targets.

"Well, not much at all," Thomas replied.

"If you're asking me out, I prefer opera," Darby smiled.

"How many movie theaters would you say you go to on a regular basis?"

Thomas thought for a while, squinting his eyes and tilting his head back. "Three. Only three."

"Would Allander know about them all?"

"No," Darby said quickly. "Two are very old—Camera 9 and The Cutting Floor. We used to take him to those when he was younger, but the other opened after he . . . after he left."

"Good," Jade said.

He pulled the entertainment section from his back pocket and smoothed it on the table. Camera 9 and The Cutting Floor were both small theaters, which didn't surprise him. He had figured the Atlasias would enjoy older, more intimate theaters rather than the huge movie houses off Highway 280. He had been banking on it, in fact. There were two movies playing at Camera 9 and only one at The Cutting Floor, a revival of Orson Welles's *Othello*.

"We're sending you to Camera 9 tonight," he said. He looked up and saw Thomas's startled expression. "Not really," he said. "Just in spirit. What do you want to see? *Peril* or *Chances Are?*"

"*Peril?*" Darby asked.

"Sylvester Stallone."

She snorted and then covered her mouth in embarrassment. "I'm afraid to say he doesn't do much for me," she said. "All the grunting and what not. I'll take Paul Newman any day." She looked over at Thomas and smiled. "Sorry, dear."

He chuckled. "She's not big on action movies, son," he said apologetically. "Never has been."

Perfect, Jade thought. The choices were narrowing.

He had Alissa Anvers on the phone in less than five minutes. He had heard her speak on TV, but she sounded different over the phone. Her voice, as haunting as her dark eyes, had a deep feminine roughness to it, as if it would be sharp if rubbed the wrong way.

McGuire had said that Anvers's mother was on the force. Jade noted in her personality the unforced candor typical of someone raised in a police family. They spoke for a little while, then she agreed to meet him to discuss his plan.

"Not promising anything, of course," she said.

"That's fine," Jade replied. "Neither am I."

Alissa pulled up to the curb in a red Mazda and strolled up the walkway. She was dressed like someone used to being on camera, in a black skirt, black high heels and stockings, and a maroon silk blouse that accented the curves of her breasts.

"Mr. Atlasia," she said, taking Thomas's hand at the door. She smiled at Jade and Darby. "You must be Jade and Mrs. Atlasia," she said, her eyes lingering on Jade for an extra beat.

"You must be very bright," Darby said. When Alissa looked at her, Darby smiled and Alissa decided she was sincere.

Jade and Alissa went into the living room to talk while

the Atlasias ate their dinner. Jade had brought a file in from his car, and it sat on the antique wooden table between them. They argued for a while, going back and forth over how they would exchange information for help. He tapped the file nervously as they spoke; time was running out.

"Is there any way you can get on the air tonight?"

"I could," she answered coyly. "If I needed to."

"Look, Ms. Anvers—"

"Alissa," she said. "Please call me Alissa."

"Whatever. For this to work, I need it on the air as quickly as possible. Your channel has had by far the most extensive coverage of this case. I think he'll be watching, and if he is, I think it'll work."

"Mr. Marlow. As I said, there are a number of professional and ethical considerations. I can't just run any story you want."

"I said it's not just 'any story' I want." Jade's voice was rising and he felt the anger and frustration coming to the surface. "It's essential to this case."

"There are important considerations at hand here."

Jade stood up and opened the file. "You want considerations?!" He yanked out a photo of Janice Weiter's body and slammed it on the table. He followed it with a photo of Henry Weiter's body. Then Theodore Johnson's.

Alissa brought the back of one hand across her eyes, shielding her view. She turned sharply in her seat, her head angled away from the pictures, her eyes lowered.

After a few seconds, Jade realized she was crying. He had forgotten how upsetting seeing corpses could be for people who weren't used to them, when they weren't part of their lives.

"Ms. Anvers, I'm tired of hearing you regurgitate your junior year *Ethics in Journalism* textbook. We need to do this if we're going to stop him."

She turned around slowly. "All right," she said. "What do we have to do? Run a story on where they're going at a certain time?"

Jade shook his head. "No way. Too obvious. We have to give him a knot to untie."

Alissa pursed her lips. "For it to be realistic, we can't have it as a main segment. It's a people piece. Maybe I'll see if they'll run it as the orphan story to wrap things up."

Jade went to check on the Atlasias as Alissa called her crew.

Darby and Thomas sat on either side of Jade that night as they watched the news, all three of them showing signs of nervousness and irritation. There was the usual update on Allander, followed by a story on an earthquake in China. Then they suffered through the sports and weather.

Jade was worried that Alissa had changed her mind and canceled the story. He had pushed her pretty hard.

Finally Alissa came on, standing outside a big commercial theater in downtown San Jose. "People complain that there's too much violence in the movies. But movies can also be a wonderful escape. Thomas and Deborah Atlasia have certainly found themselves to be the center of attention once again since their son, Allander, escaped from the Tower at Maingate seven days ago. But they're teaching us all a little lesson in human dignity. They're holding their heads high, and letting their lives go on."

Darby laughed loudly, then covered her mouth with her hand.

"Tonight, the FBI continues one of the biggest manhunts in history, calling in even more men from their national headquarters. Tonight, Allander Atlasia will find himself fleeing just that much faster. Many people are holing up in their homes in terror. And what are Thomas and Deborah doing?"

The story cut to footage of Thomas and Darby entering a movie theater. It looked like a *Hard Copy* shot of a celebrity who did not consent to be filmed. Although the theater sign was not in the shot, the camera panned past a coffee shop next door to the theater as it followed the Atlasias walking in. CUP OF CHEER, a neon sign announced in the window. The coffee shop had been there for over thirty years. Allander would recognize it, and know that it was right next door to Camera 9.

The camera cut back to Alissa. "They're at the movies," she said. "Inside sources tell us that they're finding that a healthier way to spend their evenings, at least until the storm blows over. What's on the program tomorrow night is anybody's guess. For *Channel 5 Eyewitness News*, this is Alissa Anvers."

Perfect, Jade thought. Just like they'd discussed. There was no way they could come right out and say that the Atlasias were going back to the movies tomorrow—that would have been too obvious. But Anvers had alluded to the possibility, and that, in combination with the reference to "inside sources," would hopefully be enough to get Allander's juices flowing.

Allander would think that they'd seen *Chances Are* tonight, and since he'd know Darby would never go to *Peril*, that ruled out Camera 9 for tomorrow night. It was logical that they'd go to The Cutting Floor if they wanted to see another movie, so he'd keep an eye on it for the next couple of nights. There was one nighttime show tomorrow—Orson Welles's *Othello*, 8:00 P.M.

See you there, Jade thought. See you there.

Thomas got up, turned off the TV, and headed back to the bedroom. Darby pushed one long red nail into the soft skin of her palm. It left a crescent-shaped indentation that faded quickly. She did it again.

Jade stood up, dug the car keys from his pocket, and left quietly. The front door clicked shut behind him.

There was nothing left to do except wait.

JADE chose The Cutting Floor because there was only one theater, and the entrances were in the front by the screen. There was no back door to worry about. He positioned himself in the front row several hours before the film started. It meant he had a long wait, but it was worth it to avoid being seen entering the theater.

From his seat, Jade could see everyone who entered. Sitting in the front also ensured that he could rapidly get down the aisle in either direction. If he chose a spot farther back in the theater, he was sure to get boxed in. Here he was the gatekeeper; Allander would have to walk past him to get to the Atlasias.

Thomas and Darby were going to have what appeared to be their first unprotected outing since Allander's break. Darby had already expressed her annoyance several times at having agents around the house. If Jade hadn't been open with her from the start, he was fairly certain that she would have refused to allow twenty-four-hour surveillance. She wouldn't have wanted Allander's escape to alter her whole life. Jade had Alissa allude to this during her news story by saying that the Atlasias were "holding their heads high, and letting their lives go on."

Jade bet that Allander wouldn't be surprised to see his parents on an outing without any coverage. If anyone knew about Darby's resiliency, it was he.

And his parents would be awfully tempting tonight. No cars would follow them from their house. Jade had drawn up routes for five different FBI cars so they would cross paths with the Atlasias' car on the way to the theater and follow them briefly. Each car would turn off after a few blocks, and another car would take its place at the next street. In a move that caused more than a little grumbling, Jade had also asked the agents to drive their spouses' cars. The last thing he wanted was for Allander to see dark sedans pulling out behind the Atlasias every few blocks.

He was a little concerned about the Atlasias' trip from the parking lot to the theater, since there was no logical place to position undercover agents. He had decided to disguise two younger agents as television reporters. It would appear that they had staked out the theater on a gamble after seeing Alissa's story. They would run to the car and throw questions at Darby and Thomas, who would ignore them angrily until they made it to the safety of the theater itself. It was a perfect way to ensure in-your-face FBI coverage from the moment the Atlasias stepped out of their car, while at the same time keeping them highly visible.

One of these agents would lug a television camera with its inside mechanisms cleaned out, replaced with an eight-and-three-eighths-barrel .44 Magnum pointing straight out the lens. Just in case there wasn't time to draw.

Two agents would cover the lobby of the theater. Jade had decided to disguise one as an overweight mall security guard. Allander would certainly be aware of his presence, but he would probably dismiss him as one step above harmless. He'd never suspect the mall security guard to be an FBI field veteran. Jade had learned that visible disguises were often the most invisible.

He had put the other agent in the front ticket booth. She was dressed in the theater uniform: a worn-out, ill-fitting tuxedo shirt and black polyester pants.

Jade had made it clear to all the agents that they were

forbidden to shoot to kill, unless in clear self-defense, or if Allander went after bystanders. He had obtained these provisions from Darby with little prompting. That was because she knew they weren't relevant. Allander had a short list of people he wanted to kill; he wasn't interested in offing random civilians. That would be too easy for him.

Once the Atlasias made it through the lobby, they were all Jade's. He was confident that any attempt by Allander to attack his parents would occur in the theater during the movie. It seemed appropriate to his style. Highly dramatic.

Each time Jade thought about his promise to Darby, he cursed under his breath. She had certainly made his planning more difficult. Allander would have to be ensnared in an elaborate trap—Jade had known that all along, but it worried him that he couldn't proceed in his usual manner once he spotted Allander. He was most comfortable with sheer physical collision. When it all came down to it, that, even more than his tactical expertise, was what had made Jade famous; it was what he did best.

He wasn't entirely sure that he'd know how to manage to capture Allander when the time came. In some ways, the promise to Darby meant he couldn't use his greatest strength: fearlessness. It served him best, Jade had learned, in a fight to the death.

The theater started filling for the eight o'clock show, mostly with older couples, forty to sixty, plus a few professor types with sweaters and uncombed white hair.

The conversations around him were intellectual. A woman wearing thick glasses with red frames and an oversize flowered shirt sat with friends in the row behind Jade. She looked like an owl. Jade grimaced as she rattled on in a high, shrill voice. "The use of light and dark is what you have to watch for," she said. "The sense of enclosure will take your breath away."

At one point, an elderly couple sat in the front row, probably because they were nearsighted. Jade walked over to them calmly.

"I'm sorry," he said. "The front row is reserved tonight."

"For who?" the old woman asked.

"For me."

The woman started to answer, but the man took her by the arm and they moved back a few rows.

Darby and Thomas arrived a few minutes later. They didn't look over at him at all. Darby touched her forehead with her left hand. That was their signal that everything was okay so far. She never missed a beat, Jade thought.

He kept his eyes on the two entrances, swinging his head back and forth as if he were watching a tennis match. Each entrance had a short set of stairs leading up to the theater from the door at the bottom. He figured that from the time he heard the doors open or saw the light from the lobby, it took the average person about five seconds to walk up the stairs and through the entrance.

A group of high school students filed in. Oh, Christ, Jade thought, a field trip. They sat near the middle of the theater, laughing and rustling their candy wrappers.

Jade felt a sudden rush of heat move through his body, and he realized he was sweating heavily. What the fuck am I doing? he thought. Maybe Travers was right.

He checked the entrances, calming himself by inhaling deeply and counting each breath. Catching Allander justified everything. It had to. He was too dangerous. And the only cards Jade held right now were the Atlasias. If he'd learned one thing from his father, it was to take risks while they were still available.

He pushed thoughts of Darby and Thomas out of his head and thought of Allander. That made things easier.

He would sacrifice anything to get his hands on Allander. Keep the anger, he thought. Lose the other shit.

The lights went down and the film started. Once the entrance doors closed, Jade didn't have to be so alert. If they opened, a stream of light would flood into the theater.

He barely watched the movie, but he felt it flickering overhead in grays and blacks. He glanced back at the Atlasias from time to time as Orson Welles's booming voice filled the speakers. They were fifteen rows back, the first two seats in from the left aisle. With a slight movement of her eyes, Darby glanced over at him. She winked and Jade couldn't help smiling.

He leaned back and glanced up at the screen, but he couldn't focus on it, even for a moment. Just images and noises flashing overhead. He wondered if the Atlasias could concentrate at all, sitting back there like living targets.

The door opened and Jade leaned forward. His breathing intensified as he waited to see a silhouette. He counted six seconds until the person appeared. The figure had on a dress and a woman's hat, but Jade didn't relax until he saw her face. He wasn't expecting Allander to walk in without a disguise.

He heard occasional gasps and chuckles from the audience behind him, and the kids on the field trip giggled from time to time. He kept his eyes trained on the entrances instead of the screen.

The movie seemed to drag on for an eternity. It was hot and stuffy in the theater, and Jade was sweating profusely. Finally he was convinced that Allander wasn't going to come. When he thought back to his meeting with Alissa Anvers, he felt foolish for being so confident about his plan. He sighed, leaned back in his chair, and waited for the film to end. A fat man thumped down the stairs on his right to go to the bathroom.

Jade heard some rustling behind him and turned around. Two of the girls from the field trip were headed out into the aisle. Probably just going to get a snack, Jade thought, turning back to face the screen. Whispering loudly to each other, they came down the aisle and sat in the front row, to Jade's left.

Jade wasn't concerned. They were just splitting off the group, wanting their own space. He stood up and started walking over to them to tell them to move.

The doors on both sides of the theater opened at once. The artificial yellow light of the lobby fell in triangles on the fronts of the aisles. Jade whipped his head back and forth, feeling concern take hold inside him. Allander might have waited until someone else entered the theater on the other side, knowing it would create a diversion.

Jade froze, not sure which way to move. The film projection ran over his face and torso, and he had to turn from the glare.

The screen above was almost completely dark. "Put out the light, and then put out the light," Orson Welles growled as his hand sneaked into the bottom of the screen and extinguished a candle.

People in the audience started yelling at Jade.

"Down in front!"

"Hey! Do you mind?"

"'Scuse me, sir, we can't exactly see through you!"

Jade could hear his heart pounding in his ears. He had about three more seconds until the figures would make it up the stairs and into the theater.

If Allander was waiting for the ideal moment, it was right now. And Jade was not in control of the situation. He decided to throw secrecy out the window, and he started whispering loudly to the two girls to his left.

"You two! Up! Get out of the way!"

They looked at him nervously and half-stood to leave. Jade pivoted back and forth, checking the two doors while waiting for the girls to move. No one yet.

People behind him kept shouting.

"Hey! Shut up pal!"

"Why don't you sit down instead of yelling at those—"

"—can't fucking see—"

Jade turned to check on the Atlasias and was almost blinded by the stream of light from the projector. He caught a quick glimpse of Darby's face and she looked terrified. Thomas had his arm around her and he was pulling her down the row away from the aisle, just as Jade had instructed. In case of emergency.

Jade couldn't move in one direction or the other until he saw the figures entering the theater. Now he was yelling at the girls. "Get out of the way!"

They stood still, frozen in fear. Behind him, the theater filled with the sounds of angry viewers.

Jade felt as if he were moving in slow motion. The only thing he could hear was the pounding of his heart. It seemed to fill the whole theater, drowning out even the people behind him.

He swung back to his right and saw the person entering the theater. It was the fat man who had left to go to the bathroom. A figure flashed into view to his left and then disappeared behind the two girls. It was a male.

Jade could taste the sourness of his panic along the sides of his tongue. He had to move. Whether he was right or wrong, he had to move now. If that person got past him, it could be too late.

He jumped up onto the ledge that ran in front of the screen and sprinted toward the left side, his dark figure racing across the flickering black and white of the film. Light swirled across his body like tattoos. The two girls remained in their awkward half crouch, their mouths open. A few women in the audience screamed.

The man was moving quickly up the aisle and Jade leaped over the heads of the two girls, targeting the man's back. He hit him at the waist about five feet up the aisle, swinging one arm under his shoulder and across the back of his neck, and locking him instantly with his cheek smashed to the sticky floor. He rolled him over, his fist reared back, ready to slam down. It wasn't him. It wasn't Allander.

The audience was in an uproar, yelling and swearing and running. The lights came up and the film shut off. A manager's recorded voice boomed over the speakers. "Please exit the theater calmly and slowly. We are experiencing some technical difficulties. Do not push and shove."

The man looked back at Jade, confused terror glazing his eyes, but not a hint of anger. Jade stood quickly, shoving himself up off the man's back. People ran by them on both sides and Jade started pushing his way back to the Atlasias.

I'm not going to lose them, he thought.

A large man purposely blocked his path. Jade didn't see him at first through the crowd and his face collided with his chest. A large football stretched across the man's shirt with the number 22 underneath it.

Jade looked up at the huge, unshaven, football player. Probably a college lineman. He had a confident smirk on his face and a cowering blonde girlfriend to one side. He was out to look impressive.

Jade punched him once in the stomach, dropping his shoulder so his fist would hit just under his ribs, on the rise. The football player coughed loudly and staggered forward, bent at the waist. Jade brought his elbow down in a full swing, cracking him on the back of his head. He crumpled heavily to the floor.

Shoving the girlfriend out of the way, Jade blazed through the rush of people, up the aisle. He cut down one of the rows and jumped off a seat back. It bucked wildly under his weight, but he managed to stumble into another jump, landing off balance, next to the Atlasias. He pushed them roughly behind his back and turned, shielding them with his body.

The agent disguised as a security guard burst through the entrance, flattening a pair of teenaged boys against the door frame.

Jade waved him off. "We're covered in here. Concentrate on the front."

The agent nodded and held up his arm to stop the other agents who were heading toward him. He glanced back at Jade, then disappeared into the stream of people leaving the theater.

Jade had instructed the other agents to clear the area in case of an incident, and he was angry that they had wasted time by checking on him.

Darby's nails pried into his biceps as she held her balance. The three of them waited together, breathing heavily as the theater emptied. After a while, the sound in the lobby died down.

Jade was drenched with sweat. Wiping his arm across his forehead, he cursed himself out loud. He had panicked and ruined the plan.

Darby started to say something, but Thomas shook his head, catching her eye. They stood quietly, holding on to Jade's arms, which were spread behind him protectively like a pair of wings.

Finally, Jade led them out of the row and down the aisle. They walked from the dark theater toward the bright light of the exit.

THEY sat in the living room, silently surveying the dark brown carpeting. Darby wore a glazed expression, her mascara smeared across the top of her cheek. Thomas was in his usual spot near the fireplace. With his wrinkled clothes and weary demeanor, he looked like a recently fired executive in the middle of a drinking binge.

Jade sat with his head lowered, his forearms on his knees. He had kept the windows down as he'd driven to the Atlasias', to cool himself off. He had put the FBI cars back out front for the time being. Thomas and Darby were safe again, at least for now.

A glass dangled loosely in his hands. He raised it to his lips and shook loose a piece of ice, which slid into his mouth. Lowering his head, he crunched the ice slowly.

Darby had lost her voice answering questions following the incident at the theater. Local police, FBI, press, even the fire department had been drilling her from all sides while Jade met with the other agents to see if he could uncover anything useful about the evening's events. After enduring more than twenty minutes of questioning, Darby had weaved her arm through Thomas's and had raised her head to the group of men and women interrogating them. Something in the majesty of her expression had caused the pens to stop scribbling on the notepads.

She had spoken, her words coming in fragments as her voice faded in and out of hoarseness. "You know," she'd said softly to the throng of listeners, "we're more than this." She'd swung an open hand around to indicate the throng of listeners, the bright lights, the police cars. "We're more than just this."

As she had turned to go, McGuire had stepped forward and placed his hand on her shoulder, but she'd shaken it off and kept moving. McGuire had done nothing. Jade had just returned to retrieve the Atlasias, and if McGuire had decided to detain them further, he had been prepared to step in to prevent it. Thomas had followed his wife to the car, his eyes on the ground.

Once again, they had been subjected to a terrible ordeal, and Jade had been the one to do it. All for a failed plan, he thought as he looked at Darby, collapsed on the sofa, exhausted and drained. He crunched another ice cube and his eyes hardened. All Allander needs to succeed, he thought, is for me to do nothing. I'd burn any bridge to get to him.

He stood up and headed for the door without facing them.

"He knows now," Darby said, "that I've betrayed him."

Slowly, Jade turned around. "Yes," he said. "He does."

"I'm glad you're in our corner."

Jade looked at her for a long time. "So am I," he said.

He walked quietly to the door and left.

The two men crowded against each other as soon as they saw movement at the gate. A figure scaled the fence right next to the big gold letters that formed the arching Midland Hills Cemetery sign.

"Could be him. Could be Atlasia," the shorter agent whispered to his partner on lookout. He whipped out his binoculars and tried to focus them through the trees.

The other agent leaned against him, one hand resting on the walkie-talkie looped through his belt, the other on his gun. "Is it him?" he hissed.

"Think so. He's heading for the grave." He waited as another tree trunk blocked the figure from view.

The other agent strained his eyes through the dimly lit cemetery. "It's him. He's at the grave site," he whispered impatiently. He unholstered his gun and started to step from cover. "Call it in," he said.

He got three steps from the small grove of trees when the shorter agent called to him in a hoarse whisper. "Wait! Come back. It's not him."

The other agent backtracked. "What do you mean it's not him? Who is it?"

The shorter agent grinned. "It's Marlow."

"Jade Marlow?"

He nodded.

"What the hell's he doing here?"

"See for yourself."

The agent took the binoculars and peered through them. Jade stood before the grave, his head bowed meditatively. His eyes were open and his face wore a tight, serious scowl. His lips moved, offering jumbled phrases to the silent cemetery. For an instant, his face softened, and he ran his thumb across his bottom lip.

The agent lowered the binoculars and smiled at his partner. "Holy shit! It *is* him. Should we approach?"

"No way. Not unless you wanna lose a limb."

"So what should we do?"

"Just watch him, I guess. Make sure he doesn't dig them up or anything." He laughed, a short, hiccuping giggle.

The taller agent raised the binoculars back to his eyes. Jade was nowhere to be seen.

He drove along the streets, prowling in his bullet-riddled car. He didn't want to go home, but he wasn't sure exactly where it was he did want to go. He turned on the radio and a news brief blasted from the speakers.

"—today at The Cutting Floor. At least one male was injured and—"

He clicked it off and drove in silence, listening to his tires clatter over the sewer grates. After a while, he wasn't sure where he was.

The pounding started in his head, like a vise tightening incrementally around his temples. The throbbing increased until he could almost hear it. He reached into the glove compartment and pulled out a bottle of Advil. With his left hand on the wheel, he couldn't get the top off, so he banged it against the dashboard and the round pills spilled everywhere, clinking against the windshield and scattering across the passenger seat and the floor. He scooped four of them off the seat and swallowed them.

Shaking his head and pressing one hand to his face, he kept driving, still with no apparent destination. All of a sudden, he was in his garage. He stumbled from the car and into the house.

Somewhere deep inside him, he heard the singing start again.

He staggered to the study as if he were drugged, and there he collapsed into his chair. His hand groped for the drawer, knocking the lamp off the side of the desk. It swung from the cord, light twirling around the room. Without looking, he opened the drawer and pulled out a small music box. All he could hear was the rhyme in his head, even over the tune of the music box.

Eenie meenie minie moe.
Catch a retard by the toe.
Make him holler blow by blow.
Eenie meenie minie moe.

The music box stood open, the top of the circus tent long chipped away. His hand came down firmly over the lid of the box, trapping the music inside.

An eight-by-ten picture of Allander lay on the desktop. The music box covered part of it, but Allander's brown eyes leered up at Jade as if tracing the lines of his face. They were alive, his eyes. Even here, even now.

Jade ran his hands over his face and through his hair. The pain was not subsiding. He couldn't remember it ever lasting this long. He closed his eyes tightly, pressing his thumb and finger to the top of his nose.

The circus tent on top of the little music box spun to him in the darkness. Sounds echoed in his head.

The bang of a screen door as the thirteen-year-old boy ran from the house. A crying mother collapsing against the door frame.

He's going. He's going to see Mr. Hollow.

He ran down the street.

The retarded boy finally reached Mr. Hollow and he stepped over the neat circle of rocks to see him, reaching his hand to touch the golden hay sticking out from under the loose clothes. He was mesmerized by the scarecrow—so much so that he even forgot about the boys from whom he was fleeing. Mr. Hollow would protect him from anything, he thought. His mouth hung open as he paid homage to the great scarecrow. The pounding of footsteps stirred him from his trance, and he turned to face the four boys who circled him menacingly.

The thirteen-year-old boy sprinted down the road holding on to his cap so it wouldn't fall off. He turned off the road into a large field of waving foxtails and cursed as he saw the trampled trail leading through the high weeds. Running full speed, he disappeared into them.

Eenie meenie minie moe

In the crack of a gunshot, he was back above himself, sprinting through the waving field of foxtails. He ran with quick, expert steps, leaping over furrows, weaving past dirt mounds and gopher holes. His arms pumped furiously at his sides, and the sun fell over his shoulders.

Catch a retard by the toe

He could barely make out the chanting of the children, but as his vision cut ahead and he saw his younger brother still holding dumbly on to the straw that he probably thought was a hand protruding from Mr. Hollow's sleeve . . .

Make him holler blow by blow

. . . the sound rose and his brother turned, remembering again the boys who had been chasing him, and terror crept back into his face. He heard him yelling, "Jade! Jade!," over and over as the boys circled him . . .

Eenie meenie minie moe

. . . and closed in, and Jade heard their voices now and remembered the rhyming lyrics that his brother would recite in his slurred voice as he stumbled home after school, crying, and they were his call to duty, his incitement to fists and swings. Jade ran faster through the high weeds when he heard his name shrieked; a foxtail caught him across the left cheek, cutting deeply, but he didn't notice, he just ran faster; but the four had closed in and one stepped firmly over his brother's foot . . .

by the toe

. . . and his fist reared back to strike above the loosely blubbering lower lip.

The clock struck the hour, breaking Jade from his vision. It tolled gloomily, filling the house. Jade slid the photograph of Allander from under the music box and lifted it to his eyes.

In the living room, the phone rang.

"**I** enjoyed your little ruse earlier this evening. I can't believe they actually pay you for paltry efforts such as that. So obvious. Plus, Mother hates Orson Welles. Wouldn't be caught dead at one of his films. So to speak."

Jade's entire body tightened when he heard the purring voice. His shoulders and neck tensed, his chest flexed, his stomach grew taut.

The voice sounded like two pieces of silk rubbing together. It was low, smooth, unrushed. Jade felt a tingling in his stomach as the voice calmly continued, the voice from the audiotapes and the videos, the voice he had heard rise from the written transcripts as if they were so many burning bushes. He sat down on the couch, slowing his descent by leaning on the cushion with one arm.

"I'm glad to see I caught you speechless. I've heard that's quite a feat. Are you enjoying having your miserable life filled with me? Pictures? Tapes? Files? You're consumed with me, Marlow. I've seen how you work. With my own eyes, in fact. I'd almost consider it flattering if you weren't such an amateur." Allander chuckled. "I must say, I find the title 'Tracker' a bit overblown. You're more like an errant chaser."

"I'm getting to you."

"Yes, you're just waiting at home to . . . what? Gather your strength?"

Jade strained to identify any background noises, but the line was quiet. He picked up the map of Woodside from the floor and glanced over it. "Something like that."

Another chuckle. "Yes, yes, I see."

Jade was desperately thinking of how to get a rise out of him, some way to make him angry so he'd slip up. Deny his individuality, he decided. "You think you're smarter than the rest, but you work in patterns. You all do."

"That's right, you keen little copper. Was the corpse's head covered? Were the bodies posed? Were they . . . violated?" He paused for a moment, and Jade could hear him breathing. "I know the patterns so well I give them to you gift-wrapped. And you know the best part, Marlow? You still can't catch me."

Bluff called. They both knew Allander was right.

"I turned your prison inside out and killed everyone in it," he sneered.

"Not everyone."

"Oh yes. Mustn't forget Claudius."

Allander had lengthened Claude's name to Claudius. Jade caught the reference—Hamlet's uncle, who had murdered Hamlet's father and wed his mother. Another Oedipal figure, Hamlet's rival and the fulfiller of his desires.

"Well, before I go," Allander continued, "I was hoping you could allay my concerns about something."

A beat of silence.

"I was wondering why a grown man with no children would keep a picture of a retarded boy. Couldn't help noticing when I was in your bedroom. You know, Jade— it is all right that I call you Jade, isn't it?—I detect a similarity in the eyes. Between you and the retard, that is. It's amazing what one can find out with a little research."

Jade gripped the receiver so tightly that his entire hand was white. He was shaking all over.

"Just you push me, you fuck," he growled. Not the conventional way to keep a suspect talking, but he knew that Allander would time the call out at fifty-nine seconds anyway.

"Funny, Marlow," Allander replied. "That's precisely what I thought I was doing."

Jade heard him breathing on the other end of the line again, but he couldn't think of anything to say.

"Well, I had better let you get back to your case, hero. It seems you're a bit behind. But don't worry, I'm sure something will break soon."

"Only you, Atlasia. Only you."

Dial tone. Fifty-eight seconds.

Jade held the phone tightly to his ear even after the dial tone had faded to an automated recording. He rose from the couch and hurled the phone across the room. It smashed into a framed print, shattering the glass and bringing it crashing to the ground. The phone's cord snapped, its plastic plug still stuck in the jack.

Deep inhale. From the stomach to the rib cage to the chest. Exhale. Eyes closed. Jade imagined himself sprinting. Control, efficiency. He felt his shoulders loosen up. You never realize how tense you are until you relax, he thought. He walked his body slowly down a mental ladder, amazed at how many steps it took for his muscles to unclench. He was close to his end. The end of the fuse.

Allander had called him a "hero." The word rang through his head like a crash of cymbals. There are no fucking heroes, he thought. They're all dead and we've created playthings to fill the void.

The phone shrieked and Jade pivoted to his side, yanking his gun from the back of his pants and whipping it to aim at the door. His heart jerked in his chest. He couldn't remember ever feeling so jumpy.

On the second ring, he lowered his gun, walked over to the phone that lay among the broken shards of glass, and picked it up. Another ring as he realized he was holding the smashed receiver to an unconnected line. He shook his head and walked into the kitchen to pick up a functional phone.

"It's Darby. Bad time?"

Jade looked at the shattered picture frame and smashed phone lying at the base of the living room wall, and then at the gun that he was still gripping tightly. He let the gun clatter to the countertop. "You could say that."

"I was just calling to make sure you weren't wasting your energy and our time by sulking."

"What gave you that idea?"

Darby laughed. "I don't know. Motherly intuition. You can see how well it's served me in the past."

Jade wanted to say something reassuring, but couldn't find the words.

"We don't hold you responsible, you know. Just keep doing your job and we'll keep doing ours."

"I know," Jade said. "I am."

"Good."

"Get some sleep, huh?" Jade said.

"Oh sure. Then maybe we could play a few holes of golf in the morning."

"Good night, Darby."

He hung up and stared at the phone for a few moments before picking it up and ringing Tony.

"Hey. I need to talk to you."

"Fine. Beer. Pour Little Rich Kid. Twenty minutes."

The idea of going out caught Jade so totally off guard that he actually stopped to consider it. He hadn't realized how claustrophobic he'd felt the past few days, as if the sky were closing in on him.

He closed his eyes to think, and images pressed themselves into his mind—Orson Welles appearing out of
darkness, Darby's swollen face, two graves with no grass
grown over them yet, the stretch of a scarecrow's arms. A
flicker of mania brushed against him, the edge of an obses-
sion. He needed some distance. He was no good like this.

"All right," he said. He ran his fingers through his hair
and then across the scar on his cheek.

Allander smiled when he heard the sound of the crashing phone echo down the line from Jade's house across
the street. He lowered the cellular phone and slid it into
his pocket.

At first, Allander had been content to toy with Jade, to
engage in a kind of gamesmanship with him. He had
been drawn to Jade's astounding arrogance from the start,
but more and more, he was beginning to feel an emotional outrage. There had been the whole issue of the
obscene and obviously erroneous article in that tabloid,
but there was no need to get worked up over that. Still, he
felt increasingly drawn to Jade, in a way that was more
visceral than tactical.

He watched the house for a few minutes, enjoying the
chirp of crickets issuing from the bushes around him.
Pretty soon, the living room light turned off and he
heard Jade's car start up in the garage.

Allander cut back silently to his Jeep.

Jade raced across town in his car, cutting in and out of
lanes of traffic. Honking incessantly, he revved, swerved,
and fought his way along the road, passing other cars as
though they were moving backward.

At one point, he got stuck behind slow cars that
blocked all three lanes, but he managed to cut over and

then back, threading his way through them. As he accelerated past the last one, he smiled as the road yawned empty before him, and he pierced the openness ahead, nosing his car forward around turns and up hills.

He arrived at Pour Little Rich Kid five minutes early.

Jade sat for a minute studying his own eyes in the rearview mirror. He sensed a storm rising beneath the green surface.

Pour Little Rich Kid was a yuppie hangout. Like most bars of its type, it was all windows and mirrors, a spacious loft of a building. The mirrors were essential, for the customers looked at themselves constantly and adjusted their hair almost as often as they looked around to check out members of the opposite sex.

It was not the usual hangout for Jade and Tony, but it was slow on weeknights and the ale was brewed in the back. A large sign showed a twenty-something male wearing a cardigan and holding a tennis racket in one hand. His other arm rotated mechanically, tipping a huge ale to his mouth at regular intervals.

"Black and tan," Jade said to the bartender as he swung his long legs over the bar stool, taking his seat next to Tony. The bartender's nametag had "JIM" written on it in big red letters.

Tony looked over at Jade, who was already nervously laying the coasters side by side on the bar. "Oh, I'm fine, thanks. Yeah, work's going well and Maggie's doing just great," he said, smiling as a smirk spread across Jade's face.

"Oh, I'm sorry, princess. Forgot to ask how your day was."

"Forgiven. What's the word?"

Jade shook his head. "The FBI's already maxed out on the case. I need to know I can count on you if something comes up and I need more manpower."

"Sure, kid. Of course."

Jade straightened the coasters in a line with the edge of his hand. "So, any more big-league crimes in Falstaff? Kids playing mailbox baseball? Petty shoplifting? Overdue library books?"

"Yeah, fuck you, kid. Nothing too thrilling, though, gotta admit. Some guy beat up his girlfriend pretty bad last night, but he was calm by the time we got over there."

"No action, huh?" Jade leaned forward, paying attention to Tony for the first time.

"No. Nothing." He saw the look of disappointment cross Jade's eyes. "You know, some people consider that a good thing."

Jade downed his black and tan, holding the glass upside down as the creamy head slid into his mouth. He raised a finger to Jim, then lowered it and tapped the rim of his glass.

"I had a guy a few years back who beat up real bad on his kids. I was tracking him on a drug case, wound up at this shady apartment in Oakland. Kids all cowering in the background. I got over there and he looked charged, like he wanted to go. Didn't even try to escape. I was just praying he'd try'n hit me. He came on and I dropped him to one knee with a single shot to the gut." Jade's right arm tightened as he recalled the shot, the soft sink of his fist into the stomach just below the rib cage.

"Had a blade out and tried to swipe at my legs. I broke his fuckin' check in four places with the butt of my gun." He told the end of the story gazing at himself in the mirror behind the bar. His face had the dreamy look of someone recalling a romantic interlude.

Tony watched Jade with some concern. He cleared his throat loudly and took a long sip.

"How's the kid?" Jade asked.

"Tommy?"

"Whatever."

"He still remembers that time you brought him that—"

"Yeah, well, it was left over."

Tony lowered his head and smiled. "He's good. Starts kindergarten in the fall."

"That's good. Outta your hair more, huh?"

"Yeah. Guess so. Hadda birthday party last week. Clowns and cake and all that shit. It goes by so fast sometimes you can't even see it."

Jade stared into his own eyes in the mirror again. "Clowns, huh?"

Tony glanced over at Jade's expression and laid a hand on his shoulder. "All right. This nun gets into a cab, and the cabdriver asks her what's up with the celibacy vow thing, right? So the nun says, 'Well, maybe I'd consider having an affair, but the man would have to be Catholic, unmarried, and not have any children.' So the cabbie says, 'Well that describes me perfectly. Why don't you come on up here?' And the nun goes in the front seat and gives him a blow job."

"That was quick."

"Indeed. So she finishes up and the guy starts laughing, and she asks him, 'What's so funny?' And he says, 'Well, I'm Protestant, and I'm married with two kids.' And the nun looks at him for a moment, then shrugs and says, 'Well, that's okay, my name's Fred and I'm on my way to a costume party.'"

There was a long, uncomfortable silence as Jade continued to stare at his reflection. He normally knew how far he could get inside his quarry without losing his balance, but something about this case made it hard for him to find the line of demarcation. Allander kept moving, playing, changing. It was almost impossible to nail him down.

"That's the punch line, you see," Tony said. "The nun was a guy, which provides us with good homophobic humor." He looked at Jade's serious expression and stood up, raising his hands in defeat. "Well, as good company as you've been, I'm outta here. Gotta get back to Maggie and 'the kid,' you know?" He tossed money on the bar.

"Yeah."

"See ya later, hotshot."

As the door banged shut behind Tony, Jim walked over. "Hey," he said, "we're closing up."

Jade turned slowly to face him, his eyes unfocused. Jim blanched.

"I'm gonna lock up the front then, so no one wanders in. I gotta cash out in the back. You take your time and I'll let you out when you're ready." Jim spoke slowly as he inched away, a lion tamer backing out of a cage.

Jade ignored him, gazing ahead at his reflection in the mirror. He thought of the sprawling bodies, the wash of blood on the walls, Leah's frightened little face floating above the sheets of the hospital bed. People were dying because of him. He glared at himself in disgust.

He sensed a slight movement in the mirror, reflected from outside. He wouldn't have noticed earlier, but it was late now and the streets were empty. His eyes darted to his left, fixing the spot on the mirror and focusing on the image. It was difficult given the darkness outside and the reflections of the bar's lighted interior.

It seemed like an eternity as he waited for his eyes to adjust to the image outside, but he sat like an animal, head trained on its prey. Finally, he saw the two eyes peering at him from the darkness; he could make out the sweep of the cheekbones and the casually drifting hair.

The rest of the face and body faded straight into the night, a ghostly apparition.

But it was enough for him to know.

Jade's lips moved silently. He mouthed the name once before he was on his feet and across the bar in a few giant strides, his bar stool sent spinning like a top.

FOUR

THE

CONVERGENCE

on his cheek.

Jim, the bartender, stood fearfully regarding th
age from inside the bar as Jade approached.

THE thick door was locked and Jade's arm almost ripped out of its socket as he tried to yank it open. He could have sworn he felt the big brass handle give slightly at the screws. He was locked in the bar.

Yelling at the top of his lungs, Jade seized the nearest stool and raised it above his head, charging the window. He followed the stool through the window as pieces of glass showered over him. Hitting the ground in a roll, he was on his feet almost immediately, whirling to check all around him, moving not just his head but his whole body.

Then, he stood perfectly still. Steam drifted slowly up from a sewer grate and somewhere, far away, someone tuned a violin. The streets were empty. No one. Nothing. Just the tinkle of a shard of glass falling from the window's shattered frame.

He moved swiftly to check the alley next to the bar and along the neighboring streets. As he pursued imaginary footsteps, the heat of his temper rose until it flushed his cheeks, and his breath hammered in his throat. He had lost him. He had lost Allander.

"FUCK," he screamed, kicking a metal trash can end over end across the bar's parking lot. The sudden ache in his foot returned his clarity. He took a deep breath, then walked slowly back to the bar, his fingers tracing the scar on his cheek.

Jim, the bartender, stood fearfully regarding the damage from inside the bar as Jade approached.

"Don't you *ever* lock me in!" Jade yelled. Reaching through the broken window, he seized Jim by the shirt, lifting him off his feet. He yanked him outside, hurling him to the ground. Jim skidded to a halt facedown on the street, and Jade was on him immediately, pulling his head back with a fist laced with his hair. His other hand was around Jim's throat.

"I didn't do anything," Jim said, struggling to catch his breath. "Don't . . . don't hurt me." He tried to shake his head but his chin was ground into the pavement.

A station wagon turned onto the street, its headlights catching Jade in the face. He squinted into the light. The vehicle slowed as it approached, and Jade saw a young couple gazing at him in horror.

As they passed, he noticed a young girl in the back-seat. She wore a bright yellow slicker and had one hand raised, palm open, pressed to the window. There was a look of fright in her eyes, a confused terror about the world outside.

Jade felt a flash of shame. Goddamnit, he thought. What's she doing up so late?

Her eyes continued to watch Jade as the car passed and disappeared into the night.

Jade blinked heavily, fighting through the rage clouding his mind. What the hell am I doing? he thought. He looked down at his knee in the bartender's back, his hands gripping the man's head like claws.

Like an animal squatting over its kill, Jade thought. Like a fucking animal.

He released Jim's throat and rose carefully from his back. "Jesus, I'm . . . Jesus, I'm sorry."

Jade reached to help Jim to his feet, but Jim jerked away from his touch. His chin was bleeding and Jade could see that he was crying. Jade's face was red with regret and self-loathing. He took a step forward, but Jim cowered away from him.

Jade opened his mouth but nothing came out. Silently, he turned and walked to the BMW. There was a squealing of tires, and Jim was alone in the parking lot.

Allander sucked the cool night air through his teeth. His feet swayed beneath him, dangling off the roof as he watched the black car speed away.

Jade had nowhere to direct his rage, and Allander sensed that he knew he was losing ground. I'm so far inside him I can touch him wherever I want, Allander thought.

He tilted his head back and stretched his arms before getting up to head back to the new house. *His* house.

A leg protruded from the glade of trees, a blue-and-brown hiking boot on the foot. A line of blood ran over the exposed calf, matting the thick black hair.

Allander stood with his back to the body, gazing through the last line of trees to the edge of the cliff. The sun was rising gloriously, its golden rays glittering off the ocean surface.

There was a drop of several hundred yards that ended in a small forest just outside the grounds of Maingate. The gates were laid open to the world as workers scuttled back and forth, towing out ruined materials and bringing in new equipment and tools.

What the prisoners would have done to see the gates spread like that for just a moment during their captivity, Allander thought. The entire facility was emptied of inmates for these weeks of repair. With the exception of Claude Rivers and the single guard watching him on the Tower, Allander had emptied it. He had emptied Maingate.

As he looked out over the main prison and saw the Tower in the distance, he slid his hand under his shirt to his nipples. They were hard in the crisp San Francisco air, and he ran his fingers over them, one at a time.

He had taken a new house for himself in the western hills of San Francisco. It was being entirely remodeled, so it had no decorations or heating, just bare walls and a few pieces of covered furniture. For some reason, construction had ceased, but Allander had still prepared a careful escape route in case workers showed up.

He was quite content with his new home. And how wonderful that he could keep the lovely red Jeep from his former house in Palo Alto.

He had found a small motorized saw in the front closet of his house, no doubt left there for use in the remodeling. He had used it last night, employing one of the extra-long, heavy-duty extension cords he had found, and wrapping a water-cooler insulator around the saw to try to dull the noise, since he was working out in the open, away from the protection of his home. But he needn't have worried; the traffic had drowned out everything anyway. And now it was ready—waiting, hidden. His entrance. That was for later, however. He had to focus on today, on completing the first part of his plan. There was so much to do, so many things he'd set in motion.

For the past week, he had been timing the workers at Maingate. They usually left the site at around four o'clock (bless those government workers). The guard on the Tower switched at 6:00 A.M. and 4:00 P.M. There was never more than one guard, probably because the rest had been moved to San Quentin to deal with the Maingate overflow. They were accustomed to having two men guard eighteen Tower prisoners; they probably figured one-on-one was a breeze.

Someday soon, he'd have to go down and take care of things. He'd have to wait until after they left, of course, although he had no choice but to hide his supplies there during daylight. Aside from the Tower guard and Claude Rivers, Maingate was pretty much abandoned by four-thirty. He'd have to remember to wear the pair of dusty overalls from his house, though, just in case someone saw him—that way they would think him one of the workers.

He took pleasure in the solid, unwavering path of his plans.

Walking over to the green Blazer on the path, he opened the door using a key from the carabiner key ring he had lifted from the body. He drove the Blazer far enough into the woods so that it was no longer visible from the road. Leaving it behind a cluster of trees, he got out and headed back to the body, looping his arms under its shoulders so he could drag it to the Jeep. He grunted with effort as he lifted it in the back, pushing it face-down across the seats. He would dump it somewhere down at the base of the hill.

Throwing the car into drive, he glanced over at the second body he had propped up in the passenger seat. He leaned over and patted its knee.

He would keep this one.

Jade's eyes opened; the ringing was so loud that at first he thought it was inside his head. He rolled over and lifted the phone off the cradle.

"Marlow. Travers."

He groaned and rolled onto his side. "If you want to gloat, I'd prefer a singing telegram."

"No time, thanks. We got him located. Placed a call and stayed on the phone sixty-three seconds. Three seconds too long. Must've mistimed it." Travers's voice was charged with excitement.

Jade pulled on his sunglasses in an attempt to shield the onslaught of light from the crack beneath his curtain. No way, he thought. No way he fucks up like that, not by three seconds.

"Who'd he call?"

"His former defense attorney. Made a few threats, shook the guy up pretty bad."

Jade rubbed his eye with the heel of his hand. It wasn't adding up. Allander would've known that line was hot. "Where's he fixed?"

"Mountain View. Cross section of Fisk and Glen Boulevard—4512. We have it listed as unoccupied. Perfect hideout. We're set up and we're moving in twenty. Be there in fifteen."

"I'll be there in ten," Jade said, and was immediately out the door.

The complex was surrounded when Jade arrived. It was a two-story strip of small apartments, guarded by a thick brown railing. The apartments were arrayed in two wings that met in the middle, giving a sense of enclosure to the front parking lot. Heavy green curtains were visible through most of the windows on both floors. Probably low-income rental units, he decided.

The building sat back off a fairly busy four-lane street. Jade glanced up the street and saw road workers in orange vests diverting traffic. Jade stood tall next to the officers crouching behind their car doors. FBI all the way. Flashing lights on undercover cars. He walked through the vehicles lined in the front parking lot.

McGuire looked up at him. "Get behind a door, Marlow," he hissed.

"He's not gonna shoot from far away," Jade said, surveying the scene broadly. "Not intimate enough."

McGuire yanked him down by pulling beneath his knee. "You don't know that. He's never been cornered before," he said.

Jade glared at him for a long time, biting his cheek. "Be grateful you have your title between us," he finally said, looking away.

Travers appeared at their shoulders. "Nice you could

show up, Marlow. We've been in position for fifteen minutes without response. We have snipers on neighboring buildings and men in position there, there, and there." She pointed to the black-vested men with Heckler and Koch MP5 9-millimeter full automatics scattered on the roof and under the windows. Agents were flattened against the wall near the corner apartment on the second floor.

Jade reached behind his jeans and fondled his Sig Sauer—P228, 9 millimeter. Stopping power. A lot of firepower here and probably nothing to use it on, he thought.

"We waited for you to give the final countdown, Marlow," Travers said, handing him the megaphone.

Jade waved it off. He looked at the corner apartment, shaking his head.

Travers glanced at McGuire.

"All right," he said. "You take care of it."

She moved out slightly from her crouched position behind the car door.

"Probably not a bright idea to use a megaphone," Jade said. "Just a guess, but I'm assuming you don't want to come off like an authoritative asshole during negotiations."

"It seems like you don't even think he's in there, Marlow," Travers replied coolly.

"Good point," Jade said. "What the fuck." He gestured her forward.

"ATLASIA," she bellowed through the megaphone. "WE'VE GIVEN YOU AMPLE TIME TO RESPOND. IF WE DO NOT RECEIVE A SIGNAL FROM YOU IN SOME FORM, WE WILL TAKE THE HOUSE."

"What if the signal's a dead hostage, Travers?" Jade muttered under his breath, but she didn't hear him.

"WE'RE GIVING YOU A FIVE COUNT." She paused and ran her fingers over the top of her left ear, pushing the hair back off her cheek. Jade thought he could make out the scent of her perfume.

"FIVE ... FOUR ... THREE ..." Travers looked nervously to McGuire, who nodded her on. "TWO ..."

Jade stared at the pavement. Nothing made sense—the sixty-three-second phone call, the look of the shabby complex, the fact that the apartment was on the second floor.

McGuire leaned against the car in a raised crouch, holding his gun up by his cheek. His left hand was shaking back and forth in a nervous tick. Something on one of his fingers was flashing in the sunlight. His wedding ring.

Jade's mouth went entirely dry. He heard an echo of a conversation in his head. *Where's McGuire? Actually, he's at his kids' baseball game.*

"ONE," Travers shouted into the megaphone. Everyone went into motion. Jade leaped to his feet and ran in the opposite direction of the other agents, heading for his car.

The house imploded with bodies as FBI agents crashed through the doors and windows, springing from the ground and swinging from the rooftop. They led with large black boots and pointed barrels. It seemed as if every point in the apartment was instantly covered by the agents' guns.

Travers was already up and running and she leaped through the smashed front door into the apartment. It was bare and unfurnished, with wooden floors and white walls. On the floor in the middle of the living room sat a single black phone. It was old-fashioned, its big receiver clunked down heavily on the metal jaws.

She moved slowly through the scattered agents.

"Where's Marlow?" one of them hissed nervously. She didn't know, so she said nothing.

The agents stood motionless, their guns trained on the zone of the apartment for which they were responsible. Travers felt as if she were walking through a sculpture garden. The sound of her footsteps knocked through the empty apartment like raps on a door.

There was nothing in the entire apartment except the phone. Travers circled back to the small living room and stopped. They all stood perfectly still, stunned by the silence.

The phone rang, a high, shrill jangle, startling everyone. It rang three times before Travers picked it up. Still the agents didn't move.

McGuire had stumbled into the house a few seconds after her, and he stood behind her panting as she raised the receiver to her ear.

"What?" she asked tightly.

"Ms. Travers, I presume. I've read so much about you. Could you be so kind as to place Agent McGuire on the line before you can get a tracer in place?" Allander asked. He knew they wouldn't have brought a tracer with them; they were expecting more than a phone. He just wanted to play with her a little.

"Yeah, but tell me—"

"Your time is up, Agent Travers. I need to speak to the important people now. Like I said, put your boss on." "Boss" would get to her, Allander thought. He was sure of it. "Get him. Now."

Travers realized she didn't have any options without losing the line. She bit her cheek and held the phone out silently to McGuire. His eyes lit up. "Giving his demands?" he asked, whispering anxiously.

Travers said nothing. He's playing with all the cards right now, she thought. I doubt this is about demands. He doesn't need to ask us for anything.

"McGuire here." He spoke in a gruff, efficient voice. Travers could tell he was intimidated as hell and trying to cover it with the briskness of his tone.

"Well, Agent McGuire. Let's play a little guessing game to find out where I am, shall we? I'm thinking of a lovely crocheted wall piece with dark brown beads hanging from its fringes. Looks like it belongs on the floor of a doghouse, but someone made the unfortunate decision to display it as a wall ornament. It's a virtual shrine to the seventies, as seems to be most of the house. And look, here's a beautiful blue marlin plastered above the fireplace, evincing the Hemingwayesque masculinity of the man of the house. How noble in reason. In action, how like a god."

"H N E." Three letters splashed in crimson, their boundaries marred by the drip of the dark blood. They looked ready to slide right off the window; they were drifting, living letters.

Allander's bloody fingers were wrapped around a cordless phone. He moved into the kitchen and plucked a photograph off the refrigerator, leaving a red smudge across the front.

"How cute," he said into the phone. "A photograph of Grandma on her eightieth birthday. However did you fit all those candles onto the cake . . . Agent McGuire?"

Allander smiled in awareness of the stunned silence on the other end of the phone. He walked into the living room and faced the two boys who were bound to chairs with tape.

They were about fifteen and sixteen years old, just

starting to build muscles in their chests and shoulders. Tears ran over the tape that bound their heads firmly to the high backs of the chairs. Only a small strip of their faces was visible, their eyes and a thin band of their cheeks.

Behind them on the floor lay the body of their mother. Both of her ears had been cut off and her throat was slashed. Allander had used the spout of blood that welled from the wound as his paint bucket. The blood was still warm when he dipped his fingers into it.

Firecrackers were pushed into the boys' ears. Allander had wedged them tightly into the ear canals so they would be sure not to slip.

He walked over to the counter and calmly picked up a book of matches. The boys' panic found expression only in their eyes. They were taped to the heavy chairs so tightly that even their most frenzied wrenchings barely moved their heads or bodies.

Allander watched how their eyes flicked around the room with urgency and disbelief. They were terrified. He loved having their complete attention, loved them watching his every move, knowing that their lives depended on it.

As he bent to light the fuses of the firecrackers, he looked like a mother tucking in her children. His lips brushed against the sides of their cheeks as he leaned over them.

"Hear no evil," he whispered.

Travers watched McGuire's eyes widen as he held the phone to his ear. Everyone in the room jumped when they heard the loud bangs from the phone. They echoed off the stark walls of the apartment.

McGuire kept the phone to his ear for a few moments

longer and then held it out to Travers with trembling fingers. Travers could hear the dial tone.

"Oh my God," McGuire said. "He's in my house. Oh God."

He had barely finished speaking before the agents in the living room sprang to life, clearing the house and jumping into vehicles.

McGuire remained frozen in precisely the same place, alone in the small apartment. He was still holding the telephone out with one shaking hand, and his right cheek began to quiver beneath his eye.

THE house finally quieted down. The agents had driven to McGuire's house in the city as quickly as possible after radioing in help from the SFPD. McGuire lived in the Sunset District, on Ninth and Irving.

Travers was not surprised to find Jade already there, sitting calmly in a kitchen chair. He shook his head when she and the others walked in. Too late. At least he'd gotten there before the blood could clot.

When he'd first arrived at the house, he'd been furious that he had missed Allander. He had called 911 to get ambulances on the way, then had left the boys taped to the chairs to look for him. After checking the house and yard for any trace of him, being careful not to disturb the crime scene, he had walked out onto the street.

Even though Allander had left no visible evidence, the location of McGuire's house tipped his hand. It sat on a network of wide-open streets with very few alleys. Visibility was extremely high. Since he would have had to stick to the streets, it would have been nearly impossible for Allander to escape on foot and get very far. He had come in a car. And for the first time, he had brought something with him: firecrackers. That could mean he had a base from which he was working. Somewhere he could keep the car and make his plans. Somewhere they could catch him.

Jade could feel the net tightening. Just had to pick up a few more corners to trap his prey.

He went inside to free the boys.

The ambulances picked them up and took them to the ER at St. Mary's. The body of McGuire's wife was left for further examination. Most of the agents had departed after searching the area, and only the forensics team remained.

Allander had slipped away in broad daylight, leaving no traces. It was almost as though he wasn't real; they could only sense him, like an image seen through murky waters. The other agents noticed a hint of a smile on Jade's face, though they couldn't tell why it was there.

Travers dealt with the neighbors, interviewing them in case they had seen anything, or could offer any leads. It proved futile, of course. When she returned to the house, Jade was still in the kitchen, sitting in one of the high-backed chairs, his right leg pumping up and down excitedly. A cup of ice sat on the table in front of him.

"What?" Travers asked. She was exhausted and her hair was down, fanned loosely across her shoulders.

Jade looked up, noticing her for the first time. He stood, swinging the cup of ice with his thumb and forefinger. "We know he's somewhere. He's at a fixed location now, operating from a base. We can check for clues. Get forensics in here." He turned to the door and yelled, "FORENSICS!"

Two men scurried into the room. "I want a full materials check," Jade ordered. "Fibers, particles, anything. Comb the place—the rug in the living room especially; it could've picked up a lot of shit."

The men stood there and stared at Jade.

"Well, go. What are you waiting for? Go."

One of the agents cleared his throat. "Uh. We already did. Picked up some particles. Already got the read from lab. Lead. Lead traces in the carpet, definitely a foreign material tracked in here. Also got some hairs, but no surprises there."

"Lead? What the hell does that indicate?" He looked back and forth at the two men, who shrugged. He shook his head in disgust. "All right. Good. Out."

They left.

He turned to Travers. His mind was so tightly wound he felt as if it might snap. "He's working from somewhere. Got room, got time, got privacy. Resources."

Jade ran his thumb across his bottom lip over and over, feeling it push softly to the side. "A house. Deserted, empty, or hostages. No, no hostages. Wouldn't want to leave them."

"He could've broken in, killed a family," Travers said.

Jade was struck with a sudden, horrible thought. What if Allander had used his pistol? The Glock that he'd stolen from the back counter. Jade had not yet told anyone about it. He was hoping to keep it his and Allander's little secret, at least until it became relevant.

At least he hasn't used it yet, he thought. At least not yet.

He nodded. "Could be. The average response time for SFPD to this site is sixteen and a half minutes. He would've known that we'd radio in after he called us. He probably even timed his call by it. And this is a bad neighborhood to make an escape by foot. Too open, way too open. He came here in a car, left in a car. And he would've wanted to be back to his base by the time police arrived here, even before to beat the roadblocks. I'd say he'd want to be back to his base in fifteen minutes."

Jade ran to the kitchen desk and yanked the drawers out, emptying them on the floor. He sank to his knees and dug through the papers, finally pulling out a map of San Francisco. He returned to the kitchen table and cleared it with a sweep of his arm. His glass shattered on the floor, and the salt and pepper shakers rolled in arcs on the linoleum.

Travers closed her eyes and bit her lip. Wotan had come down on her hard for bailing out of the movie theater operation. He had made it clear that she was to provide support for all of Jade's plans, no matter how much she disagreed with them. She breathed deeply as she surveyed the mess in the kitchen, and forced herself not to comment.

Jade unfolded the map on the table, spreading it out before him. He walked back over and grabbed a thick black marker from the pile he'd left on the floor.

"Okay. We're here." He circled the location of McGuire's house. "Fifteen minutes by car could put him anywhere from . . ." His voice trailed off as he sketched an approximate circle on the map with the black marker.

The circle stretched down to San Francisco State and out to Van Ness in the east. He didn't want to push the perimeter too far downtown because the traffic would have slowed Allander. The top of the circle ran up to Presidio Heights, and to the west it covered the ocean coast.

"I want a full listing of all incidents in this area in the last week. Break-ins, homicides, stolen cars, anything," he said.

"That's a big circle, Jade," Travers said skeptically.

"It's a start. Put a couple of your desk jockeys on it pronto. Call it in now."

As he headed out, he heard Travers pick up the phone.

Spring was giving way to summer, and the late-morning heat was fierce and steady. Jade pulled into his garage. He wiped the sweat from his cheek as he got out of his car, immediately stumbling over something in the garage.

He looked down and saw a growing pool of black paint

spreading at his feet. As the familiar smell rose to his nostrils, he swore loudly. After touching up his bookshelves the other night, he'd forgotten to put the paint away.

He bent over to pick up the bucket and felt a burn in his throat. He backed up, coughing. The shit they put in this stuff, he thought. Not exactly meant for breathing.

He snapped his fingers twice, ran into the house, and grabbed the phone. "Forensics. Yeah, yeah. This is Marlow. I need someone on the McGuire house from this afternoon."

He waited, his knee jackhammering up and down. Finally one of the agents got on the line.

"Yeah. Marlow here. I have a question for you about the lead particles you picked up at McGuire's. Were they pigmented?"

The forensics agent sounded surprised. "Why yes. They were dark green. How'd you know?"

"They're paint scrapings, probably from a house being remodeled. Dark green—must be exterior paint. If someone sanded it off, the lead would probably settle separately since it's heavier."

"But they haven't used lead in paint for over twenty years."

"Twenty, huh?" Jade said, scribbling down the number on a piece of paper. "I figured it was somewhere around there. Thanks."

He hung up and called Tony.

"Whaddya want, kid? Always calling me for something."

"Tony. I need you."

"Well, I never would have thought—"

"Not now. I need you to use your force for some legwork." Jade paused. "It's kind of shit work."

"Well, I appreciate your thinking of me."

"I got Atlasia nailed down to an area of San Francisco. I think he's in a house that's undergoing a major remodel. The house is at least twenty years old, and it used to be painted dark green." He told Tony the rough bearings of the circle he'd drawn around the map he'd taken from McGuire's house.

"Well, kid, you know I got the men and the time, but there's no fucking way we can search an area of SF that big just based on a remodel and a house color. What the fuck?"

"Okay, okay. Hang on." Jade was quiet for a moment while he thought. "He's in a secluded house with a lot of privacy, no common walls with other houses. He needs privacy to plan and he doesn't want to be seen. That means it's gotta be in a rich neighborhood. It's probably elevated. That should cut out a lot of neighborhoods in that circle. Call around Pacific Heights and rich communities like that, find out which companies do major remodels. It'll be a pain in the ass, but it should be do-able."

"All right. I can put a couple men on it, but obviously only when things are slow. I don't know how long it'll take."

"Great. Just move it along as quick as you can."

He had barely placed the phone back on the cradle when it rang again. He picked it up. "Yup."

"Marlow. Travers. Ever heard of call waiting?"

"Call who?"

"Forget it. I got a list of incidents in that area, wanted to run them by you."

"Shoot."

"Only three stolen cars reported in the last week; amazingly, all have been recovered. There's a long list of muggings. I'll start with *A*."

"Skip 'em. He's not a mugger. What do you have on homicides?"

"We have three. One's a drive-by shooting off Haight. Then we have another restaurant hit, but we're pretty sure it's mob. And a random shooting at the edge of Sutro Heights."

"Sutro Heights, huh?"

"Yeah. Let's see. Steven Lloyd Francis. Nineteen. Left in a parking lot. No motive. Two bullets to the head. Early this morning."

"Gun?"

"Let's see." There was a pause and Jade heard Travers flip a sheet of paper. "Looks like a forty. Both bullets made a clean exit, so that's all we got from ballistics right now."

Jade swallowed hard. His Glock was a .40. His head felt numb, as if he were walking through a dream. He cleared his throat harshly and tried to focus. "Are you at headquarters?" he asked.

"Yes."

"Call the family. I want to interview them. I'll be by to pick you up in a half hour."

Jade hung up and went to wash his face. He let hot water fill the sink, then he leaned over it, inhaling the steam. He splashed the water over his face, drawing his hands firmly down his forehead, over his eyes, and around his cheeks. When he shook his head and raised his eyes to the mirror, he realized the phone was ringing again.

"What am I, the fucking operator?" he said angrily, heading back to the living room. He picked up the phone. "What."

"Well, Mr. Marlow, I was very disappointed in your performance at the bar last night. I must confess, I had expected a little more from you."

Even though Jade had heard it hundreds of times, Allander's voice still took his breath away. So close, so fucking close. And directed right at him. He struggled to keep his voice even. "No shit, huh?" he said. "Guess we'll have to do the dance again sometime soon."

"Oh, we most assuredly will. There will be time for that later. And more. You know—the real test. I can't wait to get my little hands on them." Allander said "little hands" with a German accent—like it was "little hanz."

The real test, Jade thought. A nonchalant way to refer to killing his parents. After the movie theater fiasco, it was in the open between him and Allander. He knew where Allander was going, and Allander knew he knew it. That just made it all the more enticing.

Allander sighed. "So many loose ends to tie up."

"Look, this whole prank call thing is getting a little old. So unless you wanna chat for, say, sixty-one seconds, I don't really have the time."

"Oh. What a disappointment. And I thought you were going to undo me at last with your sharp questioning."

"I don't have to. With how you are, you'll reveal yourself."

"I see. And how's that, Marlow? Oh yes—I'll stumble into Dr. Yung's office with a severe onset of psychosomatic blindness."

Always moving, always mocking.

"Hey, Atlasia," Jade said softly.

"Yes?"

"I had lunch with Darby yesterday. She's a . . . charming woman."

Jade heard an immediate click and then the dial tone. Allander was too smart to get upset on the phone, but Jade had managed to get in a solid shot. And more important, he had known just where to punch.

TRAVERS turned in the passenger seat to face Jade. "Well, we got an interesting complaint from a bartender today. Filtered to us through the local police. Said some maniac yanked him through a shattered window and dribbled his head on the pavement."

"I find 'dribbled' excessive," Jade said.

"What gives?"

Jade looked at his hand, on top of the steering wheel. "I had an off night," he said.

"Well, it was pretty bad form, Marlow."

"I am well aware of my form, Travers. Much more than you think. Let it go, all right?"

She was surprised that he seemed upset about it, so she backed off. "Well, you don't have to worry. Someone up high is giving you all the room you need for this case. Charges were mysteriously dropped."

"You wouldn't have had anything to do with that, would you?"

She looked out the window. "No. Why would you ask that?"

"I just think it's odd that no one's checking up on me. No one at all." He glanced over at her, but she was watching the side of the road. "The reports back to headquarters must say I'm competent."

"'Competent' might be an overstatement," Travers finally said. "Let's let this go, too, huh?"

Jade nodded.

"McGuire's house was a nightmare. Atlasia's still more than a step ahead of us."

"I'm getting there," Jade said. "He's definitely gonna go after his parents. We got that in the open after the theater ruse. On the phone, he called it 'the real test.'"

Travers whistled. "I still can't believe he called you again. You really got him hooked."

"He loves talking about himself so much he can't resist. And his parents. He said he couldn't wait to get his 'little hanz' on them."

Travers laughed. "That's great."

"What?"

"It's a parapraxis, a classic Freudian slip. 'Little Hans!' Freud's most famous case study about the boy—"

"—with the unresolved Oedipal complex," Jade finished. "It's more like a pun than a slip. Allander's fully aware of the game here. But still, great call, Travers."

Her eyes darted around the dashboard as she tried not to smile. "Well, you're not the only one doing your homework."

"His 'little hands,'" Jade repeated. "He's been trying to prove how small all his victims are compared to him. Compared to his experience. He's just been building himself up psychologically to face his parents. And he's 'little' only when he faces them. David and Goliath. The final challenge is the one that scares the shit out of you."

"The one nobody else can take on," Travers said.

They were quiet for a while as the car sped across the city. It had taken some time, but Travers had finally learned to ride with Jade without gripping the door handle.

"You seem pretty excited about this lead," she said. "What makes you think it's related?"

Jade flushed. "Just a hunch."

"It's a completely different MO, though," she said.

"It was a functional killing."

"Functional?"

"Yeah. He must've wanted something specific or he would have left more than two bullet holes."

"Well, the body was moved. Abrasions on the elbows and the heels of the shoes. Left in a deserted lot on the edge of Sutro Heights, but from the twigs and dirt samples they picked up, looks like he was killed somewhere more rural. Nothing was found at the crime scene except the body."

"That's the whole point," Jade said. "We need to figure out what's missing."

"I don't get it," Travers said. "It looks nothing like Atlasia to me. Nineteen-year-old male, killed by a gunshot, outdoors, no mutilation."

"He can break character," Jade said softly.

"What?"

"He's not trapped in the pattern—his killings aren't a compulsive ritual, they're more like a performance. He can step out of it if he needs to." Jade rubbed his eyes with a thumb and index finger.

Travers looked over at him as the car bounced over a few dips. "You all right?" she asked.

"I think—" Jade cleared his throat, covering his mouth with a fist—"I think it might be my gun that was used in the killing."

"Oh God, Jade," she said. "I'm sorry. Was it . . . ? How did . . . ?"

"He took it from my backyard when he came over and dropped the note. I kept a Glock under a back counter." Jade's expression hardened again. "Look, there's nothing I can do about it now. Let's use it for what it's worth. See if it can lead us to him. That's all I can think about right now."

Travers didn't say anything, but she nodded in agreement. Jade silently thanked her for being quiet. He needed quiet right now.

Steve Francis's parents lived in Sunset, close to McGuire's house, though his body was found at Sutro Heights. Their nondescript single-story home was painted yellow and trimmed in white. For some reason, they had decided to paint their mailbox a bright fire hydrant red, post and all. Jade wondered how many dogs relieved themselves on it daily.

Travers took Jade by the arm as they headed up the walkway to the door. "Look," she said. "They've just lost a son. They sound okay on the phone, but they almost didn't consent to see us. They've been dealing with a parade of police and press all day. Why don't you let me handle the bullshit and just ask questions when they're important?"

"We'll see," Jade said.

The door opened to reveal a woman with white hair pulled back in a bun, a pair of circular spectacles perched on the end of her nose. She looked like a retired librarian. Her eyes were not red from crying.

Jade let Travers do most of the talking. She expressed her condolences to Mary and Len Francis for the loss of their son. Len was a carpenter. Jade could tell that much from the muscular arms that protruded from his starched, short-sleeved shirt, and the outline of the tape measure worn in the back pocket of his jeans.

The parents were very much in control. They were not accustomed to expressing emotion, particularly to strangers, and the strength of their suppression was visible in their tightly drawn mouths. They were not the type of people to fall apart, even over the loss of a son.

The interview progressed routinely until Travers

asked what Steve was doing at Sutro Heights. "Did he like to hike? Do you think he went there on a walk?" she asked.

Mary and Len looked at each other blankly. "No," Len said. "Steve wasn't the hiking type. Liked more thrills than that. Pole-vaulting maybe, but no hiking." He laughed.

The back door banged and a boy about fourteen came in. He looked a lot like Steve, at least judging by the crime-scene photograph.

"Hi Mom, Dad," he said.

He caught Jade's eye and walked over. "Frank Francis," he said, offering his hand. Travers smiled at his confident swagger, trying not to laugh out loud. "Jade Marlow, right?" he asked.

"Right," Jade said, feeling ridiculous for shaking a boy's hand with such severity.

"I want to be in the FBI when I grow up," Frank said. "Just like you were. Then I want to quit and work special cases." He pursed his lips seriously. "Probably homicide."

Jade nodded wearily. "That's great, kid," he said. "Good luck." He turned back to the parents. "So you have no idea why Steve was over in that area?"

"Not the foggiest," Len said.

"Hey," Frank pulled on Jade's sleeve. "Want to check out Steve's room?"

Jade pulled his arm away, yanking his sleeve from Frank's hand. Frank grabbed it again. "Hey," he said loudly.

Jade glared at him and started to speak. But he reminded himself that Frank had just lost a brother, so he held his tongue. Then he noticed that the boy was winking at him.

"Why don't you let me show you Steve's room?" he said again.

The interview with the parents didn't seem to be offering any leads, so Jade figured he'd find out what the kid wanted to tell him. He stood and followed Frank down the hall.

Once the door closed to Steve's room, Frank whirled around and addressed Jade in a deep whisper. "I know why Steve was at Sutro Heights. He went there to parachute."

"To parachute?"

"Yeah," Frank said. "Free-fall jumping off cliffs. He was crazy about it—did it all the time. It's illegal, so I didn't want to tell Mom and Dad. Might upset them, you know?" He nodded maturely, cueing Jade to agree.

"Are you sure you're not fucking around here, kid? This is an important investigation."

Frank got on his hands and knees and crawled partially under the bed. He pulled out what appeared to be a parachute pack. "See?" he said. "I'm not fucking around." He really emphasized the words "fucking around." Jade could see just how much he enjoyed using them.

"If he was there to jump, then why's his parachute at home?"

Frank waved him off. "He was a fanatic. Had like four 'chutes."

"Did he usually parachute alone?"

"Sometimes, I guess, but mostly with a buddy."

Jade turned the pack over in his hands. "Well, thanks for the info, kid."

"No worries. Just don't tell Mom and Dad. They're sort of having a hard time, you know?"

Jade nodded dumbly and turned to leave. When he got to the door, he looked back at Frank. "How are you doing?" he asked.

"About Steve?"

"Yeah."

Frank shrugged. "Okay. He was kind of an asshole."

Jade bit his lip. "Fair enough."

Travers fingered a bullet hole in the side of the passenger door, then climbed in the car. Jade flipped through the radio stations.

"What a weird kid," she said.

Jade laughed. "Yeah, you could say that. He thought his brother was in Sutro parachuting."

"Parachuting?"

"Like jumping-off-cliffs parachuting. Don't ask me, I just work here."

"That's interesting," Travers said. "They didn't find a parachute with the body."

"Obviously, if it was moved. But now we can cautiously assume he was killed somewhere in the hills."

Travers laughed. "Let's do that. Let's cautiously assume, shall we?"

Jade threw the car into drive. "The kid said his brother didn't usually jump solo, so we might have a missing body."

"I'll get a list of males from eighteen to, say, twenty-five who've disappeared in the past couple of days. It might be slow because we've got the forty-eight-hour window for reporting missing persons."

Jade nodded, watching the blur of pavement ahead of the car. Ever since he'd found out about Steve Francis, Jade had been telling himself that there was a good chance it wasn't his gun. There were a lot of .40s out there, and even if forensics discovered that it was a Glock, there was no shortage of those either. But now that the parachute was a potential lead, he found himself hoping that his gun had killed Steve Francis.

That's how these things progress, he thought. Through bodies.

He pulled out from the curb, and though she tried not to, Travers grabbed the seat to steady herself. "We're thinking about going door-to-door," she said. "Within the neighborhoods you circled."

Jade shook his head. "No way. There's too many places. Plus, he's way too smart to get caught with something that obvious. No hope."

"We're running in circles here. And the clock's ticking."

Even though her tone was sharp, Jade said nothing. She was right. The clock was ticking. He heard it all the time.

The leads had all been followed as far as he could run with them. Now it came down to waiting. And Jade hated waiting more than anything, especially with a rising body count. He had been straining to think of another proactive strategy, some way to draw Allander in, to turn the chase upside down. But he'd only come up with dead ends. And, as Travers had said, the clock was ticking.

WOTAN pivoted his great black leather chair as he surveyed the files spread on the desk before him. Picking carefully through photographs and notes from headquarters and from Agent Travers, he assessed Marlow's progress, glad to see that Travers had come to recognize the former agent's utility.

It had been difficult, but he had managed to hold the case together for Marlow. He kept the FBI's resources open to him, and he had ordered the squad's full cooperation. Stifling some of the press and police complaints hadn't been quite as easy, since they fell outside his normal jurisdiction, but he had managed.

Wotan never once doubted the wisdom of bringing Marlow in early to handle the situation. Atlasia was worse than a time bomb; he was a disease. He had to be either captured or killed before the damage got out of control.

Wotan's task was to keep the world stitched shut around both of them, to keep Marlow in the chase and in the fight. It wouldn't be so hard now that Atlasia had struck blood within the FBI.

For obvious reasons, Wotan had to find a replacement for McGuire, and had selected Fredericks, one of his senior agents. The other agents understood and no doubt shared the pain felt by McGuire; it was every man's nightmare that his vocation would put his family in harm's way. They wouldn't object to cooperating with

Marlow now. Marlow's involvement promised Atlasia's delivery. It virtually guaranteed it. Nobody knew that as well as Wotan.

Wotan shuttled the bullet slug across the tops of his knuckles. It was a holy fight. He had learned that the hard way.

Jade and Travers were exhausted. The dark circles beneath their eyes that usually came and went had taken on a look of permanence.

The enthusiasm Jade had felt at McGuire's house had faded. They had a start on locating Allander, but it was definitely a long shot. Jade had taken to counting all the dark-green houses he drove past. So far, he was up to twenty-three.

Travers pointed to the bold white letters on an exit sign. "Could get off here to eat. There's a great restaurant a ways back. A little French cafe."

Jade was quiet.

"I have my beeper in case anyone needs to reach us," she added.

"They won't," he said. "If we're dead-ended, it doesn't bode well for everyone else."

He flipped on the radio as he took the exit, and clicked through the channels, trying to find a good station. His search ended when he heard jazz pouring through his speakers. Abruptly, he pulled his head to the side and cracked his neck.

Travers directed him through some back streets to the restaurant she had in mind. It sat by itself at the edge of a yellow field that curled around the base of the Woodside hills like a sleeping cat. A rare summer storm was brewing in the heavy air, and dark clouds drifted overhead, blocking the late-afternoon sun.

As Jade pulled into the parking lot, the disk jockey started his wind-down. "That's right. We've got the golden sounds of Joshua Redman to carry us into evening. Don't forget we have a busy weekend coming up, with the Cantab Singers rocking Saturday night at the House of Jazz in downtown San Jose. And for you more sophisticated listeners, there's the annual symphony hall fund-raiser at Singspiel's Restaurant up in the city tomorrow night, followed by Haydn's *Drum Roll* and—"

Jade turned the radio off. "Joshua Redman. Great young performer."

"I didn't know you liked jazz," Travers said, genuinely impressed.

"You mean I might not be all bad?" He smiled quickly, holding her eyes with his until she looked away. They got out of the car simultaneously.

Twenty minutes later, they faced each other across a table laden with food. Jade was quiet, leaning over his plate and inhaling deeply as the smell of chicken and brie rose to his nose. He hadn't realized how hungry he was until the food arrived, and he began to eat in large, slow bites, finishing his meal before Travers was halfway through.

The waiter asked if they wanted wine, but Jade waved him off without even looking at him. He looked instead at the woman seated across from him. Jennifer Travers. She wore her hair down around her neck, and it fell in radiant, blond strokes. Her collarbone was just visible beneath the neckline of her shirt, and Jade watched it move slightly as she breathed.

Meanwhile, his mind was filled with details from the case. He didn't like the way it felt right now, as if he were chasing and not getting any closer. The leads had dried up and he didn't have much to show for them. It had been nine days since Allander's escape. With the entire state of California watching him, he was standing by while the body count rose.

"I feel terrible for McGuire," Travers said.

Jade shrugged.

"I mean, imagine. A wife dead and both children permanently impaired."

He shrugged again.

"Jade, for Christ's sake, his sons' eardrums got blown out. I mean, we should really try to do something for him."

"Why don't we get him tickets for the symphony?" he suggested coldly, looking down at his meal again.

Travers's jaw tightened, and there was a long silence.

"I don't get why he doesn't fuck them," Jade finally said, his voice loud in the relative quiet of the restaurant. A couple of people at nearby tables turned to stare.

Travers cleared her throat. "Fuck . . . them, Jade?" she repeated quietly after the waiter dropped off the check.

"The kids. I mean, he's a victim of child abuse himself, and an early sexual offender. Why would he stop now when he's got ample opportunity?"

"What do you think?"

"I don't know. Sexual insecurity, maybe even impotence."

The waiter came up in his white starched shirt and rubbed his hands together. "Can I take that?" he asked, pointing delicately at the brown check folder.

"Uh, we're not quite ready yet," Travers answered.

"Could be he's just waiting to direct all his sexual energy toward his mother. Building up for the rape, you know." His last remark drew another stare from a woman at the next table.

"We have to prevent it. We just have to stop it."

"Well, no shit, Travers. I think we're doing everything we can." Jade picked up his water glass and looked into it with one eye.

The waiter returned with a half bow. "Hello again, do you think I could—"

Jade didn't even look over at him. "I believe we said WE'RE NOT READY YET!" The waiter blinked several times, backing away.

Travers took a deep breath, trying to contain her anger. "You know, Marlow, I don't get you."

"And that's a news flash?"

"You act like no one should care about the people affected by this case, no one should care about the victims. Like it's not okay to feel badly about this. To get upset." Her voice was rising and her cheeks were flushed. People in the restaurant were again glancing at their table. "Like it's all a big fucking game. We can't ever talk like we give a shit about anyone, let's just use them as bait." She pushed her hair off her forehead. "We have a responsibility to these people, Jade."

"Responsibility?" Jade said. "You want to talk to me about responsibility?" The veins in his neck were bulging, though he was speaking softly. His upper lip peeled back in a grimace. "You think I don't care about these people? You don't think it's hard for me to make a decision to put people in the line of fire? Well grow up, Travers. I do these things because they have to be done. I make these decisions because no one else will. So don't you second guess me, and *don't* you talk to me about responsibility."

Travers took a sip of water. "Nice speech."

Jade looked away for a long time. "It's like you think I enjoy it. Putting people like Thomas and Darby at risk. And the kids, Christ, the kids . . ." His voice trailed off again. "I just can't deal with that if I'm gonna do my job."

He drew a line on the table with his hand. "It's too much. It's all too much."

Travers leaned forward and laid her hand across Jade's. "Jade. I didn't . . . it doesn't seem . . . I guess the only thing I've seen you give off is anger."

The tension eased from his face, and he raised his eyes to Travers's. "Maybe guilt turns to anger if you hold on to it long enough," he said. For one awful instant, Travers thought he was going to spill tears. Seeing his face now, she realized what it was about Jade that made him so committed, so intense.

He stood suddenly, pulling money from his pocket and tossing it on the table. Then, without speaking, he turned and walked out of the restaurant. Travers closed her eyes for a moment before rising and following him.

It was raining, a thick downpour, but instead of walking to the car, he headed across the field toward the hill behind the restaurant, ignoring Travers when she called after him. She caught up with him behind the cafe.

Grabbing him by the arm, she spun him around, planting him firmly against the back wall. Water dripped off the roof and ran over his face, dripping from his hair to his forehead and down off his lips.

"I'm talking to you," she said.

"What?"

"I wanted to fucking apologize, all right?"

Jade's eyes glinted as Travers raised her hand and traced the scar on his cheek down to the thin stream of rainwater dripping off his lips. Grabbing his head with both hands, she banged it against the wall, seizing his lower lip in her mouth and feeling the water run from his mouth into her own. Her hands were at his belt and then he was out and in her hands and her mouth went to his neck.

He lowered her onto the damp field, holding an arm in the small of her back to break her fall. His knees sank in the ooze and mud between her legs, and the water stood out in beads on their bare skin as buttons and material gave way. Travers's shirt was soaked and torn, her hair matted with mud, her elbows buried in mounds of soil. Thrusting forward, Jade entered her.

He froze. "Holy shit," he said.

Travers's nails stopped tracing their red paths up his back. "What?"

"The radio. The disk jockey. He said the symphony fund-raiser dinner was tomorrow night. Darby said they always used to go as a family. Allander will be expecting them to be there."

Both seemed to have forgotten that Jade was still inside her. Without hesitation, he pulled himself out, quickly stood, and ran for his car. Travers immediately dug herself from the mud and followed, yanking together the ripped remains of her clothing. The car was moving when she got there and she had barely jumped in before Jade sped away.

Once they were on the freeway, he looked over at her mud-tangled hair, her tattered garments, her smeared face, and started laughing. She tried not to smile but couldn't resist, and then they were both laughing, almost uncontrollably. Travers reached over and painted a line of mud on Jade's cheek with her finger. Her smile faded, her lips pursing ever so slightly, just enough to betray her thoughts.

Jade took his eyes off the road for a moment to look at her. "Jennifer, huh?" he said gently.

She nodded.

He glanced at the clock and the softness faded from his face. He took 85 to 17 and exited in San Jose, racing over curbs and through red lights.

He berated himself for not thinking of the fund-raiser earlier. Closing his eyes, he remembered the drum roll opening the classical piece he'd heard when he'd interviewed Thomas in the living room. Darby's story about the fund-raiser dinners. *Charity. Our road back to sanity.*

The shower had ended by the time the BMW squealed to a halt at the Atlasias' home. The FBI agents down the block were out of their cars before they recognized Jade.

The door swung open to reveal Darby's startled face. She looked at Jade's clothes and the mud shot through his hair, and then at Travers's ripped shirt.

"Oh. No thank you. We didn't order a stripper," she said, and feigned shutting the door.

"Are you going to the symphony dinner tomorrow night?" Jade asked.

"Of course we are."

Jade put his hand on the door and pushed it open. "Then we have to talk." He brushed past Darby and into the house. Travers waited outside, a procedure they had discussed.

"Well, Jade Marlow, before you floor me again with your plans and calculations, there's something you need to see." Darby pointed to the kitchen.

On the kitchen table was a second envelope. Same block print. Jade reached inside and pulled out a lipstick tube.

"We got the mail about a half hour ago," Darby said from the doorway. "I just left a message on your machine."

"Speak no evil," Jade said softly.

Darby raised her hand and let it clap to her thigh. "What's next?" she said, her voice cracking in a mock laugh.

Jade looked up at her, holding her eyes for a moment. "Probably an earring," he said.

"How . . ." Her words trailed off into a silent sob before she regained her composure and continued in a horrified whisper. "How can you stand this? Day in, day out." Her voice rose angrily. "How can you deal with it all day, every day? When you don't even have to?"

"Because that's what I do, all right?" Jade replied sharply. His voice rang around the room. He looked down at the floor sadly, tracing the pattern of the tiles. "That's what I am," he said softly.

When he raised his eyes to meet Darby's, he was surprised by how suddenly pale she was. She staggered to the side as if she were about to faint, leaning on the table for support. Pulling herself erect, she squared her shoulders, her eyes lit with their familiar determination.

"Darby. Are you all right?" Jade asked, genuine concern in his voice.

She nodded, then turned and left the room.

Jade started to follow her, but stopped when he got to the doorway. Although time was of the essence, he could give her a few minutes. He sat down and turned his eyes to the clock on the microwave. Five minutes. He could give her five minutes.

She was standing at the edge of the square lawn with her back to the house. She appeared to be gazing at the neat rows of flowers and plants that constituted her garden. Jade approached her cautiously and halted next to, but slightly behind, her.

"I'm sorry," she said, still not turning to look at him. Then she laughed her sad laugh, and Jade realized how accustomed to it he had grown. He wondered how often she had laughed like that before she'd met him.

"It feels like I'm doing that all the time now," she said.

"Apologizing. More than I ever have." She finally turned to look at Jade. "Believe it or not, I usually have a difficult time with it."

"I can empathize," Jade said.

"I can imagine." She laughed and he joined her.

The garden was small, but extremely well cultivated. Two rosebushes flanked the smaller plants like monoliths, one on each side of the bed of rich soil. Jade slowly became aware of a loud buzzing sound.

"What's that noise?" he asked.

Darby pointed to a tube hanging from the larger of the two rosebushes. About the size of a tennis-ball can, the tube appeared to have an inverted funnel at its base. Through the clear plastic, Jade noticed at least a dozen bees flying nearly in place, trapped inside the device. The buzz of their wings vibrated inside the tube, giving off an eerie hum.

"Thomas is allergic to bees, and this keeps them out of the backyard. There's a nectar scent that attracts them," Darby said. "They fly up through the funnel at the bottom and can't figure out how to fly down out of it."

They watched the bees fight against the plastic for a few moments, their buzzing amplified by the container. Though it was not easy for him, Jade raised his hand and placed it on Darby's shoulder. She swayed a bit toward him, but didn't turn her head.

"I will protect you," he said. The words came with such conviction that his uneasiness departed. "On my life, I will protect you."

His hand rose with her shoulder as she breathed deeply. Darby squeezed his hand briefly before lifting it off. "Well, I've had my wounded moment," she said. "Let the planning commence."

She walked back to the house without waiting to see

if Jade was following. She was not wearing shoes, and Jade found something distressing and wonderful about watching her bare feet on the grass.

Placing one shoe delicately between two rows of pansies, Jade moved closer to the rosebush and looked down into the bee trap. A piece of yellow plastic plugged the tube around the funnel, and Jade noticed the dead bees that it ordinarily hid from view, their shell-like bodies forming a grotesque bottom layer. As he watched, a bumblebee that had been struggling against the clear plastic fell to the pile, exhausted, fanning its wings in ineffective short bursts. Jade watched until the wings no longer blurred, then headed back toward the house.

SINGSPIEL'S Restaurant was in a stylish converted brewery located across the street and up the block from the symphony hall on Van Ness. The entrance was narrow, like a hallway, but the building widened into a dining area with about thirty tables in the back, positioned around a large vat left over from the brewery.

An elegant bar where customers bought drinks to take to the tables in the back ran along the corridor of the restaurant. Mirrors covered the wall behind the bottles, reflecting the space's brass-and-marble design. The bar ended just where the bottleneck of the entrance opened up to the table area. A stack of kegs marked the start of the restaurant proper, lining the edge of the bar, just beside the wooden Dutch door of the coat-check closet.

It was to be a very early dinner, since it was to be followed by a concert at the symphony hall. The Atlasias were to arrive at 5:05.

Jade sat inconspicuously at a table largely blocked from view by the brewing vat. He, however, had excellent visibility of the entire seating area, and he could also lean slightly and look straight down the length of the bar.

Jade felt more keyed up than usual, the increased tension brought on by growing pressure for him to end the terror that had begun to spread through the city. If he couldn't lure Allander in tonight, he wasn't sure he ever could. It was doubtful that another opportunity this promising would come along. Jade relaxed in his chair and tried to calm himself. There was a high probability that Allander would show up. After all, the fund-raising dinner was something of a family tradition.

Jade had pulled back all the agents assigned to the Atlasias so that Allander wouldn't be scared off. The couple would be dropped off by a cab (with an agent disguised as the cabdriver) right at the front door. Jade and Travers would cover the restaurant. He was using only one other agent, the woman he had disguised as the ticket vendor at the movie theater. She would be working the coat check tonight, which placed her in position between the table area and the front door. Jade had instructed her not to involve herself at all unless he signaled. Despite all efforts, undercover agents tended to stand out at high-society affairs, and Jade just didn't want to run the risk of frightening Allander away. He barely trusted Travers to play her part.

Jade expected Allander to hit early, intent on killing Thomas and either killing or kidnapping Darby. Maybe he'd let Darby go for now so he could catch her in a more intimate setting later.

Since Allander wouldn't recognize Travers, Jade put her at the bar to keep an eye on the front of the restaurant. Wearing a simple black dress, sitting at the bar with her legs crossed, and sipping a glass of Burgundy, she blended in perfectly with society's elite. She glanced up from her position between two girls who looked like debutantes and winked at Jade. He nodded seriously and leaned back out of view.

Travers had agreed to back him only after learning that the Atlasias were already planning to attend the event. She tried briefly to talk Jade into ordering them not to come, but she realized early that her protests were falling on deaf ears—Jade's and the Atlasias'. They were three of the most determined people she'd ever met.

Thomas and Darby were intent on not letting their son dictate how they lived their lives, and they were willing to use themselves to catch him; they had already proved that. They trusted Jade more than Travers had realized. There seemed to be an element of faith between them, something unspoken yet understood.

"I want it to end," Darby had said to both Jade and Travers earlier in her kitchen. She had looked up at Jade, keeping her eyes steady on his. "Just make it end."

The Atlasias' Singspiel entrance was beautifully natural. They walked in and ordered a drink at the bar, standing only about four feet from Travers, never making eye contact.

Thomas looked very sharp in his tuxedo, complementing the sweeping black sequined dress that Darby wore. She carried a small clutch purse, having denied Jade's request that she put a gun in it for the evening.

Jade smiled to himself as he remembered something Darby had told him. "We'll do fine," she had said. "We're good actors. We've had lots of practice."

She proved that now as they walked to their table, pretending not to notice the hushed silence that fell around them, the hands covering whispers, the curious glances that lingered a beat too long. They smiled and nodded at the people they knew as they threaded their way gracefully through the tables to their own.

They were seated in front of the brewing vat, to Jade's right. He leaned out from behind the vat and scanned the restaurant, focusing on the Atlasias' table from time to time. Once in a while, he caught Travers's eye at the bar and she shrugged, raising her shoulders and eyebrows just slightly. The agent working the coat check was doing well—she wasn't so much as looking at Jade and Travers. Jade didn't let down his guard, but he started to relax.

Travers gave him another half shrug and he frowned, bringing his hands up in frustration. What do you want me to do? he thought.

The first part of dinner was over and Jade couldn't smell any danger in the air. At this point, another fruitless evening out might be devastating for the Atlasias. Glancing over, he checked on Darby and Thomas.

Darby laughed boisterously, raising one hand to cover her mouth. An elegant pearl bracelet hung from her wrist, swaying with the force of her laughter. She sat at a table full of grinning men who looked at her with expressions of delight and amazement.

It had taken some doing, but she had won over the table. She was used to the routine. It started with awkward glances and pointed questions: Well, how *are* you, Darby? How *are* you holding up? But she had done it again. She had won another small social victory for herself and her husband. A moment of normalcy to hold in their memories and cherish.

She smiled and continued with her story. "And so I didn't know that Thomas had just washed the floor, so here I come, walking in with bare feet and—" She burst into fresh peals of laughter and some of the men began to chuckle prematurely, anticipating the rest of the story.

"—two cartons of eggs (I mean, what are the odds of all the things I could be carrying in—not one, but *two* cartons of eggs?), and Thomas was at the sink peeling carrots and he said he just heard this enormous THUMP!"

Darby banged the table with a fist to punctuate the thump and all the water glasses jumped. One fell over

into the lap of a man with a carefully manicured mus-
-tache and Darby burst into laughter all over again.

"Oh my God, I'm sorry. I'm a nightmare. See what a
nightmare I am?" Her voice was high as she strained to
speak through her laughter. "And during my eggs story."

The mustached man assured her that he was fine and
that the water would soon dry.

"But my feet went out, and I swear to God I hit the
floor flat on my back. I mean, every part of my back hit
the ground at the same time. And the eggs, the eggs . . ."
She covered her mouth, her shoulders heaving again
with laughter. "I mean, it was like a cartoon. Up in the
air." She imitated her frantic attempt to locate the eggs
above her, and then the exaggerated expression of shock
that crossed her face once she did. "All over me. My face,
my hair, my neck. All over."

Everyone at the table laughed.

"And so Thomas turns around to me slowly and says,
'Darby, honey, if you need more attention from me, all
you have to do is ask.'" She laughed and pounded the
table again. The men all grabbed their water glasses.

Thomas leaned over, draping his arm across her
shoulder. "Dear, why don't we see if the Lawrences have
arrived yet? We told them we'd catch up."

"Sure, sure." Darby pushed back from the table and
laid her napkin gracefully across her place setting.
"Gentlemen, it was a pleasure horrifying you with stories
of my ineptitude." Her voice dropped to a whisper. "Now
you know the truth," she added to smiles all around.

She followed Thomas through the clusters of tables,
the self-assured patrons of the arts, the lipsticked smiles,
the jeweled fingers, until they were alone by the bar.
Glancing over Thomas's shoulder, she caught Jade's eye.

"How are you, love?" Thomas asked.

She rolled her eyes. "What a chore. I swear to God these people all have large sticks up their asses. I feel like I'm talking to a bunch of corpses." She imitated a wide-eyed stare with an excessive head nod. "'And how *are* you, Darby? You look great—I mean fan*tas*tic. And Thomas is all right? Good, good. And has your son embalmed anyone this week? Oh. Good, good.'" She made a quick gagging gesture, bringing one finger to her open mouth.

Thomas smiled at her, shaking his head. "I recognize that the strain of being charming must wear you down considerably," he said. "But, you know, you do look quite lovely."

"Thank you, honey. I don't mean to be ungrateful, it just seems like there are no *real* people here. You know what I mean?" Her shoulders dropped. "Not many real people anywhere for us anymore."

She ran her open hands over the lapels of his tuxedo. "And you look very handsome. Are you here with anybody?" Rising to her tiptoes, she kissed him gently on the lips.

JADE watched the Atlasias from across the restaurant. They had agreed that they should move to the bar area if nothing happened during the first half of dinner. They'd be more visible there, more vulnerable.

Now that they were in position, Jade was having second thoughts. There was so much activity at the bar that there was no way he could keep an eye on everything. He drummed his fingers underneath the table and grimaced. It suddenly felt wrong again, as it had in the theater. It felt risky.

He moved to a table that was closer to the bar, signaling Travers to head outside and watch the street. He was convinced that everything was safe among the tables behind him, so he wanted to shift their coverage to the front of the restaurant and outside. Travers exited the bar casually, turning a few heads on her way.

With Travers outside, it was up to him to cover the entire restaurant. The other agent, who was casually watching the crowd above the bottom half of the Dutch door, was not to leave her post. They were daring Allander to strike. The Atlasias were dangling like bait on a hook.

After Travers left, Jade felt a sinking in his stomach. The early taste of panic flooded his mouth. As he watched the smiling faces moving in all directions, he felt his control of the situation slowly slipping away.

His sweat seemed to come in waves, as if his hammering heartbeat was pushing it through his pores. He thought of Darby outside the movie theater, her smeared makeup and tired eyes, trying to face the crowd of jostling cops and reporters. *We're more than this.*

One of the waiters bumped into Thomas, and Jade almost left his seat in a sprint, but the fellow righted his tray, apologized, and moved on.

Once they got to the bar, Darby and Thomas knew not to return to their seats. The front door opened and swung closed slowly, and Darby felt a breeze blow across her shoulders. "Honey, I'm a little chilly. Would you mind getting my coat?"

Jade had told them not to separate, but force of habit made them forget their instructions. A crowd of women headed for the bar to refresh their glasses of wine, blocking Darby and Thomas from view. Jade sat up straight in his chair to keep his eye on them. He felt a tingling down his spine as he waited for his view to clear. When the women parted, he saw only Darby.

Jade stood up, knocking his chair over clumsily and scanning the restaurant for Thomas. Darby looked over at him, concern written in the furrows of her brow. With a tilt of her head, she indicated where Thomas was. Jade turned and saw Thomas heading for the coat closet.

The restaurant flooded in on Jade, and he pivoted to try to hold the scene together, to keep control of the surroundings. The Atlasias were split apart, people hustled at the bar, the waiters and bartenders clamored around noisily. The glow of cigarettes flicked through the air, and for a moment Jade saw only the cigarettes, tracing orange lines through the smoky air. The necklace around his neck felt like an albatross.

For the first time, Jade felt doubt lower, like a cloud, over his intentions. He couldn't do it. He couldn't risk the Atlasias like this, even to catch Allander. He knew something was wrong—in his gut, in his bones, in the raised hair on his arms, he felt it. Then he realized. The top and bottom of the coat-closet door were both shut.

As Thomas placed his hand on the doorknob, Jade sprang forward shouting, "BACK OFF. IT'S NO GOOD." He wanted the Atlasias side by side, and he wanted himself in front of them. He ran toward them.

All the people in the restaurant turned to stare at Jade. He could have sworn the crowd took in a huge collective gasp of air. Then, they were still.

Thomas froze. He noticed a slight movement at his feet. Blood seeped slowly out from beneath the door, the edge of a growing pool. It rippled slightly, and as it reached his shoe, Thomas saw the reflection of the ceiling fan in its glassy surface. He released the doorknob, its click echoing through the silent restaurant.

He took a cautious step back and then the door swung open, crashing against the wall. A silver arc slashed through the air and a neat slit appeared across Thomas's tuxedo jacket and shirt. He stumbled back, a vacant look in his eyes, his hands clutching his chest. Blood oozed from beneath his fingers as he fell to his knees.

And then Allander was on him, an arm around his neck, a hand gripping the back of his head. Thomas felt the coldness of a blade at his throat, pushing the skin as far as it could go without breaking. He knew he was going to die.

How did I beget such a cursed thing? he thought.

Allander looked fiercely at Jade, warning him with his eyes.

Jade stopped in his tracks right beside Darby, feeling the backs of his knuckles brush her arm. They were about twenty feet from Allander, so close Jade could see him breathing. He fought every instinct in his body to hold his ground, lowering his Sig Sauer to his side. Allander made a jerking motion and Jade dropped the pistol to the floor. It bounced to his right. A full panic rattled through his body, but he forced himself to stay still.

He saw the smudges of dirt on Allander's chest and thighs. The crawl space, Jade thought. Allander had come up through the fucking floor. From the amount of blood on the floor by the closet, Jade was sure he'd killed the agent.

Travers was on the street, probably with an eye on the parking lot and the side alleys. Jade prayed that she'd notice the sudden stillness of the people in the restaurant.

Still on his knees, Thomas closed his eyes and listened to the silence of the room. Then the voice came, slicing the air like a sickle—the voice that he had carried in his head over the years, day and night. And now it was *with* him, inches from his ear. He could feel breath on his cheek, the exhaled air making the words sail tangibly across his face.

"You betrayed me. You betrayed me as father to the son who is father to the man. It was your responsibility as my father and keeper to protect me from trespasses, from things that go bump in the night, from the urges and yearnings of other grown men. You didn't fulfill your duty and I was sold at the ripe age of seven to a carnal circus.

"Perhaps you were just protecting your investment in Mother; I understand. But I've waited for years to stand before you not as equal but as superior, and I PASS MY JUDGMENT ON YOU!" Allander's voice rose to a yell, and he raked Thomas's head to the left, drawing the blade deftly to the right.

"WAIT!" Darby screamed.

Allander froze, the point of the knife sticking an inch and a half into Thomas's throat. A trickle of blood ran down the blade and dripped from his cuff as Allander held Thomas's lolling head in his arms.

Slowly, he faced his mother.

The restaurant was completely silent. Everyone was frozen, watching Allander with terror.

Darby looked at the blood and almost fainted. For a moment, she thought she had lost Thomas, but then she heard him emit a dry, rasping noise and she knew he was still drawing air.

Allander was planning to end her also, to drive the point of his blade through her rib cage, to stop at last the pulsing of her heart. What he couldn't possess, no one would. But the moment he saw her, he knew he would not be able to carry out his plan. He would surrender his due reward. Closing his eyes tightly for a moment, he thought of his impotence. His performance would not end as he had wished. His elaborate game, his mockery of the violence and psychology he had been forced to endure, seemed suddenly empty before his mother's eyes.

He raised his head to look at his mother, and it was just as it had always been. Allander stood abashedly before her, a naughty child. He could almost feel the years fleeing his body, the small lines departing from around his eyes, the potency draining from his organs. He was helpless again, a frightened boy lost in the forest of his own sexuality.

It was her cursed inconsistency. She was so uneven, so rounded. As he gazed on the drifts of hair around her neck, the movement of her flushed chest, the fullness of her hips, he was reduced to a weak-kneed helplessness. It was all he could do not to flee.

Darby opened her mouth as though to scream, but

nothing came out. A tear rolled from the corner of her eye. She stared at her son and felt no anger, only fear. No matter what they do, she thought. I felt him grow inside me for eight months, three weeks, and a day, and he stands before me still as my child. She understood that he loved her in some way, that this was all because of her, and she would have to carry it, alone, until the end of her days. She stood erect, almost proudly, with the force of her natural dignity about her like a shield.

Allander blinked back threatening tears and felt the softness of his emotions washing around inside him as he lowered his eyes from his mother. He was disgusted by his weakness. Glancing at Jade standing right beside her, he felt his rage reemerge, as pure and fresh as a torrent of water.

When he looked back at Darby, she caught his eyes and held them. He saw in them a coldness that he didn't recognize, as if she were looking right through him. She kept her eyes glued to his with a force he could almost feel in the air. And then, with excruciating slowness, she moved her hand two inches to her right, into Jade's.

Jade barely had time to be surprised when he felt Darby's skin against his—he was too focused on Allander's reaction. Allander's face seemed to tear itself apart in a scream as he kicked his father aside and lunged forward. He bellowed something but it was unintelligible; his throat was closed like a sobbing child's.

Jade was fully extended in the air, diving for his pistol, before Allander had staggered into a second step. He gripped the weapon by the stock before his body hit the floor, and he dug his finger through the trigger guard, whipping it to aim it at Allander's shoulder.

Jade struck the ground as he fired and the impact jolted his gun hand upward. Rolling onto his back, he heard a scream and the knife clattering to the ground. He came up in a crouch.

Allander's hand was leaking blood, but he could see that the bullet had only grazed him. Allander blinked twice, as if remembering where he was, and then sprinted for cover in the crowd by the bar. As he ran, he pulled Jade's Glock from where it was tucked in his jeans.

He fired blindly in Jade's direction and the bullet ricocheted off the metal vat behind him. People were screaming now, some still frozen in place at their tables, others standing, unsure where to run.

Darby's expression did not change, but she rocked on her feet to keep her balance. She didn't even turn her head to watch her son disappear.

"GET THE FUCK DOWN!" Jade yelled, firing once in the air.

The crowd broke, scattering behind stools and tables. More screams pierced the air. Everyone sank to the floor except Allander, who bent at the waist and scurried for the door, trying to shield himself with other people. Jade waited for a clear shot to open up, but Allander kept fading behind tables and crouching guests.

As Allander got within ten feet of the front door, it banged open and Travers swung into the restaurant, gun leveled at his head.

Allander was still pointing his pistol blindly behind himself in Jade's direction, and he didn't have time to swing it around at Travers. With a scream, he ducked behind a woman and hurled her toward Travers. She toppled forward on her high heels and smashed into Travers, knocking Travers's arms above her head and causing her head to bang against the door frame as she sank to the floor.

Jade lined his sights on the back of Allander's hip, but before he could fire, Allander had moved behind the staggering woman, jumped over Travers, and disappeared through the door.

Jade followed, screaming over his shoulder, "Someone call an ambulance." Travers was on her feet by the time he reached the door and she followed him out.

As they ran onto the sidewalk, two gunshots echoed loudly up the street. They went down over their right shoulders in exactly the same way, and completed their roll in a crouch behind a red Nissan parked out front. They glanced at each other over their weapons for a second, surprised.

"Agent down?" Travers asked.

"And out," Jade replied, straining to see up the street.

Allander was behind a taxi that was stopped a short distance down the block, and he fired in their direction a few more times. Jade grimaced as he recognized the sound of his pistol. One of the cabdrivers yelled out in broken English as Allander pulled him from his car and smashed his face with the butt of his gun. The driver sank to the pavement, limp.

Crouching behind the taxi, Allander fired again. The back window of the Nissan exploded, spraying Jade and Travers with fragments of glass. They were pinned down; with no immediate cover other than the car, they couldn't get off any clear shots. We'll have to wait until he breaks for it, Jade thought.

"I think I got him, Jade," Travers said.

Jade rolled his eyes and banged the back of his head against the door of the car. "Are you kidding me?" He turned his pleading gaze to the sky. "I'm not gonna let you do this, Jennifer."

"What did you call me?"

"Travers."

"I think I've got an angle on him."

He glared at Travers. "Look. You stay put. I'm calling the moves. This is not a time to fuck around. You are *my* backup, and I'm going to need you later. You *will* get killed if you break cover now." As if to accent his point, a bullet split the passenger window right above their heads.

She peered around the side of the door again, toward the street. "Jade, I feel it. I'm telling you I got it and I'm going."

"Goddamnit. You are not going."

Travers smiled and raised herself slightly from her crouch. "What's the matter, Jade, don't you trust me?"

"I trust you, Travers," Jade replied. "I just don't think you're that good."

She frowned at him and turned to go. Jade slipped the handcuffs from his pocket and slid them around her ankles, fastening them with a click. He threw the key into the street.

When she turned around, he saw a burning in her eyes he hadn't thought she was capable of. Her cheeks were red, her hair fell in sweaty spikes over her forehead, and her upper lip was raised in a snarl. She was absolutely breathtaking in her fury.

Her pistol flashed forward from her side. Jade knocked it out of her hand before she could bring it down on his head. She would've done it, he thought. She really would've done it. Something about that filled him with respect.

"It was no good," he said. Staring at her scowl, he couldn't resist a smile. "Try to hold on to your gun a little tighter next time."

The cab peeled out from the curb and Jade was up and running for his car, which was partially hidden behind a Dumpster in the small alley that ran between the parking lot and Singspiel's kitchen. The driver's door was snug against the wall, so he opened his passenger door and leaped across the emergency brake to the driver's seat.

As he sped away, the door kicked shut with the force of his acceleration. He turned left out of the alley and peeled past the front of Singspiel's, leaving Travers still on the ground. She rolled over to a sitting position, feeling the handcuffs dig into her flesh, drawing blood. She was unaware of any pain, however; she felt nothing but rage.

THE oncoming cars were passing so quickly that they looked like one long blur as Jade's car flew through the streets of San Francisco behind the yellow cab. They raced up Van Ness, then turned left on Geary, heading toward Fort Miley, the VA Hospital.

Allander accelerated through a yellow light and continued out toward the ocean. Jade blared his horn, as though daring the cars at the intersection to move. I still can't believe he fired at me, Jade thought as he kept his eyes fixed on the brake lights of the yellow cab. He's not a gunman.

They raced over the uneven road, bouncing into the oncoming lane to pass cars. Jade was certain that Travers would call for backup. There were probably a dozen cars and a helicopter on the way right now. The backup wouldn't have trouble locating him; a high-speed chase through the city was something eyewitnesses loved to talk about.

They crossed Twenty-sixth and Allander cut right suddenly, bouncing the cab over a curb and almost hitting a woman who turned screaming and disappeared into a corner deli. Jade hit the brakes and made the turn, gripping the steering wheel tightly and praying the car wouldn't skid out.

When he rounded the corner, he saw a group of children crossing the street two blocks up. On bicycles and holding balls and Frisbees, they looked like they were just coming back from a park.

Allander accelerated toward them and the boys scattered, leaving one little girl on a tricycle frozen in the middle of the road. Jade heard a smash as the side of the cab clipped her tricycle and then he saw her flying through the air. She landed in the road and Jade slammed on the brakes, his front tires skidding to a halt no more than two feet from the little girl.

He leaped out and circled the front of his car, falling to his knees in front of her. His heart was pounding. Another victim, he thought, this one killed before my very eyes. As he heard the first cries from the boys behind him, his hands went to the girl's chest to administer CPR. Before he even pressed down, her body shook and her eyes opened. She immediately began crying—a loud, healthy cry.

"Fuck," Jade said. He turned to the boys on the sidewalk as he ran back to his car. "Call nine-one-one. Now!"

Suddenly quiet, they stood regarding him with saucer eyes. Jade backed up his car so he could maneuver around the girl without moving her. The boys stood motionless. He leaned over and rolled down the passenger window, picking one boy from the crowd. "You. Kid with the blue jacket. Go into the deli and call nine-one-one."

The boy scampered off, leaving his friends still frozen on the sidewalk.

Jade peeled out, zooming around the crying girl. It was too late, though, and he knew it. He had lost too much time.

He patrolled the surrounding streets, making looser and looser circles around where he had last seen Allander, but there was no sign of the yellow cab. After spending twenty minutes pulling over and asking people if they'd seen a cab traveling at a high speed, he gave up.

No doubt aware of what had happened on the street

behind him, Allander had probably slowed down, turned the corner, and faded into the San Francisco traffic. Few cars were less noticeable than taxis. Since they're everywhere, no one really sees them.

On his way to 280, Jade drove past the street where Allander had hit the little girl. He didn't stop, but he saw that an ambulance had picked her up. He could tell from the strength of her cries that she was going to be okay. Bruised and scared, but okay.

Jade's shoulder was starting to swell from his dive to the floor in Singspiel's, but he did his best to ignore the pain. Removing *Sketches of Spain* from its CD case, he slid it into the stereo. He tried to calm down as he heard the first notes of the trumpet, but it would take a while. He was too angry with himself.

Another trap had been orchestrated, had been put into play, and had failed. Allander had taken the bait this time, but he had also injured, maybe even killed, Thomas, and in the end, Jade hadn't been able to keep track of him. Allander had played right into his hands, and he had lost him. Everyone had done their jobs except for him.

Even though it was unfair, Jade felt anger at Darby for forcing him to promise to bring Allander in alive. Maybe if he could've shot to kill, it would all be over. It was a lot harder to shoot to wound someone. Jade hadn't had much practice at that.

The drive home was miserable. Jade replayed every second of the evening in his head, thinking of what he could have done differently. He was furious with himself, and more than a little irritated at the complete failure of his backup support. If a helicopter had joined the chase in time, they probably would not have lost Allander.

One thing had become clear—Allander didn't panic

on the run, which made sense given the fact he'd been running almost his whole life. Now he would be almost impossible to track down.

Jade pulled down his street and turned into his quiet driveway. The house seemed dead to him as he entered through the garage. Sinking heavily to the couch, he gazed around his dark living room. It had all begun here, with Travers's visit to his house.

Allander's liquid eyes gazed out of the photographs on the walls, taunting Jade with their silent focus. Where was he? Jade wondered. Headed back to his base, no doubt, but where was that? He would wait there for a few days, recovering and plotting his next move. Or maybe he already had it all lined up. He had had time, transportation, access to God knows how many resources.

The light from the setting sun cast horizontal lines through the venetian blinds in the living room. They fell across the books and papers on the floor, the photographs taped to the walls, and on Jade as he sat on the couch.

His eyes closed for a moment and he felt a complete surrender wash over him. It was a new sensation, something he had never felt before. He took his Sig Sauer out from the back of his jeans and laid it on the coffee table.

He held his head in his hands for what seemed like hours, and then he rose to go take a hot shower. As he headed for the hallway, something in the kitchen caught his eye—the red blinking light on the answering machine.

"**ALL** right, kid. The bad news is, we had a slow week here in Falstaff Creek. The good news is, we put two men on your shit assignment. Don't thank me, I'll take payment in beers next weekend. So, let's see who the grand winners are."

There was a pause as Tony breathed heavily. Jade scrambled to find the map of San Francisco on which he had drawn the circle.

"Okay. Secluded rich houses twenty years old that used to be green in the target area. One: Presidio Heights. 223 Clay, at Clay and Baker. Two: St. Francis Wood. 311 Santa Ana, two blocks from where it crosses St. Francis Boulevard. Three: Sutro Heights. 23 Taos Drive. This one's way up Geary, winding into the park. Almost by the Cliff House."

Jade scribbled the addresses onto a pad, then marked them on the map with a big red marker. They were all in rich neighborhoods, pretty well spread out through the target area.

"That's all. If you need any more help, be sure you don't call me."

There was a click and the answering machine shut off, leaving the house quiet. Tony's voice could really fill a room, and now its absence accented the silence of Jade's house.

Jade looked at the three red circles on the map. Sutro Heights—that was where Steve Francis's body had been found, on the edge of Sutro Heights. The house was on a hill by the Cliff House, so if the kid had indeed been parachuting, Allander could have stumbled across him near there.

Jade traced his finger along the route of the car chase. It definitely seemed that Allander had been heading in that direction. At least before Jade had lost him, Allander's path had pointed straight for Sutro Heights.

Charging out to the garage, Jade hopped into his car. He was backing up when he braked suddenly and got out, leaving the engine running. He went back into the house and directly to the living room, where he grabbed his pistol, spun it once around his finger, and jammed it into the back of his jeans.

His car laid tracks as he peeled out backward from his garage. His head smashed into the headrest on his seat as the back of his BMW plowed into a car pulling into his driveway. The other car spun around in a one-eighty, landing halfway on his front lawn. Yanking the pistol from his jeans, Jade stepped out of his car and found himself aiming at Darby's head. She didn't seem to notice.

He lowered the pistol and walked over to her as two dark sedans drove up the street and pulled over on the far side of the road. A sideways glance at his car revealed that it was still drivable. The bumper was loose and the brake lights on the left side were smashed, but with the exception of a few wrinkles in the black metal of the trunk, the body of the car was surprisingly intact.

"They told me . . . they told me not to come," Darby said.

For a moment, Jade mistook her shock for drunkenness. Her eyes were glazed and her voice had a foreign flatness to it. But there was an awareness beneath the fog. She always knows what she's doing, Jade thought. Even now.

"Thomas?"

"Don't. They don't know. He's getting . . . help." She shook her head and looked around the dark street before her eyes settled on the gun in Jade's hand. "You're going, aren't you? To my son."

Jade nodded. The air seemed too thick for words.

Darby reached a trembling hand up to Jade's shoulder. She squeezed it tightly, almost lovingly, then reached across to his necklace. She wound one finger in the thin silver chain, made a fist, and yanked it. The chain broke and dangled from her hand.

"Go," she said.

Darby felt the chain swinging in her hand as Jade's car backed up and shot down the street, one of the dark sedans following close behind. She lowered her head and her mouth opened in a silent scream. Her shoulders shook with sobs.

Jade raced up 280 all the way to San Francisco and cut across town to Sutro Heights. The FBI tail followed him all the way. He knew they'd wait to see the direction he was headed and then call in backup. Hopefully, he could have a few critical moments alone with Allander before they arrived.

Eventually he pulled off the main street and moved up winding roads into the hills. It was getting hard to keep the road in view as darkness set in, especially around the hairpin turns. He could no longer spot the tail behind him. He heard a helicopter somewhere in the distance, but its noise faded away.

The car almost got stuck on one embankment, the wheels turning listlessly in the dirt for a few seconds before catching and jerking the car ahead. The road cut back and forth up the hill in fierce crisscrosses. Jade strained, his head out the window, to look up, but couldn't see where he was headed.

Finally, he saw a green sign that indicated the turnoff for Taos Drive. Moving off the road, he drove to the mouth of a long driveway that led to a secluded house. The mailbox flashed the number 23 in gold letters.

The house was shaded by a small forest that crept into the front yard. Pulling over close to the main road, Jade got out of his car and gazed through the woods. He scanned the area slowly, his eyes straining to see through the leaves and branches. Waiting. Waiting for the slightest crack of a twig or crunch of a leaf. Somewhere, a stream moved against its banks, its melodic flow tickling Jade's ear. A soft roll of thunder issued from the distance.

As he looked, Jade turned in a full circle. When he'd returned to his starting position, he headed toward the house. He moved forward and sideways, never taking his eyes off the front door.

If Allander's here, he's watching me right now, Jade thought. And something told him that Allander was expecting him.

The chopping of a helicopter sounded overhead. It approached swiftly, its searchlight zooming across the landscape. It would pick up Jade's car and direct the backup. Anger swept over Jade. He wanted this one alone.

He walked boldly up the front walk to the house, then sprinted for the door. Clearing the three stairs, the small porch, and kicking down the door with a single flying leap, he landed beside the door, inside the foyer, balanced in a boxer's stance.

He stood motionless as the dust settled around the stark interior. The furniture covered with dust cloths and the rolled-up rugs leaning in the corners of the rooms made the house look as if it belonged in a ghost town. Tools lay scattered about the floor.

A small mound of dirt was fanned in a semicircle at the base of the stairs. Jade walked over to it and pinched some in his fingers, raising it to his nose. Fertilizer. Probably tracked in during the landscaping makeover. He rose from his crouch and looked up the stairs.

Complete silence. Outside he heard another rumble of thunder, closer now.

Jade moved quickly, overturning the covered desks and chairs, smashing doors open and kicking through closets. He ran upstairs and sprinted from room to room. There were no signs of life.

Only the master bedroom remained to be searched; he looked down the length of the hallway at the closed door. With his Sig Sauer leading the way, Jade stalked toward it, cushioning the sound of his footsteps by walking toe to heel.

The door left its hinges entirely when he kicked it, crashing to the floor. The light from outside was fading rapidly, and much of the bedroom was cloaked in shadow.

An antique mirror stood in the corner of the room, next to an enormous maple wardrobe with intricately carved handles. Jade aimed his raised pistol at the wardrobe. He was ready. He approached it slowly.

His finger was white-knuckled against the trigger as he nosed the wardrobe door open. It swung outward on creaky hinges. He leaned back and fired once into the dark interior. A single wire hanger dangled from the bar, lit with the flash from Jade's shot. That was all.

The house was empty. It had all been a wild-goose chase. In his excitement, he had forgotten that the green paint and remodeled house only had been part of a theory, and that this had been one of only several possible houses.

Rage filled his body, and he spun to face the room. Catching his dim reflection in the mirror, he glared at himself—his hard, green eyes, his ineffective body.

Cursing, he hurled the pistol at his reflection. The mirror shattered and the wooden board behind it swung to the side like a window shutter, held there by two bent nails. As the mirror fell away in shards, it seemed that Jade's reflection still remained, his eyes peering back at him. Then the eyes blinked when his did not, and a smile crept across the face of Allander Atlasia.

THE element of surprise decidedly in his favor, Allander stepped through the shattered frame and pounced on Jade, pressing the point of a screwdriver to his throat. Jade swallowed roughly as the probing tool dug into his Adam's apple.

Allander smiled. After all this time, he and Jade were together. Here at the new house. *His* house. Allander felt a chill teasing his legs, and his testicles tightened. The dance had begun.

The noise of sirens outside escalated, and red-and-blue lights flashed through the window. Jade tried to talk, but the screwdriver was pressed so tightly against his windpipe that he only choked.

He looked into Allander's face, savoring the feeling of his flesh against his own. After so much distance and time, the two men were finally touching. The beat of Allander's heart pounded in Jade's ears, and for a moment, he could not distinguish it from his own.

"Not a movement, not a word," Allander hissed in his ear. "At last, Marlow, we're together. I know you've waited desperately for me to come out of hiding. Or should I say, out of repression."

Jade saw the dried blood covering one of Allander's knuckles where his shot had grazed him in the restaurant. There was another smudge of blood on Allander's cuff, but it was lighter, a cherry red. It looked like paint.

Jade struggled again to speak, twisting his neck until he could force out a few words. "Kill me if you're going to. Just don't waste my fucking time."

Allander eased the pressure from the screwdriver just enough for Jade to continue.

"You're done, Atlasia. We got cars, agents, 'copters. And you've got a fuckin' screwdriver."

"And your gun, Marlow. And your gun." Allander reached for the Glock tucked in his jeans.

The moment he moved, Jade seized the hand gripping the screwdriver and dropped all his weight off his feet. As he collapsed to the floor, he twisted Allander's hand across itself until he felt the elbow lock. Allander screamed in pain and swung the butt of his pistol to the back of Jade's head, dropping him to the floor.

The death grip on his hand eased and Allander pulled it to freedom, sending the screwdriver skidding across the floorboards. In seconds, he was through the door and down the stairs.

Jade pushed himself up on all fours. The bump on his head was painful, but the skin wasn't split. He grabbed the pistol he had thrown through the shattered mirror and stumbled after Allander, gripping his head and banging forcefully into the door frame with his shoulder. The stairs and the floor below were quiet.

Walking unsteadily from room to room, Jade planted his hand on countertops and walls to support himself. He was familiar with this drill, the disappearance. He knew Allander had to be in the house somewhere, especially with the FBI barricade outside. He tried to focus, but saw only blurry images.

He had a haunting feeling that Allander had spared his life. It was the worst thing he could imagine—charity from a murderer. If Allander had wanted to kill him, he would probably have done it right away, sending the screwdriver through his neck to the handle and watching his blood spray the floor.

Jade's vision was getting worse. He knew he had to get some fresh air or he would pass out. He staggered over the flattened front door, blinded by the searchlights that covered the front yard. Most of them, at this moment, were angled directly into his eyes.

The clicking of gun hammers greeted Jade as he stumbled off the porch. Still gripping the back of his head, he shouted, "Relax! It's me, Marlow. He's pinned down on the property, so hold your positions." He walked behind the phalanx of cars. "I need to sit down a minute and then I'm going back in."

A tall agent stormed over and bent down like an umpire, hands on his knees. Jade recognized him as Fredericks; he'd last seen him at the meeting in the federal building. Evidently, he had replaced McGuire. "Until you bring me up to speed," Fredericks yelled, "you're not going anywhere, Marlow."

Jade reached over and grabbed Fredericks's tie, yanking his head forward. He tried to make his eyes focus as he spoke. His voice was low, calm, and surprisingly tired. "I don't think you should push me right now."

Fredericks stumbled back when Jade released his tie. "We *will* discuss this later, Marlow. I don't have the luxury right now." He backed off and pretended to busy himself by repositioning a few of the snipers.

A row of FBI agents dressed in black swept past Jade as they rolled into position. Same game as at the apartment. Agents around the house, on the roof ready to rappel. Snipers in the trees. There was no way out for him. Not this time.

Jade pulled himself to his feet. He checked his pistol,

clicking the chamber and glancing down the hard shaft as he pointed it at the ground.

"Put on your condoms, gentlemen," he said. "We're going in."

As he turned to move, a shoulder blocked his path, striking him in the ribs. His eyes still on the ground, Jade noticed an ankle loosely wrapped in a bandage.

Jesus Christ, he thought. She must've tried to run with her ankles cuffed together.

He raised his eyes to Travers's. "If you don't get that thing looked at there'll be no more ballet lessons for you."

She snapped his head all the way to the side with a right to the cheek. The pain compounded that of the earlier blow to his head, tearing through his temples and forehead. He clenched his teeth and shut his eyes to avoid showing how much it hurt. He made sure he loosened his features before he swung his head back to face her.

"It's too bad you don't—"

An explosion lit the house, sending glass and debris flying through the air. The agents flung themselves to the ground and ducked behind cars. Flames roared inside the first floor, quickly consuming the interior.

Jade fell to the ground near Travers. She covered her face and he rolled beside her, unwinding the bandage from around her ankle. As he ran for the front door, he yelled over his shoulder, "Ambulances, fire engines, backup for roadblocks. Get 'em here now."

Several agents had caught up with him by the time he'd reached the front doorway. He peered around the corner, backing quickly out of the way. Pressing Travers's bandage over his nose and mouth, he headed in.

When he entered the foyer, he realized that the blast

hadn't reached far beyond the kitchen. He led the agents into the kitchen, shielding his face from the flames rising from the floor and table. A charred body sat at the table, completely engulfed in flames. The flesh was burning off the body, leaving only a darkened husk. The corpse was about Allander's size and build.

"Holy shit," one of the agents yelled. He pointed to the pantry, where the door had been blown clear off the hinges. Three large metal drums sat dangerously near the flaming wall. GASOLINE was stenciled across them in red letters.

"Move 'em out," Jade yelled. "If they blow, they'll compromise the crime scene. Move 'em. Now!"

The agents ran forward and grabbed the barrels. They gasped for breath as they rolled them quickly out through the flaming kitchen.

"And tell the fire department it's a Class B," Jade shouted after them.

He stepped forward and stared at the body, the flames singeing the collar of his shirt and curling the ends of the bandage he held across his face. The body seemed grotesquely casual, as if it had just finished eating breakfast. The flesh crackled beneath the flames.

Jade crouched and picked up a twisted piece of metal as Travers stumbled in.

She buried her face in her sleeve. "Jade, let's go. Get out of here."

Behind her, several firemen sprinted in with extinguishers. Clouds of smoke and Halon filled the air. One of the men doused the burning body with foam. There was no need for hoses.

Jade raised the piece of metal, looking at the flap of duct tape dangling from it. "Basic microwave bomb. Open jug of gas, roll of aluminum foil, tape the door shut. Douse the kitchen and body, set the timer, and boom."

"Looks like our boy went out with a bang," Travers said.

Jade followed Travers outside, his eyes troubled. The front yard was clogged with agents, cops, and firemen. People sprinted back and forth, screaming into radios. The first few media vans had pulled up, and the reporters were putting the finishing touches on their makeup while their crews readied the cameras. Three ambulances pulled into the driveway, sirens screaming.

Jade approached Fredericks, seizing him by the shoulders. "Get men throughout the house immediately to see what they can turn up. And I want the corpse to the lab to check dentals immediately."

Fredericks pushed Jade's hands roughly aside. "Relax, Marlow. We have the body."

"We have *a* body."

"If that's not Atlasia, you wanna tell me exactly how he slipped through the blast? Because I didn't see many gaps in our coverage here."

Jade glanced over at the gasoline barrels at the edge of the woods. The agents had thrown them well clear of the burning house. "We don't know that he didn't—" He noticed that the red lettering across one of the barrels was smeared. His stomach lurched as he remembered the red he'd seen on Allander's cuff—red that looked more like paint than blood.

The cluster of agents watched Jade as he took a few steps toward the barrels. "They're decoys," he said.

"What the hell are you talking about, Marlow?" Fredericks said. "We've got the body."

"The barrels are decoys."

"No, sir," one of the younger agents said. "We rolled

them out. He filled them only halfway, to leave room for the vapors and everything."

"They're not full of gasoline," Jade said.

"What do you mean? What else would be in there?"

"It doesn't matter, Marlow," Fredericks said. "We have the body."

Jade pulled his Sig Sauer from the back of his jeans and aimed it at a gasoline barrel. A female reporter screamed and three of the agents nearby leaped for cover, diving across the hood of a car. Jade fired and the bullet entered the barrel with a ping, sending a stream of liquid shooting into the air. He shot the barrel beside it and another fountain of water sprang up. When he shot the third barrel, there was nothing, just a dark hole.

Jade glared at Fredericks. "There's your fuckin' body," he said.

Jade turned and looked across the front yard. There were over thirty vehicles parked haphazardly from the street to the driveway, and dozens of people were running around. He watched helplessly as an ambulance and two fire trucks backed out of the driveway and drove away. In the confusion, Allander had probably crept from the gasoline barrel and hidden in one of the vehicles. He would be long gone by now.

Jade turned to face Fredericks, but Fredericks was still crouching in anticipation of the gasoline explosion. Travers was standing behind him, so Jade addressed her, ticking off the points by bending back his fingers. "Hold all these vehicles and search them. Send out an APB to SFPD ASAP, have them set up roadblocks on all streets leading out of here. Call the fire department, hospitals that dispatched ambulances, and news stations and have them radio any vehicles that we already missed and direct them back here or to the nearest police station.

Call the police stations so they're expecting them. Call headquarters and have them alert the agents at the Atlasias' house. I'm guessing the body in there is Steve Francis's parachuting buddy, so get that missing-persons list we talked about, interview the closest relative— scratch that—interview the *friends* of all males matching the demographic profile. Find out if any of them parachuted or knew Steve Francis." Jade and Travers both stared expectantly at his next finger, but he couldn't think of anything else. "Got it?"

"Yes," Travers said.

"Oh, and Travers?"

"Yeah?"

Jade touched his cheek gingerly. "Nice right." He turned and walked away.

Travers glanced down at the crouching agent. "You can stand up now, Fredericks."

When Jade reached the barrel lying on its side, he picked up the lid and saw that a handle had been soldered on the inside so that Allander could hold it shut while he was being rolled out to freedom. There was a small puddle on the ground beneath the lid; Allander had also put water inside his barrel so the agents would hear it sloshing around as they rolled him out.

Beside Jade, the other barrels still leaked water from the bullet holes. He cupped his hands in front of one of the streams, then brought them up to his face. No way Allander would have put explosive barrels on either side of himself.

Jade rose and hurled the lid at a nearby tree trunk. He had ordered them to move the barrels out. He had practically freed Allander himself.

Jade walked into the woods, cursing. Where would Allander go now? Back to Darby? After his failed attempt tonight, he'd know that security would be tighter. For the time being, Thomas and Darby were out of reach. Alex, the younger kid from the second house, was already safe, in witness protection.

Would Allander try to establish a new base? Leave the area? What were his aims? Jade rubbed his eyes with his thumb and forefinger. Allander was obsessive, obsessive about finishing what he'd started. That was why he'd returned to Darby after all these years. *So many loose ends to tie up*, Allander had said to Jade on the phone. Were there any other loose ends that needed to be tied up?

Jade searched his brain for anything he could have forgotten. Allander had to have weaknesses Jade could use to his advantage. What was it Jade had told Travers earlier? *I thought about the emotion that most overwhelms him. That's his Achilles' heel. His jealousy.* Who would Allander be jealous of?

Studying the leaves on the ground, Jade stepped between two trees and almost toppled over the edge of a cliff. He jumped back and gazed out across the forest below. The last hint of daylight shone from beyond the horizon, and highlighted the Tower against the backdrop of the sea.

Of course. Claude Rivers. Claude, who had already raped his mother, if only her corpse. Claude, the only survivor of Allander's rampage. Claudius, the fulfiller of Allander's desires. The other loose end.

Jade leaned over the edge of the cliff, peering along its curve. Its steepness lessened drastically to his left, and he thought he could make out a path zigzagging beneath the trees. A sudden concern washed through him regarding Claude Rivers and the guard on the Tower. He had no radio, and he'd lose too much time running back to the house and finding Travers or someone else to call over and warn the guard. He'd have to rush to the Tower himself.

He turned back into the forest and ran for the path, crashing through branches and leaves. Even if Travers realized that he had disappeared and called in a helicopter, he would lose it under the cover of the trees.

Just the two of us now, he thought. It's what we've both been waiting for, isn't it Allander?

ALLANDER gazed at the clouds rolling across the full moon and wondered when the rain would come. Now that he had the ground beneath his feet, he felt himself drawn inexorably toward the Tower. In a sense, he was going home, and that was what everything had been about.

The Tower was not visible from any point within the forest, but Allander sensed its location as if aligned by an internal compass. He broke through the last line of trees and walked through the entrance to Maingate. Repairs were still underway, so the grounds were deserted, with only one guard out on the Tower. And one prisoner.

It had been a mere ten days since his escape, though it seemed like years. No one would be on guard against Allander. They were only concerned with people trying to break out of prison; they would never think anyone would be so insane as to break in.

Earlier in the day, Allander had left a bag of supplies hidden at the base of the small guard tower on Maingate's grounds. He removed a dent puller and channel-lock pliers from the bag, and scaled the short ladder. The small window to the door was double-barred. Glancing out across Maingate and the ocean, he figured that the Tower was over a hundred yards away.

Inserting the screw end of the dent puller into the doorknob lock, Allander carefully tightened the screw. Then, with a single jerking motion, he pulled the metal slide toward the handle. It gave, and he removed the entire lock assembly from the knob.

He clenched the channel pliers on the dead bolt, twisting it with all his might until he felt the retaining bolts break. Then he removed a pick from his back pocket and, using a thick hairpin for a torsion bar, jiggled the dead bolt open. He whistled "Heigh Ho, Heigh Ho" as he worked.

The lock on the weapons cabinet was easy, and he soon had the Win Mag .300 in his hands. It was a substantial weapon, laying heavy against his shoulder. He stepped out onto the deck, resting the gun on the railing. It was a bolt gun, holding four rounds in the mag but only one in the chamber.

He saw the black dot of the guard patrolling out on the Tower and raised the gun, leveling the scope's crosshairs on the back of his head. He squeezed the trigger slowly until he felt the gun jerk back against his shoulder. The bullet must have kicked wide because the guard never broke step. Allander ducked as the guard swept around the far edge of the circle and headed back, facing the mainland.

Allander watched him through the scope, pausing to manually recock the gun. The wind gusted strongly, whipping his cheeks, and he realized that he hadn't adjusted enough to take it into account. He peeked through the scope again, finding the back of the guard's head. Taking a deep breath and aiming a touch to the left to compensate for the wind, he fired.

The guard's arms flared and he was down and out of sight instantly. Allander smiled and lowered the gun to the deck. He continued whistling as he descended the ladder, looped the weighty bag over his shoulder, and headed out to the dock.

Jade ran off the path and sprinted through the rough terrain, cutting through the forest in the direction of Maingate. An incredible pounding started in his head as he ran along the top of a small ridge in the forest, carefully avoiding the forty-foot drop that sloped dangerously to a creek.

He felt as if he were going into the twelfth round of a boxing match. The tender burn across his face, the bruise on his cheek from Travers's blow, and the raised bump on his head took his attention in turns, each greater pain momentarily distracting him from the others.

But he recognized his headache and knew it could not be blamed on recent injuries. The systematic thudding through his temples welled from something not entirely physical. He gritted his teeth and kept running, trying to ignore the needles of pain that his footsteps sent up the back of his neck. And as he ran, the furious pumping of his legs brought him back again to the terrible day of his frenzied childhood run.

Moving swiftly through the foxtails and ignoring the blood streaming down his left cheek, the boy heard his name cried again: *Jade.* It was a doleful, wavering sound, and he ran more quickly, until his breath burned in his throat.

The four boys had surrounded his brother in the clearing by Mr. Hollow, and one had already knocked him down. They tore into him, kicking him about the face, the head, the arms.

Eenie meenie minie moe

There was no sign of Allander and Jade moved faster, his run edged with panic as his feet expertly gripped the uneven ground, propelling him forward. He finally caught sight of a broken sapling just on the brink of the ridge and he ran past it, barely glancing down.

Saliva drooled from his brother's chin as he struggled to his feet.

Catch a retard by the toe

One hand went to the straw by Mr. Hollow's cuff (a hand, I swear he thought it was a hand) and the other reached out toward the sun setting atop the rolling hills, showering the foxtails with orange. His mouth was awash with blood and spit and he opened it and screamed a word, one word, his last word: *Jade*—a sound that would echo in Jade's memory for years.

Make him holler blow by blow

A fist closed the mouth as it yelled and Jade burst into the clearing as his brother toppled backward, his hands moving dumbly in the air, one holding tightly to a few loose strands of straw. He saw the panic in his brother's eyes as he reeled backward and heard the crack as his head struck one of the jagged stones framing the site, and heard a grunt—a low grunt, like an animal's—and then that was all, and he knew he had lost him. Then he was a whirlwind of knees and fists and elbows and he had lost his hat on the ground and he didn't even know what was moving his body, but when he reached his brother there were four boys lying around him coughing blood and whimpering.

Jade ducked and dodged reflexively, his eyes straining in the faint light to spot broken branches and trampled bushes. He rounded a tree at full speed and a jagged limb caught him across the left cheek, slicing along the line of his scar. Once again, he felt the hot blood oozing down his cheek.

His focus on the path ahead was so intense that the cut barely registered. He came to a clearing and halted, unsure in which direction to continue. In the dim glow, he spotted a broken branch, and he sprinted past it, back on course.

The boys were clutching their legs and stomachs, and tears streamed down their bruised faces. The boy who was Jade knelt down in the clearing and looked into the blank eyes of his brother. He felt the hole across the back of his head when he put his hand there to hold him against his chest, and as he sat with his dead brother under the brilliant sun, he felt the blood spreading stickily through his clothes and across his stomach.

Eenie meenie minie moe.

Jade pounded through the brush. He felt exhausted, but also somehow purged. It had finally come flooding through him, and he realized for the first time that his brother's panicked cries had long ago blended with the cries of other victims. Though Jade couldn't save them all, he had spent his life making sure that they didn't die on *his* shift, on *his* time.

Fear had propelled him, whipping him: *What if you're not there, Jade? What if you can't stop another life from slipping away?* He had to oversee all things dark and dreadful—he had to reign over it all. Fear was his bedmate and his lover. Fear was his anger and his hatred. Fear was the burden he had carried ever since childhood, just as it was Allander's.

He felt as if he were stirring from sleep, lost in the aftermath of a dream. A few lingering cries still rang in his ears. He heard them behind him now, and he picked up his pace, feeling adrenaline pumping again and thinking of Claude Rivers and the guard ahead. He was sprinting so fast he couldn't really see where he was going.

Bursting into a small clearing, Jade whirled around, searching for signs of Allander's path, desperately trying to remember in which direction the Tower waited. It was silent here except for the noise of his own labored breathing.

He sensed that the ridge he was running was parallel to the Maingate entrance. He looked at the trees ahead, then turned and faced down the slope. From his angle, it looked almost impossibly steep. The creek running below wasn't moving very fast, but it looked rocky. He glanced back up along the ridge, and suddenly realized he had to change direction.

"The quickest distance," he said in a low, growling voice as he stepped off the ridge.

He tried to keep his feet ahead of his torso as the slope carried his body to a full sprint, but about halfway down, his shoulders passed his center of gravity and he tumbled over, hurtling out of control down to the river below. The thick weeds that ran along the creek slowed his fall before he crashed into the icy water, but since he couldn't see it coming, he gasped at the shock. He pulled himself up, feeling heavy in his wet clothes, and sloshed through the creek to the other side. The pain of a thousand different bruises stung him, but as far as he could tell, he hadn't sustained a serious injury. It took him a few steps before he could feel his legs under him again, and then he ran into the forest, leaving the creek and the ridge behind.

Twenty feet later, he broke through the trees, and the steel gates of Maingate lay open before him. He saw a shadow flash, deep within the prison. He had been right—after all the struggle, Allander had returned to his starting point.

Jade sprinted through the gates.

Allander threw the bag of supplies in the speedboat, untied the rope mooring it to the dock, and revved the motor, edging the boat out into the turbulent water. As he pulled away, the rope slid from the dock to the water, where it trailed the boat like a slippery eel.

Loud, hammering footsteps sounded on the dock, and as Allander turned to look, he saw a shadowed figure take flight after the boat. He screamed and jerked the throttle all the way down.

A sudden peace washed over Jade as he broke the water's surface. He had aimed his jump at the retreating rope, so he was not surprised to feel its coarse fibers against his palm. It jerked suddenly away and slid through his hand, tearing the skin along his palm. Despite the pain, Jade squeezed down tight on the rope. His body lurched forward, and he was off in a spray of bubbles.

Bound together, even through the jagged waters of the inlet, Allander and Jade headed for the Tower.

As he steered the boat, Allander noticed the drag of Jade's weight, and he could see a figure outlined beneath the surface of the water. He thought of the inevitable pain spreading through Jade's arms, tightening his shoulders and tensing his stomach. And the burn, Allander thought. The burn in his lungs must be divine.

As the boat approached the base of the Tower, Allander steered a tight semicircle. Jade, who had been struggling to get his feet in front of his body, hoping to pull himself into a skiing position, felt his feet sinking as the sudden turn yanked his body forward. His torso half-broke the surface as he was flung into a new trajectory. Although the water slowed him, he was almost airborne as he saw the stone wall of the Tower rushing directly at him.

Bringing his knees to his chest, Jade struck the wall sideways, his body in the fetal position. A loud crunch in his hip and he knew the bone was shattered. He slid down the wall into the water's embrace.

Allander brought the boat forward, crashing hard into the side of the steel ladder that crept up the side of the Tower. It was low tide, so the lowest rung was above water. Straining, he pulled the bag up across his shoulders and seized the ladder's side rail. Laughing now with excitement at being so near his goal, he began the steady climb up. The strap from the bag dug into his shoulder, but he was too wired to pay attention to the pain. As he climbed, he stared up at the full moon, his face splitting in a grin.

Below him, a hand reached out of the water and gripped the bottom rung. Climbing hand over hand, Jade pulled his body from the sea. He was unable to use his legs, and they dangled uselessly below him. The rope burn on his palm stung horrifically, first with the saltwater and now with the pressure of his own weight. The ladder shifted under him, loose on the bolts from the speedboat collision. If he slipped, he knew he'd never be able to keep himself afloat in the water.

When Allander reached the top, he turned and looked back, noticing Jade struggling after him. In the dim light of the moon, their eyes locked for a moment. Allander smiled, then blew a kiss. He drew himself up from his crouch, his head momentarily framed by the full moon. Intoxicated by his sense of complete power, Allander threw back his head and laughed. Then he doubled over, shaking with childish laughter.

He noticed that the speedboat was drifting out to sea a little bit. He'd have to hurry through his plan before it floated farther away. Hearing a scraping noise, he turned and saw the guard lying near the Hole, gasping, his hands cupped around his throat. The bullet had nicked the side of his neck—a deep wound, but not lethal. The man's whole body heaved as he drew air, his limbs jerking almost mechanically. His hands were speckled with blood to the wrists, and his submachine gun lay on the ground a few feet from him.

Allander stormed over and kicked the gun down the Hole, then drew Jade's Glock and pressed the muzzle to the top of the guard's head. His eyes looked up at Allander, wild with terror, but he couldn't speak or even move away from the gun. He wheezed and sputtered, trying to hold his blood in his throat.

"Well, that wouldn't be very sporting, would it?"

Allander said. He lifted the gun from the guard's head. "I've got better plans for you."

He walked to the edge of the Hole and peered down. "And for you, you fat wretch." He could see Claude's hands around the bars of Unit 11A, his face a fleshy white orb staring up at him. "You didn't do it, not as I'm going to. What's the fun of fornicating with a corpse? It's about cognizance—it's about looking into the eyes of the one who conceived you, holding sway over her, over life itself. It's in her knowing, you unworthy simian, not just the deed." The anger in his voice surprised him. "It's in the knowledge of what you're doing!"

He ran to the edge of the Tower to check on Jade again. He was still barely above the water's surface, hanging on and gasping for breath. Allander had time. He had plenty of time.

He walked over to a large diesel drum, hauling the heavy supply bag; he had watched them haul the drum up earlier in the week to refuel the water pump. He removed the large plug and noticed that the drum was almost empty. Pulling a tube from his bag, he siphoned some diesel fuel from the water-pump tank, sucking on the end of the tube to start the flow and spitting out a mouthful of the bitter liquid. After a certain amount of diesel fuel had poured into the drum, he yanked the tube out, letting the fuel wash over the top of the Tower. Then he removed three bags of fertilizer from his bag, raking them open with a knife. He dumped them into the drum, one after another, aiming the spill through the large plug hole.

Of course, he wasn't able to measure precisely, but he knew ANFO mixture well enough—7 percent fuel oil to 93 percent ammonium nitrate, found in common fertilizer.

Still clinging to the ladder, Jade shook his head,

attempting to clear it. The water and the Tower were spinning crazily around him, and he tightened his hands around the rails, gathering the courage to raise his head. The ladder seemed to stretch up forever. He bit down on his lip and began the climb, the ladder, loose from being struck by the speedboat, shaking with his movements. He crawled willfully, steadily, pulling his straining hands closer to Allander's throat.

For the first time, he noticed how much he really hurt. He counted his injuries with each rung. The gun to my head, the cut in my cheek, the fall down the slope, the Tower up my ass. He felt for his pistol, but it was gone. He was not surprised.

Aware of the need to act quickly, Allander sprinted over to check on Jade once more. He was down about forty rungs, moving slowly, but moving nonetheless. Allander knocked the drum on its side and rolled it a few times, mixing the diesel and ammonium nitrate as best he could.

He'd taken a stick of dynamite from the site at Maingate because the only blasting caps he could find were eights, which weren't too reliable when used alone with an ANFO mixture. The his and hers cell phones he'd stolen were lying side by side in the bottom of the bag, and he picked them up, sliding one of them into his pocket. The back panel was already removed from the other one, and he had pulled out and stripped the two wires that ran to the ringer. He intertwined each one now with a wire from the blasting cap, then wound the phone, the primer, and the dynamite in electrical tape and dropped the whole thing into the drum. It landed on the ANFO mixture with a wet thud. He hammered the large metal plug back into the drum, then rolled it over to the edge of the Hole.

He crouched over the choking guard, gently peeling back the guard's blood-drenched jacket and removing the elevator control from his inner pocket.

With a click of the button, he lowered the elevator platform to roof level, then pushed the big drum onto it. He walked back and kicked the guard once in the side as hard as he could. The guard gasped as he rolled onto the platform, his head clanging against the drum.

Jade still inched up the ladder, rung by rung, ignoring the pain through his cramped arms. He had to make it. He had to get his hands on Allander, but he was still a good twenty yards away.

Allander pushed the red button and the platform started to descend into the Hole. They'd done an admirable job of repairing the elevator, he thought with a snicker.

Claude watched the bomb and the wheezing guard descend past him, his expression unchanged. He scratched himself, then looked up at Allander with unfrightened interest. The guard's rasps echoed inside the Tower, bouncing off the hard stone walls.

The platform clicked to a halt when it hit Level One. Now it was all set. Once he was a safe distance away, Allander would call in with the cell phone in his pocket, and the current would trip the primer, which would trip the dynamite. With the diesel drum containing the initial explosion, the whole thing would go. The shock wave should blast the walls right off the Tower. And Claude and the guard along with them.

A squeal rose in his throat, and he ran back to the edge, looking down at Jade.

"The dance ends here, Marlow!" he shouted. "We bring this show to a close upon the same stage on which it began." He screamed his words to be heard over the crash of the waves. "There are three things I have on you right now, Marlow," he yelled. "Just three."

Jade looked up at him, but couldn't muster the strength to speak.

"A bomb . . . a detonator"—Allander held his arms up to the moon, the cell phone glinting in his hand—"and your gun." He pulled out the Glock and waved it in the air.

Jade clenched his eyes until he saw white dots dancing across the darkness. Of course. Blasting caps and dynamite to blow out the rock from the cranes back at Maingate. Fuel from the water pump. The fertilizer scattered by the stairs back at the house. A Timothy McVeigh special. How could he have missed it?

They had practically given Allander all the pieces of the bomb right here. Right at the prison.

He glanced down and saw the speedboat knocking against the base of the Tower. Allander could dive in, swim to the boat, and dial in to detonate once he was a safe distance away. And Jade was too weak to do anything but watch him.

Allander stepped from the parapet to the top rung of the ladder, fanning his arms to balance himself. "I am Allander Atlasia!" he yelled. He lowered the pistol so it was pointing at Jade's forehead, taking a long, last look into Jade's eyes. "Hope you said your prayers."

A wave of terror flooded Jade's body for the first time since he had begun the case. Allander was going to shoot Jade and escape. He'd be free, leaving nothing behind but a watery blast. Jade looked up into the bore of the pistol, tightening his hands around the steel railings until his biceps felt as if they were going to burst. Shoving with his legs and arms, he jerked back on the loose ladder with all his might. It shifted, rolling under Allander's feet.

Allander screamed, his arms flailing madly. The pistol fired once up into the air, kicking from his grasp and falling away. He tottered on the rung, trying desperately to throw his weight back toward the Tower. When he'd resigned himself to the fall, a calm washed over him. He tapped the bulge of the cell phone in his pocket, smiled, and leaned forward in a dive.

Jade roared as the body flew toward him, Allander's eyes open, a serene smile curling his lips. Jade could tell he would pass inches out of his reach from the ladder and would land in the water mere yards from the boat.

Seeing Allander escape was too much agony for Jade to bear, and before he was aware of what he was doing, he had wedged his leg against the stone behind a steel rung and had pushed his torso away from the Tower.

Allander's eyes went wild with fear as he saw the impossibly outstretched arms and clutching fingers shoot at him as he neared. He let out a high-pitched scream as Jade caught him, his fingers grasping Allander's shirt and pants. Jade's torso was extended horizontally from the Tower wall, his leg the only thing keeping him from dropping to death by water below.

Jade held Allander weightlessly for a moment, savoring the feel of the fabric between his fingers. Then, as the force of Allander's fall pulled them downward, Jade tightened his leg with all his might and rotated both their bodies around the point of his wedged knee. Bellowing, he let Allander's momentum carry him down and into the stone wall.

Allander's face met the stone of the Tower and came apart instantly, his nose driven back through its hole, his cheekbones shattering, his forehead giving way to the cracking lines of his skull.

The moment Allander's face struck the Tower, Jade's

leg snapped. He heard it before he felt it, heard it even over the dull thud of Allander's head imploding, and the pain was unlike anything he had ever felt. He released his grip on Allander's body and it drifted away from him, down to the ocean.

For a moment, the ocean buoyed Allander on its breast, his shirt flapping in the wind like a wounded bird. A pool of crimson flowered from his head. Then, with excruciating slowness, the body sank from view until, from his upside-down perch near the top of the Tower, Jade could no longer discern where its outline ended and the ocean began. Dangling from one grotesquely bent limb, he watched even the body's wake disappear into the swells.

He was suddenly struck with an overwhelming exhaustion that left him too weak to consider moving. He prayed that his leg would not give way entirely. Every time his body swayed in the wet wind, a pain beyond description tightened its grasp on his insides.

He hung from one thin steel rung for over ten minutes before, through the thick haze clouding his mind, he heard the chopping approach of a helicopter.

DARBY woke up alone in bed for one of the first times in thirty-eight years. She instinctively turned to her left to extend her arm across Thomas's chest before she remembered he wasn't there.

She rose from her bed with the routinized motions of a woman living alone, and pulled on a robe. She went to the kitchen, put coffee on, and called the hospital, just as she had done every day this week.

"Good morning, love. How are you feeling?"

Thomas's voice was not quite right. It would never be right again, never the voice that had wooed her and carried her in sickness and in health. But that seemed a small price to pay to have her husband alive, so she buried her sorrow beneath her gratitude.

His larynx had been severely injured, and it had taken a delicate surgery to get him to the point where he could speak at all. But he had remained optimistic all the way through, reassuring her with his eyes when he couldn't with his words.

"Oh, great. Or should I say, stable?" Thomas laughed a dry, croaking laugh. "Just three more weeks in, love."

Darby smiled. "And one more operation."

Thomas tried to laugh, but it came out a dull wheeze. "Oh yeah. Nose job, right?"

Darby laughed softly and tears moistened her eyes. "I'm leaving in five."

"Okay. I love you."

Her voice cracked and she struggled to keep it from shaking. "I love you too."

She hung up and sat on the couch in the living room, sipping her coffee. The very couch where they had met Jade time and time again, she realized, where he had helped them in his own guarded way.

She had come to care greatly for Jade. She had come to respect him and almost love him. She knew that some part of her emotions had to do with his role in protecting them, and some part had to do with her son. Though she didn't understand, entirely, her feelings for Jade, she sensed them, as if through a fog that wouldn't lift. It saddened her that they would never see Jade again. There was too much there for her, too much there for them. He had freed them, finally and painfully, from a lifelong ache, but she could never forgive him for it.

She heard the soft rattling of the mail truck outside and she rose and went to the door. It was a splendid morning, she thought as she moved down the walkway to the mailbox.

Turning to face the sun, she fanned through the mail. Mostly bills and mailers. At the bottom of the stack was a plain white envelope, her name and address written neatly in black.

Opening the envelope confirmed it: a single earring.

Placing it back in the envelope, she crumpled them together into a ball and walked over to the trash can at the end of the driveway. She lifted the lid and tossed the small ball of metal and paper inside.

She whistled softly to herself as she headed back inside, closing her eyes and tilting her face to the sun. It *was* a splendid morning.

THE room was dark, as always. Once again, Travers sat in the gloom, across the desk from Wotan. She held a thick folder in her lap.

She inhaled deeply and continued. "Well, sir, that just about covers it."

"Very well," Wotan said softly.

"We've placed Marlow's money in an account that he can claim when he gets out of the hospital." Travers cleared her throat. "Although we're not really sure when he'll get out, sir. I put in an order to cover his full medical expenses."

"Very well."

"He did . . ." Travers tilted her head back a little, biting her bottom lip. "He did a good job, sir."

Wotan nodded once, running his fingertips over the dry socket of his eye. "Put the file to rest," he said, turning his attention back to some papers on his desk. A long silence ensued as Travers watched him work.

"I didn't understand it before, sir. Your faith in him. Marlow. How did you know?"

The room was quiet for so long that she began to wonder if Wotan was going to respond. Just as she was rising to leave, he looked up from his desk. He picked the bullet slug from the ashtray and held it up in the dim light.

"Do you know what this is, Agent Travers?"

She shook her head.

"It's a slug. Early in my marriage, when my wife was still alive, my girl was kidnapped. She was my . . . our only child. Four years old. She had just learned to ride a bicycle with training wheels alone to the end of the street." He spoke with no emotion at all, as if reciting a memorized passage.

"Marlow was a young agent at the time, fresh out of Quantico. It was his first kidnapping case. He pursued her kidnapper with such determination and vengeance that I could have sworn the burden was his instead of mine."

Travers listened tensely. "And he saved her, sir?"

"When he found her kidnapper, my child had already been raped and killed." Wotan stared directly into Travers's eyes, refusing to flinch.

Travers finally looked away.

"When they meet the devil, they always bring something back," Wotan said. "Marlow brought this back to me." He held the slug between his thumb and forefinger and then gripped it tightly in his fist. He looked back down at the papers on his desk. "Do you think we'll be seeing him again, Agent Travers?"

Travers looked down at her hands, in her lap. "I hope so, sir. I hope so," she said, then stood and walked to the back wall. She twirled the combination lock through a series of numbers, then used a key that she'd removed from her pocket. She swung the metal door open and rolled out a tray with raised edges. It protruded into the room like a small morgue slab. Laying the file carefully inside, she tapped it once with an open hand and then slid the vault shut, slamming the door.

She walked across the room to turn the large metal wheel of the exit door, and left without saying a word.

Wotan sat alone, the darkness settling around him

like a cloak. In the dark, he cracked the knuckles of his right hand with his thumb. They snapped loudly, the sound echoing off the hard walls. He made a fist with his thumb inside and tightened it, cracking the joint. He repeated the same ritual with his left hand. Then he stood and walked to the door.

The light cast from the small fixtures in the room did not touch him. He did not maneuver to miss the light, but it seemed the shadows came to meet him, laying themselves over his body and across his path. He turned the wheel and the lock disengaged with a click.

He stepped out into the corridor, and just before the thick metal door closed behind him, his hand crept back through the small gap into the empty room. It groped on the wall for a moment, then found what it was looking for. He flicked the wall switch and the room was flooded with light.

WITH his lower body wrapped in a hardened cast, one leg in traction, stitches threaded through his left cheek, and an incessant hammering in his temples and ears, Jade looked at the bare white walls of his room and the single plastic tray before him, and wondered why he was alive.

So far, his only happiness during his days in the hospital had come from his recollections of the case. He had heard the shattering of Allander's skull, he had felt it in every muscle of his body, and he still heard the gory crunch and felt the dull vibration in his dreams and his drugged hours awake.

He knocked the tray across the room with a hand wrapped in a soft bandage and winced in pain as it clattered on the tiled floor.

This room was his new home, it seemed. He pictured his house sitting empty, an occasional breeze blowing through the back screen and shaking the pictures taped to the walls. It seemed so far away.

He thought that Travers had come to see him, but now he wasn't sure if it had been a dream. It had seemed real; he thought he remembered her oddly sad face looking at him, the lingering touch of her fingers across the scar on his cheek.

She had smiled at him, though her eyes remained sad. "You beat yourself up pretty good, Marlow. Guess you don't need me around to do it for you."

And he had tried to answer her, but his voice had been thick with sleep and drugs. It was so hard for him to turn to face her, to shift out of the indentation his body had pressed into the mattress. After what seemed an eternity, he made the words come out: "Maybe I didn't handcuff you just to piss you off."

But having spoken, he realized that the room was empty, that Travers had left long ago, maybe hours, maybe days, and for the first time that he could remember, he felt like crying.

He gazed through the metal screens that guarded his window, looking out at the night sky and the trace of a moon—the same moon upon which he and Allander had once fixed their eyes. It seemed that a lot of time had passed since the dance, and now more time would pass with him here alone, trapped with his thoughts and with Allander in the shadows.

Full fathom five

He saw Allander's grown face on a child's body, popping out of a jack-in-the-box and dancing around the room. Allander sang to him through red-painted lips that stood out starkly against the pasty white of his cheeks.

Full fathom five thy father lies

He skipped around the room and Jade saw that he was dressed in the baggy pants of a clown. Big red suspenders with large buttons stretched across his skinny, little boy's chest.

Jade's bed creaked as he shifted his body. His right-lower eyelid twitched slightly. It was just from the pain and the painkillers, the nurse had said, and it would go away when he got better. When he got better.

The boy-Allander stopped at the foot of the bed and stretched out an arm, a disproportionately large, white-

gloved hand directing Jade's eyes to shift to where he
pointed. Jade followed the arc of the hand and looked at
the bare tiles of the floor, and as he watched, they dis-
solved into a garden scene. A small group of people
stood before a rectangular hole in the ground: a man and
a woman with their arms around each other, and a row of
people sobbing into handkerchiefs.

Alone, under a tree on the far side of the grave, stood
a boy in an awkward black suit with a cap worn backward on his head. He looked angry; he looked mean.
The parents did not look to him and no one stood near
him. He did not cry.

The boy-Allander stepped into the scene on the tiled
floor and walked past the open plot in the ground to
stand next to the lone boy under the tree. Taking the
boy's hand in one white glove, he led him slowly away
from the other people. They did not look back, and
gradually, they faded from view.